TRANQUEBAR PRESS
KASHMIR BLUES

Urmilla Deshpande lives in Tallahassee, a place of swamps and Spanish moss, a writer's paradise. This is her second work of fiction, and, having discovered the writer in herself late in life, she has no time to lose. She is working on her third novel, and a book of short fiction. Although she writes for herself, she loves nothing more than when the book is published and then belongs to every reader, to experience and interpret as they please.

KASHMIR BLUES

Urmilla Deshpande

TRANQUEBAR

TRANQUEBAR PRESS
An imprint of westland ltd
Venkat Towers, 165, P. H. Road, opp. Maduravoyal Municipal Office, Chennai 600 095
No.38/10 (New No.5), Raghava Nagar, New Timber Yard Layout, Bangalore 560 026
Survey No. A-9, II Floor, Moula Ali Industrial Area, Moula Ali, Hyderabad 500 040
23/181, Anand Nagar, Nehru Road, Santacruz East, Mumbai 400 055
47, Brij Mohan Road, Daryaganj, New Delhi 110 002

First published in TRANQUEBAR PRESS by westland ltd 2010

Copyright © Urmilla Deshpande 2010

All rights reserved

10 9 8 7 6 5 4 3 2 1

ISBN 978-93-80283-32-6

Typeset in Goudy Old Style by SŪRYA, New Delhi
Printed at Gopsons Papers Ltd

This book is a work of fiction and any resemblance to events, or people living or dead is incidental.

This book is sold subject to the condition that it shall not by way of trade or otherwise, be lent, resold, hired out, circulated, and no reproduction in any form, in whole or in part (except for brief quotations in critical articles or reviews) may be made without written permission of the publishers.

ACKNOWLEDGEMENTS

Without the dedicated reading of the first draft by my brother-in-law Paul Mitchell, and the detailed reading of the last by my editor Prita Maitra, and her (gentle) insistence on getting it right and not letting me get away with vagueness or laziness, this book would not be what it is. My heartfelt thanks and love to you both.

My sister Meithili Mitchell was part-time editor as well, not always voluntarily, and sometimes even under (vague and unspecified) threats. My love and thanks to you.

Nikhil Khosla, my friend who happens to be my brother-in-law, thanks for sharing your knowledge.

Thank you Lu Vickers, for all your help. Your comments and suggestions were invaluable, and I know the book is better because of them.

My friends who gave me valuable criticism and welcome praise. You make my writing better, yes, but also me: Urvashi Khosla, Richard Bush, Sheila Curran, Joseph Hellweg, Jane Macpherson, Julia and Philip Sura, Robert Draper (who also took out the garbage and changed lightbulbs), Tracy Sumner, Shashi Deshpande, Suhael Merchant.

Sukhi, Tissa, Ashish, and Saheli, your patience and

tolerance sustains me, and your encouragement and expectations make me reach beyond my own perceived limits. In writing and in life.

Frank-Udo, I used your name without your permission. This Frank *is* named for you and not any other. But there the resemblance ends. I did not know you were in the world when I wrote it, just hoped that you were.

PROLOGUE

Early spring, 1881

A man may wonder, lost in the Himalayan winter, if he has gone blind, and if blindness is, in fact, not dark, but unending white. When the cold begins to seep inward and lodge in his very marrow, he may not wonder about anything at all. His frozen mind will respond to nothing anymore. Not to the infinite solitude sought here by the rishis of ancient times, nor to the beauty that kills him even as he discovers it in the sparse shades of white and sapphire. He may not feel the loss of colour and air, and finally life, in the shadow of those oblivious, eternal mountains.

Men of the north do not wander in the Himalayan winter, they know they will suffer and die. They know this land well enough to stay away in this season of sleep. Blankets of snow and sheets of ice cover the earth's skin. The ground is unpredictable, treacherous, cleaving into impossibly deep crevasses, graves for the foolhardy or unlucky. A frozen wind screams down the peaks, carrying shards of glass water as it rakes through the valleys and plains leaving nothing alive.

Spring always comes back. It reclaims lost territory. Toward the end of winter, warmth is a promise on the still cold air. Then the snow melts willingly, its time past for now, and feeds the seeds in the ground. A rainbow lies on the once dry browns and ice tones of the season gone by. It sets blues against yellows and pinks against purples in a happy riot of colour and texture, enough to fill any snowblind traveller's head with dreams. The lower valleys fill with grass for grazing. Snow flows off the high peaks, the valleys rasp with swift water. With the full retreat of winter, this land becomes pleasant and welcoming, full of small game for the nomads, sweet fodder for animals, and drink for all.

Winter waning, tribesmen set out from the north. They cross mountain passes to trade with villages south of the mountains. They travel by day and camp by night, sometimes staying longer at places with more grazing, or, just for their pleasure, at the sweeter spots. There are small hollows near the mountain walls. Tents are pitched close to them, shelter from always cold night winds. These travellers find their way instinctively, probing the passes for a way, sometimes having to wind back and forth before they can break through to the south.

This mule train has wound its way around the spurs at the mountain's base. Children run around the mules, chasing each other and hiding in mounds of gravel on both sides of the narrow path. It is no longer cold enough to keep them on mules, and their parents let them run free, after so much restraint during the long journey. There is still snow on the ground in shallow patches. Unlike with the deep snow of higher altitudes in the earlier part of the year, they enjoy it now, they throw it, eat it, lie in it.

The group comes into a small clearing, large enough to set up camp for a few days. They will sleep on the unmoving ground here, eat some hot meat, and rest until it is time to go again. The men tether two of the mules and leave the rest free to graze. There is plenty of water, streams flow from the peaks that ring their temporary home. They set up the tents, covering the ground with huge wool carpets they have made along the way, on this and other journeys. Their sheep they pen quickly, unrolling fences of light wood stakes and rope. Fires are lit, one to every three or four families. They have had a good journey, all the way south from the heights, they have lost very few animals, and only one grandmother, early in the spring. They had been high in the mountains and that night proved too cold for her old, thin blood.

Four of the men leave camp to hunt. They plan to search into the evening. If they catch something, even a few rabbits, it will save them slaughtering one of their own sheep. They backtrack the way they have come. One of them had noticed a cave high up the ridge on the way in, and they agree that they should go up and see what they might find there. There is no path, no one lives at these altitudes, and it is too early in the year for shepherds to drive their flocks up that high for grazing. They clamber into the gravelly mountain, looking at the ground all the time, watching their step lest they slip. The majesty of Hagshu La peak rising high above them, her crown hidden from them by huge white clouds, is lost on them. Luckily, there is no wind at all, the sunlight and exertion makes them all sweat as they edge closer to the cave.

The youngest of the four hopes it is not a large cat up there in the cave, but rather a wild goat or ram. He knows perfectly well that goats and sheep do not live in caves, and he does not speak of his fears to the other three men, one of them his father. He wants to marry soon, he yearns for a certain girl back home—bright eyes, dark hair, sweet mouth—she could not come on the journey that year because of her mother's health. He thinks his thoughts, he does not speak of his fears so that his father will see him as a man, and so not refuse permission for him to bring a bride into their family.

They follow the natural steps on the mountain wall. It leads them in a wide curve ending right above their own camp. They stop to rest awhile, and look down at the camp. The tents, squat, fat creatures alien to that landscape, sheep in their pen, women collecting the freezing water from the stream, children running and screaming as they always do, exploding their energy. The three older men sit on their haunches, fill up their pipes, and have a slow smoke, exchanging a few words about their journey, making plans for the time they will set out again. The young one dreams of his bride, and some mysterious feeling that he does not understand fills him. They have with them the best hashish in the world, from their home in the south of Afghanistan, enough to last all of them until they get back home. Once, they were nomadic shepherds, but they had found a market in the south, in India, for their hashish and carpets. They had soon found out that the profit was well worth the risk. Some of the older men have done this journey as many as nine times, all the way through Kashmir into Delhi and then back to their home and their other lives.

The men finish their pipes and stand up. They have seen several rabbits in the rubble around them as they sat. The little creatures are unused to men, quite unafraid of them, and would be easy to catch. A dozen or so would feed all of them, when the women cooked them up with cracked wheat. The talk of hot stew for dinner makes them all energetic again.

They begin to walk slowly on the ridge, all of them on the same four- or five-foot length, when they all stop. They have felt the impossible movement of the ground. The ledge which has been solid under their feet slips away, carrying them down a hundred feet into the camp. Time takes on a dead quality, they fall, almost float down. The stones, earth, thunder of breaking rock fills the air around them, and the dust chokes them as they fall, but yet, still, they all remember it later as a gentle, slow, dreamlike falling: not violent, not frightening at all.

After the thunder of the fall, there is a momentary silence. Then the men and women and children of their families are upon them, digging and pushing away the small stones and mud, clearing away debris, but mercifully not touching or trying to move them. One of the tents and everything in it is entirely buried under rubble, but it is a small loss considering that no one below is hurt. Even the mules and sheep are untouched. The four men are not injured either, so mellow from their drug that they hadn't tightened up in fear and panic. They had fallen, consenting to the will of the mountain, bonelessly, just debris on the huge slab of the mountain itself. They stand up uncertainly and test their arms and legs.

They are awestruck by the size of the slice of mountain that lies there. The children resume their running and screaming, they pick up large pieces of bluish rock that emerge from the heap. The entire group, released suddenly from the wonderment of their brush with death, joins the children's frenzy. The blue stones seem to be everywhere in the landslide's dusty debris, and they are so pretty. One of the men picks up a pebble to take a closer look. He tries to scrape away the milky scum that envelops it. When he has whittled it away, there is a blue within. Like Himalayan sky, Himalayan pools, cornflowers in springtime, a velvety blue like he has never seen before.

When they are done with the rubble, they scrabble around in the slab itself, where they find even more buried in the soft rock. These are pried out easily, and they have a child-high pile of them by the time the camp is back in order. They take the pile of stones with them into Kashmir, and trade them for enough meat and salt for their journey home.

When Maharajah Ranbir Singh first heard of and then saw the sapphires that had found their way down the mountain, he had

them traced back to the villages that the northern nomads had
traded with. He had every stone he could find there taken away,
and harried the villagers for more. He had them watched and
hounded for years until he had taken every smallest blue chip from
them. Finally he found the source in the mountains and had the
area dug and scraped till he had every last grain of blue that could
be found there. Rumours about the Maharajah's sapphires
abounded: he had the largest collection of sapphires in the world.
He had eighteen thousand carats of gem-quality stone. One of the
stones was a foot long. No one had actually seen his whole
collection, so the rumours grew and grew.

The nomads never knew what they had unearthed. They went
back to their home without ever knowing what had been revealed
to them by a whim of Shiva, gazing down at them from the great
mountains: they, who had never asked, never wanted, and so were
never harmed by the stones. But though the tribesmen's story
ended there, the Kashmir Blues had been brought to the notice of
the world.

These are the tears of Shiva. They carry within them more than
just carat weight, more than just the superstition of bad luck.

ONE

Samaad got off his metal cot and folded up his bedding. He filled his old paint can with water and went out into the field behind his house to relieve himself before Fajr, the first namaaz of the day. He watched the sun rise. He got no pleasure from it, he only watched it because he was awake when it rose outside his kitchen window as he made his tea. He was done with his morning prayers, and with the ritual of rolling up his precious old rug and putting it away. That rug was part of him, it went everywhere he went. The profound red in it came from madder root. The plant had to be at least a decade old, mixed with milk and fermented exactly thirty days. He sometimes wondered if it was the feel of that rug rather than any true religious feeling that brought on the reverence he felt while performing his ritual. He had used it most of his thirty-six years, or at least since he was old enough to pray. His father got it from his grandfather, they had all used that rug for a long time. Someone far back in the family had made it when they were still nomads, wandering the North-West Frontier of India with their goats.

As the water began to steam, he saw the dust boiling up on the path to his house, backlit by the early morning light that came in through his window and dappled his mud floor. He added two cups of water for the tea and went out to greet the two men as they stepped out of the battered and dusty Jonga. They were both dressed in the knee-length shirts and loose pants worn by the men of the North-West all the way from central India into Afghanistan. Samaad hugged the older man, leaning into him side to side in the traditional way. The younger man he just nodded at. They walked over to the Jonga and began to unload it. They talked as they worked, about how old the vehicle was, how neither the Japanese nor anyone else made things the way they used to, this one had a hundred thousand kilometres on it, each one hard-earned on those unforgiving Himalayan gravel roads. They talked of the death of old Abbas bhai in the village. He had been shot in the thigh as he walked home after locking up his chai-beedi shop, as he had done through those same fields for most of his life. He had lain there, not fatally wounded, but in shock, had gone to sleep in the cold dark. He had been found frozen the next morning, not twenty steps from help.

Then, of course, talk turned to the state of their beloved home, the slow death of the local businesses, how there were no European or American tourists. No one came anymore to honeymoon in the old houseboats, once splendid old ladies decked in silk curtains and carved walnut screens, now rotting or rotted, abandoned on the great Dal lake and the banks of the Jhelum, their owners and all the artisans gone south to make their homes and set up shop among the Tibetan diaspora, new refugees among those old ones.

Not even Indian tourists came to see the heartbreaking colours of the flowers in the Kashmir valley. They said,

after soldiers and freedom fighters had died there, the
flowers bloomed with colours like never before, stained
vivid by their blood. 'In Flanders fields the poppies blow/
Between the crosses row on row', Samaad thought, the
Great War. Those battlefields, having hosted murder and
death, lay asleep all winter under the cold quilt of snow,
and then, come springtime, poppies bloomed like great
drops of blood, the earth ridding itself of the life-blood of
young soldiers that had soaked into the ground as they lay
dying. They talked of this and that, more matter-of-fact
than sad, the older men ignoring the occasional outburst
from the younger one. He was very young, after all, no
more than seventeen. They both remembered being that
way at his age. Sometimes Samaad wondered about his own
lack of outrage. He sometimes wondered if he had lost it
along the way, in England, where his father had sent him
to school and college. He had wanted his son to be
indistinguishable from the people who came to buy their
carpets, or to vacation in their houseboats. But Samaad
knew it was there, lying dormant, feeding his life, feeding
everything he did. It was better this way, pent up, a trickle
of the fury, that would last him his whole life, rather than
a gush that would send him into open conflict and take
that life away in a single moment of violence. That young
man would be recruited soon enough, for some quick and
dirty operation that would likely end his life. Then his
blood, too, would feed the earth.

When they were done unloading, they went into the
house, got their tea, and then sat on their haunches and
sipped it while they smoked their beedis. They talked some
more. Then the older man said goodbye and drove away,
leaving the boy to help Samaad.

Samaad got to work then, opening each bag one by one, with care, taking out each carpet, unrolling it onto one of his own that he had laid out on the floor. He went over each one, turning it this way and that, looking at it from each side of the little room, measuring, counting knots, making notes, making more notes, and finally writing a number beside each column, a code for the price that only he knew. There was nothing special, no spectacular carpet in the lot. None that he could take to those special buyers in Bombay and New Delhi who would pay whatever price he asked for. But there were some good ones, some old ones in very good condition. He would make what they needed that quarter. He would pay the men who would visit him four months hence, in the earliest time of day, when it was all night and fog, when no one would see them. When they had come and gone, then even he could not say for sure in the bright light of morning that they had been there at all.

Businesses willingly and sometimes, as in Samaad's case, unwillingly, funded the insurgency in their area. They really had no choice but to pay for 'protection'. Samaad tried not to dwell on the fact that radical fanatics from the north were taking over not just the land, but the businesses, and everything that was once his father's, his brother's, his. He tried not to dwell on the erosion of his religion—tolerant, mystical, spiritual, and therefore easy to push aside: to ridicule. His way was hated by these radicals who came quietly like snakes and rats through the passes. They said his beliefs were so distorted from the real Islam that they did not consider it Islam any longer. It had been tainted and mixed with Hinduism and Buddhism over the

centuries, the radicals said, and this was true. But Samaad
knew that his beliefs were what had kept their land, their
people together. Not harmoniously and happily at all times,
rubbing along with some friction, but at least together.
Now, the warp and the weft were being pulled out of that
great carpet of diversity that was Kashmir. The Pundits had
been driven out, the Sufis were being killed, the Buddhists
had retreated to their corner, it would soon all fall apart.
He tried not to, but did dwell on it more and more. A
thought was growing within him, a glowing cold blue
ember. He knew something was calling him. He had heard
it that day on the mountainside. He had heard the great
conch of Shiva, his footsteps sounding in the hills. He had
heard the songs of the qualandars, those old men who
followed the truth of Allah above everything else, whirling
in the eddies flowing out of Shiva's dreadlocks, calling to
him to protect this land, to keep it pure and safe.

At noon they ate the food the boy had cooked, huge
coarse rotis and lentils and fried green chillies. Samaad
went back to work, keeping at it all that day and most of
the next, with only a few hours of sleep. Then the older
man came back in the Jonga, collected his boy and a list
from Samaad.

'Salaam ale kum, Hamid bhai,' Samaad said to him.

'Wale kum salaam,' the old man replied, 'be safe, Allah
is always with you, my boy.'

They embraced, and then he and the boy drove away.

TWO

Ali carefully eased his way down the slope. It was so steep
it was almost vertical. The gravel made him slide down
again and again, making him howl and cry out in pain, his
cries answered only by the eagles treading thermals overhead.
He had tied his broken arm to his torso, but that helped
hardly at all. He would have lain down where he was, if
there had been any surface that would hold him. He was
almost empty from the continuous agony. He kept going,
sliding, stopping, breathing, thinking of his friend with
both legs broken. The injury on his friend's head seemed
even worse to Ali than the legs. The skull had felt pulpy
rather than bony, and though there was no blood, it gave
Ali shivers. The thought of his friend lying on the cold
mountain ledge waiting for help pushed Ali on. He knew
Samaad bhai lived close by, and could help him. He kept
climbing down. He knew the man only slightly, as an aloof,
solitary man. But it was enough to keep him going.

Samaad came out of his house at once. He picked Ali up
in his arms, carried him into the house and laid him out
on the bed. Ali moaned. Samaad hushed him and untied
his arm, holding him down by putting his own weight on
him. He moved the arm experimentally, ignoring the
groans. Then, with a snap, he cracked it back in place. Like
a miracle, the pain left Ali as if it had never been.

'It was just dislocated,' Samaad told him, laughing quietly.

He had no sympathy for these men, but they were young
and perhaps stupid, and so didn't deserve his hatred. He
knew why they crawled over the mountains into Kashmir.

He knew what they wanted, what they had been trained to do. And he hated what they did. They had money, he had seen it spent lavishly on other young men in the villages. These were recruits to an angry cult that made strangers of everyone who was touched by it. And he saw, each day, his land burned by embers spilled from the fires of their hatred. And he felt impotent, helpless. He had no water to pour over these flames, their fuel was too strong, too intense. These young men felt illuminated, bathed in power, and they scorched everything around them to cinders. Then they left with their new brothers, their new comrades, initiated and ready to receive more. Months later, trained, indoctrinated, they would return to collect more kindling to feed the pyre that his home had become.

His arm fixed, Ali decided to make the journey back with Samaad to rescue his friend. They had water, blankets, a rough stretcher that Samaad had rigged up, a first-aid kit, food. They made it up the mountainside easily. Samaad knew his way around perfectly well, and Ali followed him. He told Samaad what had happened as they climbed. They had started towards the village on the other side of the mountain, and instead of going around the base, had decided that it was late enough in the season to go over the mountain. This was a normal thing to do when crossing over, it was a whole day's walking shorter, and many younger men took that route once the winter snow was gone. On the climb down, they had been standing on a ledge that had slipped out from under them, carrying them and half the mountainside violently to the rocks below.

Hours later, they were almost on the ledge where the injured man was. Samaad was walking ahead of Ali, leaning on his walnut walking stick. His much taller and larger frame made it easier for him, and Ali was about a hundred feet behind him. He could see Samaad, but could no longer hear him. Samaad could see the broken hillside, the exposed organs and veins of the mountain. He could see the blue blood running through those veins. There was a great wedge off the mountainside, cracked open by the fall. He stared at it, its blueness confusing him. His steps got faster. Somewhere deep in his mind, comprehension had come even though he did not consciously know it. His whole body knew something he did not.

He came right up to the broken body of the man lying on the ledge, covered in Ali's jacket, barely alive, shivering and moaning from some deep animal pain that kept him alive and made him wish he wasn't. Samaad took in all this mechanically, but his eyes were on the blue piece of mountain. He sat down beside the man and began to examine him. He saw that Ali was right, his legs were broken, he was mangled like a doll thrown from a height. He had landed badly, his head was broken too. His pupils were dilated, making his eyes dark and without vision. Samaad knew that he was beyond their help. He shrugged. These men came with money to recruit other young men like themselves to their cause. Samaad was sure they were used to losing a few. He could not find any great regret in himself for the loss of one of them.

He stood up and walked out to the mound of gravel, and picked up a handful of it, separating the red earth from it, cleaning and blowing away everything but the blue. He looked at his hand and knew what he held in it. He looked at the blue slice of mountain again and knew why it was blue. He closed his eyes and took a quieting breath.

Ali came panting around the corner. He was puzzled when he saw Samaad standing some distance away from his friend. 'Is he all right?' he asked. 'What is it, Samaad bhai?' and then he came closer and saw what Samaad was doing, what he was holding in his hand. He knew that blue too, though he had never seen it before. He had grown up there, he had heard the legends, he had probably scrabbled around rocks as a child, hoping to find what Samaad held in his hand. His eyes changed, and Samaad saw that he knew.

Samaad walked up to him and pushed him hard over the edge that he was standing on. Ali screamed, a thin and long wail that went on for ever, taken up by the eagles and passed on and on till the sound filled the small valley for long seconds. Samaad watched the thrashing, flailing descent of the body and its ultimate, silencing impact on the valley floor. Then everything was silent. Samaad checked the pulse on the other man. There was none. He rolled the body easily to the edge and thrust it over. He knew its destination, and didn't stop to look this time, turning back to gather the blue shards strewn on the ledge. He wrapped the sapphires in his handkerchief and put them in his jacket pocket, turned, and walked slowly back down the mountainside to his house.

THREE

That year had been hard for the villages in the valley. The short summer stretched out, full only of the usual hardships

of life, but without the hope of renewal, without the peace
that accompanied each sundown, without the knowledge
that the passing of days and years meant children growing
into men and women, meant grandchildren, meant a
continuum of the life they had always known, and expected
to live. The slow leak of young blood, the loss of the
strongest, of the future, from the valley made it difficult, in
body and soul, for those remaining to tend to families left
behind, to find food and firewood before the great cold. It
was the oldest and weakest who were left to do it, the most
hopeless and helpless. Winter was upon them before they
were ready for it, colder and harsher than the last. For
Samaad, the carpets had brought some money, barely
enough to see him and his family down in the village
through the season. Samaad did not want to have to touch
the money from his father's Swiss account. There was
enough there to see them all through many winters, the old
man's glory days as the owner of a fleet of five-star houseboats
had seen to that. But Samaad had never taken any of that
money, and he didn't think he ever would. It was a matter
of pride.

One day, a day warmer than most, old man Hamid's boy
had driven up to Samaad's house unexpectedly and
announced that the old man was dead and had left
instructions that the Jonga be returned to Samaad bhai, so
here he was. The boy had asked if he could stay with
Samaad, perhaps do some small jobs for him, and get fed
in return. Samaad had sent him down to the village to his
brother Jabra, thinking how little they had to offer the
young men of their land, thinking how this boy too would
soon be lost to them, snatched up by the insurgency.

He had done nothing with the little package that lay in a hole under his bed. He had not met or talked to anyone for a month after he came down from the mountain that blue day. He had not gone down to the village even to meet Jabra, who came himself finally to see how his reclusive big brother was doing up in the lonely house. Samaad was rinsing his teacup when he saw Jabra from his window, absently kicking the tire of the Jonga as he walked by it. They had talked all day that day. Samaad told Jabra about his visions, about the dreams that ran through his head all those days alone. He had walked through those hills and valleys all that summer, as was his habit. He knew everyone, and they all knew him, at least by sight, at least enough to say 'Khuda hafiz, Samaad bhai,' as he strode along with his walking stick. He had seen the shrunken villages, he told Jabra, he had seen the empty homes with broken roofs, and little children running aimlessly between them. He had seen the old men with sad eyes, and young mothers and old grandmothers doing the jobs of men. One day he had seen a large mixed flock of domestic goats and sheep high up in the mountains, with no shepherd. He spoke to his brother of dreams, of thoughts, of plans, of how he would abandon those half-empty villages in the valley and move those remaining into one big village right into their own land. He would surround it with armed and trained men that would guard them against the men from the north. They would build a small mosque, and a Shiva temple and anything else that their people wanted. They would grow rice, and vegetables in the summer. They would have work for the young men, so they would keep those who were still there, and bring back some who had left. They would corral those goats and sheep that had wandered off into the wilderness. Jabra had listened respectfully because Samaad was his older brother, and because Jabra had always listened to him. But he had begun to think, by the end of the day, that his brother had gone mad from his self-inflicted solitude. The image of the two of them hunting for a lost tribe of goats made him certain that his brother was no longer quite right of mind. But Jabra was a simple man, and he said nothing. Finally, Samaad had drawn out a little bundle from under the cot and opened it. And Jabra, like Samaad, had known in that instant when he set eyes on them, that his brother was not in some hashish-induced dream, conjuring up some impossible future for them. He knew at once what he was looking at. Samaad had burst out laughing when he saw Jabra's light brown eyes go wide. Jabra had laughed too, because he knew their life had changed from that moment on. And then the brothers had gone together to that place on the mountain, and dug through the rubble till their fingers bled, scrabbling with their bare hands, not noticing the blood or the pain, till it was dark, and they had a small mound of stones to bring back down. They walked home in the moonlight, talking and laughing as if they had just had a long and satisfying banquet, getting back as the sun paled the dark sky.

The months passed, another spring and summer came and went, and the night air began to show hints of the coming winter's chill. Samaad and Jabra made do with what they had, and it was hard because they had so little, but easy too, because they knew now it would not be this way long. They were getting closer to their goal. Along with men intended as mine workers, they had about a hundred men from the neighbouring villages and small hamlets in the area. If Samaad did not put them to work and start training them, and then pay them, they would begin either to leave or become unruly. They were fed and housed, the men and their families, but they had to have work, a livelihood, and with this would come the feeling that it was a real life they had there, a permanent home. They needed a school, a teacher, a chai shop where the men would gather and talk. They needed to think of this place as their home, something they had built and would defend from anyone who tried to take it away. They had to have something that was their own that they would not abandon or betray.

Most of the militia men they had hired to train their own people wanted to be paid in euros. These men could use or exchange this through Afghanistan and the north into southern Russia. They had figured out over the last two decades of conflict that their lives were unpredictable, and their time would be bartered only in hard currency. Samaad had been very careful about whom they hired from the wild men that came around when they heard there was work, and even more careful what he told them. They made sure that those who left there had nothing with them in terms of information. There were not too many questions from these men, the work was safe, just weapons training, compared to what was available further north and west, in Afghanistan and Iraq. They ate a lot, slept a lot, trained Samaad's men, took the money, and then left. There were some that stayed, a handful, and became his men. These men were grateful to have found a life with him that

seemed, at least for the present, safe and easy. These were
men who had seen nothing but guerrilla war since they
were young boys, and they stayed because they were tired
of it. They believed in Samaad from the bottom of their
hearts, because all they had known was what he was
fighting to keep out of there. These men were loyal to him,
they would give their lives for him, and he felt safe
knowing they were there to defend him and the rest of his
people against any enemy.

'We need a few more men, Jabra.'

Samaad sat on the carpet, legs stretched out in front of
him, back against the wall. He passed the chillum to his
brother, who accepted it and took a long drag from it before
he spoke, using the time to frame his answer to Samaad.

'If you are willing to accept everyone who comes in, we
can have enough men by the end of the month,' he said
softly, carefully, watching Samaad's eyes behind the smoke.

Samaad took the chillum back and took his time too,
puffing out the smoke after holding it in as long as he
could. The men at the far side of the room by the door
kept their faces turned away from the brothers, looking out
into the dark. Samaad pointed his chin at the men and
Jabra called one of them over and handed him the pipe.
The man smiled, showing broken teeth and ruined gums
that made Samaad shudder.

'Jabra, I will tell you this one more time. And I will tell
you again and again as often as you need to hear it. We will
not have people here who are not part of this. We will not
have mercenaries help us get what we want. We will have
to pay them a lot more than money. They will take us over,
them and their laws, their ways.'

He let the emotion take him over, he gave in to all those sentimental, belly feelings that he always held apart from him. He had always thought of himself as someone who followed his heart on a path dictated by his head. He had tears in his eyes when he spoke again.

'Do you remember Abba? No, I mean do you remember what he was really like? How he followed the way of Sufi, how he felt that there was nothing above Allah, truth, and love? For everyone? That's how this valley will be, Jabra. Full of love and truth. There will be no jihadis with their black ways, their iron wills. There will be peace here, for everyone who wants it. And we will have none of those dogs telling us what to do. We will train our own to fight, to keep them out. We will have a voice, and they will listen. When we are done with this, they will all listen. Don't forget what we started out to do.'

He was quiet then, and his brother waited for more, but there was no more. Samaad had closed his eyes, their fire hidden from his brother, always burning inside.

Samaad had had thirteen stones cut and polished by an old cutter and lapidarist in Bombay's diamond market. Their perfect cornflower blue, the soft glow of the unheated gems, the sheer size of the gem-quality stones, made them prized above all other sapphires, and sometimes even over other gemstones. He could see why, when he had first held those polished stones in his palm. His heart had lurched, his breath had stopped in his throat at that first sight of them. He had seen them raw, but this was the real thing. They were divine. This was what they were meant to be. So this would be his first big sale, the first large lot of uncut stones, and he would have the cut gems to show as samples.

He knew he would have to be careful, very careful. It was not only governments that he had to worry about. Now there were powerful organisations that would do harm to get their hands on this. He imagined he could have the resources of a UNITA or an al Qaeda, that they could purchase enough weapons and power to make them a force to be reckoned with. And once they had the village fully built, they would move in the families, women and children, make it look normal, like any large village in the area, and they would be temporarily, at least, immune from danger. He had to consolidate their control over the mines as soon as possible. He had to get a large consignment of the stones out and so have the funds to get things moving faster. As he sat there in the dark, planning, thinking, working toward his ultimate vision, he felt that he had been given the gift of the stones for this purpose. He knew he had a higher power behind him, one that would guide him to success.

FOUR

The winter was short and not very harsh. In fact, it was the mildest winter of his memory. The work had gone well, both at the now complete camp, as well as at the mines. They had managed to collect a small amount of sapphire before the area became snowbound, enough for Samaad to take down to Bombay, just to see what the market would give him. This was the perfect time to go, when the days were short, the mines were inaccessible, invisible under snow. There was no danger from anywhere that he could think of.

Samaad had intended at first to establish a chain of trade with those first small sales he had made. He wanted to sell small quantities of raw stones to a single buyer that he would cultivate. He would then use the money to buy euros from a currency dealer. Then he realised that, though harder to do, it was safer and almost untraceable if he sold to a different buyer each time. He wouldn't attract attention this way. His stones would be passed off as Sri Lankan gems, he thought. Those stones were heated to mimic the very hue that came naturally to the Kashmir sapphire, the process even produced banding that mimicked its characteristic occlusions. The irony was not lost on him that he was hoping to pass off his originals as copies, and that he was devaluing them a thousandfold by doing so. But he saw no other way. By the time the sapphires got to someone who recognised their true value, the lead to him would be cold. This whole transaction was tedious and also meant that he got far less for them than he should have, but he consoled himself that it was temporary: once everything was ready and in place, he could sell to the highest bidder. He would sell in Europe, in Antwerp, or Paris. He knew there would be many buyers, after they saw what he had. He thought perhaps Jabra would do the job of selling the stones. He felt he could not go himself and leave his people without their leader. But he realised that it would have to be him. Jabra could more ably represent him there at home. They all knew he was Samaad's brother, and so accepted his leadership. Jabra could not negotiate with the corrupt and powerful men in the diamond and

gem market of Bombay or Europe. He did not have the
sophistication and subtlety that would be required. No, he,
Samaad, would have to go himself. They had enough
stones now, and they urgently needed the money to buy
the equipment to be able to get more raw gems out faster.

Samaad pulled his huge iron trunk out from under his
cot. It was a military green, with a strip of garish pink and
yellow flowers stencilled on it. The lock had rusted a bit,
and he had to struggle with the key, jiggling and pulling on
it till it gave. He took out clothes, a grey suit and a blue
shirt, a tie, socks, shoes, all of a quality that showed their
age, that they had all been made at a time when everything
was not made in the thousands in China. The suit had
been made for him in Hong Kong by an old master tailor
who had moved there in the Seventies with a very wealthy
Pakistani family. Then he took out his father's fine leather
travel case from inside the trunk. It was old, handmade
buffalo hide. It had its own story. The old man had
selected, after hours in a luggage store in London, a fine
travel case that suited his needs in every way. Time came to
pay for it when the store clerk commented on the supreme
quality of the pig skin. The old man was outraged, his
devout Islamic sensibility was offended, and he actually
burst into tears. Samaad found this part of the story, told
to him by his mother, hard to believe. The manager of the
store, to their surprise, apologised profusely for the lack of
sensitivity on his clerk's part, gave him the best case in the
store, assuring him it was buffalo and not pig. Samaad
smiled to himself when he thought of his beautiful little
old father, who said his prayers five times each day, lived
as devout a life as he could, upset by a pigskin case.

He pulled the cot away from the window and dragged it across the door. He picked up the piece of slate he had uncovered, and put it aside. Then he took a small spade and started digging up the packed earth that was his floor. When he hit metal he dug carefully around the square box and set the spade down. He lifted the box free and dusted the earth off the top. He opened it and took out the jute bag that was inside. It had a rough picture of Shiva and 'Himalaya Best Basmati Rice, 2 kg' printed on it. He carried this to his case and placed it inside. He put the suit and his other clothes in the buffalo hide case too, packing meticulously, rolling things so they would stay somewhat wrinkle-free, tucking underwear and socks into corners, wrapping a bottle of Burberrys cologne in underclothes so it wouldn't break, rearranging the clothes around the rice bag to cushion it. Finally, he put his prayer carpet on top of everything, closed the case and turned the numbers to zeros. He replaced the metal box in its hole and covered it up, the slate went back on it and then the trunk. He pulled the cot back to its spot under the window.

He went to his kitchen sink and boiled enough water for tea, and a shave. Then he unrolled his father's shaving kit, a gift from one of his royal guests on the houseboats. He laid it out on his cot with the hot water, a shaving cake, and a mirror with very little silvering left. The mirror was one of the few things of his mother's that he had in his own house, so he kept it in spite of its relative uselessness. He first clipped his beard and moustache short, looking in the fogged glass, but working mostly by touch. Then he lathered his face with the ivory-handled shaving brush. He shaved then, carefully cleaning and scraping and enjoying the technique of the strokes, the ivory in his fist, the straight razor cold and sharp on his skin. He took off all the beard and moustache that had grown in the two months since he had been home. He rinsed and wiped the razor dry, put it back into its place, rolled up the kit and put it on his case to take with him. That done, he drank his tea, threw a tarp over the thirty-six carpets that lay in the corner of the room, wrapped and ready for their journey. He had been in the business of carpets for almost fifteen years. It was the perfect cover for anything else he did. He attracted no attention to his activities because everything he did was the same as it had always been. He stepped out into the evening, to walk to his brother's house.

He let his mind wander where it would, chasing random thoughts, alighting on some, brushing past some. It had been two years since Ali had come down the mountain and led him up to his destiny. They had mined the sapphire as best they could without calling in experts that would expose the discovery. They had only peeled the skin off the mountain. He knew there was more deep inside, but didn't have the means, yet, to do anything about it. He knew he would, soon. Very soon. He hadn't thought, after all, that all that he had accomplished would have come to pass in so little time. They had a home now, where they could live in some safety. They had an everyday peace that surrounded them, and it was a good feeling for the most part. They all knew that things could go bad one day, but at least the fear they had lived with each day had left them now. All the scattered enclaves and little houses in the valleys had been moved—people, sheep, and all—into the high but large valley that once had nestled only Samaad's own house.

There was only one way in, so even his small contingent was easily able to guard the valley in spite of having so few trained men. Ill-intentioned people from the north had tried to come in at first. After a dozen or so men had been killed and two severely wounded ones had been allowed to return, they stopped. They would be back, he knew, but they had understood that they would need more than the usual minimally trained rag-tag fanatics to break up Samaad's camp. By then, he would be ready for them. They had begun to buy weapons from the bazaars up north. In small quantities, so they wouldn't attract attention to themselves, going singly, mingling with others. Getting the weapons was easy, there were people who would actually deliver to them in the small towns or mountain passes. It was the ammunition that troubled him. They had to drive in trucks, sometimes convoys, to buy ammunition. This was probably what had turned eyes on them. It took large amounts of money to buy large amounts of ammunition, large amounts of money attracted attention. It attracted curiosity as to its origin. The traders were just that—traders. They traded everything and anything to the highest bidder, or sometimes first buyer. Information was often the most profitable commodity: there was no investment, it came free with their trade, so they could sell cheap. Samaad himself bought as much as he could. He thought about the strange disconnected bits of news that he had paid for, how he had to wait weeks, sometimes months to make sense of it all, putting it together as it trickled his way. He never wrote anything down, he carried this information to its destination, to the man he gathered it for, in his head.

He had fought to stop his home from being affected by

the changes that had filtered up from the south and down from the north. They were slow to reach them, high in the Himalayas, but reach them they did, and they were hard to take for those who had lived easily and peacefully for decades—centuries—in those mountains. But he had to force change to stop change, and the irony was not lost on him. He thought of Brainiac, enemy of Superman, who had shrunk the whole city of Kandor and put it in a giant glass bottle. He had tried to do the same. He smiled at the absurd thought and turned into the compound of his brother's house.

The children were playing outside Jabra's house, a small cloud of high energy, a brown dog among them. They came chirping around him, hugging and jumping and clutching. Jabra's children, he gathered, had eaten, their mother had cooked mutton, he might get some if he went in the house, and then they ran off again, with the dog. 'The innocent and the beautiful have no enemy at all,' he thought, wrong-remembering a line read a lifetime ago. But it felt right.

He went inside and sat down beside his brother. Jabra touched his face with the back of his hand. He knew this would be a long absence.

'It is time to go already?' he asked, needing no answer.

FIVE

Naia stood on the deck of her parents' home, watching their boxer on the beach, frantic, chasing the huge brown gulls. Her father's word 'galumphing' came to mind, and tears came to her eyes once more.

The wind chimes tinkled, clattered, rang, hissed in the morning swirl of Pacific wind. Her eyes burned with the salt from it, or her tears. She hated those wind chimes. Her mother had bought them everywhere, some she had made herself. The slightest lift in the air brought on a discordant cacophony drowning out all talk. This day there was no talk, and she was almost grateful for the conversation of the wind chimes amongst themselves. The one with the long rice paper scroll was from Kyoto, where her father had studied Japanese pottery for a year before she was born. The kanji was still visible on it, a shadow of writing. She knew it said 'long life'. The clacking wooden one was from Bali. It once had a sun and a moon face painted on it, cobalt and gold. She could still see it, though the paint had long since peeled away in the salt air. The ceramic one with dolphins and starfish was from down the coast. From one of those cutesy shops at Ventura harbour, or the awful weekend art bazaar at Santa Barbara, where aging hippies sold artsy sculptures, paintings, photographs, and other aging hippies, like her mother, bought them.

She pulled her mother's soft morning coat closer and hugged herself. Her mother's smell was all around her. She had read about people smelling their dead loved ones' things, she had seen it in movies. Here she was, smelling her mother's smell. It came to her as a blend of images and feelings around her, confusing her, and bringing on the gasping sobs that calmed her for a time after they were done, ridding her of built-up grief until it filled her up again.

She took hold of herself and ran a get-up-and-go thought through her soggy sorrow, like a comb through her unruly hair. Everything had become blurry at the edges, and she held hard to the moments of clarity. She used those to do everyday things. Make and drink coffee. Bring in the newspaper if not read it. Feed the dog, for whom she stayed in her parents' house in spite of how much she wanted to go back to her apartment where she could pretend that Dad would call her, say, 'Your mother wants to talk to you', always a laugh in his voice, and hand his darling wife the phone.

They had died instantly, the policeman had told her. The truck had been carrying bees. Yes, bees, he had repeated patiently. He must have known he would have to. One must have somehow got out of its carrier, into the cab of the truck, and stung the driver, who had gone into anaphylactic shock. The truck had rolled gently across the grass median, met her parents' Volvo, carried on across, turned on its side, and had lain there for three days. They had been unable to get to the trucker's body because the swarms of bees stayed and hovered around the wreckage. The policeman had told her this part of the story too, he had seemed fascinated by it.

The phone had been ringing, blending with the wind chimes, and she ran to get it, reached for it, when her mother's hesitant voice filled the room. She snapped off the answering machine and said hello.

'This is Adam, Naia?'

'Yes?'

'I've been calling every number I had for you. I should've called this one first, I guess.'

Uncle Adam. Long blond hair, brown eyes with blond eyelashes, dusty-looking. Adam Hairy-eyes, that's how she had thought of him. Uncle Adam, always with gifts for her mother, and sometimes for her. She had a flash of an image of him being hugged by her father in that very room one afternoon, looking at her over her father's head, with his brown hairy eyes. She remembered Adam's hand on her father's back, a thick gold band on his thumb. Her father was stroking his head, he must have been comforting Adam, she thought. The image puzzled her, remembered now, though she had no memory of any childhood misgivings. She hadn't met him in a long time, she didn't remember how long. But he was one of her parents' closest friends, always at their impromptu gatherings on lazy summer afternoons at the house, always barbecuing earth-smelling portabella mushrooms and slimy eggplant slices for her vegetable-loving mother. Adam had been in love once, her father had told her, he had lost his love, and never wanted another. She had always meant to ask more, and never had.

'I'm barely ten miles north up from you.' Of course she knew where he lived, and felt a little guilty that it had been so long since she had been to see him. He gave her the address and directions anyway. 'Could you come now, with Leon, please?'

She paused, full of questions.

'I'll have dinner ready, you can bring the dog, okay?'

'Okay.' The questions would be answered if in fact there were any left, and she would be happy for the company of Adam, a friend of her parents for as long as she could remember.

As Leon and Naia drove up to the house, the sun was low. Vees of pelicans sagged over the water in their heavy flight. She had asked her father one day, as a little girl, why it was so sad to see birds at sunset. He turned to her, puzzled, and she had thought then that it was not a universal feeling. But bird silhouettes at twilight always closed her throat, brought on a bitter longing, a human sadness, something that she knew was not hers alone, in spite of her father's reaction.

She saw a black and white motorcycle, lights flashing blue-red, blue-red, and a thunderbird convertible pulled over. That car had to have been speeding. She slowed down, and passed the policewoman, big, blonde, muscular, in the formidable inky LAPD uniform, a blur of metal and black leather in the right places, very dark shades, very firm mouth.

Naia adjusted her belt and glared at the speeder in his T-bird, his lips quivering, unable to hold his polite smile when she said from behind her aviators, hand on her hip, 'Licence and registration, please.' She smiled at her own little fantasy. She had never actually wanted to be an LAPD officer, or any of those other things she imagined herself as. They were just little indulgences, like a piece of baklava, lives as mind mirages. She felt that rising sadness, thinking of all the lives her mother must have wanted to live, or even had lived in the short time she had had. Lives that Naia had never known, and now would never know. She thought about how quickly she had wanted to leave that cold room in the morgue. Her parents' bodies, what was left of them, were laid out side by side on shiny steel slabs. The policeman with her had told her a friend had already identified them, but she had wanted to see them one last time. She wished she had not. She wished that she had left her parents intact in her mind, laughing, the way they were the last time she had been with them. They were broken, the bruises on her mother's creamy skin must have formed after she had died. Once, an EMP at a helicopter crash site she was covering had told her that the body would continue to bleed, to bruise, even grow after it had ceased to live. As if the message of death hadn't reached all its parts. She had reached for her father's hand but snatched hers away from his when she felt the cold. Of course he was cold, he was dead, she had thought, and had turned and left. Leon had been waiting for her outside, in the sunshine. Nothing could induce him to look at dead people unless it was through a lens.

'The only dead person I'm going to go look at is my mother. To make sure she's never coming back,' he had told Naia, who had smiled in spite of everything.

She turned into the driveway of Adam's house. The orange sky showed right through the huge windows. When they went inside, it was just as she remembered it. Like a song comes back as it is sung, word by word, Adam came back to her, and she was surprised how much of him she had forgotten. It hadn't been that long. She was disoriented from grief, exhaustion. She examined his face carefully, now that they were seated and she had been released from the long crushing hug that was as much for him as her. His bitter cologne was in her hair. He was not a golden man now, more straw, his eyes were still hairy, but lighter, faded. He was looking at her too.

'Naia,' he said. 'Naia, Naia, Naia.' And she remembered that too, about him. That he said her name a lot. She had always found it funny.

'The real beauties don't change much,' he said. 'They look the same all their lives.' He smiled a little, but his face seemed unused to it, and quickly reverted to its sadness.

'Back in a minute,' he said, and left the room.

Leon had said almost nothing on the drive, but finally said what he must have wanted to for a while.

'You look like shit.' He was pissed off, he never could hide it. She had to smile, and she, too, felt odd muscles shift in her face. She knew she should have told him she was going to her parents' house. He hadn't said anything to her about her two-week disappearance, and his comment on her appearance was his little revenge. He had probably known where she was all along anyway. His irritation came more from the fact that she hadn't wanted to be with him than from not knowing where she was. On reflection, she realised that he had certainly known where she was, he had just left her to herself, and that must have been very hard for him. He was, now, all she had left that could be considered family. He was like a brother, but more. She had no siblings, so she didn't know for sure, but she supposed that Leon was probably as close to her as a brother would have been. Maybe closer, because they had met as adults. They had avoided the history of childhood and adolescence that sometimes ended in enmity between siblings. Neither of them had figured out who was the older sibling in the relationship, they just played that part by ear. He was an only child, so he had no training in sibling behaviour either. He had adopted Jim and Anne as his parents because he preferred them to his own, and they let him pretend. If he was hurting, he was dealing with it better than she was. She felt guilty again for not having considered his feelings.

'You look like shit, too,' she said.

'It's okay, no need to wallow in guilt or apologise. Get this dog out of my crotch, Naia, I swear I will kill him.' He rubbed at the globs of drool on his rumpled khakis and frowned despairingly at the stain darkening exactly the wrong place. She just smiled. Dog and Leon loved each other. Leon and her father had brought him home from the pound when he was a runty bow-legged puppy. They had gone there to fulfil a promise her mother had made to the humane society about finding volunteers. They had no need or desire for a dog, but they had both been afraid no one else would take him.

The coffee table was a hunk of pink-red stone with the top surface hand-rubbed to a dull sheen. Adam came and put a large, ugly Burmese box on it, black lacquer covered with fine scrawly orange brushwork. It looked like one of several that her father had in his studio.

'Leon, let's go get dinner ready. Naia, you take your time and look at all that stuff, it's why I asked you over. Dog, come here.'

Dog gave him a one-eyed sneer and turned over on his back.

Naia opened the box. The first thing she saw on the stack of papers inside was a thick envelope with her name on it in her father's writing.

SIX

The Goa boat rocked violently as they clambered off the ramp onto the grey slushy ground. It wasn't really a boat—

more like a small passenger ship with two decks and a few cabins for first-class passengers. Anne had been seasick most of the twenty-four hours it took to go up the coast from Goa to Bombay. The only time she had her own colour back was when Jim rolled her a joint from some of the very fine hashish they had bought in Vagator. He didn't even have to burn it before crumbling it. He wished he had his pipe so he wouldn't have to add any tobacco to it, but it had rolled off the deck into the Arabian Sea sometime in the night, with the pitching and rolling they had been going through. The captain, as stoned as the few passengers on board, had assured them that this was the last trip the boat would make until the monsoon was over, not that it did them any good.

The taxi ride to the Great Samrat Hotel was mercifully short. The first three letters on the neon sign had leaked their argon, so the sign now read, in glowing blue, 'Great rat Hotel'. Jim hoped this was not a sign of what was under their bed, but their room wasn't bad at all. It was quite large, on the second floor, overlooking the sea, and if they went out on the balcony, they could see the Gateway of India. Almost as good a view as if they had been staying at the Taj, the five-star monstrosity a mile down the road from where they were. The owner-waiter-cashier-concierge told them stories about it he had obviously told a thousand times, but they were fascinated anyway.

He sipped the cinnamon-and-clove-laced tea that had been sent up as soon as they were settled in, with toast and 'jam' which was what they called the fruity, extremely tasty jelly that was eaten sparsely spread on toast. Anne loved it. She had it on her list of things to take back home: 'Kissan

Mixed Fruit Jam', it said in her pink custom-bound notebook. She had already bought enough stuff to load a ship container—spices, grass mats, silver jewellery, saris, sandals in all hues and materials, reams of handmade paper, a mountain of clothes in cotton and silk, bales of vegetable-dyed muslin with handprinted motifs, even grass and bamboo brooms. He had pottery from every place they went to. He had found some excellent blue and white in Goa, and had bought a sample of each thing ever made in the whole state. Anne was no help, pointing out more and more pieces to him, none of which he could resist. They were going to have to retrieve all this from the house of an accommodating friend and send it home by sea, as the Russian writer on the Goa boat had suggested they do. It seemed a good idea, and really their only option. They had a long way home, via Marrakech, Torremolinos, and then all the way across the country when they finally made it back to the east coast. And they would surely accumulate more trinkets all the way there.

Jim was glad they were not like most of the hippies on the road. They had funds, they had provided for their trip and their return and didn't have to forage and scrounge or slum if they didn't want to. This did mean that they sometimes had to buy meals and hashish for people who were less fortunate, or, as Anne called them, the real thing. But nothing cost very much in India, and they were doing fine. Plus, Jim had orders enough for a year's worth of work when he got back, from four new restaurants who wanted his signature on their dinnerware. So they could pretty much use up all their liquid assets without fear.

Anne had been sleeping for two hours. Jim had run out

of useful and useless things to do. He dragged one of the armchairs out into the balcony, rolled himself a fat joint, and settled down to watch life go by on the street below. The sky hung close to the sea, sullen and grey, and the small white birds wheeling on the wind didn't look anything like the gulls back home. There was a connectedness here, he thought, you felt you were part of the rest of the world, not alone, as when you stood at the edge of the Pacific Ocean looking out to nowhere. Here he could see the ships lined up waiting for dock space, the bustle of international commerce, comings and goings from Europe and Africa, people, animals, spices, carpets, gold and gemstones. It must have been this way for centuries, very little had changed.

He watched people strolling, eating peanuts from the vendors that hung about the promenade. They carried baskets strung around their necks with broad sashes, they had little coal braziers for heating the nuts. He was about ready to go try some. He turned to look at Anne, so asleep, her sheet moving with her breathing. He stared at the sky for a while, watching it swirl and change, rain and stop, lighten and darken and lighten again. Eventually, he came in and lay beside his wife, draped himself over her, and fell asleep looking at her, his face so close to hers that he couldn't focus.

They both woke up from hunger early in the evening, refreshed but disoriented from the strange yellow monsoon light in the room.

'Dinner?' Jim asked her.

They dressed and walked out into the city, looking for something exotic and spicy to eat. They usually followed their noses, which had hardly ever let them down. They found a roadside 'restaurant'—there were wooden benches to sit on and more wooden benches to put their plates on, there were several barbecues and several cooks and the smell of tandoori spices overwhelmed them in their hunger, and they ordered a lot more than they could eat. They ate for a long time. There was red tandoori chicken, tender, hot and juicy, charred black bits on it that crunched undertooth, with raw onions sliced so thin they had to eat handfuls, long lamb kebabs with hot mint sauce, omelettes— huge, eight inches square, stuffed with ground spiced lamb, breads like fine unbleached muslin draped over their plates, even barbecued cauliflower, because Anne thought there should be a vegetable in every meal. Finally, when they were done, they could not stay seated anymore. They strolled slowly along the seafront hand in hand, looking at the lights of boats in the harbour. There were small islands quite close by, one of them was floodlit. The Gateway of India stood majestically at the mouth of the harbour in all its Gothic gloom.

'What is it for?' Jim asked Anne, she was the one that pored over tour guides and had bought *Lonely Planet* guides to everywhere 'in case we go there'.

She seemed happy, almost high. 'Short or long tour?'

'Long,' he said, 'what else have we got to do?'

'Okay, you got it. It was built in the Indo-Saracenic style, designed by George Wittet, English, of course. The foundation stone was laid in 1911, it was actually completed in 1920. What for? For you and me to kiss under, what else. It was built for King George V and his wife Queen Mary, to commemorate their visit to Bombay.' She turned her face up at him for a kiss.

'Wow.'

'There's more. I'll tell you just the fun stuff. By the time the Government of India had built this hulk, there was no money left to build the road that was supposed to lead up to it—which is why the road approaches at an angle and not straight to it. And—this is the best part, I think—the last British troops to leave India in 1948, after Independence, left from here. The Somerset Light Infantry. Imagine that— they sailed from here, right here, having said goodbye to their dark, long-haired loves, taking nothing of India with them but the scent of cinnamon and clove, which wouldn't last even till they got home to England . . .'

'Okay, alright. Where on earth did you get all this stuff?'

'The brochure in the hotel lobby.'

Jim laughed. She must have been there for less than ten minutes, and already she had swallowed, digested, and then come up with her own version of what was probably a dry history of the monument. He delighted in her romantic imagination. She always had a lovers' tale for him. If it didn't exist, she made one up.

That first night was the only one they enjoyed in Bombay. In the following days, although the food was the best they had ever had, and they met fellow travellers from Cadiz and Cologne and Cape Town, and the monsoon had made the usually naked, sun-bleached city romantic and mysterious, Anne could see only sadness. He showed her happy cows holding up traffic, she showed him an armless man. He pointed out a saffron Hanuman temple, she saw a woman and her babies huddled in a doorway to keep dry. He delighted in unidentifiable antique brass gizmos in Chor Bazaar, her eyes were on children with hungry eyes in filthy rags.

The children really bothered her. Jim would tell her that they were smiling, that they were always in groups, chattering and laughing even while they were begging for 'one rupee please mummy-daddy', but something had snapped in her, and there was no comforting her constant misery. She didn't eat much, she hadn't shopped for anything in days, and she would give money to every beggar that asked her, and of those there were many. Jim was both impatient and indulgent, and thought of all this as part of the experience. None of it bothered him very much, he tended to take it all in his stride. He was aware that he had a lot to be thankful for, but routinely and without guilt, a reflex action of an American in the Third World.

There was a French kid that hung around them for a few days, probably because they were generous with everything and he was on the verge of being quite broke. He was into India in a different way. 'The pain, man . . . it is just maya . . . *toute illusion* . . . *quelle bordelle*,' he would say in stoned French, and would point out all sorts of horrors to Anne—a leper holding a banana in his mostly fingerless grip, a small kitten with an infected eye, two babies playing in a huge mountain of festering, stinking garbage. All this would send her into a state of silent weeping. Jim was ready to send the kid on his way when his money arrived and he moved on. Things improved only marginally after that.

They had gone to the lumber market behind a huge mosque to buy hashish one Sunday morning. They sat among piles of wood and stacks of bamboo poles sampling what Mushtaq bhai had to offer. He owned the lumber shop, and business went on around them as they passed the chillum around and drank tea. People mostly ignored them. Some struck up the usual 'Where from? Why no children?' conversations that had initially amazed Jim by their total disregard of his privacy. He was quite used to it now, and he happily answered questions about his parents, his country, his and his wife's fertility or lack thereof.

What had Anne's complete attention was an enormous billy goat that had sidled up to her and was eating the remains of joints that littered the ground. He was rank and hairy, and stared at them with his square goat pupils. Anne watched his progress with a big smile on her face. Then Mushtaq bhai came out to check on them. He emptied the pipe onto his hand, which he held out to the goat, who licked up all the crumbs and smoky bits with such obvious relish that they all cracked up.

'He eat charas, he get hungry, he eat lot of food, he get more big and fat. Every year I want to eat him for Ramzaan, but he look at me, and I think, next year more mutton. Eight years old this goat. Next year I eat him. Good biryani for forty people.'

Anne turned to him in horror and disbelief that was almost funny in its predictability. Jim saw the outburst coming.

'He's joking. The goat is his pet. He's just joking. Aren't you?'

Mushtaq bhai saw and heard Jim's plea. 'Of course, joking. He's my pet, I can't eat him.' He rubbed the goat on the neck for effect, and winked at Jim.

'What's his name?'

Mushtaq bhai shook his head. 'His name? Whose name? Goat?' He started smiling and then laughing and then explained to all the passers-by and employees and customers what Anne had asked him and they all smiled and laughed.

'You Americans are crazy. Name? For mutton goat? Crazy.'

Anne was devastated.

She told Jim in the taxi to the hotel, 'He's going to be eaten. He's not a pet, he doesn't have a name.' And then she wept all the way back. Jim wondered if she had somehow gotten pregnant.

The next morning, when the hotel guy came up with their breakfast, she invited him to a cup of tea. Jim listened to their conversation through the open door of the bathroom as he flossed.

'Why do so many children have no arms and legs?'

'So that people will give more money when they begging.'

'Do you mean they only use children without arms and legs to beg?' She was puzzled by his reply.

'This is very bad thing, madam. The parents tie wire when the child is small baby.'

'They maim them? Their own children?'

The man was embarrassed and annoyed at himself. He stood up and hovered uncertainly for a minute.

'I have to go down to front desk, madam. Sorry. Thank you for tea.' He left hurriedly. Anne was quite pale and shaken.

And just as Jim thought his wife would spiral down into darkness, Adam arrived in the city with his beautiful and pregnant wife Naia. They had been visiting Naia's parents in Hyderabad, and were on their way back home to California. They wanted to be home for the delivery. They moved into the room next door to Jim and Anne for the few days that they would stay. Naia carried her pregnancy gracefully, without any trouble, as if that was how she always was and always would be. She had no aches or pains or sickness or complaints. Anne fussed over her nevertheless. It took her out of herself, Jim thought, and was relieved for a time. They spent hours just sitting in the coffee shop of the Taj, watching the sea, the four of them, talking of life after the child was born.

'It's a girl,' Naia would say, 'I just know it is.'

Anne had, it seemed to Jim, retreated from the abyss she had been moving toward. She was fascinated by the pregnancy. She touched and stroked Naia's belly, she asked her endless questions about her mind and body, so many that Jim wondered if he was the only one who thought his wife went too far. He knew he was right that her fascination came from the fact that she would never have the experience of pregnancy herself. He didn't want to bring up the subject, he knew it would start painful conversations—it was not something she fully acknowledged. She seemed so calm, and Naia didn't seem to mind, so he didn't say anything. Adam and Naia would leave soon anyway.

And then, early on the morning of the day Naia and Adam were to leave, Jim woke to frantic hammering on the door. Naia had gone into labour prematurely. They called a taxi and rushed her to the hospital. What had begun as a morning of hope and impending delight ended in death and a sorrow that Jim was unable to grasp. He held Adam in his arms as he wept in agony and confusion, inconsolable, saying Naia's name like an invocation, reaching again and again for his wife in his moment of pain, and finding again and again that her absence was the cause of it. And would be forever.

Adam was looking at his tiny being through the incubator

glass when they asked what name should be put on the birth certificate. He was confused by the question and said once more the only word he had spoken in those hours in so many hopeless broken ways: 'Naia'.

They had been lucky that the hospital closest to them had the city's best neonatal clinic. The girl child had survived just long enough to have a name, even if mistakenly, and long enough to be issued a birth certificate, before she went to sleep one final time. The human lungs are late to develop—the foetus swimming in its mother's womb doesn't need to breathe. She was just not ready for the world.

The next days, while he watched over Adam, who barely spoke, Jim neglected Anne. He found her sitting on their bed one morning, just staring at the wall.

'Let's go for a walk in that nice park we saw yesterday, you'll feel better. Let's go find a nice steak for lunch.'

They left Adam in his room and instructed the staff to look in on him and make sure he was cared for. The staff was aware and they all assured Jim that they would not forget.

Jim picked up their tickets and passports from the hotel safe so they could make their forward bookings at the airline office. He thought, 'It's time to leave Bombay. There's no joy here anymore.' They would all travel home together, as soon as possible, Anne and Adam and him, there was nothing left to do, and no desire left to do it anyway. Jim wanted to take his friend home, to be there with him and for him.

The park was beautiful, high on a hill with a heart-stopping view of the city. They could see the whole curving bay, the cluster of tall buildings at the end. On a day as clear as that day was, Jim imagined he could see over the Arabian Sea all the way to the dark shores of Africa.

'The shores of Africa must always be spoken of as dark,' he thought.

It was an old park, landscaped in a hodge-podge English fashion, full of unfamiliar plants and trees. Very old gardeners in government-issue khaki shorts and shirts slowly made their way around snipping a leaf here and there.

Thankfully, the park was free of beggars to beleaguer Anne at that hour of the morning. Jim wondered if they had regular hours, like people going to office. He thought briefly of asking her views on the subject, but didn't bring it up. The trees and grass and sky were washed and scrubbed clean by the rain and thunder and lightning they had heard all night. The wind had blown away every trace of the usual smell of Bombay ('It's like being in a smoker's mouth,' Anne had once said to him), and the air felt like it was cooling and cleaning his lungs with each breath.

They walked around for a few hours, taking in the sea, full of monsoon roil. The clouds were slowly beginning to march in and deploy for the next battle, children were playing around their grandparents, a few men were taking a shortcut through the park on their way to office. Jim bought hot batata vadas and fried green chillies from a vendor at the gate and sat on a bench to eat them. Anne was definitely not herself yet, but then, Jim thought, this was part of herself too, this darkness that took hold of her. It came on more often than it used to, and lasted longer each time. He sometimes let himself call it depression, and wondered if he should take her to a doctor. He wondered, too, if all the drugs they had tried had anything to do with it. It was a good thing, he thought, that they mostly smoked hashish or ganja, not much of anything else. This time there was a real reason, but it was one more thing on something that already existed within her.

They had been in the park an hour, and had walked a lot. They were both hungry again and ready to go find that steak he had promised. They held hands and strolled toward the gate, when Jim saw an arrow-shaped sign on a tree saying, 'Toilets'.

'Hey, I need to pee,' he said. 'I got the urge when I saw all those "Do Not Urinate" messages on the wall.'

They started down the path, and then followed the smell. There was a men's and a ladies', but Anne, though she badly needed to, refused to go in. She sat down on the old wood and wrought iron bench and held her nose and crossed her legs. Jim went in the men's, and did the best he could to hold his nose and pee at the same time. The place stank, and the floor released his shoes reluctantly. He shuddered, did his business quickly, and came out. Anne was standing halfway down the path, clutching a large bundle to her chest, and yelling at him to hurry up.

He ran down the path towards her.

'What is it?'

'We have to go now, Jim, now!' She was frantic, running ahead of him still saying, softly but urgently, 'Come on, come on!'

They ran all the way to the gate, and she quickly got into the first taxi in the long line at the gate, and told the driver the name of their hotel.

'What is it, Anne? What's wrong? What?'

They were both quite out of breath. She was still clutching

the bundle of clothes. She nodded toward the driver and put her finger to her mouth to quiet Jim down. Then she carefully put the bundle on her lap and pushed the cloth away.

Jim felt himself gulping like a fish, but couldn't stop.

He looked at the tiny brown baby asleep in his wife's lap.

He looked at his wife. She was looking at the baby, and he thought she was smiling, but he couldn't be sure, because it was not an expression he had ever seen on her face before.

SEVEN

Naia was exhausted from crying. She had been in emotional overdrive for too long. She was overwhelmed and then numbed and then, eventually, finally, calm as she went through the things her father had put in the box. There were her Valentine's Day cards to him from kindergarten until eighth grade, bus tickets from when they went to a Native American pow-wow, backstage passes to a concert and a signed photo of Madonna (he had gone with her to that concert in spite of being thoroughly mortified about being the only grown man among a gaggle of screaming teenage girls), the tag from her first bra (Christian Dior), postcards from everywhere from her to them and from them to her (she was guilty that she never collected her parents' letters, and was glad that her father had saved them for her), black and white photographs of her mother bathing her, walking her, reading to her, even one of Anne changing her diapers, and the newspaper clippings from browning Indian newspapers, some in Hindi, which she couldn't read.

She turned to the last page of her father's fifteen-page letter to her. She had read each page twice, carefully.

'. . . and returned home. Home wasn't the way you remember it. It was just one room then, with a kitchen and a bathroom. I built most of what you grew up in with the help of Adam, and a couple of other friends who stayed with us sometimes, visitors from here and there—you know, you met some of them.

'Your mom got a lot better. The therapy and new medications worked miracles, so that by the time you were five or six, you'd never know she had ever been sick.

'I don't know whether her sickness came from her inability to have children, or whether that just made it worse. But she never admitted that she was sterile until she had you. It became possible for her to accept that fact, and somehow find peace within herself and such happiness in you.

'Naia, I never showed her all this stuff that you're going to see. I didn't want her to know any of this. I didn't believe that your mother could have dealt with the guilt of what she had done, and I didn't think she could have dealt with the pain of giving you back. I was afraid that she would go back to being sick, to the therapy, to the medications . . . actually, I didn't think that she would get better if she got sick again. I love her very, very, much: I don't think I would have been able to take it.

'So, my love, if you are reading this, it means we are both gone. It means that I was not brave enough to have told you all this face to face, and probably that you are not yet an old lady. Because I had promised myself that when you were thirty, I would sit you down and tell you everything. Because I thought that was *when you would be able to take it all in and not hate me and your mother. And my poor Adam, though he helped me with your adoption, he knows nothing of your birth-parents, if I could call them that. To him, as to your mother, you were an abandoned baby in the city. He had so much pain of his own. I love him, and wanted to care for him, as I did for your mother.*

'I hope that you will forgive me for lying to you all your life, and in time be able to think of all the good times we had together. I had nothing but good times after you came into my life, we all did. Remember, when all the anger is gone, that your mother did nothing wrong, from her point of view. She rescued you, she brought you home, she loved you and did everything she could for you.

'I love you, my darling girl, and want all the best for you, and all the love and happiness in the world. I am grateful and proud that you were mine.

'I am, and will always be,

Your Daddy'

Naia called Adam and Leon into the room. They had been coming in and checking on her every so often, and she could tell that they were hovering just outside the door. They were relieved to be asked in.

'Did you know all this, Adam?'

'All what?' he said, looking at the box. 'That box was for you, Naia, I never even opened it. I promised Jim. I've had it since we came back from India with you, that's when Jim started it. He kept putting stuff in over the years. How can I tell you about it all?' he was almost sobbing. 'It was a lifetime of knowing them, being with them, loving them . . . a lifetime of friendship . . . we all grew up together, you know, they were my family. Jim, he was my father, my brother, my friend, he was my angel in my darkest times . . .'

He put his head in his hands. Naia watched huge tears fall through his fingers, splash onto the pink stone surface of his table and pool there.

His eyes were all shiny, his eyelashes looked unnaturally long, the tears making them stick together.

'So that's how mascara works,' she thought, and a little worm of guilt came out of the fertile soil of her mind, confusing her.

'But did you know all this stuff about them? About me?'

'Whatever it is, it wasn't for me.' He seemed puzzled, and so sad that Naia let it go. She believed he really did not know.

'What is it?' Leon said. He had been very quiet for a very long time, something not easy for him to do.

'What's in the box? Can I see now? Please?'

'No, Leon, you cannot.'

He was deflated. He had never understood the need for secrecy in any relationship. He said it gave people power over other people. Knowledge had to be free and available to everyone, according to Leon. Even knowledge about other people's lives.

'Well, why? What's in the box? Why can't I see?'

'You just can't. Because it's mine, for me, left for me by my parents. It's about me, it's private, it's stuff they wanted to tell me about—where I'm from, and who I am. Will you just leave it alone? I cannot believe you, Leon, stop it.'

He was actually wrestling with her to get to the box. Adam stood by watching and wringing his hands. Naia looked at him and all the tension and misery left her. A

giant bubble of laughter started welling up inside her, and
she had to let it out, like a burp. Leon and Adam were
both aghast, thinking she was hysterical, or ill.

Her face was wet from laughing and crying. They waited.
Every time she came up for air, the sight of their bewildered
helplessness sent her back into paroxysms that cleaned out
her head, like throwing up after a hangover. When she was
done laughing, and thankful that neither one had slapped
her to stop her hysteria, they sat quietly together on the
couch. Adam brought out the soup he had made for
dinner, some chewy, roughly-cut, dark bread, and the most
delicious wine she had had in years. Then, finally, she gave
them free run of the box. Leon was thrilled. He read out
newspaper clippings, giving them views of chewed-up bread
and chowder. He dug through envelopes stuffed with bits
of paper—receipts, bus tickets, postcards, business cards. It
was like he had found the treasure he had been looking for
all his life. He did not seem to care much that it was not
his life.

'"IFS officer's baby stolen from city park" . . . wow. This
is the *Times of India*—page three. Naia, you're famous
without even knowing it! Amazing, girl, this is amazing.
What's IFS anyway?'

'I think it's the Indian Foreign Service,' Adam said. 'I'm
pretty sure I've heard it somewhere—probably from Jim. He
was always on about India.'

Naia knew that too. 'Yes, they both were. You know, I
thought all those times they took me there was just to show
me what my roots were. But I guess there was much more
to it. Or not.' She shrugged. 'I haven't been back since I
was thirteen—that would make it, what—sixteen years? I

wonder if all the friends they made knew about me? About how they got me?'

'I am absolutely certain they did not. Nobody knew but Jim. Nobody.' Adam rubbed her back like her father used to do.

'Are you okay?' he asked her. He seemed almost disconnected, she thought, in spite of his words of concern. His words and gestures were automatic, stunned, somehow. 'I am, Uncle Adam,' she said in a mock-child's voice, smiling a little. 'You know, all that crying was more about realising that they were gone than anything else, that there was so much to ask them and no way to get answers to my questions . . . it wasn't because of what I found out. I'm going to miss them forever now, aren't I?' She began to tear up again, and Adam did too. They sat close, sharing the moment, but she had the sense that they were not sharing the same sorrow. There was something about him she didn't know, but she felt it was beyond her. Again, there was that nagging childhood image of him with her father, and she thought about bringing it up, but didn't. There was really nothing negative about what she remembered, and she had had enough finding-out for a lifetime.

'You do realise that we have to go and find them, don't you?' Leon was getting very loud and excited, still rummaging through the box. 'Your birth parents. We have to go to India and find them. India, Naia. I've never been to India!'

Naia did not even bother to point out that she might not want Leon around for that. She knew perfectly well that she didn't really have a choice in the matter. It must be his turn, she thought. She just sat back, had her soup, drank her wine, and watched him take over her life, as he had the first time she met him.

EIGHT

Naia felt no pain, just the impact of a body hitting hers, and then both of them lay in a heap on the concrete sidewalk. There was silence, as if everything had stopped. Then she heard people shouting, sirens, too much noise. Her hearing was the only sense working. Then it was all silent again. She awoke in a bed with heavy green plastic curtains around her. A hospital bed, just like in the movies, she thought. She had a large plaster cast covering her left arm, and some of her shoulder. She found a switch by her bed, and when she tried it the curtains whispered open and she saw she was in a ward and there was someone in the bed right next to hers. He had a thin pale face, brown limp hair, and from what she could tell through the sheet that covered him, a very long, thin, bony body. She figured he was a sick or hurt person sharing the room. But there was something familiar about him. Right on cue, he opened his eyes and looked at her. She looked back at him. He looked at her like he was reading a book, scanning all over her face, puzzling out something. She thought she could hear his brain glopping about. She had always thought that the ticking of brains was an absurd notion. How could something as fatty and soft as brain tissue tick? Then he spoke, in a soft, sweet voice that was very alive, but still very tired, 'Hi, Naia K, I'm Leon. I am really sorry I hurt you, I didn't mean to. Thank you for saving my life.'

She was at a loss. She had no idea what he was talking about. He saw that she was confused.

'You're not sleepy, are you? Because I really should tell

you why we are here before anyone else does. So wake up, okay, and listen. Oy!'

Naia was a little taken aback. 'Oy? What d'you mean, oy? I am awake, so tell me. Because the only thing I remember is getting out of my car, walking a long way because parking space is so rare downtown, feeling very relieved to have made it to my interview on time, and then this.'

'You were about to enter the building, that's right, and just then I jumped from the second-floor window of my boss's office because he fired me. I landed on you, Naia K, broke your collarbone, and lived to tell you. I was trying to die. Or at least, frighten bloody Elijah into giving me my job back. But really, I am really thrilled to be here. So thank you, Naia K, for being my uh—trampoline.'

He laughed softly, and started singing, very softly, 'Suicide is painful—it brings on many changes . . .'

'Who the hell are you? Why do you keep calling me Naia K?' She was getting angry, reality was beginning to set in, due in part to the itch she could feel building up somewhere deep inside the plaster cast. Listening to him wasn't helping her very much. Listening to him, she could feel another itch building up, somewhere in her mind, as unreachable as her arm inside the cast. 'Also, stop laughing, because none of this is very funny to me. I mean it, cut it out.'

He just smiled and said, 'Or what?'

The doctor and a nurse came in then, followed by her mother, all pale and wrung out. She sat down beside Naia, stroking and fussing and breathing small shallow breaths anxiously into her hair.

'Are you okay, baby?' was all Anne could manage to say, and then she began to weep.

Naia, usually patient with her mother's dramatics, was at the edge of her patience already, and thought she could not stand it anymore. She gritted her teeth and waited while the doctor stood looking at Leon's chart and the nurse took his vitals.

'Nothing wrong with his vitals,' thought Naia, hoping he would either get very ill or completely well, in either case he would leave her room.

The doctor came over to her, having pronounced that Leon would have to stay for further observation.

'That big pile-up on the freeway has all the beds full . . . that's why we opened up this ward, K . . .'

'Is everything okay?' Anne asked him. 'Does she have to stay longer? Or can I take her home?'

'We'll wait for the blood work,' he replied, neither answering her nor giving her any more information. He had evaded an answer casually, in the usual way of doctors. He read the chart a while longer, asked her if she needed any more pain medication, nodded perfunctorily at her, and left. The nurse followed him out, after wishing everyone a good one. They all sat in silence for five very long minutes, and just as Naia thought things could not get any more awkward, the door swung open with violent force. A very thin woman with a turban of orange hair, a huge basket of fruit and several bags, strode in. She had a very large nose, it looked all the larger in her pinched face. Naia held back from saying anything, especially in the presence of her mother, who was frowning at her and shaking her head. She knew Naia too well, she knew her daughter was perfectly capable of being rude without a qualm.

Anne, always polite and proper, introduced herself.

'Hi, I'm Anne. Naia's mother . . . this is Naia,' she said, holding out her hand.

'Carla. I'm his mother.' She jerked her chin at Leon. She sat down and rearranged Leon's pillow. She had ignored Anne's hand. If Naia had hoped for some entertainment, she was soon to regret it. She scrunched up her face, drawing her eyebrows together.

'Does anything hurt?' her mother whispered. 'I'm going to take you home soon, Naia, don't you worry.'

Leon's mother gave them both a look, abruptly stood up and drew the curtains closed around the bed.

Naia gave Anne a look of disgust, shook her head and sighed, 'Some people . . .'

Before Anne could reply, Carla's shrill voice came cutting through the curtains. 'What is wrong with you? Have you stopped taking your medications? Are you even keeping your appointments? If your father could understand anything, he would deal with you, Leon. You don't know what this does to me . . . I cannot sleep, I take pills for that. Then I cannot wake up, they give me pills for that too. Now I have this tremor in my hand, thank God it's the left one, I can still do everything for your poor father . . . Now this . . . Can you not just get over all this nonsense, Leon? Why don't you meet some of those girls I introduced you to? I tell you, marriage and children, you know, that will cure all this. When you have responsibilities of your own. Only then will you know what it is like to be in my place, always worrying, worrying . . . Your father, he only lives in the hope of a grandson, you know. You should really think about him, about letting him die in peace, and then I will not have these burdens . . . You are grown up now, and still it is my job, Leon, to look after you . . . Now the doctor says you could have killed that silly girl, why she should be walking about at that time of day . . . these girls these days . . . You are lucky they didn't call the police, they say Elijah said it was an accident . . . You are going to die without an heir, Leon, and I will survive you and your father. I will be alone and wretched, wretched, wretched . . .'

At this point there was a strangled sound, and then the woman started sobbing and wailing quite loudly, and her monologue continued, but was beyond their comprehension.

NINE

The flight to Bombay had been uneventful, and comfortable, because of the empty seats between them. They both slept most of the way. Leon had watched old episodes of *Candid Camera* being shown at mealtimes, laughing loudly and annoying many passengers. None of them did more than send looks his way, but that had never bothered Leon, if in fact he noticed. Naia's excitement, which had waned over the days of preparation, began to rise in her like a snake in the pit of her belly as the landing gear thumped out. She reached across the seats and held Leon's hand.

'What are you, scared? You should be, take-offs and landings are the most dangerous part of flying.'

She wanted to smack him. She just squeezed his hand hard, making him turn and look at her a moment. 'It will all be fine,' he said, 'as long as I don't get some vile stomach virus, and then I'll shit myself to death.'

Still, she didn't say anything. She knew he was trying to distract her from her own misgivings. She let him ramble on about third-world diseases and filth in the streets without interruption, paying just enough attention so she would not have to think her own thoughts.

His camera bag sat at his feet, the largest piece of luggage he had. Security had tried to check it in, when he whipped out his press card and threatened bad publicity for some invented slight. Even in this age of terror, he got away with more than was fair or safe. There was something about him, she thought for the thousandth time since meeting him all those years ago. She was never able to define it, but everyone that had ever met Leon had felt it. He wasn't charming or handsome or even particularly tall. But people responded to him as if he were all three. As if he knew things that they did not, and did not care. Then there was his photography. It showed more than should be seen, said more than should be said. He was among that small group of people that ran toward something that everyone else was running away from, the camera between himself and whatever was happening, removing him from the scene, protecting him, giving him a sense that ordinary people lacked. His lack of fear of death helped too. No, she thought, he didn't just not fear death, he actively sought it, again and again. But not in a long while. Almost long enough that she had finally begun to feel safe. Maybe, she thought, after all, death would come to him naturally or in some way not of his own doing.

The sensory overload was immediate when they stepped out of the concrete terminal. The smell of the great city hit them like a solid thing. It was exactly as Naia remembered.

You could tell from looking at a person what their perfume might be—floral, musky, modern, synthetic. This city had the smell of humanity, naked. You could smell the people in all their living. You could smell them eating, working, reproducing, dying, cleaning their toilets, cooking, smoking, living. Yes, she thought, you could smell them living. It horrified and disgusted her. She turned to Leon in panic. He threw his head back on his neck till his Adam's apple pointed at the sky. Then he sucked a long slow stream of air in through flared nostrils, filling his chest. He breathed in so long she thought he would pass out. Then he whacked it out in a gust and said, 'Awesome,' in a voice filled with genuine delight. Naia closed her mouth and swallowed her words. They sat in separate silences in the back seat of the taxi as it made its way through impossible knots of traffic. They could not hear much of the outside through the closed windows and over the music and the constant chatter of the cabbie.

'You staying in hotel? I can show you cheap hotel in Colaba, clean room. Toilet paper coming free.'

'No, man, we're staying with friends. At the address I gave you. But I could do with some good ganja man ... ganja? You know, to smoke?' Leon was frantically sucking on an imaginary joint in order to make the man understand.

'You want charas? Not good for you. Baba says these things not good.' He pointed to one of several pictures of a heavily bearded old man, naked but for the beard, with piercing eyes that would frighten any follower into submission. Leon persisted, still pumping and sucking his air joint which was getting realistically smaller and harder to smoke.

'Okay, I take you to. You check in hotel first, then I take you.'

'No hotel, thank you,' Leon informed him. He told him the address again.

Naia lay in an exhausted stupor against the taxi's velvet seat covers. The ocean was on both sides of them.

'Is this a waterway? Leon? Like in Florida? Like in the Keys?'

'No, doesn't look like it,' he said, and asked the cabbie whether they were on a bridge.

'Not bridge. Reclaimed land. Bombay all islands, joined together.'

They gathered that the swamp on their left was brackish water, an estuary. It was so thick with mangroves in some parts that the ground seemed treacherously solid. During the riots of the past few years—police riots, Hindu-Muslim riots—many lakhs of dead bodies were thrown in the swamp, and that was why it stank so, the cabbie informed them. Leon was further delighted with what must surely be an urban legend. He watched a brown dog padding busily on the sidewalk till it was out of sight. Naia just closed her eyes, afraid of the time they would have to stop and leave the safety of the taxi into the vile air she knew waited for her outside.

Tara's house brought back memories. Good ones, mostly, but those were just as hard to take as if they had been bad ones. Naia ran her hand along the banister as they climbed up the five wide marble steps in the foyer. Her hands knew that place, and her feet. She reached up to the doorbell, but the door was open before she could ring it. A powder-headed bird-woman was standing there. Her hands flew up to her mouth to hide the flash of stained teeth that filled her happy mouth. Naia knew her, but it was too distant a memory and she couldn't grab hold of it.

'She's here, they're here!' the woman trilled into the depths of the house, and Tara hurried down the hallway, arms out, just the same as she had always been in Naia's memory.

'My dear girl,' she said, and hugged Naia and then pushed her away to look at her. 'Well. Here you are, just the same as ever.'

'You too, Tara,' said Naia, surprised that she remembered, that it all came back so easily, everything she had put away where she thought she wouldn't find it. She began to cry, there in Tara's arms, pushing her face into the soft worn-ness of the cotton sari, with its smell of food, and sandalwood soap, and talcum powder, wishing for the sound of her mother's voice coming down the passage, calling to her to come and eat, or just to give her a kiss, the slap-slap of her father's flip-flops that he would wear only in Tara's house because the terrazzo was too cold for his large pink feet.

Leon stood and waited, he knew this would end soon and he would get to eat. Naia had told him about Tara, but she had forgotten or omitted to tell him how obviously wealthy she was. He peered past the two weeping women into the house. The hallway was wide and lined on one wall with carpets. He had been around good carpets enough to recognise the jewel colours of Persia and Balouchistan. The opposite wall was a giant glass pane, hung with bamboo blinds of the most delicate quality, filtering out the loud afternoon light. Rooms led off the passage, at least six. He was standing on a carpet, he realised when he took off his shoes, it was so large that he had thought it was tiled floor, until his bare feet were on it. It was a giant runner, with no border, like it had been a part of a larger carpet. It had worn patches on it, and the pile was very low. It must be very old, he thought, and valuable, but he didn't know enough to know how valuable. Tara was still patting Naia, clucking and saying something under her breath, and then she remembered Leon.

'Come on, come on, let's get you settled in, you must be tired, and hungry, and jet lag will get you soon. You should try and stay awake, eat an early dinner, and then you'll be just fine.'

She led them both to the very end of the hallway to the room at the end. It was huge, and there was a thick mattress on each end. Cushions of all shapes, colours, textures and sizes were everywhere, covered in pieces of old carpet. Low shelves lined the length of the wall below the window, the surface was strewn with coloured rocks, arrowheads, and prehistoric stone tools. It was a beautiful room, bathed in the same filtered light through the bamboo blinds that covered the many windows, and there were some marvellous carpets on the walls and floors here too. A balcony led off the room, and Leon went out to see. He came back in a rush.

'There's a pool out there Naia—come and look!'

'I know,' she said. 'I used to swim there as a child. I think I learned to swim in that pool.'

'So, where did Jim and Anne meet Tara?'

'In Japan—she was a visiting professor at the university where Dad was learning pottery. Kyoto. Before I was—born.

Before he met Mom. Tara's the one that sent me all those tribal things and arrowheads—and those huge hideous heads from Kenya.'

'Zimbabwe, dear,' said Tara from the doorway. 'I think they are hideous too, they gave me the creeps. Did you tuck them away somewhere dark?'

'So, why did you send them to me?'

'To get rid of them. Plus, your dad loved things like that, and I thought you might take after him.'

'No.' Naia thought that was ironic. 'Maybe I take after my real father?'

'Naia!' Both Tara and Leon had turned to her in not a little anger. 'You know, you have no idea what you are saying now, so I will let it go.' Tara put her tea down hard on the marble table, spilling some. 'Bai!' she called out, and the bird-woman came in and mopped it up with a cloth she pulled out from the waistband of her sari. Leon watched this performance and said nothing. It had distracted them all from an outburst that could have gone anywhere.

'How is Adam?' Tara asked, and both told her in unison that he was fine.

'You were named after his wife, Naia. He lost her so tragically. But I suppose you know that, of course.'

'No, I didn't,' Naia said, and thought, here was one mystery solved already, however small. She wondered why no one had ever mentioned it. Perhaps it was just too painful for Adam.

Dinner was an experience for their taste buds and noses. They both enjoyed the textures and tastes and smells of everything. Leon spent a long time over each bite, first looking, then smelling, then tasting and chewing. Tara and

Naia tired of watching him and chatted about everything, especially Jim and Anne. There was so much Tara knew about them over so many years, and she tried to tell Naia as much as she could remember. She asked about Naia's love life, if there was anyone special in her life. Naia told her about Raoul. Tara had actually met him once on a visit to Jim and Anne. He drew a soft admiration from anyone he met, left a light but distinct impression. It was no different with Tara.

'Jim and Anne were hoping he was the one. That's how Anne put it—"the one"—in fact Jim said you had never been that way with any of your other boyfriends. They really liked him. And he seemed so happy there. He was visiting them when you weren't even there. I remember he had brought flowers for Anne. Or was it something else? I don't remember.'

'I thought he was perfect for her. But I didn't think about whether she was perfect for him,' Leon interrupted her. 'They looked so fabulous together. I shot them together on Anne's hammock out on the beach, great black-and-whites. The light was perfect for black-and-whites that day. I made the most amazing prints, remember, Naia?'

She smiled. She did remember. She still had the ten-by-twelves that Leon had given them some days later. And then, soon after that, Raoul had accepted an offer from Tokyo to play a series of concerts with the Tokyo Philharmonic at their fabulous new concert hall. It was preliminary to their final offer, a two-year chair. That worked out too. They had a single tuba in their orchestra, and his talent combined with his beauty and gentle persona was irresistible to the Japanese. He was the first non-Japanese to be hired by the Tokyo Philharmonic Orchestra.

'I guess his music—his career—came first. Clichéd, but true. I have to say, Tara, if he had asked me to go with him, I would have.'

'Bullshit,' Leon said. 'That's what you think. You would have considered it, you would have freaked at the thought of being in a country where no one spoke anything but Japanese, then you would have decided I would be too far away, and, finally, you would have said no because you couldn't bear to be that far away from Jim and Anne. Tell me if I'm wrong.'

'You're right,' she said, 'except for the part about you. What the hell do I need to be close to you for?'

'To tell you what to do next.' He laughed out loud, and Tara and Naia did too.

In the morning Tara offered them her car and driver, but they declined, preferring to go with their airport taxi driver who had promised them a tour of the underbelly of Bombay. Leon was ready with his camera strung about his neck. He fiddled with his spare batteries as they ate a large breakfast around Tara's enormous ebony dining table.

'They made it for me when I was in Central Africa, as a goodbye present. I know it's hideous, and it's really heavy. So much trouble bringing it back, but I've grown used to its ugliness, and I don't cover it like I used to when I first got it.' She dug bits of food out from the edge carving.

'It's magnificent,' Leon said, surprising them. He didn't usually voice his opinion. His photography was his voice.

Their taxi driver, announced by Mira bai as 'Kartar Singh', arrived at Indian Standard Time, about twenty minutes later than the agreed time.

TEN

Kartar Singh turned the music slightly down, at Naia's rude request. He got that Leon liked it, he understood a lot more American than he could speak. Naia turned her face to the window. She watched the city pass by them like a travel video, without the soundtrack or the smells that she knew were right there, only the thin glass of the window kept them from her. She looked at the colours, so different from Los Angeles. Even the sky was a different colour. She had never noticed this before.

'It's the way the light comes through the atmosphere,' Leon said. 'It comes straight down here, in California it comes slanting down, but it comes through less pollution. It's crisper in California, with a high actinic quality, but brighter here. Too, the light's colder in California . . .'

'What-ever, Leon, I never get what you're saying,' Naia interrupted him, and then regretted it. He shrugged and carried on fiddling with his camera, looking at everything, holding it up this way and that. Then he looked at her face, and started taking shots of her, hair all frizzed up by the intense humidity, eyes dark with irritation, squinted to keep out the bright white sunlight, even that early in the morning.

'Oh, stop' she said, but smiled a little, looking deep into his lens.

An hour later they turned into a small side street, and all they could see on both sides was wood. Logs, strips, poles, planks, all standing up in rows upon rows lining the whole street. Kartar slowed and stopped by a store just like the

others, with a couple of charpoys out in front, two very old
men sitting and sipping tea from saucers. A brown dog ran
out from amongst the poles and disappeared between two
buildings across the street, flashing by them so quickly that
Leon wasn't sure he had actually existed.

'Mushtaq bhai. Good charas,' Kartar informed them,
and then wandered off around a stand of bamboo poles.

They got out and looked about.

The old men moved to one bench and gestured for them
to sit on the other. He pointed at his camera at them.

'Shooting? Cinema?' the younger of the two asked,
glowering and growling at Leon.

'No, photos.'

'Take, take,' the other one said, silencing his friend with
a gesture. 'This,' he said, pointing at his glum partner, 'is
Shankar. I Abu. I am hundred and six years old.'

Leon was first startled, and then laughed, thinking the
man was joking. 'Okay, Abu, we'll put your picture in the
Guinness book, man, smile.'

He began to shoot the two old men on their cot, one
with a white turban, mouth closed, eyes glowering, not
happy to be photographed, but obviously younger, and not
in charge.

Naia stood fidgeting on the sidewalk, holding her pants
slightly off the ground. She had put on her Oakleys. Instead
of eyes there was a flame reflection of everything she saw.

'Can we get what we came for and get going?' Leon
wondered if she was aware of the whine forming in her
throat. He pretended not to hear, and kept shooting.

Then he sat down on the bench, and patted next to him
for her to sit. She shook her head.

'I'm going to ask for tea,' he said. 'You may as well sit.' She sat.

'I am hundred and six,' Abu said again with a definitive nod of his ancient head. Leon looked at him closely. He didn't look a hundred and six, but then, Leon did not know what a hundred-and-six-year-old looked like.

'No, you're not,' he said. 'You can't be a hundred and six, man, no one is a hundred and six.'

'I am,' Abu said firmly. 'My oldest son died now one week.'

Leon was alarmed to see Abu begin to cry fat tears which he wiped dramatically with the back of his hundred-and-six-year-old hand.

'I am so sorry, Abu, man,' was all he could say, over and over. He shrugged helplessly at Naia.

Abu stopped crying abruptly, and said, 'I am hundred and six.'

'Okay, then how old was your son who died? How did he die?' Naia asked abruptly, hoping to end that conversation.

'He died of old age,' Abu said triumphantly. 'He was eighty-eight years old.'

Unsure whether to congratulate or commiserate, Leon stifled his laughter and avoided eye contact with Naia. He had heard her sharp in-breath and knew they would both explode if they looked at each other.

Kartar came back just then. The man with him was much taller than him, about sixty-ish, and walked with the grace and confidence of a movie star. He was handsome too, in a Semitic sort of way. Naia had seen this type before, but couldn't remember where. He had oiled-back hair, a carefully carved flaming orange beard that flared out from his cheekbones and came to a point in front of his chin. It gave him a slight hauteur that disappeared as soon as he grinned at them, exposing a mouthful of light brown teeth. Kartar introduced him.

'Mushtaq bhai,' he said. 'Sorry, he was little busy—namaaz—you know?'

'Yes,' they both said together.

Mushtaq nodded and smiled. 'What you drink? Tea? Coffee? Coldrink? We have ThumsUp. Hungry? Good batatawada, very hot.'

'I'll have tea, and the hot baba thing, sure,' Leon said, unsure whether to mention the ganja. Naia just shook her head and said nothing.

Mushtaq bhai shouted into the stack of poles. A small boy came crabwise out of a crack and took their order. Several small goats followed him out and began to wander around them.

Naia felt the bile in her throat. 'They smell vile. Like meat!' she said to Leon, who whipped off his lens cap and began to shoot again. He was happy as a clam, she thought, he couldn't hear or smell anything from behind the lens.

They sat around and ate what turned out to be hot potato fritters with fried green chillies and fresh baked rolls, and drank tea, and talked to Abu and Shankar and Mushtaq and Kartar, and finally, after what seemed like hours to Naia and seconds to Leon, Mushtaq took a clay pipe and a box of matches out of the pocket of his flowing white cotton shirt. He lit it and took a few short puffs to make sure it was coming through, covering the end with his sleeve as he did so.

'You try, if you like, you can buy. Sorry, no ganja.' He

handed the pipe to Leon, who grinned and sucked on it.
The smell, fresh and green and warm all at the same time,
was like nothing he had smelt before. It didn't have the
depth and muskiness of Afghani hashish, or the spicy spike
of Thai stick. It was mellow, more like ganja than hashish,
he thought, and mildly flowery.

'This is great,' he said to Mushtaq bhai, coughing out a
cloud of green smoke, like a baby dragon.

'Made from Kerala,' said Mushtaq bhai.

Leon passed the pipe to Naia, who took a short drag to
be polite. Before she could hand it back to Leon, Shankar
leaned over from his cot and took it. He cupped his hands
around it, held it up to his forehead and said 'Jai
Bhambholenath', and then sucked very hard several times,
eyes tightly shut. Eyes still shut, he handed the pipe to
Abu, still holding his breath. Abu didn't have any, and gave
it back to Leon. Leon and Naia were watching Shankar,
who after what seemed like five minutes, finally released
his breath slowly, and for an impossibly long time, a
locomotive engine steaming. Then he opened his eyes.
They were blood-red.

'Fuck,' Leon said, awestruck.

They sat on the khaat for a long time.

Leon stared about him, his eyes were bloody too, like
Shankar's. As the morning grew old, beautiful slant-eyed
girls emerged from the buildings across the street. 'Nepali
whores,' Abu told them. They were just sweet, giggling
schoolgirls, betraying no sign of their profession. Leon
slowly took his cameras from his bags and put lenses on, all
without taking his eyes off the street. His movements were
fluid from of years of practice, he didn't do these things

consciously anymore. He just went from seeing with his eyes to recording on film, and now on the memory card of his fabulous new digitals, what he saw. What he saw was not visible to most beholders.

Leon loved streets. When they are laid down, the streets don't know what they are going to be. This street, he thought, was what every street, highway, byway, lane and path wanted to be when it grew up. This wasn't just a smooth tar surface rolled over by impersonal SUVs and trucks. There are sinuous mountain roads in California embracing the curves of huge sleeping mountains. They curve around the mountain's cheek, down her throat, her breast, her belly (a brush of Scottish broom at the junction of her stony thighs), the road slips lusciously by all this, at last, to her ankle, depositing the lovers in their top-down convertible, lost in their own curvy thoughts, to the end of Decker Canyon road. It ends at the Pacific Coast Highway, now there's a road: forever wedded to the ocean, caressed by her at high tide and low. This lane in Bombay's hood was no simple macadam either. Life was lived on this street. The bare feet of children playing cricket on humid Sunday afternoons. The slap-slap of fish women dripping oyster juices and melting ice from the baskets on their heads. The soft scrapy paws of packs of brown dogs that nobody owned, running in the early morning to get at garbage heaps before they were carted away. The soft-hard rubber tires of those giant garbage trucks with their drip-drip of ancient decaying slush. This street had been slept on, spat on, shat on, lived on, loved on, the stage of millions of little dramas, tragedies, comedies and romances. Leon was entranced, and more than a little stoned. This was no coastal highway, or Main Street, USA. But this was what they all wanted to be in their next life. He would, if he were Peachtree Avenue. He was still looking, and driving his motor drive, when Naia said, as she used to years ago, 'Have enough film?'

'Film?' he said, confused, and she just laughed. She had his attention.

After they had left Mushtaq's, they stopped to photograph the lights of Marine Drive from the Hanging Gardens. Kartar dropped them at the gate and said he would wait for them in his taxi. The park was dark, the lamps were lit but only threw light in a pool on the ground below. There was nobody around in spite of it being not very late. The empty wrought iron benches had been recently painted and were shining. The whole place smelt like a public urinal, but when they had walked past the 'toilets' sign, the sea breeze started up and the smell was gone. At the viewing place, Leon set up his tripod and mounted his camera on it.

'I once photographed Liv Ullman. She was odd. There was nothing remarkable about her. But she could act beautiful—pretend. And you believed her absolutely. She looked beautiful in just about every frame. That's how Bombay is at night—pretending to be beautiful. At night you can't see the rot and the lepers and the lung-black smack addicts. Just this amber necklace around the throat of a Portuguese queen.'

Naia listened quietly and a bit apprehensively to all this. Leon had been reading obsessively about Bombay before they left LA. She thought again of the Spain assignment. She hoped he wasn't going to refuse to get out of bed the next morning.

'Leon, are you in love?'

'Yes,' he said, 'of course.'

ELEVEN

They got back to Tara's house just as dinner was being brought to the table. Leon had shot all day and was still high, more from the company and the experience of the day than from any substance. Naia had a headache. She was unaccustomed to anything but California chardonnay, so the hashish and jet-lag had caught up with her. She went to their room to take a shower and a pill.

Leon sat at the table with Tara, consuming the hot rotis as they were brought to him by the tittering Mirabai. He rolled them up and dipped them into a different bowl of curry for each bite, and was unable to stop eating. His tongue felt tingly, as if it had grown new taste buds, or had been rid of a layer of numb cells that he had never known he had.

'Is this all vegetarian? Even this potato-cauliflower curry thing?'

Tara laughed. 'Yes, everything. No animal product, except the ghee on your rotis. I have been vegetarian all my life. Except one time. When I was in Germany doing my PhD, they had nothing there I could eat—in the winter, all they had was these salted great lumps of beef, and a bit of boiled cabbage. This was back in the day, you know. I'm sure there are supermarkets everywhere now, with rice and daal.'

'You ate beef? Isn't that like eating the holy cow?'

She laughed again. 'Holy cow! Yes, but I am not a practising Hindu. It was more of a habit, something I had never done, but not for any reason. I said to myself, I am after all, an anthropologist. And then, I have to eat something. Or I have to go back to India without my degree. So I ate the holy cow that whole winter, but never again. I have to be honest, though, Leon, if I had liked it, I would not have stopped. But it was just so much chewing. And then I would get so constipated . . .'

Leon held up his hand to ward off the rest of what was coming. 'Too much information,' he said. 'You Indians are obsessed with your bowel movements. This guy I had never met in my life before started discussing the bowel movement he had had this morning. He said he was a hundred and six.'

'Well, he has lived to be hundred and six probably *because* he has been obsessed with his bowel movements all his life,' Tara said firmly, and Leon felt a lecture coming on, when Naia joined them looking fresh and washed and a lot happier than he had seen her all that day.

'Naia. Eat something, you look so thin. When are you going to start looking? Make some calls?' Tara asked.

Naia didn't say anything. Thus far, she had made no effort to do the thing they had come this far for—find her birth parents.

'Do you really want to do this?' Tara asked her. 'After all, what good will it do you? I mean, I have heard of other people looking for their birth parents and finding out that they don't even speak the same language—I mean literally. After all, they must have been very poor, or you might find that your mother was a young unmarried girl who got pregnant and gave you up for adoption . . .'

Naia took a long breath. She was going to have to tell Tara the truth, and there was no point in waiting. She pushed her plate away, and asked Mirabai for a cup of tea.

Later, Tara sat in stunned silence for a few minutes, as if unsure what to say to Naia. Then she shook her head, stood up, and began to pace the carpet. Naia and Leon exchanged looks, but said nothing. It was not surprising that she was upset and shocked. Jim and Anne had been close friends, and no one had as yet even internalised their passing in that brutal and unexpected moment. Their concern was also because of her age.

'Naia, you don't understand—I know these people! This is just unreal, Naia, I cannot believe any of this. Jim and Anne have been my friends for decades, not just years, and I knew nothing of all this—I know these people!'

Naia pulled her down next to her. 'Tara, we all think we know people, you can't know everything about your friends—look at me, they were my parents and I didn't know . . .'

'No, no, Naia, you don't understand—I know the people that Anne took you from—I know your actual parents.'

Naia looked at her without any comprehension.

Leon got it before she did. 'No way,' he said. 'There are over a billion people in this country and you personally know the very people we're looking for? Yet, why am I not surprised? You know, nothing is ever going to surprise me again, I'm all surprised out. For the rest of my life. Wow.'

Naia closed her mouth and opened it again. 'Tara, are you telling me you know my real parents?'

'Yes, Naia, I am. Your disappearance in Bombay in the mid-'70s was a big story. But apart from that, the man, that is, your father, is high up in the diplomatic service, and his wife, I mean your mother, never let anyone forget that her baby was lost—stolen from her. She gave many magazine and TV interviews over the years, more as her husband flew up the ranks, and she never failed to mention the tragedy of her life—the loss of her precious child—in each and every one.'

'You sound like you don't like her very much,' Leon said.

'Oh no, Leon, it's not that . . . I didn't mean . . . well, okay, I admit I don't. But then who am I to judge or even understand someone who had that happen to them? I mean, I don't even have any children. The closest thing I have to a child is you, Naia.'

Naia hugged her.

'Have you met them, Tara? Do you actually know them?'

'Yes, I have, many times. And, oh my dear, you have a brother. His name is Karan, he is actually older than you. He is in England, I think, studying in Cambridge or something.'

Naia just sat and took in the information. She didn't really respond emotionally to it, it didn't mean that much to her, not yet. She was excited, but not as much as she should have been. She supposed, and Tara agreed with her when she said this, that she was emotionally exhausted from dealing with the death of her parents, numb, and it was probably a good thing too.

'Leon, this may sound odd to you, because, like you said, there are over a billion people in this country. But really, there are a few social circles, and they all overlap each other at least a little. I belong to the academic circle, I suppose, and we overlap with the diplomats sometimes.'

'Could be because you're so damned rich too, right, Tara?' Leon laughed.

'Leon. That is totally none of your business.' Naia was clearly embarrassed by her friend's comment.

'No, Naia, he's absolutely correct in that. It is because of my ancestral wealth that I am very well connected. He is right. Being a mere professor would not have got me invited to all those dinners and functions that I go to, nor would I have got all those appointments in universities all over the world without my connections in New Delhi.' She paused and turned to Naia, and stroked her hair. 'This is all so strange, Naia. I am dazed, I can't imagine what you must have felt when you found out. I loved Jim and Anne, and I knew them so well for so long. Now that I think about all this, I can't say that it entirely surprises me. I mean, it does, because it is an amazing story, but I knew Anne. She must have thought she was rescuing a beggar child, giving you a better life . . . and Jim adored her, so he went along, and then when he found out it was too late, he couldn't take you away from her.' She had tears in her eyes, her gentle face lost in the past, remembering her dear friends.

'So, what do you want to do about this? How do we go about getting you together with them?' she asked Naia, still stroking her hair, looking at her in a kind of wonder.

The next evening found them back at Mushtaq bhai's lumber shop. Naia was tired from following Leon through the streets of Bombay all day. They had started the day at the fishing villages out in Versova, at the northern end of the city, where he had got Kartar to drive them at four in the morning. Naia refused to go out to sea on the boat with Leon, she slept in the back seat of the car till he came back.

He smelt fishy and salty and sweaty when he got in the seat next to her, tired and happy. He laughed when she complained and refused when she suggested a detour to

Tara's for a shower and change. She had seen him like this before, the high before the fall, and hoped fervently that all this war on his senses would not spiral him into a depression that would stick with them like a third person until she wearied of it and him and sent him back to LA, as had happened in Spain.

They were there to do a magazine story on a retiring bullfighter, a man who had been a star in Spain: elegant, strong, restrained, a throwback to some other time when the Moors ruled, and brought their sport to Spain. A perfect story for Leon. He had found it, and asked to do it. He photographed the final fight, a masterpiece of shadow and light, beauty and blood, a perfect kill, the sword glinting in the sunlight, the man and the black bull tied together by life and death in an intricate incomprehensible flamenco, the indrawn breath of the crowd, a wave of the judge's white kerchief, a perfect end to a perfect career. Naia had never seen a bullfight before, and she took a long time to get over the horror of it. She didn't see any beauty in an armed man, assisted by more armed men, no matter how graceful or popular, tormenting and then murdering a majestic but ultimately helpless animal. She thought that would get to Leon, that it would wring his heart as it had hers. But it did not.

It was unbelievable to her, but in Spain it was the beauty, the pure unrestrained beauty of Sevilla that sent him into first a high, and then a full-blown episode where he refused to get out of bed or even allow her to open the curtains of his room to let in the light—he said it was too perfect, too demanding. She loved him dearly, but wished he would get a hold of himself and take his medication like he was supposed to. She knew, too, that she loved him just the way he was: manic, depressive, riddled with complexes and borderline OCD, and the most seeing photographer she had ever known.

Naia had realised early in her career that she was not ever going to be a great writer. She was adequate, and Elijah would keep her on because she was reliable, yes, but mainly because she worked well with Leon. Elijah loved Leon, but was at the end of his patience when Naia had come in to be interviewed. She didn't think she would have got the job had Leon not decided that he was indebted to her for saving his life. He had an instinct for a story, and if she followed him, she would get to write it while he took the pictures. With those pictures, it didn't matter who wrote the story. She was lucky she did. She thought of herself as a piece of gum stuck to the chicken's foot. She got across the road because Leon chose to cross it. They were good for each other in different ways: he was the leader at work, she did the dealing with people, especially people in authority. Now, although he was here because of her, she wondered if she would have come at all, had it not been for him.

Mushtaq's shop was deserted but for Shankar and Abu on their cot. Leon jumped out and walked quickly to the rear of the shop, behind the poles and stacks of lumber. Naia sat down on the cot next to theirs. Abu was talking endlessly, Shankar was listening, or at least nodding every so often. Naia fiddled with her hair and sat there. The two old men paid no attention to her except for one small nod. She didn't want to talk to them either, it was too much effort to try and understand what they said, and even more to reply. Leon could spend hours communicating with the ancient pair, using gestures, sounds, facial expressions, even words. It occurred to her that they may even be quite deaf. It was painful to watch them, and when she asked Leon what had been said after an hour-long performance, he replied, 'Stuff'. So she definitely didn't think it worth the effort.

About the time she had reached the limit of her patience, and had become intimately familiar with each splinter and hole in each pole in the stack beside her, a taxi pulled up. The man in the back seat bounded out. Not so tall, pale-haired with the pale face of a recent arrival into the sun, in jeans, a navy blue shirt that had seen better days, and most definitely Caucasian. He smiled vaguely and nodded, and then, like Leon, parted the poles and disappeared into the rear, or store, or whatever was back there. She neither knew nor was curious.

A few more minutes passed in foot-swinging, and the new arrival came out with Mushtaq. They seemed to be having an argument. He sat down beside her, grumbling in what sounded like German, and took out a cigarette from a plastic bag he was carrying in his shirt pocket. He held it tilted up, as if to keep the tobacco from falling out, and then lit it. A smell like a synthetic flower fragrance hung in the air, not actively unpleasant, but not pleasant either.

Mushtaq gave Naia the cup of tea he was holding and assured her that Leon would be out and ready to go before she finished it. She was hungry but didn't want to ask for anything that would further delay their departure.

'My name is Frank, from Germany—hi.' He had waited for Mushtaq to be gone before he had spoken to her.

'Hi Frank, Naia, from LA,' she said.

'Na-ya? Los Angeles, California?' he dragged out the first syllable of every word, and clipped everything else. He offered her the cigarette he was smoking.

'You smoke hashish?'

She nodded, 'Sometimes'.

'This is better. You feel to try?'

'What is it?'

'You try,' he took a drag and then held it out to her. 'Very special.'

She took it, and took a small exploratory puff, remembering the first time she had smoked, thirteen, girls' bathroom, Santa Margarita Middle School. A bitter-metal taste filled her mouth, as if she had smoked a rusty key. She didn't like it. The flower smell was there again, like fading air-freshener in a public toilet. She had a sudden feeling of panic, wondering what she had smoked, and felt stupid for not having asked.

'Thanks.' She handed it back to Frank.

'You want more?' he asked.

'I'm fine.' She stood up to stretch her legs. Nausea licked up from her stomach, and she sat down heavily, thinking it was her hunger again.

Leon came out just then, all in a hurry to get going, as if she was the one making him wait.

'Come on, let's go. I'm all done. Have you said goodbye to Mushtaq? I told him we were off to Delhi tomorrow.'

He noticed something off about her. 'Are you okay? Sorry I made you wait,' he said.

He nodded at Frank, went over to their taxi, opened the door for her and started yelling for Kartar, who came running out from the back. She looked back at Frank, and waved goodbye. He didn't seem to notice or care.

Leon went over to Abu and Shankar, and, to their visible surprise, hugged them both and ran back to the taxi before any conversation ensued.

'Are you okay?' he asked her again. 'You look all sleepy and tired, and your eyes are red. Are you hungry?'

She said nothing, but felt curiously excited and alive, and ready to take on whatever was coming next, so she turned and smiled at his sweet concerned face. He smiled back. Then, since he had procured what he had come to Mushtaq's for, he proceeded to roll himself a joint. Naia was outraged.

'Are you kidding me? Do you want to get arrested? Stop it, Leon, now.' Kartar turned right around and reassured her that no one was going to even stop them, let alone arrest them, and it wasn't really illegal in the strictest sense. She gave up the issue and concentrated on the tingling she felt all the way to her bones.

They stopped to watch the sunset on Chowpatty beach on the way back. Standing at the edge of the water, Leon was oblivious to the floating matter that Naia didn't even want to think about. He was also quite unaware of the plastic bags, glossy magazine pages gone soggy with food and wet sand, coconut shells, orange peels, all mostly degradable but nevertheless ugly mounds he was standing in. Naia watched it go in and out on the waves.

'It's not the same, you know, standing on the Pacific coast,' he mused. 'Standing on the beach at Oxnard never gave me this cool connected-to-the-world feeling. I could start swimming and be in Africa in a week. America is such a lonely place.'

He stared at the great sun ball as it fell toward the sea slate. Just as it touched the water, he hissed, startling Naia. 'My mom always did that when the sun set—like it was sizzling.'

'That's the only time you have ever remembered something nice about her.'

He turned on her, almost in a fury. 'Nice? It was not nice. After that, she would tell me that the sun had melted into the water and would never come back. I eventually stopped believing her, but there were enough times when I didn't sleep all night, worrying about eternal fucking night.'

Naia was always aghast at his mother stories. She sometimes thought he made them up, but then, what else could have made him the way he was?

They talked about this and that all the way back, but didn't mention the reason for their being where they were, didn't talk about what they were about to do or how, Naia because she didn't want to confront it, Leon because he didn't want to confront Naia with it. Not that he couldn't. But he was having too good a time to want to change anything just yet.

TWELVE

Leon was fast asleep with his head against the powder-blue laminate wall of their compartment. His mouth was open, and she watched the stain on his shirt expand from a spot to a map, and began to drift into an open-eyed doze. They

had been on the train only four hours, and she was already
stir-crazy, wondering how she was going to make it through
the thirty-six-hour journey from Victoria Terminus in the
heart of Bombay to New Delhi station. She gave in to her
tiredness, laying herself full length across the bunk with her
duffel bag for a pillow. She felt the lumps of her wallet and
rolled-up socks and panties, and soon, the metal on metal
chakachakachaka jabbering yammering of the train put her
out.

Tara had managed to get them tickets on the slowest
train to Delhi. Leon had insisted on travelling that way,
even suggesting that Naia fly if she preferred not to go with
him. Tara was to meet them in Delhi. There was no way at
all that she was going to agree to take a thirty-six-hour
journey on a train, even if it was first class. 'Not at my age,
certainly not at my bank balance,' she had said, laughing at
Leon and his total excitement. He had a thing about trains.
He took one whenever he could. He said you could see the
veins and sinews of the land from a train, and you could
meet the real people that lived there. He found the slowest
trains, the locals that said 'stopping at all stations', sometimes
getting off before their destination when things looked
interesting. It was true what he said about seeing things
and meeting people.

His train journeys had been published several times in
travel magazines and he even had a book from his journeys
through the former Yugoslavia. She remembered being
terrified the whole six months he was gone. She would sit
glued to the radio listening for his name amongst the list
of dead reporters and photographers. And then he had
come back, changed and worn, numbed and aged from the

things he had seen people do to each other, and he had it all on film. He did get a unique perspective from trains. Sooner than she had thought possible, though, he was ready to go somewhere else, preferably somewhere he might not return from. When she tried to stop him from taking assignments that might kill him, he refused to discuss it, and got her dad to talk to her. Jim had bought her a book. The author, a reporter for fifteen years, spoke of the need in him to return to the war zone repeatedly, and had seen the same in many others. Leon, like that writer and the many others that had lost their lives chasing war, had 'the lust of the eye'. He went back again and again to get his fix, and he brought his images back for an audience that was hungry for them. She didn't understand because she didn't want to. All she knew was that she didn't want to lose her little brother. Or her big brother. Or her best friend.

Naia had suffered less dangerous train journeys with him all over Europe and once in Canada. But she still hadn't known what an Indian train would be like. Her parents had always flown everywhere with her. Now she was grateful to them for it. She hadn't thought about how many people would be at the stations, or in the train itself, threatening to pour into their compartment every time Leon slid open the door. She had been to the bathroom at the end of the passage one time, and as she squatted on the toilet and watched the tracks slam by below her, she had decided she would not eat or drink anything until they got to New Delhi. She had refused all the food, and sipped sparingly from her bottle of spring water while Leon scarfed everything on both their trays with absolute relish. After the first meal he had told the waiter to bring both the vegetarian and non-vegetarian options for every subsequent meal, so he could try everything they had on the train. He also made several trips to the dreadful toilet with his toilet paper, returning quite calmly each time, so she didn't think his prophecy of shitting himself to death was on its way to coming true as yet.

Early on the second morning Naia woke up to find Leon outside the bars of their window drinking something out of a brown earthen pot. He grinned at her as she poked the corners of her eyes. 'Tea? It's really, really good. This crunchy yellow stuff's great too—it really beats eating bagels and cream cheese.'

'Get back in the train. What if it leaves?'

He just laughed some more. 'You've been sleeping endlessly. You should eat something. The restrooms are really not that bad. A guy came in and cleaned them all up at the last station.'

'Did he cover up the hole in the ground too?' she asked him, pushing away the long yellow wafer he offered her. 'I am not eating anything on this train, let alone off that station. What town are we at?'

'Mathura,' he said, and walked off into the crowd leaving her straining to look through the bars of the window to catch a glimpse of him. She was suddenly overwhelmed with a feeling of loss and confusion. She found it hard to put together who she was, and where and why. She looked around her, at the blue walls of the compartment, at Leon's bunk, strewn with peanut skins, his joggers, his lens caps, and wondered what had happened to them. She was the messy and untidy one, not him. Her own bunk could have been unoccupied except for her bag sitting neatly in the corner like a punished dog.

Leon came into their compartment long enough after the train had started to give her a tension headache. He put his cameras down and began to fiddle with his stuff.

'What's wrong with you?' he said. 'Are you afraid? Because, you know, you don't have to do this if you don't want to. You can just go back home. You can always come back when you feel ready.'

As usual, he had put into words a thought that she had refused to think.

'Will you come back home with me?'

He didn't even pretend to hesitate.

'No way. Why? You know, you don't have to go back, you can just travel with me, we can find everything there is to be found. I'll photograph the whole country and everything in it, and then when I'm old, we'll go back.'

The very thought hurt her. Not of being with him, that was not something she thought of in terms of choice anymore. But of travelling in this country, in this way, with no clean food, with no place she could put her stuff down without thoughts of bacteria-laden saliva, unwashed hands, disease, dirt, garbage, so much humanity that there were no individuals, just a mass. She wondered not for the first time how her parents had loved this country so much, and how they had protected her perhaps without intending to from all that frightened her so much.

'No, Leon, I am going to meet my parents, and then I am going to go back to my life in California, with or without you.'

Leon shrugged and lit up the joint he had been working on. 'Okay,' he said, with a happy smile on his face.

'Let's go sit in the door. It's an amazing experience. Come on, Naayo, feel the wind in your face, come on.'

Naia sat in the door of the train, crushed between the side and Leon, their legs hanging into air. She tried to ignore the eight or nine smokers behind her, the smell of their beedis nauseating her. It was exhilarating in a Leon sort of way, she supposed. She was beginning to enjoy it a little bit when they started going over a river, and Leon dropped his shoe. Before she could react, quick as a whip, he got up, took his other shoe off, and, to her horror, he held the vertical steel bar on the side of the train, leaned out so his body was more off the train than on it, and flung the shoe backwards in the direction they had come from. She heard him grunt hard as he did it, but didn't see where it went. He sat down again. 'Don't you want to know why?' he said, grinning his stoned grin at her. Her stomach went cold when she realised how dangerous what he had just done was, when she realised he was as high and out of control as a bit of paper flung on the wind.

'Gandhi,' he said, and she decided he was even higher than that.

'One day, Gandhi was in a train going over this river, just like we are. He was sitting here in this door, with his feet hanging over the edge, just like we are. He dropped his sandal, and then, just like me, he threw the other one out too. I just did what he did.' He waited for her to ask why, and she did, to humour him, but also of course, because she was curious. He was not a storyteller, but India was bringing out things even he didn't know he had in him.

'He figured that the person who found the one sandal may as well have the second. You know, what was the point in two people having one sandal each.'

'So did you accidentally drop the first one, or did you throw it as well?' She regretted the question as soon as she asked it, and even more when he got up and left, pushing through the people that were crowding the passageway.

A few hours to New Delhi station, and people began piling their luggage into the passage outside their compartments, shouting instructions to each other, passing the bags and sacks into the area by the door. Leon insisted on having the door open so that he could watch everything and take pictures. Sleep and tiredness and a furious hunger were threatening Naia's sanity, and she closed her eyes and leaned her head on the window, carefully pulling the hood of her jacket over her head, putting the velour between her skin and what might be on the bars and siding. The train was rattling hard, and occasionally she heard a surprisingly sweet but insistent wail from the horn. She thought of Raoul. She had forgotten to call him and tell him about Jim and Anne. She wondered if someone else had told him, but could think of no one.

Raoul felt like he was from so distant a past, another life, almost. It wasn't that long ago, though, not even a year since she had last seen him, and not more than three since she had first met him. Leon had introduced them, in fact Leon referred to Raoul as his birthday present to her. He brought him to Jim and Anne's where they were having her birthday dinner. They were all thrilled by his elfish face, his understated but distinct Cuban accent, his unobtrusive intelligence, and finally, his music. He had gone to his car, she remembered, not at all reluctantly, but as soon as Leon asked him, and come back with the most enormous case she had ever seen, taken out an instrument that she had never actually seen before, and played unbelievably sweet music. She had always thought that a tuba would be loud and brassy, but he nixed all those assumptions when he played it. He was the best birthday present she had ever got. Except she didn't know when her birthday really was. That thought brought her back to the present, the train, New Delhi station, Leon shaking her gently out of her stupor, saying, 'Come on, we're here!'

Naia and Leon watched Tara as she held the phone to her ear. Naia held her breath. She blew out with relief when Tara said, 'Hello? *Sa'ab hai?*'

Neither Naia nor Leon understood anything she said in the next few seconds. Then she hung up.

'They are out of town for the next week. See, I told you we should have called before coming here. Well, never mind, I have things to do, and it's a good thing I borrowed my sister's cook and driver. She has gone off to their home in the hills. Now I will get the house all cleaned up and the kitchen going, you two go shower or rest or whatever you need to do. Naia, are you ill?'

'She didn't eat anything on the train. I mean *anything*. Ask her why. Ask her.'

'Shut up, Leon,' Naia punched him in his shoulder. 'I went and saw the restrooms, Tara, they were scary as shit.'

Tara burst out laughing. She and Leon proceeded to whip each other into hysteria, and Naia figured it was a good time to go shower and change.

'Don't be too long, I have someone coming to show me some carpets, you might enjoy that,' Tara shouted at her departing back.

Naia stood in the shower a long time. She had sat on the

pot a long time too, though there was no reason for her to, she just wanted to feel the luxury of it. She never thought she would be so grateful to see a roll of toilet paper. She washed her hair, she shaved her legs and armpits. She scrubbed herself with what she assumed was a scrub cloth and found it was a very good one. She conditioned her hair, and soaped herself again while she waited for it to work. She put anti-frizz serum in her hair. She combed it and put lotion all over herself. She filed her nails. She arranged all her hair and body and face products carefully on the expanse of black granite. She went into her room in her mother's morning coat and unpacked her clothes and hung them up in the closet. Then she pulled on a pair of her mother's soft cotton pants even though they were pink and flowery, and her own white t-shirt, and then took a good look in the mirror. She remembered what her mother used to say: 'Smelling good can lift your spirits a little.' Her spirits were not lifted, but she smelt a lot better.

She went out into the vast sitting room. She had been too tired to notice much when they had arrived from the station. The room was like Tara's home in Bombay, but there were plants in this room, huge plants in brass planters, making it look like a tropical jungle that had been cleared to make room for divans and brass statues of Buddha and Lakshmi. The statues were the height of small children, and seemed old even to Naia's untrained eyes. The carpets were here too, on the walls, along with a wall full of original paintings and collages. The room was in three sections, and she had to walk through two to get to the third where Leon, in clothes she had never seen before, and Tara, sat on the divans, and a third man sat on the

floor, all of them drinking chai and eating parathas. Her
stomach nearly leapt out into her mouth, she was so
hungry. Tara handed her a plate and she got to eating the
hot paratha, trying to be lady-like but not really succeeding.
It had been too long since she ate. Her gobbling ruined any
impression she might have made when she had come in all
clean and fresh and pink-smelling. They waited for her to
finish eating before they introduced her to the visitor.

'This is Noor Khan, Naia, he is Mirabai's son-in-law.'

'Wow, wouldn't that be like—inter-religious or something?'

'Yes,' Tara said. 'My Mirabai is very progressive, even
more so considering her background. There is no way any
other mother would have let her daughter marry a Muslim.
They had a lot of trouble, poor things. When Arpana
converted it became even worse for them, and then Noor
decided to move back to Delhi. Poor Mirabai was quite
upset until she realised that she could visit her daughter
whenever I came to Delhi, which is at least once a month.
Actually, Bano is back in Bombay right now, she's pregnant.
You guys were too busy, or you could have met her. She is
living with Mirabai in the quarters downstairs.'

'Wait, now, who is Bano? Does he have two wives?' Naia
was confused.

'No, no, Arpana had to change her name to Bano when
she converted and became a Muslim.'

Leon shook his head. 'So, she had to change her first
name and her last name? Wow. She, like, became a
different person! I don't know whether that is good or bad,
man, Noor.'

Noor Khan just laughed. He was what could easily be
called jolly. He wasn't fat, but he had a round face, and

smiled at everything that was said. He seemed incapable of taking offence, and the lack of lines on his face said he never had.

'So where are the carpets?' Naia asked.

'Samaad bhai coming tomorrow. I have some carpet, Samaad bhai has very good carpet. He will bring direct from Kashmir, direct from Iran, Iraq, Afghanistan, direct to Pakistan, and then bring here. Direct.'

Leon laughed and pushed Noor Khan. 'Man, that is too dai-rect.'

Noor Khan just smiled sweetly. 'Yes, yes, direct,' he said, bobbing his head from side to side in an arc.

'You have seen Qutb?' he asked Leon.

'What? No. What is that?'

'Qutb Minar . . . don't have English,' he said, still smiling and nodding.

Tara helped him out. 'It's this monument. You two should go out and see the city. I have things to do, so you could take the car and driver—Avatar Singh will drive you— and see all the sights of Old Delhi. I am sure Leon would love that.'

Leon was visibly excited. Naia was sure he would find the drug lord of the Indian capital as soon as he was out of Tara's sight. Naia was grateful that he hadn't lit up in her presence, and decided to warn him not to as soon as they were alone.

'Lunchtime, you meet me. I tell Avtar,' Noor Khan said, and then said goodbye all around and left.

Sure enough, the first stop they made was in a small lane, not even wide enough to be called a lane, where Avtar Singh parked them in the middle, turned off the car, pocketed the keys, and disappeared into a blue door. He came out in under a minute, and handed Leon what he needed.

THIRTEEN

Naia tried to pull her pants higher so they would not touch the street. She tried to keep her eyes off the street too, away from imagined and real filth right there by the food and vegetable and trinket vendors. Her hands were full of Leon's stuff. He squatted down on that same street, undisturbed by the muck.

'We are breathing shit as we speak, Naayo, so you may as well chill out,' he said, startling her by reading her thoughts. She wrinkled up her nose and pushed her sunglasses up for a second. It was too bright. 'Shit lays about the streets, and then it dries up, and then it floats up into the air—that—we—breathe.' He seemed delighted by this idea.

He was photographing a banana-seller. He was very tall, not very dark, with piercing eyes under his yellow turban. He smiled, startling them both with his fantastically crooked and mostly black teeth.

'Shit,' he said, waving his hand in the air, signalling that he had understood at least the gist of what Leon had said.

He thrust a bunch of bananas at Naia. 'Have, have, madam, very sweet, honey . . .'

Naia nearly gagged, but took the bunch. She gave the man a five-hundred-rupee note for his fifteen minutes of posing, and picked up her pants, the bananas, Leon's bag, and then ran to the car.

Leon was still shaking the man's hand, hugging him goodbye when she slammed the door closed, shutting out the dust and heat and the shit in the air.

He got in the front with Avtar Singh, his new best friend.

'Lunch? We have to meet Nooky.'

'Who?' she asked, but she already knew who. Leon always distorted peoples' names. He didn't often call her Naayo, because he knew she didn't care for it, but anyone else was fair game.

'Noor Khan. And his friend. Who is going to show us carpets. Shall we eat with them?'

Naia wasn't sure that she wanted to eat with a carpet salesman. But she didn't say that to Leon. Avtar knew where they were to meet, and he drove them to a side street lined with little dives.

Naia couldn't help her hunger welling up from the smells of the food, the spices and baking naans and charring meat.

As the trays of food began to arrive at the table, Leon started eating. She watched him for a while before she ate, thinking it rude to start before Noor Khan got there. But she couldn't control her hunger anymore, and gave in. It was one of the best meals of her life. The chicken was sunset-orange, the chutney was leaf-green, and though it cooled the temperature of the chicken, it raised the spice index, taking the skin off the roof of her mouth.

Leon had ordered enough for six, because he ate for two. They were lost in silent appreciation, almost reverence, for

the simple pleasure of eating, when Noor Khan walked in
with his friend. Naia's first thought was 'wild-looking'.
Although he was meticulously shaved and very neatly
dressed in polyester and had clean but old-fashioned brogues,
there was something about his eyes that betrayed an
uncivilised arrogance. But they were beautiful eyes. The
thought came to her as unexpectedly as a hiccup, it was
almost the first time she had found beauty in anything
since she left California. A carpet salesman's eyes. She
smiled at him, and he smiled back.

Noor Khan and Leon were having a time trying to
explain themselves to each other, Leon with his New York
American, and Noor Khan with his irreparably broken
Bombay-Delhi Hinglish.

'Is this Samaad?'

Noor Khan apologised and introduced him.

'This is Samaad. From Kashmir. He has good carpets for
Tara madam.'

Leon shook Samaad's hand. 'Kashmir? Like the Led
Zeppelin song?' he said flippantly.

'Yes, exactly like the Led Zeppelin song,' Samaad said,
and then Naia stared at him, almost open-mouthed. He
sounded distinctly English.

'You sell carpets? Where is your family? Where did you
learn to speak . . . no, I didn't mean . . .' she stopped,
annoyed and embarrassed at herself for babbling. 'I'm
sorry, I didn't mean it like that,' she said, trying to repair
her gaffe.

'Never mind,' he said from between his teeth. He sat
down and signalled the waiter for a plate. He helped
himself to a large piece of chicken and said no more, eating

with concentration and occasionally throwing in a grunt when there was a pause in the loud incoherent chatter of Leon and Noor Khan's laboured communication with each other. The gluttony finally did come to an end, and they ordered two cups of tea. Naia hadn't said much through the meal. She wondered what she was doing with this bunch of people. She wondered what Samaad was doing with Noor Khan, the husband of her godmother's maid's daughter. She was ashamed of herself, of how easily she had accepted the societal divisions of India and how she had placed herself at the top. She saw that Leon had taken without hesitation the saucer full of tea that Noor Khan had poured out of his cup. There was a crack down the middle of the saucer, and she shuddered. She thought, not by any means for the first time, that she simply did not share Leon's delight in the unfamiliar.

'That is called a "cutting",' Samaad said to Leon. 'When we get one cup of tea and share it like that.' Leon slurped it out of the saucer in two long pulls and put the empty saucer down. He leaned back, and his meal was actually visible on his middle.

'You have scrawn, Leon, instead of brawn,' Naia told him.

He just laughed. Then Naia remembered the envelope Tara had given them for Noor Khan, and she took it out of her bag and handed it to him. He opened it at once, and began to count it. It was a lot more than she had thought it would be. Those were not one-hundred-rupee notes, they were five-hundred-rupee notes. She had some in her own wallet, but hadn't looked closely before. There was a portrait of Gandhi on the face. She asked to see one.

'When were you in India last?' Samaad spoke directly to her.

'Fourteen, maybe fifteen, years ago—not since middle school. My parents had brought me here to learn to play the sitar . . .'

He laughed. 'Did you?'

'Did I what? Oh, learn to play the sitar? No, actually, but my mother did. She played the guitar too. They died last month, my parents. My adopted parents.' She seemed unable to stop once she started talking to him.

'I am sorry. Well, what do you think of our money?'

She was confused, and then remembered the note in her hand. She didn't understand his question.

'Gandhiji must be turning in his grave,' he said, and Leon sensed his suppressed anger. He turned at once to look at him, like a dog that had heard a silent whistle.

'Why?' he asked him.

Samaad shook his head as he spoke, but he knew his Americans. Not many that he had met knew very much, but they were unafraid to ask questions. They were not ashamed of their ignorance, and were willing to admit it and learn. Like children. Innocents.

'Because he was a man who owned one walking stick and one pair of glasses. Because he wore what he could spin himself, because he ate only enough to sustain his body. What kind of *bhenchodh* came up with the idea of putting that saint's face on money?'

'What was that word, man?' Leon heard the anger out loud now, and he would go for its core, down the worm hole that it came from, till he got to eat the worm.

'Sister . . .' Noor Khan answered him, making a gesture

to translate the profanity he had not enough English for, or perhaps because he was in polite company.

Samaad was not done yet. 'It is an insult to the memory of a great man and everything he stood for.'

Naia couldn't take her eyes off him. His English accent peppered with words she did not understand, his strangely familiar clothes, his eyes, everything about him had begun to fascinate her.

'Do you think he was right about Hindus and Muslims being brothers?' Leon asked him.

'No, I don't. But that does not mean he was not a great soul, he just said what he wished for. You know, he would have made it happen if he had lived, if he had been allowed to live. Because people's love for him would have made it happen. No Pakistan, no Kashmir as we know it now . . . well, I have said enough. We must go now. I will come to the house tomorrow evening, around six.' Leon stood up to shake Samaad's hand, but he was too late, Samaad was striding out without saying goodbye. Leon was disappointed. He knew he was onto something. He would have to wait.

When they got back to Tara's, she was waiting for them. 'They are back, Naia, and they returned my call. I didn't answer the phone, I wanted to wait for you.' She turned on the answering machine and Naia listened to her father's voice for the first time.

Samaad opened the windows to the small dusty apartment. He checked that the carpets were as he had left them, bundled up in burlap and heavy plastic sheeting. He had put his suitcase on the kitchen counter, it was the only clean spot in the place. He took off his clothes and hung them up in the bathroom. Then, dressed in only his underwear, he dusted, swept, and swabbed the floor until it was clean and habitable to his satisfaction. He had a wash by filling water in the bucket and pouring it over himself with the plastic pitcher. He washed his underwear and draped it to dry on the faucet. Finally he unpacked and took out his prayer rug.

Four men came to his door as the sun set. There were only four chairs, so he had to sit on the windowsill while they conducted their business. They took out the euros from the bag they had brought with them, and laid out the bundles on the table. He inquired about the exchange rate. They had answers ready for him, this was their business, after all. Samaad counted it as they counted the rupees he gave them. Then they opened up the cases for the second part of their transaction. They showed him the guns he had asked for. This time he only needed two small handguns for himself and Jabra. These were not of the old left-over Russian stock they got at the bazaars and from the northern traders. They were new, German-made, for their personal use. He would not have much trouble rolling them into any unsold carpets and stitching them up, away from prying eyes. He did not go through any checkpoints on his way to Delhi and back, so he did not have to worry about the law, but he had to be careful. He didn't want to draw any attention to himself.

He then gave some of his newly-bought euros back to the men for the guns, and for more supplies that he would collect when he stopped there again on his way back from Bombay. They would not take rupees. He had lost in this transaction, but he was used to that. The black markets in

Delhi and Bombay were far more expensive than the arms bazaars in the north, and for currency exchange as well, but it was more anonymous, safer here where no one knew or cared where he came from.

Their business done, the men left without goodbyes or any other personal conversation. It was as he preferred it. He liked doing business with this group, and would continue to use them if nothing went wrong.

He had a week in which to sell as many carpets as he could before heading to Bombay to find buyers for the sapphires. He wanted to take those as far south as he had time for, as far away from the source as he could. But he felt uncomfortable away from home, away from the clean mountain air. The press of people bothered him, and it had become worse as the years went by. He could feel people in the apartment next to him, and over his head, and on the lower floor as he slept on a mattress on the floor. He could hear the traffic all night, and the murmur of people living and breathing and moving around him, in his space, intruding into his thoughts with their noises and smells. He thought about Bruce Chatwin, who wrote that when human beings stopped being nomads, stopped moving and built cities, they stagnated in their own filth, disease and rot. He had been overwhelmed by the obvious truth of that theory. He believed it absolutely. He wished he, like his own direct ancestors, could keep walking, walking, anywhere he chose, without encountering any buildings, cities, roads—he sometimes wished not to see even people.

He unrolled the mattress and spread his clean white sheet on it. Then he lay on his back, eyes to the ceiling. There were cobwebs in the corner. He didn't mind spiders, they gave him comfort, busy in their own world.

He thought about the pair he had met that day. The girl was attractive, but so wrapped up in her own self and her misery that she had nothing of relevance to say. Leon, now there was a man he might have bothered to get to know better in another life. Leon was a Jew ('Yehudi,' he thought), but American, and so not really a Jew, somehow. They were easier for him to deal with because they had everything they needed, they were rich, richer than they understood. They did not have to fight for everything. Not anymore, anyway. Americans were innocent. They could be turned around and made to face the opposite way from which they had come, if you convinced them that was the right way. They could be made into instruments, and sometimes they would give up anything for a friend. Even their beliefs. Even their Jewishness, perhaps. All that apart, Samaad had felt Leon's genuine interest in him, and the world, and a genuine absence of self-interest. He had to admit, he just liked him. It didn't matter, really, he thought. They would probably never meet again, after tomorrow. He realised he was looking forward to seeing them again, not just Leon, but the girl as well. He could not remember her name.

FOURTEEN

They got out of the car at the far end of the driveway. Avtar smiled reassuringly at Naia as she walked past him. Her heart beat hard and fast, and she put her fingers up to her throat to feel her pulse. The house was huge. Two cars stood in the driveway, white-uniformed chauffeurs leaned against them, talking. She held Leon's hand tight. He returned the squeeze, and then let go, steering her gently into the house. They stepped through oversized doors into a cavernous room full of velvet and damask, couches, over-stuffed chairs, carved side tables, and carpets. Fabulous carpets, even to Naia, who had no knowledge of them. They made Tara gasp. They lay everywhere, large and small pools of silk and wool. Traditional Bokharas with their repeating geometrics. Naeens, sky and wheat twisted together in curvilinear medallions. Balouchis, quieter, but as compelling, Tara knew some and just gaped at those she didn't. Naia wondered if Samaad had sold any of these. They had all stopped and were looking around them, reluctant to step on these artworks. The man-servant pulled apart the heavy drapes giving them an astonishing view of another splendid carpet outside. A vivid living outdoor carpet, lovingly and painstakingly created with flowers and variegated leaves, mimicking the pleasing geometrics of Persian weaving. Leon had wanted to bring his cameras, but Tara had forbidden him. They were all taken in by the beauty and natural good taste in the house. Nothing looked contrived, everything was there because it was wanted, loved by whoever had put it there. It had an incongruously homely air, in spite of the obvious opulence.

Naia's father was tall, very tall. And dark. She saw her face in his as clearly as if she were looking into a distorting mirror. Leon said, 'Bloody hell' not enough under his breath that she didn't hear him. She hoped no one else had. Her mother was small, much smaller than anyone else in the room, and much thinner. She had sharp, bright eyes, large, black, so the pupils were indistinguishable from the rest of the eye, sunk deep into her small skull. Her lips were so thin as to be invisible, a slash in her face. They walked in, the two of them, nothing in the world like Jim and Anne. Naia thought of a wildebeest walking slowly, majestically with a little bird flitting about its head. Her father and mother. Everything about her mother was small, thought Naia, her hands, her mouth, even her ears, with their tiny seed pearl clusters, and when she spoke, her voice was almost a whisper. Where she was small, he was large. That mouth, under the white bristle, was hers, Naia's. She wanted to hear him laugh.

It was an awkward silence, but it wasn't as long as Naia perceived it. Time was stretching out for her. Finally she heard him speak.

'Hello, Tara, how are you . . . hello, hello, do sit down, I am Viren. You know Saroj.' He held out his hand to Naia, and then looked to Tara for introductions. Tara was at a loss. She just mumbled, 'Hello, Viren, how are you, hello Saroj,' and said nothing more. Viren must have been puzzled. But he was a diplomat, and he just smiled all round and invited them to sit.

Leon spoke then. 'Viren, Saroj, pleased to meet you, I'm Leon, and this is Naia.' He paused for effect, or to gather his thoughts, and then stood up again. It was clear to Naia that he was agitated, but no one else knew him, and so no one else noticed. 'Tara says you lost your daughter some years ago . . .' he started haltingly, and before he could continue what was becoming a very difficult speech for him, Viren cut him off angrily. 'Tara, what do you mean? What is this? Who are these people?'

Tara looked tired. She took a deep breath. She put her hand on Naia's head. 'I have no other way to tell you this, Viren, Saroj. This Naia, she is your daughter. She is the child you lost. That is why I came here today, to bring her to you.'

Saroj clutched at her husband's hand. She put her little hand up to her mouth, moaned gently, and then just fell over limp. He stood up, towering over everyone and called for help. Naia fanned desperately at Saroj with a magazine, and she began to open her eyes. She seemed incoherent, though, and the two chauffeurs and Viren helped her to her feet and walked her out of the room, a big maid scurrying after them with a pitcher of water and glasses on a tray, leaving just the three of them in the room, looking at each other. Leon said 'Bloody hell' again, this time loudly enough for all of them to hear him. Then they did something they all thought back on later with consternation. They all burst out laughing.

They stood up when Viren came back into the room. He was visibly angry, eyebrows pulled together. He addressed Tara directly. 'Saroj is not taking this well. I have called her doctor.' Nobody said anything.

'How have you come to this conclusion? That this girl is the child I lost?'

Tara sat down. He did too. Finally, so did Naia and Leon.

'I will tell you everything I know. But before that, Viren, just look at her. Don't you know that face?'

Viren turned to Naia and, for the first time, really looked at her. His eyes began to tear, and he brushed at them angrily. But he didn't take his eyes off Naia.

'Tell me,' he said. And they did.

The garden was dark by the time they were done talking, and he had asked them all every question he could think of, from Naia's childhood, Jim and Anne, Leon, every school she had been to, to her favourite song, movie, colour, everything. He took his eyes away from her only when he had to. He told them about himself, where he had been in the world, how he had lived in Tehran, Tel Aviv, Lusaka, Tokyo, Madrid, how he had to pack up and go to any place that had an Indian mission. He told them about the outlines of his life, but, too, he told them what it was all about, how he felt, what he liked, the people he had met, the food, and he told them about his special love, his carpets. His carpets brought a gentle fire into his eyes and voice, and he took them around the house and showed them his most precious ones, mounted on walls, some in glass, not even whole, just fragments held together by nothing more than a few threads that wouldn't let go. He didn't say much about his wife, Naia noticed, and when she asked him a question about her he gave only the barest of answers. Tara and Leon offered to go and leave them both alone, but neither Viren nor Naia wanted that. They were not, neither of them, ready for it.

Later, when they had eaten dinner in a small private dining room, he took them outside into his garden, and had the lights turned on. It took their breath away. The lights were perfectly placed to make the carpet glow, and when Naia squeezed her eyes out of focus, it looked for all the world like a real, giant carpet. They were all clearly delighted, and this pleased him.

'There was a Persian king, Khosro the first,' he told them

in his pleasant, soft baritone that made Naia think of an Indian James Earl Jones. 'He loved carpets. He had one made for him that was ninety feet square. It was woven for him by the best weavers in his empire, and they were supplied the best materials anyone could get. The king gave them great jewels from his treasury, rubies from Burma, like pomegranate seeds, emeralds, green as frogs, sapphires, the most beautiful bits of Ceylon Blue. And gold and silver thread. All this they wove into the king's garden carpet. When it was made, they laid it out in a quiet room, with windows so the sun would set the carpet ablaze. The king would walk on his carpet, looking at the colours, strolling on it like it was a little garden.' They listened to him, as they strolled through his garden carpet, transported to some other time. Strangeness overcame them all in some way.

'Do you want to know what happened?' he asked, with a little smile, lowering his voice even more, being deliberately dramatic.

'Yes,' Naia said, laughing a little with him.

'Twelve Arab tribesmen banded together, attacked the kingdom, defeated Khosro, and then divided up the spoils between them. The carpet? Well, that was cut up into twelve pieces, one for each of the tribes, and was never seen whole or in pieces again.' He got the gasp he was expecting, from all three of them.

'That's a beautiful and strange story, Viren, is it true?' Tara asked him.

'Yes, it is, actually. I heard it when we were in Tehran. An old carpet man told it to me, when I was in there buying my—I guess sixth or seventh carpet. I spent all my money

on those carpets. I didn't make that much then, I was very
low on the embassy ladder. Saroj didn't like it at all, you
know, she was always trying to make ends meet. But you
know how it is, Tara, don't you, with carpets?'

Tara laughed in agreement.

It was late when they got back to Tara's apartment.
Saying goodbye was awkward at least, and very confusing
for Naia. He had hugged her and held her for a moment,
and then let her go, not knowing what else to do. She
thought she might have stayed if he had asked her to, but
was glad he hadn't. She wanted to be alone with Leon, to
talk to him about everything that had happened. She
needed to ask him what he thought and how he felt about
it all. And, Samaad was coming to Tara's the next day. She
wanted to see him again.

Naia turned from one side to the other. She pushed her
arm under her pillow to find that cool-cotton spot that
disappeared too soon from the heat of her skin. She put a
pillow between her legs to cool off her thighs. She closed
her eyes and tried to shut out the laser beam of moonlight
that pierced through her too thin eyelids by thinking black
thoughts. She searched restlessly for that elusive sweet spot
of sleep, like searching for an orgasm in the midst of all
that activity of sex. She thought of Raoul, and wondered,
only because she was weak from sleeplessness, if what Leon
said was true. That Raoul had left her. Not obviously, not
consciously, but he had looked for a job away from LA, or
even out of the country, because he wanted not to be with
her.

'You're a snob, Naayo, and Raoul recognises that. And
you're a bigot. He doesn't actually see it or acknowledge it,

because Raoul doesn't acknowledge anything outside a false note, and, god forbid, address it. But he recognises it. So, he didn't tell you because he didn't tell himself that he didn't want to be with you. But, he did go away.'

'You're full of shit, Leon,' she had told him.

'That too,' he had said, and no more.

But tonight she wondered about it. Why Japan? Why hadn't he taken the jobs in Europe? He had said there was too much Beethoven in one of the positions available, and Beethoven hadn't written anything for the tuba. They had never talked about anything permanent. But neither had they talked about their relationship being over. Then, like that elusive orgasm—when you don't concentrate, it's there, and she was asleep.

When Naia came out of her room at eleven the next morning after a night full of strange dreams, Tara and Leon were at the table wondering whether to have breakfast or go straight to an early lunch. Leon wanted to have both. So after tea and toast, they sat around the table eating rice and kadhi with crisp fried okra, talking about the night before.

'He's a nice man,' was Tara's only comment, and then she couldn't get a word in because Leon had to tell them everything he had seen and felt and deduced.

'She's like a little bird, your mother, Naayo, maybe she's not really your mother even. I couldn't see anything about her that could possibly convince me she is.'

Naia laughed. 'What about your mother, Leon? Anything of her in you?'

They got hysterical over nothing, laughing and remembering and making connections, eating and happy

to be together in that moment. The day went by in the easy
companionship of friends, and when Tara went in for her
afternoon lie-down, Leon and Naia swam in the quiet pool
shaded by flaming gulmohar trees. Orange petals settled on
the blue surface. Leon floated on his back and watched
crows that watched him. Naia examined the bottom of the
pool, allowing the long-lost familiarity to return, her mother's
voice coming to her from memory, saying nothing more
profound than instructions about perfecting her breast
stroke, muffled underwater even in memory.

Samaad came in the evening. He was dressed in the same
clothes he had on when they had met him first. His taxi
driver and Avtar lugged in a great roll of carpet and laid it
out on Tara's living room floor. He untied the ropes and
unrolled the carpets. He had a stack of at least fifteen. He
began to talk, telling them about the topmost one in his
soft, cold, precise English. It was a beautiful carpet, red and
gold, with flecks of sapphire and emerald in the florals. He
sat beside it, tracing the curves of the design with his
fingers, and Naia noticed how large his hands were.

'These are like the flowers in my home in springtime.
Poppies, white and red, golden flowers, little blue and
purple ones ... I will be there soon.' He spoke almost to
himself.

'Isn't there a war going on there?' Leon broke into his
thoughtful monologue.

'War? No.' He laughed. 'That is not a war, when there
are two big guys fighting over a treasure. Two dogs and a
piece of meat. No, that doesn't explain it. I don't know
what it is. I just know that what was once the most
beautiful place on earth is now also the most dangerous.

But you should see the flowers. They are so beautiful. I think they are more beautiful to me now because I feel it might be the last time I see them.' He seemed genuinely sad. Leon didn't hear any of the anger of their last meeting.

'They may be more beautiful now because soldiers have trampled the earth they grow on. Like Flanders' Fields,' Leon said.

Samaad was startled. 'What do you mean? Like in the Great War? Poppies sprang out of a field where there had never been poppies before. It was because of the blood of the dying soldiers. I thought of that not too long ago too.'

Leon laughed. 'It wasn't the blood of the dying, man. It was because the war had trampled and turned up the earth, and turned up old seeds that had lain dormant for ages, and then when the snow melted in the spring, they all bloomed, and, you have another legend.'

Samaad was impressed. 'So I was right about the flowers near my village. There was a big skirmish, we lost enough people that four villages have shrunk to just one. After the winter, you should have seen the fields. I thought I was going to die that year, and it was a sign. I am still here, though. And I guess there is no mystical reason for the flowers. There's always a rational explanation for such things. It's when you don't find it that it becomes legend.'

He turned the carpet over to expose the one below it. Leon hovered over them with his camera, taking shots of everything and everyone.

'Can I go with you? To see your flowers?'

Samaad looked up at him and smiled his secret smile. 'Yes.'

FIFTEEN

'Forty-three people killed, 113 injured in a bomb blast in New Delhi,' the anchor read in a monotone. The bus had been moving at a slow speed through a crowded market. The bomb was hidden in rolls of carpet on the luggage carrier on the roof of the bus. The bus originated in northern Kashmir.

Viren and Naia watched the early morning news as they drank their morning tea. Graphic images of the carnage filled the screen. It surprised Naia. They didn't show stuff like this on CNN, she thought. Viren shook his head repeatedly. 'I have seen this all my life. It never ends, it never stops. This issue is one of those unhealed wounds of humanity. Like Palestine.' He looked so sad that Naia reached out and held his hand, surprising and embarrassing them both. It had been three months since she had moved into one of the many guest rooms in the big house. There was not much awkwardness between her and her father, there had been little from the beginning. With her mother, however, there were strange undercurrents of emotions beneath her unfailingly polite exterior that Naia felt but could not comprehend. She felt invisible around Saroj. At worst, Naia felt that her reappearance had taken away the central purpose of Saroj's life—to mourn the loss of her daughter. But then she realised she was being callous, and perhaps misunderstanding a woman whom she had never known, whose loss she couldn't imagine. As always, when she consciously thought about Saroj, she ended her musings with a mental, and even physical shrug. She didn't care

enough about her to go into it any deeper. Nor did she try
to actually get closer to Saroj herself. She avoided spending
any time with her alone.

Leon had been with Samaad all that time. He had left
immediately, Naia thought, he had escaped from her and
everything that she was feeling and saying. She was
unfamiliar to him, and he didn't have the desire to be part
of the changes, of the discoveries that Naia was making. He
had been back just once for a day. He had stayed with
them, but that had only added to Saroj's odd behaviour.
He had felt it too, of course, and had ignored it, as he
always did. He attributed it to Saroj not being able to
define or understand his relationship with her daughter,
perhaps even disapproving of it. He would be coming back
to Delhi soon, to upload his images, to buy more storage,
perhaps just to see her, to make sure she was doing fine.
He had to drive a long way to make a phone call, so she
didn't hear from him but that once. She was looking
forward to seeing him again, more than she thought
possible. He didn't say anything about missing her, but she
missed him every day, she wished he would stay. It occurred
to her that she might go with him. It wasn't winter
anymore, it couldn't be too cold. She decided that she
would at least bring it up, see how he reacted.

She had been driving around in Karan's car. It was lucky
Viren had never gotten rid of it, it had been serviced and
worked fine. It had belonged to one of the UN missions,
an old Toyota land cruiser with the UN blue emblem still
visible through the thin layer of white paint-over. Lucky for
her it was an automatic, she had never, in spite of Jim's,
learned to drive a stick shift.

She sipped hurriedly at the tea, wanting to finish it and go out to the Red Fort where she would hang out with some of the American journalists and photographers, and maybe bump into Frank again. It had been a big surprise to see him in Delhi, after all that time. She hadn't recognised him at first. She had been disoriented and was feeling particularly lonesome and wishing for Leon when he came up to her grinning, 'Hey! Naa-ya from Los Angeles! What are you doing here?' They had had tea and some of his special smoke, the same thing he had offered her at Mushtaq bhai's in Bombay. She had had a good time that day, and the next, when she had met him again, and every other day since. That had been a month ago. She thought suddenly that she had no address or phone number for him. She was confused by the sudden onset of physical panic that came over her at the thought that she may not see him that day. She would get a smoke from one of the others there, was her first thought, and then the realisation that it wasn't Frank but the smoke that she wanted, sent her into another thrill of panic.

'Are you feeling unwell?' Viren was peering at her with his eyebrows in a knot.

'No, I'm fine,' she answered a little too quickly. 'I'm fine,' she repeated a little more firmly, and wondered if she wasn't trying to reassure herself somewhat. She did feel pale and shaky. She put the teacup down and got up.

'I have to go,' she told him.

He looked disappointed. 'What, now? So early? Where?'

'Oh, I met some people yesterday, I told them I would come see them again today . . .' She was intentionally vague. Viren looked puzzled. 'Will you be home for lunch? Karan is coming in today, I hope you remember?'

Karan. She got a small jolt in her gut. Her big brother. She had seen many photographs of him, and scraped up all the information about him that she could from Viren, and Saroj, and from some broken English from the maids, drivers, gardeners. All she got from these sources was that he looked exactly like her, and that he was the best human being ever to be born on earth. She had been waiting to meet him since she first learned that she had a brother, but that desire had faded over the last few weeks, and she couldn't remember how or why.

Fortunately, there were no members of the press lurking at the gates that morning. She knew that Viren had tried to keep the publicity about his lost-found child to a minimum. This had not been easy because Saroj's need for public sympathy over the years had kept the story alive. Naia had had to meet writers from a few of the major papers, and some of the society glossies. She even did an interview on TV. The story was an absolute delight to a population brought up on a diet of Hindi movies, in which children are regularly misplaced at rural fairs and twins are tragically separated at birth. Everyone is magically and dramatically reunited at the end after three hours of drama, melodrama, music and dancing, vicious fights and sugary romance. The siblings, of course, love each other on sight, the end. So the return of Naia was an irresistible story, more so because it was true life. She had had to endure being photographed, she told Leon later, 'smiling endlessly, sitting between Viren and Saroj, posing in that finally-reunited-now-living-happily-ever-after kind of way'. It had grated on her very being, but she knew Viren had made her do it as little as possible. She had heard him arguing with Saroj as she came to breakfast one morning, and had stopped just out of their sight but within earshot to eavesdrop.

'But why? What is wrong with people knowing? Why won't you let me tell them the truth?'

Viren's anger was palpable, though he didn't raise his voice. 'They were her parents, Saroj, she loved them and they loved her. You will not defile their memory for her, and this is how the story will be told, or not at all. I do not want to discuss this matter ever again, or I will put an end to all this. It is all nonsense, I have been telling you for years.'

Her reply was tearful. 'So, after stealing my precious child, causing me all the pain and suffering I have had to endure for twenty-seven years, they just get to come out unscathed? Nobody should know what despicable creatures they were? They just get away with what they did?'

Viren's voice was so quiet, Naia almost didn't hear his final words. 'I lost my daughter too, Saroj.' There was a long pause and Naia thought he was done. 'And, they did get away with it. They are dead. You can't hurt them. You will only hurt her. And I will not let you do that.'

Naia waited a few minutes before going in, she made sure the conversation was really over.

The story was all over the press for the first whole month after Leon left with Samaad. It started with the newspapers as a short corner frontpage news item. After that Naia was on several magazine covers, sometimes alone and sometimes with Viren and Saroj. Finally, Viren, tired of photographers trampling his garden and his precious carpets, hired a photographer himself. The man was a news photographer, but he was an old friend of Viren's and had a small staff that could handle requests for photos in the future. He did a whole portfolio of pictures. Naia actually enjoyed herself once Saroj had done her bit and left with a headache. The man was articulate and extremely funny. She wished Leon had been there to meet him.

She threw her bag in the back seat and took off into the traffic.

She got to the tea shop outside the Red Fort and sat down at a table from where she could see the street. No one paid her any particular attention, this shop was the hang-out for ex-pats and working foreigners rather than tourists. She ordered a cup of tea and settled down to wait, watching the comings and goings of cars, autorickshaws, trucks, dogs, cows, vendors of snacks, socks, cigarettes. She began to think that Frank wasn't coming that day, when she spotted his occasional companion. She had never spoken to him, he had never joined them, but she smiled at him anyway, hoping that he would give her some information. To her surprise, he came right up to her table, and sat down.

'German not coming today,' he said. She was quite startled and a bit uncomfortable. She didn't say anything because she didn't know what she could say. 'You want to buy?' he asked her tentatively. 'I give you two packets half-half one gram.' He named a price. 'If you want, I can give delivery at home. You give me phone number.' She just nodded yes, and he got up and went outside. She left money on the table by her empty teacup and followed him out.

He was waiting for her at her car, and got into the

passenger seat as soon as she unlocked the doors. She wasn't too happy, but got in and started the car anyway. He gave her a packet of cigarettes, and told her to check if it was okay. She opened it and looked inside, and saw it was empty save for two small cellophane bags with brownish stuff in them. Not ever having seen the drug in this form, she didn't know what to do with it. He sensed her indecision, and, mistaking it for displeasure, said hurriedly, 'I can get more tomorrow, if you come same time. Or I give you home delivery. Okay? You pay me now?'

She nodded and reached in the back seat for her bag. She paid him the money, and he got out and walked quickly across the street looking as surreptitious and shifty as a drug dealer should. She wondered vaguely if there were any policemen about, and before she knew it, she was in a frothy panic. She threw her bag in the back without looking where it landed, and drove nervously home.

Once there, she avoided everyone, went quietly into her room and locked herself in. She went to the bathroom to figure out how to smoke the stuff she had bought. Then she almost actually kicked herself. She didn't own a lighter, or foil, or even cigarettes because she didn't smoke, and Frank had been providing her with what she needed, so she didn't know any better. She began to feel oppressed and sweaty in the bathroom, though it was a bright and large room. She saw the clock reflected in the mirror and realised it was almost time to go pick up Karan at the airport. Which meant that her father would be knocking on her door any minute to remind her. She splashed water on her face and combed out her hair. If she left right away, she would have enough time to buy some cigarettes and maybe park in a secluded spot so she could have a smoke, and still be back in time. There was a loud knocking on her door.

She yelled 'Coming!' and let Viren in. Saroj was with him.

'Hello, dear, are you feeling well?' she asked Naia, deadly polite as usual, not really wanting an answer.

'Yes, I'm fine,' Naia answered anyway, feeling her mental teeth on edge. She had trouble thinking of Saroj as her mother, but she didn't really expect herself to. She quite often had the deep and then painful urge to talk to her dead parents and tell them everything, ask their advice, just see them. She had to teach herself anew each day that they were not a phone call away, that she had to make do with imagining what they would have said to her. She had known them all her life, and was confident that she got it right most of the time. And then again, she thought, what did it matter if she didn't? Who was to correct her?

Saroj was sipping her tea in her lady-like manner. She was not as harmless as she liked to act, or as lady-like. She got under Naia's skin. She needed to talk to Leon, or Tara, or Adam. She felt a stab of loneliness. And the uncomfortable sweaty panic too. She wanted to find her German and get herself a smoke, she knew that would make her feel like herself again.

New Delhi airport was crowded. Many international flights landed at that time. Viren pointed out Karan to her through the glass of the upstairs viewing gallery overlooking the customs area. From what she could tell, Karan was as tall as his father, their father. He was dressed in jeans and a white t-shirt, and red shoes. His hair was very long, at least shoulder-length, tied back in a ponytail. She could see him moving around with ease through the crowd, parting people without touching anyone, gliding like an ice skater, with the leggy grace that some very tall people have. He bent down slightly, intimately, toward an official in a white uniform, saying something to him, and then put his hand on the man's shoulder. The man nodded several times, and then Karan walked out of their view. Viren took her hand and led her to the elevator. Her stomach was tight, and she swallowed what little moisture she could find in her mouth. The elevator doors opened just as she started rummaging in her bag for Altoids, and there he was. Standing in front of them.

They stood and stared at each other for a few seconds. He spoke first.

'Hello, little sister, I would have known you anywhere.'

She laughed, a little hysterically. Viren was smiling, standing back and watching the two of them, putting that moment away in his memory. He would take it out and look at it many times in his life. It was something he had imagined, but never believed would ever happen. Karan took a step toward her and enveloped her in a hug.

He smelt Euro, she thought, no guy in LA smelt like this. She was overwhelmed, and confused, and had a sense of losing and finding and falling away and being born. She felt like she was in a new place with a new start and everything that had gone before was gone, forever. And then she began to cry, because it was gone, her life, her parents Jim and Anne, and Raoul and Adam, Elijah. Even Leon, her friend, her conscience, her tent peg, had upped and left her for something or someone she didn't understand.

Karan just held her and patted her back and said, 'It's okay.'

They talked and talked all the way back home, father and daughter in the back seat and Karan in front with the driver, turned around to face them the whole way, rubbing his neck occasionally. She found out that he had been in boarding school most of his life since he was six years old, brought up by old school masters and housemaids in an atmosphere of old British public school discipline, and high academic demand. He went to live with his parents in the school holidays. This was in a different country each year, depending on where his father was. One year he had stayed in the school with a boy whose parents had died in a plane crash, because Viren was in somewhere too dangerous. 'Where was that?' he asked his father.

'West Africa.'

She watched them with each other, easygoing, friends. They had hugged at the airport, and again before they got in the car. They obviously adored each other.

'How's Ma?' Karan asked his father. And then she saw that little frown, the hesitation, the grit in the teeth.

'Fine. As fine as can be hoped, I suppose.'

Naia took a breath for courage. 'Is something wrong with her? I mean, is she ill? Or something . . .' her courage faded and she didn't say any more, hoping for, but not really expecting any answer from, either of them.

Karan turned his face to look out the car's front window. 'No, she's not ill, she's just neurotic,' he said firmly, more loudly than necessary.

'Karan, that is not quite true. Your mother has suffered a lot and she is a little sensitive, that's all,' his father said, frowning at him. Karan seemed exasperated more than anything else, and he shrugged and made no further comment. Naia wished that Leon was there right then, to hook into that little eel of emotion before it wriggled away into the murky depths of this unknown persona. He would have yanked everything out of Karan without his even knowing it. And she thought just how much she missed Leon. The months he had been gone had been full of newness, she had had to learn to live with new people in new relationships, a new city, a new country even, and though she was too exhausted to even dream each night, there were a thousand moments in every day when she had something to ask or tell Leon.

They got home and Saroj was there at the door, waiting for them. She ran out and clung to her son with a little cry. He held her for a moment, and looked at Naia over her head. Naia thought of Adam and her father again, and she wondered why parents needed so much comforting.

They spent the next day talking and eating and finding out about each other, and she found that she liked her new big brother. She liked looking at his familiar face. She had known it all her life. She talked to him about his life. He had been brought up by the domestic help mostly. When he was very young his mother had been 'ill'—he made the quotation mark gesture with his elegant fingers as he said it. As he grew older, she got busy with the duties of the wife of a diplomat rising through the ranks of the service. Eventually, they put him in a boarding school so that he wouldn't be dragged around to all the countries that his father worked in. Some places had no English or International schools. His school was in a picturesque hill station in the south, and he had had a good time there most years. After school, he told her, he was so unused to living at home that had looked for his further education away from New Delhi, even India. He went to King's College in London and had been in England ever since.

'I guess I'll finish my PhD one day, just not yet. I'm not ready to come back and live in India, and I doubt I will ever be. I'm having too much fun in the student life. It's not like I don't work hard, I do. But I'm happy there now. It's home, for now.'

Karan spent some time with Saroj. They all ate breakfast together, Viren and Saroj, and Naia and Karan. Saroj asked him inane questions about his health, which he answered with a restrained patience that belied his irritation. He was never actually rude to his mother, but Naia thought of Anne and Jim and their life together, and couldn't remember ever feeling so tense in their presence, not even when she was in trouble at school or had a bad report card. She wished desperately for them, her sweet parents who had brought her up in a house full of love and easygoing friendship. She had eaten more banana bread and drunk more carrot juice than any other child she had grown up with, she had worn some outlandish handmade clothes to school and sometimes got laughed at, but in southern California, she was hardly the strangest child in school, or the most exotic. She felt a huge surge of love for them, her parents, and especially her mommy, without whom she would have been right there, between Karan and Saroj. Only the fact that she had gone out and found Frank early that morning made it all easier to take. She just needed that one smoke each day to keep easy, no more.

Karan had invited her to go out to a favourite restaurant of his for dinner. She knew it was a way for them to spend a little time alone. It was a pleasant evening, but she had become irritable halfway through the meal. He had sensed it, but couldn't understand why. She drove them back home saying it was just a bit of a headache.

'Can I have my car back?' he asked Viren plaintively. 'Or have you given it to your new favourite child?'

Viren had laughed at him and put his arm around him and said, 'No, that is her car now. You can have your mother's, she can have mine, and I will call a cab when I need to go anywhere. I'm thinking I should come and spend a couple of months in London when you go back. What do you say, Naia? Shall we go?'

Naia was taken aback by his invitation, and didn't know how to respond. He sensed her confusion and smiled in his diplomatic way and said, 'Think about it, you don't have to tell me now.'

That morning she had Frank show her how to make her own smokes, so she wouldn't have to go looking for him every day, and she still had what she had bought from the shifty salesman. Frank had laughed. He said she had been charged too much, but the amount, especially in dollars, was not enough to bother her. He had looked drawn and ill, and he kept scratching himself. He tried to do it surreptitiously, but she noticed. He told her he was going back home the following week, he was almost out of money and his assignment had been done months ago. That was the first time she had been curious about what exactly he did. He said he worked for an NGO, and she didn't realise till she was thinking about it later how vague he had been.

They had met so many times, and every time, all they talked about was her. She decided she would talk to him about it when she saw him next. He had promised her they would meet before he left. Later, after dinner, everyone went early to bed. Naia made herself a smoke in her bathroom. She felt she had earned it because the day had been stressful. She told herself she wouldn't smoke more than once a day starting tomorrow.

She couldn't sleep and went out to walk in the garden, and look at the garden carpet. She walked slowly in the dark, she hadn't wanted to turn on the lights for fear of disturbing anyone. And she wanted to be alone. Halfway down the path, she had a whiff of something that made her think Leon was somewhere close. She followed her nose to a wrought iron bench, where Karan was stretched out, face up to the stars. She came right up to him and saw that his eyes were closed, as he brought his joint up to his mouth for a drag. She watched him for a minute, and when he had exhaled, she leaned close to his ear and said, 'Boo!'

SIXTEEN

Leon poked at his eyes. He was quite over his initial reactions to the high altitude. He didn't have headaches now, and the dullness was gone too. He drank a lot of the delicious water that Samaad kept next to him in a red earth pot with a little faucet on it. All the mountain rice, fresh-killed mutton, and vegetables from the village gardens, all the walking, miles and miles every day, had contributed to his sense of wellbeing. It had been three months since the day he and Samaad had parked the Jonga in a dip in the ground behind the house and covered it up with a tarp. A brown dog had wandered up and started digging, Samaad had shooed him off.

Samaad's house stood apart from the main village, and on higher ground. The house was Leon's now. Samaad had moved into one of the new rooms that had been built in the months that he had been there. There were six rooms all in a row, small individual brick boxes roofed with corrugated aluminum sheeting, large stones weighing them down against winter wind storms. A mile down the path stood four enormous warehouse-like structures, flat with low ceilings that didn't jut out of the landscape. They had been meticulously painted so that they would not be visible from the air. Leon had watched these being built while he was there, watched them being slowly stacked with supplies, grain, ammunition, explosives, blankets, medicines. He had asked very few questions. He photographed everything, but was careful. He framed every shot with thought and devotion in a way he had not since he had first started his career, poor and film-starved. He didn't have to worry about film anymore, but he certainly didn't want to run out of space on his drive. He never asked permission to shoot, and Samaad never stopped him from pointing his camera at anything. This arrangement suited Leon fine. He used the generator Samaad had given him sparingly, only to charge his batteries and turn on his laptop once a day to transfer each day's images.

He woke up and stretched, unzipping the sleeping bag by pushing his foot hard against it. It was worn out and a bit

torn, but it was warm and comfortable. Leon had had the
best sleep of his life in that room. His book lay on the floor
next to him. He remembered what he had been reading
before he fell asleep. It was the story of Krishna and Arjun
at the battle of Kurukshetra. The warrior prince and his
charioteer, a mere god. Samaad had given him a translation
of the *Mahabharata* when he had said he needed something
to read. He had been surprised and pleased, he had half-
expected to get an old newspaper lining from the bottom
of some old suitcase. He felt alive and happy, ready to
climb the mountain. Samaad had promised to take him up
finally. He had refused for three whole months, saying
Leon was not yet ready, the walk would kill him, the
weather up there was too treacherous. Leon had ranted on
about New York winters and war zones to no avail, but on
reflection he knew Samaad had probably been right about
his abilities. Or, he had first wanted to know who and what
Leon was. Whether to put his trust in a stranger, in a
'Yehudi'. All he told Leon was that there was a camp up
there, high up in the mountains. He may have just not
wanted to show this Jew his army. There had to be one,
Leon thought. It made sense. All those guns and
ammunition had to be for someone, and the few men in
the village, though capable of shooting a gun, were no
army.

There were twenty or so guards in what Samaad now
called the camp, which was separate from the village that
occupied the lower part of the valley. Some patrolled the
mouth of the small valley, some watched over them from
narrow ledges on the mountains around them. There were
always two men outside Samaad's room, and Maqbool was

Leon's special man. He had spent time with them, and knew most of them by name, although he didn't pronounce a single name right. They had spent much of their time together trying to teach him, and there had been much mirth and derision at his expense. 'Muqtadar' and 'Gulabudeen' were beyond his American-trained tongue to manage. He had photographed them on duty, with their AK-47s slung across their shoulders, serious and intense in their protective gaze over the valley, and off duty, hanging together and smoking hashish from massive clay pipes, laughing and talking, faces creased by the brutal sun and their own good cheer. Samaad had introduced him to them as 'Yehudi', and that's what they all called him—'Jew'. They were gentle, soft-speaking, large men, all bearded and with turbans, all dressed in the same dust-coloured long shirts and flowing pants that Samaad wore. They all wore sweaters too, huge wool cable knits that he and Samaad had bought on the way up, in a small town market.

'What do you think of the book?' Samaad was slurping his tea in the usual noisy way that Leon imitated, first in jest, and now habit. Samaad found it hilarious. They drank their tea together every morning. Samaad would bring it for him and wake him up. That was the signal for Maqbool to put his gun down inside Leon's door and go off duty for the day.

'It's interesting. Don't ever ask me to pronounce any of the names. Honestly, has anything really changed? I mean, this book is how old? Everything seems just the way it was then. People fighting over stuff.'

'Yes, that's the whole point. Some of these classics are classics because they talk about human nature. Which is never going to change, is it?'

'Human nature? Come on, Samaad, you of all people surely don't believe there is such a thing. You mean conditioning? Greed? Fighting over land and cows? Wanting a reasonable life?'

Samaad was quiet a moment, and then said, smiling, 'Yes, Yehudi, you are right, of course. Land and cows. And a reasonable life.'

Leon shook his head slowly in that Indian way that signifies resignation. Samaad looked at him sitting like that on his haunches and sucking his tea, and burst into an uncharacteristic gale of laughter.

'Look at you. You belong here, my friend, you really do. You look happy, rested, there are no lines on your face, and that beard looks good on you. And . . .' he reached into the side pocket of his shirt, 'I have something for you. The best from over the border—Afghani.' He threw Leon a baseball-sized hunk. Leon just stared. It was dark and richly organic, with a sweet, almost chocolatey smell, a fragrant piece of fertile earth. He had never seen hashish so perfect or in such a pleasing amount before.

'Have a good smoke before we start up the mountain, you will need it. It will be a five-hour climb, and I think we will stay up there for the night and tomorrow, and aim to be back here by nightfall tomorrow. We can leave in an hour, that will make it six. Okay?'

'Okay.' Leon was excited, and began to roll up his sleeping bag. Samaad had offered him the easier alternative—Jabra could easily drive him up most of the way. He had refused, thinking, and everyone confirmed this, that he would see and feel a lot more on the walk. He welcomed the chance to be with Samaad all that time too, instead of Jabra.

The climb was not as exhausting as he had thought it would be. It was not too steep, because they went winding up the mountain rather than straight up any face. A lot of the walk was through small valleys and ledges on mountainsides, giving Leon views of azure lakes set like sapphires in gold-rimmed mountain crusts. They walked in fields of wildflowers rippling like rainbow water in the mild morning breeze, the aura of the flowers clinging to their clothes long after they had passed out of their sight. And always, the peaks high above them, mocking their slow ascent to the foothills. Leon didn't shoot as much as he thought he would, or even as much as he ought to. He just wanted to take it all into his mind, through his eyes, imprint all that awesome beauty on his ever-living soul. He didn't want the lens between him and the world. He startled himself with this thought. He had not felt this way often. He hoped that there was another life after this one. He hoped that he would be able to find this valley then, and this friend would walk by his side.

They had walked hours, stopping only for short breaks to eat or just sit on the edge of a cliff and look below for a breather. Leon was beginning to tire when they came up to the first guard. Leon didn't know him. It was cold. The warmth of the afternoon sun had faded, and then left them entirely as the evening came upon them. There were tents scattered everywhere, they looked like growths in the rocks. There were enough for at least fifty men, more if there were two to a tent, Leon calculated, and there were probably more than that. He was frankly amazed. He hadn't known what to expect, nor did he expect anything so big. In spite of his tiredness, he set up his tripod and took a few shots of the camp. With the lamps lit inside them, the tents looked like glowing amber jewels in a velvet box.

That night in the camp, they sat around a large fire pit. The off-duty men were there, sharing a pipe and talking softly amongst themselves and Samaad. Samaad translated for Leon when he thought something would interest him, but mostly it was the latest news about movie stars from Bombay, the price of weapons around the border areas, and where there was recruitment going on for the kind of work these men engaged in. Later into the night, the conversation got more interesting. Many had been in the conflicts with Russia, Leon could see that most of them were old enough and scarred enough to have been in one war or another, and there had been many in that area.

He was amazed by the way these men accepted their lives the way they were. There was no anger or resentment that he could discern. They talked of lost families and friends and entire villages, they talked of acquaintances gone to Yugoslavia to fight in the wars there. Leon knew what it had been like there, he had met these men, their brothers, seen their bodies like discarded clothes on fields, on roadsides. At the end of hostilities, some of them had managed to get Bosnian citizenship papers and had slipped into western Europe and even the US. These men were available for work even though they now lived unremarkable lives. In fact, their desirability was in part because they were unexceptional. They had faded into the background, hidden from the eyes of the law.

Leon's mind began to reel with the implications of all that he was hearing. The reality and enormity of where he

was and what he was watching unfold before his eyes
began to coalesce quickly in his head. He wondered if
Samaad would ever let him go back to where he had come
from. He wondered if he would even want to. His life and
everything he had known and done seemed like a low-
budget documentary film: short and badly directed and fast
fading from memory. He blew out a long stream of smoke
and turned to Samaad to speak to him, but Samaad spoke
first. 'You should go and sleep, my friend, you are tired
from the walk. Things will look different in the morning,
the light here is clearer and cleaner than anywhere on the
planet. Go on, go and sleep. I will be in, too, in a few
minutes.'

In his tent, Leon fell asleep on a thin mattress under a
warm blanket to the sound of gunshots—the men target-
shooting in the night. He didn't hear Samaad come in and
make his bed next to him.

The next morning Samaad was there to wake him up with
a cup of tea as usual. They didn't talk much, just slurped
in a friendly silence, and then it was time to go. Two men
walked with them, one behind and one leading them. They
wound up the mountainside on an ever-narrowing path. If
Leon had been any less calm, if he trusted Samaad any less,
he would have been nervous. The thought crossed his
mind, but peripherally. He paid no attention to it, that he
was alone in the mountains with armed men and their
leader. He felt it distinctly here that Samaad was the leader
of these men. There was something about the way they
acted, an unspoken deference, something between respect
and fear of him, that the people in the village did not
display except in very small measure. And these men were

different from all those back in the valley. They were somehow stronger, wilder, barely under control. Leon began to understand what Samaad was, what it must take to have such men accept him as leader.

They had walked less than a mile from camp when Samaad stopped. They stood on a narrow ledge at the end of the path. The two guards sat down to share a smoke. Samaad put his hand in his pocket.

'Here,' he said, holding it out to Leon, a closed fist. When Leon looked down he opened it slowly. Leon had seen gemstones before: diamonds in Angola, rubies in Burma, emeralds in Brazil, both rough and polished. But never anything like this. The stones lay softly in Samaad's rough hand. Leon was silent. He had no words for such beauty. Samaad smiled. 'You know Shiva has a third eye?'

'I've heard.'

'Shiva lives in these Himalayas, here on top of the world. He walks in these mountains. King cobras ride on his shoulders. The Ganga flows from his hair, and he smokes his charas. Those clouds are his exhaled breath.' He looked toward the blinding white blanket hiding the tops of the great range from their eyes.

'Then, sometimes, when he is angry—and he's only a god, so he does get angry—he opens that eye.' He stopped, waiting, wanting to know he had Leon's focus.

'Go on,' Leon said, entranced.

'When Shiva opens his third eye, everything burns.' The white light off the mountains illuminated Samaad's eyes as he spoke. 'Everything burns. Rock turns liquid, into molten lava fire. And then, when he is cool, and turns away from the world, that burning liquid runs deep inside the earth and cools too. And turns into rubies. Bloody, perfect rubies.'

Leon looked back into his feral eyes. 'These aren't rubies, Samaad. And you are . . . Muslim, and you don't know shit about Shiva. Or gemstones.' His words were flippant, perhaps intending to discharge the electric mood. Samaad set his palm against Leon's mouth. This intimate touch had once made him uncomfortable, but no more. He was used to being touched by Samaad. It was part of his language. Leon obeyed him, and was silent. They stood very close to each other. The ledge was barely wide enough for them both face to face. Samaad pushed Leon gently ahead of him to the front of the path. Too close to the edge. He said, 'Look.' Leon looked down. The ledge fell away steeply, and Leon felt his feet crawl. He saw fifty men at least, far below them, working the rock's side, deep inside the combe. There were still more men on both sides of a thin silvery river that ran along the bottom. He could hear them, now that he had seen them, talking and shouting and the metal against rock sound of their tools.

'You're mining? For what? Did you find rubies here? Where did you get these? These are cut and polished gemstones . . . Why are they blue?' He stopped his rush of questions. Samaad said nothing. Leon turned around to his friend. 'So tell me,' he said.

'Sometimes Shiva looks at the world. And he sees the misery and the ugliness and the greed that we live by. And he remembers how the world was without men. And then he cries. And his tears fall to the earth. They go deep, and stay there forever. Unless we find them.' He opened his palm and dropped the stones into Leon's. Leon closed his hand around them.

He looked into Samaad's luminous eyes. 'Do we use them to buy more misery and ugliness?' he asked. For a flashing moment, Samaad was angry. So quickly did it come and go that if Leon hadn't been looking into them, he might have missed the slight darkening of those eyes.

'You know nothing, Yehudi,' he said, laughing now. 'Do you think I do this for myself? Do you think I want power and wealth, Leon? I cannot change the world, I cannot change this country, I cannot even really change the way things are in this place. But I have to try. I was given the chance, I was given this.' He closed his big hands around Leon's, enclosing the stones.

'You see in black and white, good and evil, dichotomies. It is not what life is, Yehudi. We don't want—I don't want to be a leader, I don't want to kill or die for this. But what choice do I have? I just want, for however long it is possible, to give these people some comfort, some sweetness. Some hope. There has to be hope, Yehudi. It has been so long since they had any hope . . . how can we live without hope? Do you understand?'

Leon said nothing. Samaad's voice was an incantation, soft and insistent. Leon didn't think in terms of right and wrong anymore. He never had, really. He just knew that his friend had a purpose and would do everything he could to see it achieved. Even kill and die for it, despite what he had just said. Not many people find such a purpose in their lives, nor the strength within themselves, nor the means to achieve it. Samaad was right, in a way. He had to do what he was put on earth to do. Or he could have walked away from it, and been nothing and no one. He could have ignored his calling, turned his back on everything that stood around him and within him, his people, his forbears, his intellect, his heart. He may as well have been dead then.

'I will not hold you here, Yehudi. Now you know everything. You can stay or go, it is up to you.'

Leon breathed the clear Himalayan air, he felt it on his face. His own life had wound itself around the world. He had searched, unknowingly, for so long, to be right where he was. He felt the call of something older than himself. He felt the sense of belonging, a bond with this man from another time and place that he had never felt with anyone before. He remembered something Naia had said to him years ago: 'You don't have to follow a snake into its hole, Leon, you can just catch it and pull it out and look at it in the safe light of day. I'm telling you, one day you will go down a snake hole and never come out.' He couldn't remember what she had been so mad about then, but it didn't matter now. This high mountainside didn't look much like a snake hole, but he knew he had found one. No, he thought, correcting himself, it was not a snake hole at all. It was home. Samaad was home. He looked down at Samaad's hands, still holding his, the sapphires warm within them. 'I am here, Samaad. I wouldn't miss this for the world,' he said happily.

SEVENTEEN

The bus was right on time. Naia saw Leon before he saw her. She hadn't recognised him, until she saw his camera

bag. His clothes and hair made him one of the crowd. His
bearded face and skeleton-gauntness shocked her. He spotted
Naia, waved, and bounded up and surrounded her in a hug
that surprised her. He didn't usually display his feelings
overtly. He didn't care for physical contact for as long as
she had known him. He smelt very clean in spite of the
long journey, like his clothes had been washed in a river.
She felt better when she had examined his face. He looked
so healthy and happy in spite of the weight he had lost.
And she realised too, that he wasn't that thin. He had
turned from a scrawny guy into a lean, stringy one. Hard
muscles were right below the surface of his skin, she could
see them every time he moved. He was darker as well: he
looked more like a jihadi than a Jew, she thought.

'How is it? What's new? Are you getting along with
everyone? What's Karan like?'

She answered all his questions patiently, enjoying the
sound of his voice, the new look of that familiar old face.
'It's all fine. Karan is awesome. You are going to get along
with him fine. Are you staying with me? Tara is here, she
said you could stay with her if you prefer, we both could.
I could really do with a break from the house, especially
when Karan is gone. What are your plans? Should we book
our return tickets soon?'

They were getting into her car. Leon waited to answer
until she had started driving.

'I'm not going back with you. I have to go back to
Samaad. There's too much to see and do.'

She didn't say anything for a few minutes. 'You've been
there three months, almost. What are you doing there?
And if you are going back for a few weeks . . .' She stopped,

unsure how to ask him. And then she just did. 'Can I go with you?'

'Samaad will come down tomorrow, you can ask him yourself. He will have to agree, there is no way you or I could go there without his protection.'

'Protection? From what? What's going on there? Where exactly are you staying?'

Leon turned away from her, looking out of the window. He watched the street, the other cars so close to theirs, people weaving around the vehicles at every traffic light. A man on a bicycle leaned on their car, resting his arm on the window, almost touching Leon as he waited for the light to change. Leon shifted his elbow to make contact with him. The man didn't notice.

'There is no concept of personal space in this country. No one cares if you invade theirs, they don't think about yours. It's wonderful. It makes me free!'

'Leon, you have to tell me what's going on with you. Don't change the subject.'

She drove into a little lane and parked the car.

'What's this? Where are we?'

'I have to do a little errand,' she said briskly, 'then we can have some lunch and do your shopping. Wait here, I'll be back in a minute.' She picked up her bag from the rear and disappeared into a space between two buildings, not wide enough for the car. She was gone only a few minutes when a familiar man came sauntering out of the lane. Leon had seen him before, but he couldn't remember where. He let it go, thinking perhaps the man just looked like someone else he knew.

Naia came out and got in the car. 'Did you see that guy?' Leon asked her.

'What guy? The one that came out before me? That's Frank, the German. We met him at Mushtaq's in Bombay, remember? I hang out with him sometimes. And smoke with him sometimes.'

'Smoke? You went in there for a smoke?' Leon was laughing. 'You should have said—I have the best hashish money can't buy, all the way from Trenchtown—I mean Kandahar, Afghanistan ... shall I make you a smoke?'

She smiled and made a face at him. 'No, thanks. You do your thing, I'll do mine,' she said mysteriously. They had arrived at the restaurant, so he dropped the subject, but she knew he would gnaw at it till he had the marrow.

They both saw the changes in each other. They talked about her relationship with her family. She was grateful to be able to have him back for that, if nothing else.

'I can't stand Saroj,' she declared, pushing the food around on her plate. He was eating fast, and a lot.

'Does she bother you? I mean, does she actively do anything to upset you?'

'No, it's just that I feel like I'm invisible around her. I don't think she wants to acknowledge who I am.' She paused, thinking about what she really wanted to say, or how to put her feelings into words that would explain them perfectly. She watched him eat. 'Have you been starving? Isn't your friend feeding you up there?'

'Not really. They have to ration the food a bit. It's good stuff. Rice, fresh veggies, lamb—no, goat. I mean I am not going to die for lack of food, but it gets monotonous. There's a limit to the variety. And there's one guy that cooks for us, so limited repertoire, limited supplies, you know. I'm going to stock up on eating pleasure while I am here. Go on about Saroj.'

Naia was still thoughtful, almost reluctant to say anything that might cause him to misunderstand. 'I feel like she wishes I hadn't shown up. Like I took away the reason for her misery, which maybe was the reason for her existence ... like she forgot to do anything with her life other than mourn the loss of her child, and now she doesn't know what else to do.'

Leon nodded. 'You're probably right about that. Plus, you have to understand, your return as an adult hasn't brought back the child she lost. You know what I mean? She's never going to be able to dress up her baby girl, or take her to school or comfort her when she's sick, or tell her about puberty and periods ... that baby and child are gone forever, and now she has no one to blame. Imagine this—she can't even blame Anne to you, because Anne was your mother, she loved you and you loved her. She has lost everything, and now she has to give up even that—the loss itself. You know?'

Naia was again struck by how he could, without any effort, get to the heart of the matter, the heart of a person. She did understand. She did see what he was trying to tell her. But she couldn't bring herself to feel anything more than pity for Saroj. Not even compassion.

She drove him around, he bought t-shirts, sweaters, socks, cans of meat, toothpaste. He was surprised at how comfortable she was driving in the streets of Delhi. She seemed to know her way around, and expertly read a worn-looking map whenever she needed to. She didn't even bother to park on the side, she just stopped in mid-traffic, ignoring the honking that would start up each time she did.

'It's obvious I'm not from around here—this car advertises that for me. It isn't always an advantage, but I'll take what I get.'

They got to the house after dinner. Naia had made sure they would get there after Saroj's bedtime. Karan and Viren were sitting at the dining table drinking brandy from huge snifters. Viren was smoking a cigar. They both stood up to greet Leon and Naia. Viren introduced Karan and Leon. 'My son, Karan. Karan, this is your sister's best friend in the world, Leon.'

Naia smiled. Leon certainly was that, and it pleased her immensely that Viren had acknowledged it. Leon said, 'I know Karan, I read about him in the *Mahabharata*. Is that where you got your name?'

Viren smiled, impressed by Leon's knowledge. 'My wife's favourite character in the *Mahabharata*,' he said, correcting Leon's pronunciation. 'Do you know what Naia's name really is? I mean what it was?' He paused, looked around, and said, 'Menaka'.

There was a sudden and deep silence. And then Naia said, 'Well, I'm Naia now,' and laughed. And the moment passed as if there had never been any awkwardness.

They sat around the table and talked. They made small talk, polite conversation at first, Karan's life at college in England, Leon's work, Viren's newest carpets. And then Viren turned to Leon.

'What are you doing up in Kashmir?'

'I met this guy at Tara's. He's a carpet dealer. He has a place up in the mountains, right in the foothills of the Himalayas, actually. I mean, if you go any higher you'd be in Ladakh. He doesn't stay up there in the winter, he

comes down and sells carpets. I was just, you know, excited
by his descriptions of his home. So I went up with him, it
was a chance to photograph a part of the world that I have
never been to, and with a person who knows it so well. I
came down to see Naia. And to shop. I'm going back in a
couple of days. The landscape is spectacular, and I like
Samaad.'

Viren sat bolt upright. When everyone turned to him he
said in a voice designed, Leon thought, to take the attention
away from his startled response after hearing the name,
'Samaad? I know Samaad. I have bought some good carpets
from him. He's an interesting man . . .'

'Samaad? The one with the carpets, yeah? I know him
too!' Karan interrupted his father. 'You remember I met
him two years ago and we discovered we were at the same
college? He looked vaguely familiar, and I couldn't place
him until he opened his mouth and spoke the Queen's
English. Remember, Dad?'

Naia was amazed. 'You all know Samaad? I should have
mentioned his name. It didn't occur to me that you might
know him . . . but I should have connected. Your carpets.
I've been preoccupied. He gets around doesn't he.'

Viren laughed. 'I know a few people like him. Kashmiris.
They have been cornered by both India and Pakistan. We
want Kashmir because . . . well, whatever my opinion, the
causes have become unimportant now. But people like
Samaad should have been living the best lives in the world.
This man should have been running his father's business—
they had the most luxurious houseboats on Dal lake. He
should have been a socialite, married to some European
heiress who lost her heart to him on her Kashmiri skiing

vacation. He should have been the playboy of the East, with his looks and fine mind. Not selling carpets, like a frontier nomad.'

Everyone was quiet. Leon's radar was up, his eyes were narrowed, on Viren. There was something there, and he would get to it. Viren knew what he was talking about. This was his work. He must have encountered people like Samaad in the course of his long career as a diplomat. He had worked in some of the most troubled spots of the world. He must have a compassionate nature, but that did not explain his response to Samaad, whom he knew as a carpet salesman. He said something under his breath about 'wasted lives' that Leon caught, and stored away to ask about later, at a more opportune time.

'Isn't it dangerous up there?' Karan asked Leon. 'Are you in the border area? Line of Control or something?'

'No, that is further west from where we are. It's not particularly bad where Samaad lives. I think he mentioned that there were skirmishes there before winter set in. Now the snow is melting fast and the passes are mostly open again. He says sometimes people come down those passes from across the border. That they are given cover fire by the Pakistani army.'

'Wow. Have you seen any of this activity?' Karan's voice was full of concern.

'No, not really. Samaad keeps me looking at flowers and mountains and rocks and rivers. Listen to this one, though. He said that last spring they "saw off"—that is what he said, "saw off"!—two guys that had infiltrated the village pretending to be from the west. They were selling handguns and ammunition, and some people from Samaad's village realised they were from across the border. I really think it was Samaad himself who saw them off, actually.'

All three of them were looking at him in varying degrees of horror, and he started laughing.

Naia was instantly enraged. 'What's so funny? Are you nuts? Do you want to get killed up there? How will we know what's going on with you? Leon, stop laughing, I mean it. Are you serious, you think Samaad has killed people?' Leon nodded yes. 'And you're actually going to go back there? What if he decides to kill you next?'

'I'll die then, won't I?' he said to her, trying to defuse her anger. She stood up and punched him in the arm as she passed him.

'I'm tired, you guys—I'm going to sleep. See you in the morning.'

If they were surprised by her abrupt departure, none of them showed it when they said goodnight.

'Tell me about Kashmir, Viren, please. It would help to know what it's all about. I've always known that it is one of the hot spots of the world. But you know us Americans, we depend on CNN, and if it doesn't affect us directly, we tend not to hear about it. So now, since it affects me directly . . .' he laughed self-deprecatingly, and they did too. Leon really wanted to pick Viren's brain. He couldn't believe his good luck at being able to spend some time with someone who knew so much about it. Viren was quite happy to have his brain picked. According to him, Kashmir was once the jewel in the crown of India. He thought it could be that way again, but if, only if all the issues were resolved. He didn't think that they could be, though. It was too late to reverse the damage done, too late to re-educate the lost youth in the Kashmir valley. He felt that they were mutilated by fanaticism, Islamic fundamentalism from across the border, economic devastation in their state, and a feeling of isolation from and abandonment by the country that they were a part of.

'Isn't that the root of the problem? That they don't want to be an Indian state?' Leon asked him. Viren frowned. It was the first time Leon had seen that expression on his face, but it was oddly familiar.

'I guess you really don't know much. It's not as simple as that,' he said, a bit condescendingly, Leon thought, but he didn't care, as long as he found out what he needed to.

Viren started from the beginning. 'After Independence— you know what that is?' Leon smiled and nodded. Viren's tone softened. 'There was Partition. India was to get the Hindu majority states and Pakistan the Muslim ones.'

'They could do that with Israel and the Palestinians too,' Leon interrupted.

Viren frowned at him again. 'No, they couldn't. That is different. But don't start on that now. Let me finish,' he said, holding up his palm to ward off any more interruption.

'There were two states that were problematic. Hyderabad in the south, with a Muslim ruler, went to India because of its geographic location deep within the country. Sind, inside Pakistani borders, though Hindu, went to Pakistan. Hindus left there in the thousands, leaving behind everything that they couldn't carry on their backs. These were very prosperous communities, you have to understand. They left a lot behind.'

'So the Hindus from Sind were like refugees in India?'

'Yes, and they still haven't forgotten it. Some of the

fundamentalist Hindus today are from that lot of people. There are some terrible stories, of loss and families being separated . . . you know, there are tragedies in every upheaval of that kind. Anyway, so that was that. Kashmir, however, was different.' Leon wondered if Viren was tired or sleepy and felt a little guilty. But Viren was in his element, and his enraptured audience of at least one kept him going.

'Kashmir was majority Muslim. But had a Hindu ruler. And bordered both India and Pakistan. So there was a problem there. Maharajah Hari Singh, on top of all this, had delusions of grandeur. He wanted independence for his state. Even after Indian Independence, he kept the issue of accession undecided. Both sides, the Indians and Pakistanis, tried to get him to accede, but he wavered endlessly. Or stalled. Until . . .'

He eyed Leon and then Karan to make sure they were paying attention. The brandy had softened Karan's spine, he was low in his chair. 'Let's move to the sofa, Dad,' he said, and they moved to the living room with their glasses.

'Until?' Leon reminded Viren, when they were all settled comfortably.

'You will find this part interesting. Until Pathan tribesmen from the North-West Frontier areas had some small revolt. Then Pakistani troops took advantage of this opportunity, joined with them, and took over Muzaffarabad. This is a city in the north-west. Then they started to move south to Srinagar, the capital.'

'Why did Pakistan join them? Wouldn't Kashmir have become part of Pakistan anyway? Since all Muslim majority states did?' Leon asked.

Viren seemed to like him a little better after that question. He smiled.

'Yes, probably. But Pakistan jumped the gun. Anyway, the Maharajah panicked, and sent word to India asking for help. India was in a bind. They didn't want to move any Indian troops there. Nehru, then prime minister, as well as Lord Mountbatten, who was our last British viceroy, waited and stalled too. Eventually they did send in the Indian army, but only after the Maharajah ceded to India.'

'Blackmail,' Leon said, and then he wished he hadn't. Viren took it badly. He screwed up his eyebrows and glared at Leon. Leon was taken aback at first, and then started laughing. 'You look just like Naia when you're mad,' he said. Viren's face opened instantly. He glanced at Karan, who had passed out on the couch and heard nothing after the first minute.

'Tell me more,' Leon said, sensing that Viren would.

'You can call it blackmail, but look. The Pakistanis weren't going to be able to help. They pretended they had nothing to do with helping the rebellion, in spite of proof that they did. Besides, the Maharajah didn't ask them for help. He asked us. The Indian government, rightly, didn't want to send troops into what was not our territory. That would have been illegal. There was no other way.'

Leon shrugged. 'That's like the Israelis getting US aid against the Palestinians.'

Viren put his hands up in that typical Indian gesture that was a mixture of annoyance, total incomprehension, and a conviction that the person across the aisle was an idiot. Leon got that a lot.

'What sense does that make?' Viren said.

'Never mind. I guess I don't have much of a clue there either.'

'When you come back, Leon, I will explain the Jews and the Palestinians to you. Until then, let's stick to Kashmir.'

'Then what? After the accession?'

'There was actually an important clause in the instrument of that accession. That the people of Kashmir would have to ratify that decision. That there would be a plebiscite. There has never been one, of course, since 1947. They kept waiting for the situation to settle down. There cannot be one now. The situation has changed too much. The Pakistanis will have to give back territory. They gave China thousands of square miles, they can't have that back. They would have to get Pakistani nationals out of the valley. They have funded a lot of those madrassas—there are so many Muslim schools in Kashmir now.'

'What if the Kashmiris wanted independence? Not to be with either side?'

Viren sighed. 'Precisely. Another reason why there cannot be a plebiscite. Neither India nor Pakistan would agree to that option. It's called "Panoon Kashmir"—"our Kashmir". There's a movement there for every viewpoint.'

Viren felt that the Indian government had let things go too far and for too long. He felt India should have been more aggressive on the social front and less on the military. He felt that diplomacy had let them down. Successive administrations had pandered to the popular but destructive ideologies and ignored the obvious expanding chasm opening up in the valley. They should have educated the youth. They should have worked at the grassroots to eradicate insurgency and Pakistani infiltration. He felt that the army had failed them. 'Yes, there are individual heroes in our armed forces, yes, the terrain is treacherous, but we couldn't keep them back, we couldn't stem that constant trickle of Pakistani fundamentalists over the border. The Islam in Kashmir wasn't like that. The Sufi way was different, mystical, almost like Hinduism. Now fundamentalist Islam has taken over. We failed Kashmir. We let it go, and we can never make it the way it was.'

Leon was surprised at the emotion and frustration in his voice.

'*Kashmiriyat*—that means "Kashmiriness", is gone,' he said.

'Is that like Jewishness?' Leon asked him.

'No. Jewishness is narrow, a thing based on religion, after all. Kashmiriyat is much bigger. It is the character of Kashmir that existed in spite of the many religions, in spite of the differences. Like a carpet. With different coloured yarns, different motifs, different directions, but holding together by the language of weaving. You understand?'

Leon nodded, slightly awed by what he had opened up.

'They all speak the same language?'

'That is the biggest ingredient of Kashmiriyat. The language. All those religions and cultures and regions speak the same language. It's not the only language there, but it was a base. But it's all gone now. I don't believe that there is a miracle big enough to weave that carpet back together. The moths of Muslim fundamentalism have eaten it away.'

The picturesque description moved Leon. He had an image of an unravelling skein, coloured dust falling everywhere, blown carelessly into the wind. He remembered the story Viren had told them when they first met, about the Persian king's carpet, divided up amongst marauding tribesmen.

'The first time I went there was on my honeymoon,' Viren said, and his face looked misty and wistful to Leon. It could have been the brandy and the beautiful glowing lighting in the room, but the mist was in his voice as well. He paused for a moment in some nostalgic reverie. 'You know, Karan, you were probably conceived in that houseboat on Dal lake,' he said with a laugh in his voice. Karan looked at his father theatrically out of the one bleary eye he had managed to open and grunted. Viren laughed again, and Leon and Karan joined in. It was a very private thing to tell them, and Leon decided that this time it had to be the brandy, which was all gone.

They said goodnight then, and Karan took Leon to the guest room next to Naia's, and staggered off to his room somewhere in the huge house. Leon pushed open the door and went in to check on Naia. She was lying on her bed, fully dressed. Her shoes were still on. He shook her shoulder gently at first, and then harder. 'Naayo? Are you okay?'

She grunted and then sat up abruptly. Her eyes were unnaturally droopy and there was an odd smell on her clothes.

'What the hell are you smoking?' he asked her. 'Naia. Answer me. You don't look good. Do you want . . .'

She got up abruptly and ran into the bathroom. She slammed the door shut, but he could hear her heaving the contents of her stomach into the toilet. She came out scrubbing her face dry with a towel, looking better. 'I feel fine now,' she said to him. 'You can go to bed, and I will too. I'll see you in the morning. We'll talk then, I promise.'

He waited in her room till she had changed and got into

her bed. He covered her with the beautiful quilt which was kept folded at the foot of the bed, and then went to his room next door. It was almost morning. He drew the heavy velvet drapes shut so the sunlight wouldn't wake him too early. He showered for a long time, savouring the hot water and fragrant sandalwood soap. He wished for a hot bath, he hadn't had one for such a long time. There were no bathtubs anywhere in the country as far as he could tell. He lay down to sleep on the soft white cotton sheets. He dreamed Samaad had thrown him off the mountain to kill him, but then caught him as he floated to the rocky bottom of the valley.

It was late in the day by the time everyone was up and about and ready to face the day. Karan and Naia tagged along with Leon to his rendezvous with Samaad. Karan wanted to see him again. His curiosity had been aroused by their conversations of the previous night, and he was footloose so he could do as he pleased. Naia got a tingle in her belly again, something she hadn't felt in a long time. She wasn't going to pass up this opportunity. Besides, she was the driver now, so she felt useful, and drove them where they had to go. Leon gave her an address that took them on a long tour of the city. They got lost on various Ring Roads, turned up at some marketplace, and had to ask for directions. Leon was happy to be lost. It gave him the opportunity to see more of Delhi. The Mughal structures they encountered every few miles delighted him. He would hang out of the window begging Naia to slow down so he could photograph each one. They came upon the President's palace and Parliament complex. Naia drove in as far as she could, turning into sidelanes when massive wrought iron gates barred their way, and she managed to get far into the complex.

She parked so that Leon could get some shots, when they heard a whistle and two uniformed men who could have been policemen or presidential guardsmen came sprinting out of the hedges yelling at them to leave. Naia took off as fast as the old car would go. She was quite nervous. She parked in a spot under some trees to calm herself. 'They could have shot us,' she said indignantly. Karan laughed. 'No, they couldn't have shot us, they don't carry guns. Even the Indian police don't carry guns.'

Leon gave him a sharp glance. 'Most don't, but these do, Karan. They didn't used to, but since the attack on the Parliament by terrorists—you know what I'm talking about? Since then, they pack. Naia's right. They could have shot us.'

'How do you know about that?' Naia asked him.

'Samaad. He knows everything about everything, I think. Which reminds me, we need to find him. He's got some errands to do, and then he's going to be at that address. So let's go. It's about time.'

When they rang the doorbell of the apartment, Samaad opened the door with a grass broom in his hand. He put it down to shake Karan's hand. 'Karan—you are Viren's son. We met the year I sold him that huge Naeen. And you were at King's College the year I left?'

'Perfect memory.' Karan was impressed.

The place was bare but for a table and a few chairs, and clean. Samaad had made tea, and he poured it out for them. 'I was only expecting Yehudi, so there's just a half-cup for each of you. Do sit down. I'll just sit here on the windowsill. I like it. I can see the street from here, and anyone coming into the building.'

Naia abruptly asked to go to the restroom. It was attached to the bedroom. She closed the bedroom door on her way through, and they heard her shut the door of the bathroom as well. Still, they could hear her running the water in the sink. Though the walls of the building were concrete, it was a very small apartment—just the two rooms and a tiny kitchen. There was no real privacy.

Samaad and Karan exchanged news and views about London. They talked about the campus, restaurants old and new, clubs, pubs, professors, the Queen. Samaad suddenly held up his hand to stop the talk and went to the bedroom door. He put first his ear and then his nose to the crack between the door and the wall. Then he opened the door and went in and sniffed at the bathroom door. He came out and shut the door and returned to his window sill.

'Naia is your sister, right, Karan?' Karan nodded yes.

'And your friend, Yehudi?' Leon nodded too, waiting, because he knew Samaad, he knew that gravity in his attitude. He knew Samaad was going to say something important, delicate. He seemed to want to say it right the first time.

'Do you both know what she is doing in there?' He looked at their puzzled faces and shook his head in disgust. 'I think you do not. Well, I guess I should tell you then. She is smoking hack. What is that? That is impure heroin. The very dregs of heroin. Rubbish. Smack. Also the most addictive substance known to man. I ask you, Yehudi, where in the name of God did she start this habit? Because I am sure it could not have been in the US.'

Leon looked at him, stricken. He turned to Karan for help, but saw that he wasn't going to get any. Karan didn't look as if he had any idea what was going on.

'She's just trying it out right? I mean, I smoke ganja and hash all the time, man, I can stop anytime I want. You know this, Samaad. She can stop too, right?' He knew he was wrong. He had suspected it since he had laid eyes on her at the bus station. He had known for sure soon thereafter that something was not right with her. But he had been too busy with what was happening in his own life to go after the obvious. He was ashamed of himself then. He had never let her down before. Samaad saw the distress on his friend's face.

'Yehudi, it's not your fault. Don't worry, my friend, I have seen worse. She has not been doing this very long, and she is not doing it very much. We can help her.'

Leon stared at the floor. His vision was blurry. Samaad reached out and ruffled his hair. 'You have a very big heart. She is your friend, and you love her. You are my friend, and I will help you. Look at me, Yehudi.' He lifted Leon's face and made him look into his bottomless eyes. 'I will help you,' he said again, and Leon felt something in the back of his neck. His mind flickered between relief and apprehension. He trusted this man so completely, and yet he was afraid.

Karan watched them quietly without saying a word. He felt strangely disconnected from what was unfolding in front of him, and he was content, relieved even, to stay out of it. He felt like if he took one step in, he would be drawn in all the way, and he didn't want to stray from his path, even if it went nowhere. He was safe. He would go back to

London, he would work on his PhD, he would be far away from this Samaad. He had stood at the top of one of the Trade Centre towers once, and there was a tingling in his feet that he felt would go away only if he jumped. Samaad made him feel that way. He knew no reason why, but he didn't question his instinct. He knew too, that Leon had jumped, and was going down fast, though he had not yet achieved terminal velocity.

Naia—she was his sister, but what obligation did he have to her anyway? It was not as if they had any bonds like she and Leon had. After all these years of separation, it was just an accident of birth. Irritation with her promptly surged up and buzzed around in his head like a gnat. Who was stupid enough to smoke that stuff? She should have known better. What was he going to tell his father? It was, of course, out of the question to say anything to his mother. Or perhaps not. Perhaps it would give her something to worry about, and put the meaning back in her life. Thinking about his mother depressed him in a disconnected way. He was rarely depressed or even disturbed by anything, but she could make him feel like life was pointless. As a child, when her self-flagellation was at its peak, he would wish that it had been him that had been stolen, or that he would be taken away to live with his lost sister. He didn't hate his mother, just the feeling of despair that surrounded her and touched everything around her. Thinking about her made his irritation surge again, but this time it was directed at himself. He wanted to get up and leave, but he just sat there, doing nothing, saying nothing, revealing nothing.

Almost forty-five minutes later, when Naia came out of the bedroom, she found the three of them sitting on the floor engaged in a complicated conversation about the use of diamonds as currency to fund a war in some west African nation. All three greeted her return with indifference and continued on with their exchange. She knew nothing and cared less about it, and so she sat on the now vacant windowsill and stared at the street below. She felt more like herself, she thought. Her stomach hurt a little, her throat was raw from the retching that sometimes came after she smoked, but she felt better when she smoked than when she didn't. She decided she wouldn't smoke anymore until the next morning.

'Naayo, were you serious about going with me? North?'

Surprised, she turned away from the window, toward Leon first, and then Samaad. 'Can I come?' she asked him directly. 'Will you protect me?'

Samaad laughed. 'From what? Protect you? What has this guy been telling you?'

'Nothing, he just said I should ask you for protection.'

'I will protect you,' he said, suddenly serious. 'From anything that might cause you harm. Are you sure you want to be protected?'

All three men were looking intently at her. She knew that Leon knew something he had not known before. And she wondered for a split second what had happened amongst them while she was in the bathroom. She knew he wanted her to go with him. She did not know why, though, when she said to Samaad, 'Yes, I want you to protect me. I want to go with you to your home. Can I come?'

Samaad didn't hesitate.

'Yes.'

Leon's intended two-day stay in Delhi had stretched to

two weeks. Naia had to convince Viren to let her go. She could have upped and left, she was not really bound to do what he told her. But she pretended, and she didn't really want to hurt him. He knew this too, and tried to talk her gently into not going. His distress came through his patient persuasion, though. They would walk in his garden after dinner every day, sometimes with and sometimes without Karan, and he would talk to her of this and that, inevitably coming back to the subject of her intended departure. He had just found her again. He was afraid more than anything of losing her. But he was, if nothing else, a diplomat, and he knew when he had lost. That last night before they were to leave, he said nothing of her not going. He just told her to be careful, to have a good time, to look for beauty and inner peace. That surprised her, but she didn't ask him what he meant.

Naia was relieved that he did not bring up Saroj as a reason for her to not go. 'She will be upset, but I will talk to her,' was all he said about it. Naia was grateful. She had not tried to get to know Saroj better. She found her depressing to be around, and avoided her when she could. It wasn't hard in a house that size, to not bump into her more than was absolutely necessary, which was at mealtimes. These were relatively painless because some combination of Viren, Karan, and now Leon was there to blunt the edge.

Leon had spent the weeks stocking up on cans of tuna, packets of orange Tang and cartons of cigarettes for his friends at the camp, photographing parts of Delhi that he had missed on their earlier stay, and spending time with Karan getting high and eating, two passions they had in common.

Samaad arrived early on the day of their planned
departure to pick up Leon and Naia. They were sitting at
the dining table. Viren, Saroj and Karan were at the table
too, it was breakfast time. There was a tightness in everyone's
attitude. The only sound in the room was the conversation
between teacups and spoons. When Samaad came into the
room he brought with him a legitimate reason to pretend
normalcy and resume polite conversation.

'Samaad. It's really good to see you again. It's been a long
time. Would you like some tea? You have time for a cup?'
Viren shook Samaad's hand and patted him.

'Yes, it has been a long time. I haven't been to Delhi very
often this year. And I didn't have anything that would
interest you—you have special needs. Thanks.'

He took his cup from Saroj and sat at the table next to
Naia. There was a small silence, into which, quite suddenly,
was thrust the sound of a hissing sob from Saroj.

'Do you have to go?' she asked Naia, wiping away tears
that had begun to stream. Naia was perplexed. She had
screwed up her face, knit her eyebrows, and was looking
down at her lap. Neither husband nor son did anything to
comfort Saroj or defuse the situation. Samaad looked
around at the miserable group, making a decision to say
something. He put his cup down on the saucer but
misjudged the distance. It clattered and tipped over, startling
everyone. Saroj was momentarily distracted from herself,
and he tried to lead her further away from her misery.

'Ma'am, she will be fine, and she will come back soon.
The mountain air will do her a lot of good. It is very
beautiful in Kashmir. Have you been there?' His voice had
the desired effect. She stopped crying for a minute, quieted

by his matter-of-fact tone. Then her distress returned in full force. 'But why does she have to go? Why are you going?' she turned on Naia again. Naia was at a loss. She wasn't prepared for this direct confrontation.

'I would like to go with Leon. He said it was amazing. It's nothing personal or anything like that.' Then she was annoyed for having to defend herself. Karan finally spoke. 'Ma, you should leave her alone to do what she wants. It's no big deal, she's just going for a couple of weeks. It's a great opportunity to be able to go with Samaad, who knows that area so well. Not as a tourist. I really think you should look at it from her point of view. Try.'

Leon and Naia made eye contact. Viren's normal diplomatic self had deserted him. He was drinking his tea nervously, running his hands through his hair, and fidgeting. He seemed to be trying to get his own emotions under control, and he didn't want to deal with his wife's as well. Leon watched him with some puzzlement. He saw him glance in Samaad's direction, and they nodded at each other. Something passed between them that was meant to be just between them, but nothing escaped Leon, and he filed it away for later.

'Are you all packed and ready?' Viren asked Naia. Saroj, hearing this, put her head down in her hands and started wailing and sobbing. Karan got up and went to his mother. He tried to pat her back and say soothing things, but that only made it worse.

'You had better go,' he said to Leon. 'Dad and I will take care of her. I am really sorry, I don't know what comes over her . . .'

Leon and Samaad went to get the bags. Viren walked

Naia to the door. He put his arm around her. 'I'm sorry about Saroj,' he said. 'She doesn't know what to do with her emotions . . . she never got over losing you. Now she hasn't got over getting you back, and she has always had this sense of doom, so she probably thinks she will never see you again. She'll be okay in a bit. But you take care, and come back soon. I'll miss you. Call, if you get the chance. And if you need anything.'

Naia just nodded at everything he said. She didn't really know how to respond to his matter-of-fact kindness. She remembered he was her father, then, and hugged him.

'I'll be back soon. I just want to go see what it's like up there. Leon seems to love it. I wasn't trying to hurt her, or even get away. You know I'm going back to LA soon, after I get back . . . I have to get back to my life, my work . . .'

He held her gently, but she felt him take a deep shaky breath. And then he pushed her away. He said, 'We'll talk when you get back. Go on, have fun.'

Karan came running out of the house just as they were about to leave. He made Naia get out of the car and hugged her and said a cheerful goodbye that was a relief after all the drama. 'I'll be here when you get back, I think. If not, go back via London and come see me.'

Father and son watched the car drive out of the massive wrought iron gates, and then turned and went back into the house, Karan to read and laze, Viren to look in on his wife, to make sure she had taken her medication and was calmer, and preferably asleep. He found her sitting by the window in their bedroom staring out at the garden. She didn't turn or show any sign that she had noticed his presence, so he left, closing the door softly behind him, leaving her to her solitude.

EIGHTEEN

The banister was old, it felt smooth and warm as she ran her hand down it to the bottom of the sweep of stairs. She pushed the gold-flecked glass doors and stepped out into the street. She was almost instantly overwhelmed by the alienness of her surroundings, and yet, the sounds were not so different from those she heard on the streets at home. She stood there for a few moments, wondering which way she should go, or if she should go at all. She looked around, taking in the faces. She was struck by how attractive every man, woman, and child she saw was, how vividly coloured, how differently dressed from what she was used to. She noticed, too, the feeling of opulence that came off the women, all wearing gold, like at home, and she remembered that the Spanish valued their gold as much as they did at home. She didn't know how long she stood there, and then remembered that she had promised herself a meal and a glass of wine that day, after staying indoors out of nervousness for so many.

She took a few steps to her right, and then, on impulse, turned around and began to walk the other way, towards the bridge, where she could see the river, and the dome of the great mosque-church. She turned towards the church, and began to walk along the cobbles, avoiding the huge piles of horse manure. Even that utterly familiar smell could not quell her fluttering pulse. What if she couldn't find her way back home, she thought, but kept walking anyway. She saw a row of little bars, and began to worry about which one she should go into. She decided it would be the third on her left after she had passed the next one. But when she came up to the next one, she saw a little gate, and a courtyard beyond it that she would have missed altogether had the gate been shut. She quickly went inside and sat at one of the wrought iron tables. No one came for a long time, and she began to think no one would, when suddenly, as if a bell had gone off, people began to stream in and sit down at the tables around her. The place filled with chatter and laughter. A waiter came out and threw down menus at all the tables. Bottles of sherry and glasses of red wine, bowls of enormous olives and chunks of cheese and ham came out on huge trays, and she began to get very nervous all over again. She stopped looking around, stopped enjoying herself, and stared at the menu, thinking she would have her order ready before the waiter came to her table.

'¿Puedo sentarme yo aquí?'

She looked up, startled. She found herself looking into a chaotic face with aggressive black hair, and his eyes, because he was standing up against the blue Mediterranean sky, looked like holes in his head.

'Si, si,' she said.

He smiled. 'Thanks. I am in a bit of a hurry, and saw you, and figured you wouldn't mind. You're the new attaché's wife, eh?'

She was so relieved to hear a familiar language that she did something she never did. She reached out and touched his arm, drawing it back almost as soon as she touched the dark hair on it.

'Yes, we got here two weeks ago, and I've been too scared to leave the house ...'

He laughed. She looked again at his eyes, seeing that he was looking away from her for the waiter. They were a clear blue, fringed with dark smoky lashes. She was fascinated. This was one colour that did not occur at all in India, as far as she knew. There were greys, greens, of course browns and hazels. But not this cold, clear, cloudless blue. No doubt in the blueness. No adulteration by any other hue. She suddenly wondered what it would be like to look into those eyes from even closer. She shook her head, thinking she must have gone a bit mad from the smell of the orange trees. He looked back at her, and she looked down.

'So what do you want?' he asked her.

'Want?' She was alarmed by his question, and it puzzled him.

'To eat? And maybe a drink? It's the least I can do, buy you lunch, when you let a stranger sit at your table.'

'Oh. Yes. No, it's okay, I was going anyway . . .' she began to push her chair back, wishing she had not worn that silly dress, that she was back in her sari, back in her room, back . . .

He put his hand on hers, and she knew then that there was something very wrong with her responses that day.

'Hey, sit down. Your husband won't be pleased if I don't look after you. Have a glass of sherry, it's really lovely.'

The waiter came to their table just then, and he ordered in his obviously Irish-accented Spanish, and she laughed, and when the man was gone, she regained some of her lost composure and asked him his name.

'I'm Gabe Hallam,' he said. 'And you?'

'Saroj.'

'Sa—? I don't mean to be rude, but can I call you Sara? I'm just not good with foreign sounds.'

She wondered why he had to call her anything, she didn't think they would ever meet again. But she nodded.

The sherry was crisp and cold and smelled of fresh bread at the same time. She had two glasses, and the ragout he had ordered for them both, with hunks of dark bread and a salad with leaves she had never seen before. He told her about the church, how it was a mosque when the Moors were there, about the river, muddy and in a turmoil, about his home. She listened, not saying much, watching his eyes, the expanse of his gestures, his laugh, his voice, everything about him was big and aggressive. He was nothing like Viren, her husband of a mere year. She hadn't known any other man, nor been alone with any other, so he was her only comparison.

'I thought you were in a hurry,' she said into a lull in the conversation.

'I was. But . . . would you like to walk down to the river?'

'Yes,' she said, and he paid the bill, and took her hand in his, and walked her out. He started to let go of her hand when they were on the street, but she held on with the slightest pressure. He stopped, and looked down at her, puzzled again, and then walked on, saying nothing.

He didn't stop, didn't say anything, until they were at a small building with an ornate stoop. He pulled a small flower off the bush there, cupped it in his hands, and held it to her for her to smell.

'Close your eyes and take a deep breath,' he said softly.

She did, and reeled from the heavy sweetness of the fragrance. She didn't open her eyes.

'Will you come upstairs with me?'

'Yes,' she said, with the out-breath, releasing the perfume from her lungs, ready for the first and only love of her life.

As she lay in his crumpled cotton sheets later and watched him, naked, huge, too big for her in every way, she wondered who and what she was, and a sort of restrained panic began to fill up her lungs, and she began to breathe rapidly. He came and lay beside her, stroking her from her breasts to her thighs, touching her with a familiarity and disdain for shame that she had never seen or even thought possible.

'You're so bloody small,' he said, 'did I hurt you?'

She shook her head, not daring to move in case he stopped doing what he was doing. His hands were definitely moving her legs apart, he was actually putting his hands, his fingers in places she had not even touched herself. He pushed her legs apart and got up and knelt in front of her. She was speechless and breathless and hopeless and faithless, and he was tasting the sweat and slime he had made in her, and she tried to stop him and herself, and instead found herself opening up and giving him more and more, and found herself in a sheer panic and confusion and delight of convulsions from something she simply had not felt before. She thought she was surely dying, and put her hands in his strong black hair and moaned from her very soul, as if it were the first and last and only sound she would ever make.

He lay quietly for a while, and then slid up and looked at her, propped up on his elbow.

He said, laughing slightly, 'Has no one ever been here before?'

NINETEEN

The journey was obviously rough on Naia. She hated the trains in India. She decided she would walk all the way back if she had to. Several times on the way she wondered what she was doing there, why she hadn't just stayed in Delhi in Viren's comfortable house, or even gone back to Los Angeles. Then she remembered that her parents were not there any more, were not anywhere but in her heart. She felt like there was no reason for her to go back, there was no one to go back to. Yes, there was the house on the beach, the wind chimes with no one to listen to them, and Adam who didn't need her, and Dog who did. Elijah would be happy to have her back, especially if she brought Leon back with her. And then there was Raoul. He wasn't in LA anymore, but she had to see him again, ask him why he had gone off to live in Japan, where he was almost totally inaccessible to her. She had to know if what Leon said was true, that he didn't want to be with her. But Leon had said that was subconscious, so how would Raoul know the answer to that? And how the hell would Leon know what was in Raoul's subconscious? She had to get to the bottom of it.

She had bought enough hack from Frank's dealer to see her through several weeks if she made sure she didn't increase the amount she smoked every day. She had promised herself she wouldn't. She only needed it three or four times, and she wasn't going to go over that. She knew she wasn't. She panicked while thinking about it. What if it wasn't enough? How would she manage? Where the hell were Leon and Samaad, and how long did they expect her to sit and wait on top of their pile of luggage in the middle of nowhere?

The train had brought them to Srinagar. From there a bus ride of nearly eight hours through some spectacular and harrowing roads had ended at a signpost on the road. She was too dazed at that time to notice, but other than that sign which said in large black letters, 'Absolutely NO Sleeping While Driving', the asphalt, and the bus that brought them there careening violently and now shrinking fast into a speck on the horizon, there was no sign of human existence around them. She sat there blinking in the blindingly bright light, trying to focus, while Leon and Samaad went off to find their transport onward. It had been fifteen minutes, she had had a smoke as soon as they had gone out of smelling distance, and she felt fine for the moment. But she was not happy to just sit there in what she was sure was not just the middle of nowhere, it was the outer reaches of nowhere. If she had been her normal self, she would have noticed that the road curved around the mountainside, and just where it disappeared around the bend, there was a broad dirt track going up at a steep grade. She would have seen the wildflowers carpeting the side of the mountain, cut off only by the ribbon of road. She would have seen the flowers littering the ridge below, like a New Orleans street the morning after Mardi Gras. She would have seen Leon and Samaad on the ridge just above her where the dirt track curved up and carried on around the mountain to where they were going.

They dragged the camouflage off the Jonga and folded it into a neat giant sausage. They then tied it to the back.

Samaad crawled under the car and came out with a large
gun. It looked to Leon like a toy. Samaad loaded it with
ammunition from the glove compartment. He got in the
passenger side, put it under the seat, told Leon to drive.

'I'll ride shotgun,' he said, and they both started laughing.
The sound carried down the mountain.

Leon started the old vehicle. He had done all this when
they had come up the first time, but that time Samaad had
not asked him to drive.

'How old is this thing? And what is it?'

'It's a Jonga. Made by Datsun. Must be at least thirty
years old. It's very easy to keep in working condition, and
very reliable. I don't really know where it came from. It
may be one of my father's, he had a lot of cars.'

They went banging down the track to pick up Naia and
the stuff, and came banging back the same way. She didn't
say much, she seemed to them to be almost asleep in the
back. They exchanged meaningful looks, and Leon made a
smoking gesture to Samaad. Samaad nodded.

'It'll be fine,' he said.

Leon was enjoying the driving. He was quite at ease with
the vehicle. It was windy and a little narrow—if someone
came down from the other side, they would have to back
all the way down and start over—but Samaad assured him
that they had the only vehicle in this part of the world. As
suddenly as it had begun, the path ended in a broad flat
plain, a large valley with mountains rising up from all sides
of it.

'You know the way, I'm going to take a nap. Stop a
minute so I can take a piss,' Samaad told him.

Leon just stopped right where they were, and both men

got out and stretched their legs a bit. It had not been more than an hour, but it was harder on the body because of the lack of road surface and the age of the vehicle. They drank water, tried to wake Naia, and started on their way again. It would be four or five hours before they got to Samaad's house. Leon wondered how all those men had got there, how they had transported all the machinery, food, supplies that were needed for their living. Samaad looked as if he was asleep already, so he didn't ask right then, but he knew he would as soon as he got the opportunity. Leon wondered too, about Viren and Samaad. How long they had known each other, and for what. Because carpets alone did not seem enough to explain their connection. He felt it, and it was more than that.

Samaad was not asleep, just resting with his eyes closed, re-charging himself for his part of the driving. He thought of Naia asleep or comatose in the seat behind him. She had fallen over onto the tarpaulin and seemed oblivious to discomfort in spite of the contorted position she was in. She was beautiful in her own way, he thought. Not the kind of woman he usually found attractive—white, very thin, free of the encumbrance of intelligence. Naia was definitely different from that type. She was dark with a very generous wide mouth that he imagined was unattractively open and quite possibly drooling just then, but he didn't open his eyes and turn his head to confirm this image. Her hair was a dusty brown, almost the same colour as her skin, giving her an all-over brown appearance, like a chickoo. Her light brown eyes were lighter than her skin, and so looked like windows in her face, letting out the light from inside her head. They were such bright eyes. It was a pity that she had found the drug she had found. Without his help it would dull those eyes, and the mind shining through them, forever. He was surprised at himself then. He had never really cared about any woman before. But then, this one was Yehudi's friend. He obviously adored her, she was his family. Samaad had seen Leon's stricken face when he had found out. Her real brother had not even flinched. He had just sat there. Leon loved her and would do whatever it took to get her off it. He admitted to himself that it wasn't just Leon's love for Naia that made him want to see her clean. She wasn't his type, at all. But she did have fine eyes.

There had been a woman, many women. College, London, he was pretty enough then, and just different enough from the other Indians and Pakis to be exotic but not threatening. His eyes drew them in, but he meticulously weeded out those who might want to take things too far. They had an obsession with kissing. He just wanted the sex, the physicalness of them, the give of the flesh beneath the skin, the succulence of breasts and thighs, the hair. Not the mouth thing. That bothered him. Morag, with the smutty eyes, had said, 'So how come ye put yer dokey in me throat, but ye won't kiss me.' And he had kissed her out of a pure but fleeting affection for her. His unresponsiveness bothered them, he knew. But he got his share, and moved on. There had been the ones he wanted to talk with, to listen to, and he didn't have sex with them. When he thought back on it now, it seemed as though he knew he had something else waiting for him. He could have had his father fix him up a wife: at least his daily meals would be cooked, his clothes washed. But he had said no to even that. The price would be children, and that was too high. With his father and mother gone, there was no one craving grandchildren anymore. His parents had enjoyed Jabra's children at least, he thought, assuaging his own guilt.

He woke up an hour later. He had gone to sleep after all. They were parked under an outcrop of rock. Leon was asleep with his head on his arms on the steering wheel. Naia was still passed out in a way that Samaad didn't like the look of. He looked around them and saw that Leon had driven a lot. They had covered a lot of kilometres and had not too much left. He was relieved. Naia looked like she needed some help. He hoped that the French pills he had asked for had been delivered. He would have to start her on them as soon as possible. He woke Leon gently by touching his face. He moved him to the passenger seat and took over the driving. It was easy for him, he knew the road home intimately, and so did the old Jonga. They were back at the village very early in the morning, almost twenty-four hours since they had left Viren's house in New Delhi.

Men ran out to meet them. Leon helped Naia out of the car and to her feet. She was staggering a bit, groggy from too much sleep and rattled from the journey. He took her to his room. The sleeping bag was rolled up where he had left it, but there was a metal cot in the room, with a new mattress and pillow on it. She sat down on the mattress and rubbed her eyes.

'Where the hell are we?'

'In my room, in my house, except there was no bed when I left. I guess it's for you.'

She fumbled in her bag and took out a pack of Marlboros.

'You smoke? Since when?' Leon asked her, but gently.

She didn't say anything. She took out a piece of aluminum foil and a small plastic vial from the pack. She poured powder from the vial onto the foil. She rolled a hundred-rupee-note and used it to suck up the sublimate that came off the foil when she held the flame of an orange Bic lighter under it. The smell which filled the room was not at all unpleasant, but it gave him a whole body panic like he had not felt since the first time he had met Naia, when he had woken up in a hospital bed afraid that he was either dead, or badly hurt. He just sat there watching her, not saying anything either.

Samaad barged into the silence, opening the door and bringing in the bright morning air, banishing the smell, and with it, the feeling of helplessness that was threatening Leon. Samaad took in the scene in a glance. For some reason Leon did not understand, Naia dropped the piece of foil and tried to hide the rest of the evidence by pushing everything into her open bag. Before Leon could do or say anything, Samaad snatched her bag and emptied it onto the bed. Thirty or so vials of the kind Leon had seen fell out along with her tampons, a ballpoint pen, aspirin, passport, wallet, many lighters in bright colours, other girly things that were a blur. Either because she had just had her fix, or was so shocked by this audacious invasion of privacy, she forgot to respond. She just sat there, eyelids slightly drooping, and watched wordlessly as Samaad took every vial he could find, sorting carefully through the pile till he was sure there were no more. He put them in the pocket of his long flowing shirt and said to Naia, 'If you have any needs, come and see me. Yehudi will show you where I am.'

'Can he do this?' Naia spoke at last, turning to Leon for help.

'Can you?' Leon asked him. Samaad smiled brilliantly and answered them both, 'Sue me.'

She felt like water that had lost its container. She was flowing out of control, her self was getting scattered and lost and she was afraid she wouldn't be able to put herself back together again. And that was only in her head. She could hear voices outside her room, but the windows were closed and the door was locked. She knew there was a man with a large gun outside. She couldn't speak. Her throat seemed to have closed up. And she didn't think she was asleep, but she couldn't wake up, or open her eyes, or move her arms. She tried to move them. They were heavy and had lost the elbow joint and become like sticks. Anne was yelling something at her but she couldn't understand, she was speaking in Kashmiri. Her whole body began to itch, and that broke her out of the dream-paralysis she was stuck in. She sat up on the bed. The room was filled with a clear golden light from the open window. It would have been beautiful if it wasn't for the unbearable itching. She couldn't scratch herself enough. It was everywhere, even her scalp was crawling. She took a sip from the steel tumbler someone had put on the windowsill. She was pulling her pants up her leg to reach new itches when the door opened and Samaad came in. She pushed the pants down and rubbed herself through them in as polite a manner as she could manage.

'We have to talk about this,' he said, sitting down on the far end of the bed, putting as much distance between them as was possible.

'Leon and I have to go up north for two days. I will give you some medicines. You have to take them and drink all the water you can. Lots of water. Naia, are you listening?'

She had begun to cry, still scratching herself wherever she could without undressing. Even her eyes itched.

'Can't you just give me back my stuff? It's not going to last that long . . . then I will have nowhere to get any and we can do this then?'

He sighed and shook his head. 'Look, Naia, you know this is going to be hard. We are not going to talk about that now. The shit is gone, I burned it. So you know that option is out. You will just have to do what I tell you. We will talk again in a week. No, don't cry, or cry if you have to, it makes no difference to me. Yehudi isn't going to come and see you. I told him he couldn't. We will be back in two days. I have those pills for you. They will help you feel a little better.'

He got up and moved closer to her. She stopped scratching herself and put her head in her hands. He sat there a while, watching her, and then raised his voice just a little for his man to come in. A heavily bearded man in blue came in and gave Samaad a Ziploc bag. Samaad held out one pill with the tumbler of water.

'These are French, they are not methadone. This is a better way, you won't get attached to these.'

'Where is Leon? I need to see him. I don't know you, and I don't want to know you, and I don't want to take anything. You need to give my vials back to me. You really do. You can't do this to me.'

He jerked his chin at the door and the man left. He said nothing for a few minutes. He waited for her to go on, but she was done. She put her head back in her hands.

'I will ask Yehudi to come in and see you, but only if you take this,' he told her, when she said nothing more.

She was in some discomfort, but her anger was greater. 'No. I don't want to take anything. And stop calling him that stupid name, his name is Leon. I want to see him. Now.'

'If you take this one pill, Naia, you can see him. Do your muscles hurt? In your calves?' She nodded miserably. The fight had gone out of her as quickly as it had come. She held out her hand for the pill. 'Drink some water first. Now put it under your tongue. Let it sit there and dissolve. That will take about ten minutes. Try not to swallow or speak or anything, don't even open your mouth. Breathe through your nose. Go on, put it under your tongue. Here, I'll do it.'

He took the pill from her and she opened her mouth and tilted up her head, turning her tongue up. He placed it there and tapped her chin to let her know to close her mouth. There was a musty sourness on her breath, but he didn't show any sign of having smelled it. They sat there then, in complete silence. Her mouth began to hurt in about three minutes, filling up with saliva that she couldn't bear not to swallow. Then her jaw went into a lock that panicked her and she reached for his hand. He nodded at her, showing her his watch, nodding reassuringly all the time. She looked at his eyes and looked into them and held them with hers, looking deeper and deeper but seeing nothing, just polished granite with blue glints where the light went through, or perhaps came out of them. Everything faded into a blur, except those eyes, everything in the world faded away. All she needed was to look into those eyes. She didn't mind dying then and there, she thought, if she could just keep looking in those black depths, looking for those sapphire sparks.

'Here, you can have a drink now, it should be dissolved,' he said, and she realised she was holding his hand with both of hers. She let it go and took the water.

'Can I see Leon now?'

Samaad stood up. 'I'll send him in, but just for a few minutes. You say goodbye to him, we are going north. We'll be back in a couple of days.'

'Yes, you said. Why? Why does he have to go with you? Can I go?'

He was patient, but seemed in a hurry to go. 'No, you can't come with us. You aren't well enough. Yehudi brought you up here for this reason only: he wanted to get you off this stupid habit you have picked up. So you will not leave until you are off it. Do you understand me?'

She stared at him in shock. No one had ever spoken to her that way before. She was more than a little afraid of him, but that didn't stop her from speaking her mind.

'What gives you the right?'

He smiled sweetly at her. 'Not what, who. Yehudi is my friend. If my friend wants you cured, I cure you, *bas*.' He snapped his fingers.

'What?'

'Nothing. Anyway, he is going north with me because he wants to. I do not tell him what to do.'

She was angry now. 'Except when to see me?'

'That is our agreement. That is because I am going to get you off this shit that you are smoking. Once that is done, he can see you whenever he pleases. And you can see him whenever you please. He can come back and live here if you like. This is his house, actually. But not yet.'

She smiled. 'We are not—you know . . .'

'I know,' he said, and then went out, leaving her suddenly alone in the fading melancholy light.

Naia sat there on the mattress, her back against the whitewashed wall. It felt hard and bumpy even through her thick sweatshirt. She wondered how she had got to where she was. She almost didn't remember the journey. A single bee, she thought, an absurdly small thing in the world, had ended three lives, and sent so many other lives into directions that they could never have imagined. She hadn't found out who she was, but on her journey to do so, she had found out who she wasn't, and had lost everything she was before. She was reborn, and free to be anyone and anything she chose. She could live any of those lives she had lived in her head since she was a little girl. She probably wouldn't ever be a surfer, or an LAPD officer or a potter like her father, or a diplomat like her other father, or a movie star in Hollywood. Or even a writer, which she actually had tried to be. But she might be a soldier in a war. Or at least the lover of a soldier. And that's where she stopped short and took a breath. Lover? How had that come about? When did he slip into her head in that way? And then she realised she wasn't feeling particularly uncomfortable even though she had not smoked in twelve hours. He really was going to put her right, then, with whatever magic medication he had given her.

She wished she had paid attention to what she had been doing with Frank. He seemed nice when she first met him, and he was still nice when she got to know him better.

Only, he was a heroin-user. He was very controlled. He used fresh needles and never ever shared any equipment with anyone. He said he had been doing it for six years almost, and took great care to control his usage, to do his work, and have his money come in every month at the American Express office. He worked for some German NGO. Or maybe it was American, she didn't remember. Those three months without Leon to talk to, to hang with, to complain to about the weather, Saroj, the city and the dirt, they had been hard. She had been glad for Frank's company in that loneliness, even though it wasn't much. He didn't know her or care about her, and she had really needed that when the feeling of loss overcame her.

No one saw it, not Viren, of course not Saroj. They wouldn't have known what to look for. Though Viren loved her just for being his daughter, he didn't know the signs of her downfall. He had never seen her any other way. Jim and Anne would have known, and they were gone. Leon knew, but he had lost his heart to a mountain lion, and had left her to fend for herself. By the time Tara visited her that one time at the end of the three months, it was too late. She probably saw that something was wrong. Naia could see the concern in her eyes, but knew she had attributed it to the newness of her situation, the discomfort of getting to know Viren and especially Saroj about whom she had had misgivings from the beginning. Tara had bought the story.

So there had been countless strained breakfasts, and then she would escape to the international café and meet someone new each day. Frank was a familiar face in an unfamiliar world, and he was happy to see her too. They had hit it off. He was a caring person, essentially, and he shared his addiction with her, and she was hooked before she understood the danger. Karan was a delight when he showed up, but her nerves had been dulled to all but that first smell of hack each day. She would make it up to him and herself when she saw him next, she thought, she promised herself. Her back ached and she stretched herself out on the mattress. The pillow was perfect for her, and she fell asleep.

The silence of falling snow terrified her. She didn't know she wouldn't hear it, it had no sound like pattering rain or howling wind. It was dark, but the snow was visible to her, white, like a thousand ghosts hanging together in the still cold air. She shivered and stared at it, and it blurred into fireflies, swarms of them, falling like stardust all around her. They didn't make a sound either, and she strained her ears wishing for the sound of a voice. She was alone in her dreams, and lonely, wishing for her mother and her father. But there was only silence, and their voices were only in her memory.

When she woke up it was dark outside, and she could see the glow of firelight. She got up and rattled the door. It was opened immediately, and the man outside put his gun down when she came out. He said something to her she did not understand, so he signalled her to follow him.

There was no snow.

They walked some way through the camp. There were men sitting around small fires and smoking and talking in deep voices, and most of them ignored her. A few looked at her frankly, eyes following her as she passed them. She hadn't known until then how many people were there with

them. She was a little frightened and wished they would get
to where they were going, hopefully to see Leon, or at least
Samaad. The man stopped outside one of the buildings
and spoke to the guard outside. The guard knocked and
said something. Samaad opened the door and pulled her
inside.

'Leon . . . I waited and waited for you.' She turned on
Samaad in a fury. 'You said he would come and see me.'

'I knew you would sleep,' Samaad said quietly. 'You have
been asleep for six hours. Both of us have been to see you
several times. I told my man to bring you to us as soon as
you awoke.'

Her anger left her. 'Aren't you guys going somewhere?
What are all those stones?'

'Are you okay, Naayo?' Leon asked her. He got off the
rolled-up sleeping bag he had been sitting on and came up
to her and hugged her. 'Do you feel ill or anything?'

'I feel fine, actually. I am really hungry. Is there anything
I can eat?'

'I'll go get you some food. There must be leftovers from
dinner. I'll be back. It may be fifteen or twenty minutes,
they will have to heat it, or maybe make something.'

He put on his shoes without untying the laces, pushing
his feet in and smashing the backs down. He went out,
leaving her alone with Samaad.

Samaad kept doing what he was doing. He seemed to be
sorting pebbles and rocks into piles by size and colour.

'Thanks for that pill. I didn't feel any pain at all.'

'You're welcome,' he said. 'You will need another in a
day or so. I will give it to you and you can take it when we
are gone.

'Where are you going?'

'To the border, I need to do some business.'

'What border? What business? What exactly are you doing?'

'You don't need to know all that just yet.'

She was getting testy. 'Why? What harm will it do if I know? I know you are up to no good.'

He stopped what he was doing and carefully put the stones down. 'Up to no good? Okay, I'll tell you what we are doing here. I found sapphires in the mountains above us to the north. These are the finest sapphires in the world. I am mining them. That takes an immense amount of money. To start with, I got the men from my village to help me dig out a pile. Then I took them down to Bombay and had them cut and polished. Then I showed them to buyers. I didn't even have to sell them. All I did was show them, and I got the money I needed. I bought men and equipment and started the mining operation the right way. I have paid those buyers their money back, and have enough to fund my little country here. We are going to control the sapphires, and therefore this piece of the earth. When someone comes, and I know they will—one side or the other—we will be ready for them. They won't take this from us. That's what I am doing here. You think that's no good?'

If Naia was expecting something, it wasn't this. She was speechless. She was in someone else's life, she was certainly not in control of anything anymore. She knew that he was not going to let Leon go, he was not going to let her go. The thought did not fill her with dread or horror, she didn't yearn to be back home or in fact anywhere. She was sitting there on a sleeping bag in a room in a mercenary camp in the Himalayan foothills. She returned Samaad's quiet unblinking stare with her own, and knew that there was nowhere on earth that she would rather be. She realised that she needed no drug, no friend, no parents real or found, no memories old or new. She could be here with this man. She could die here today, she was fine with it. She had found her place on earth, or it had found her. And then she understood what had drawn Leon here, and what had kept him here. It was just Samaad's eyes. With those sapphire sparks. Once they had found you, you couldn't live without their light. She shivered a little at her own fanciful thoughts.

'Are you cold?' he went over to an ugly green steel trunk and took out a shawl and put it around her. It was the softest thing she had ever felt against her skin, and it warmed her quickly. There was a filigree of pink flowers embroidered at the corners.

'Thank you, this is beautiful ... whose is it?'

He smiled. 'Mine. I love dressing up.' He paused for effect, watching her, knowing she would scrunch up her face. She did, and he smiled. 'No, I'm just taking the piss . . .'

'Taking the what?'

'Nothing. I sell carpets, remember? Well, some of the carpet makers will sometimes bring down shawls that they have made or someone in their village has made. I have a couple, just in case. It's shatoosh. That's wool from a species of mountain antelope. Do you like it?'

She listened to him, as always fascinated by his accent and intonation. 'It's beautiful. And very warm.'

'It's yours,' he said. 'Happy birthday.' He didn't tell her

that the mountain antelopes were shot and killed for the wool, there was now a government ban on that, and that she might be arrested for owning shahtoosh. She was probably better off not knowing, he thought.

Leon came in with her dinner. She was grateful and literally fell to eating. They watched her for a while and then Samaad went back to his sorting. Leon talked to her as she ate, telling her about what he had been photographing since they had come. He was happy and calm, she thought. Not like she had ever seen him before. He always got twitchy and nervous on assignments, fiddling obsessively with his lenses, checking and rechecking his meters against each other, rearranging his equipment in his bags when he was not actually shooting. His movements had lost that rapid edginess. His gestures had become slow and deliberate, as had his speech. He took his time saying and doing everything. He was in the moment, as it were, instead of always itching to move on to the next thing, impatient to be done with whatever they were doing. He seemed to have relinquished control too, and was as okay with it as she was. She ate everything on her plate and drank all the hot tea he had brought her. It was fragrant, and unlike any tea she had had before.

'When are you going?' she asked him.

He turned to Samaad for an answer. 'Very early tomorrow morning,' he told them. 'We should have left earlier today, but the people we need to see will be there for a week, so there's no hurry. Tomorrow will be fine. No, you can't come with us, Naia, you're not well enough. You rest here. By the way, there is a Spanish guy expected here one of these days. Shall I leave instructions for him to be brought over to meet you? You might find him interesting to talk to.'

She was pleased that he would think of her needs, that he cared about her enough to think that she might like some company. Then she was curious. 'Why would a Spanish guy come up here? A friend of yours?'

'A friend of a friend.' And that's all he would say.

'Where exactly are you going?'

He was quiet for a moment, thinking about his answer. He seemed to come to a decision. 'North. To get some supplies. We'll be gone two days. You'll be looked after well. You will have a bodyguard. He will be with you at all times. The men here are not all my men. Some of them are here only to train my people. So don't go anywhere without your guard. You can talk to the Spaniard, if he comes, but avoid the others. My man will give you a pill in twelve hours, you will need it by then. You can walk around the village as far as the first pass, but don't go beyond that. I don't think you will be up to it just yet. Naia, are you listening?'

She was speechless with anxiety and nerves after hearing his little lecture. But she did notice that he had called her by her name. She didn't think he had ever said her name before.

'Are you listening to me? Are you going to follow my instructions? You should, because if you don't, you will not be safe. The men here are not like anyone you have ever met before.'

'Yes, I will do exactly as you say. What about food? Can I go and eat at the kitchen building?'

'No. You cannot. Never eat in public. Never. Maqbool—that's my man—will bring you your meals.'

She sat quietly for a while. Watching him. He worked efficiently, his beautiful hands separating the milky pebbles into piles by size. When he was done, he had five mounds of stones. He took out a leather case from his green trunk. Inside it were several black suede pouches. He put the stones into them, placed them in the case, then closed and locked it. Then he put the case back in the trunk and locked that as well.

Leon was done with packing his equipment. Naia looked over at him, she had not heard a word from him in a while, and saw that he was fast asleep.

'You should go back to your room. Get some rest. The more you sleep, the faster you will get all the toxins out of your blood, the sooner you can live normally,' Samaad told her. She began to laugh, surprising them both. 'Normally? Like I can go back to Los Angeles, to my life? I don't remember who I was there, Samaad, I wasn't who I was. I guess I am not making sense. Can I go back? Will you let me?'

'Me let you? Why would I not? And how can I hold you here? You are free to go, Naia, and so is he.'

She didn't question him anymore, they both knew he was lying.

TWENTY

Naia awoke to soft rapid knocking on her door. Before she could get off the bed, the door was opened softly. Samaad came in. She saw his silhouette in the moonlight in the

open door. She sat up quickly, her heart in her throat. She
had wanted him to come to her room, but now she was
afraid.

'Come on, get up, we have to get out of here.' His voice
vibrated with urgency, but he spoke softly. He pushed her
toward the door, but then went out ahead of her, hugging
the walls. She followed him out, and she could see the
place alive with shadows, all the men flat against walls,
moving quietly and with stealth. She heard a low hum over
the sound of the blood throbbing in her head. It definitely
was the hum of approaching aircraft. She couldn't tell
which direction it came from, but it terrified her. She
stood close to Samaad, her whole side against his. He put
his arm around her waist and held her closer, still flat
against the wall. There were others close to them, whispering
to each other. She couldn't think of anything but how
close he was. The fear, and his touch, and all the confusion
of waking suddenly, not being quite awake, produced a
remarkably pleasant sensation somewhere inside her. She
hadn't felt like that ever. The obvious danger of their
situation made the mix heady and delicious, like a glass of
rough red wine drunk too quickly.

'Where's Leon?' she asked Samaad, a little guiltily for
having taken this long to remember him.

'He went up to the mine with some of the men after you
went to bed last night. Said something about photographs
at sunrise. He wanted me to pick him up from there when
I left in the morning, it's on my way. He'll be safe there,
don't worry. I think you will have to come with us.'

'But . . .'

He suddenly put his free hand over her mouth, shutting

off her words and her brain with the pleasure of it. She
didn't understand why she should thrill at the feel of his
hand over her mouth, but she didn't question it. She was
only feeling, not thinking at all.

Men were crawling on the ground in front of them, on
their bellies with weapons. The planes were closer. Samaad
suddenly lay down on the ground, pulling her down next
to him and covering them both with the tarp that lay on
the ground. There must have been ten or twelve small
aircraft. They went over them very low.

'I should have thought of this, I should have been ready
for this,' Samaad said softly. His anger was with himself, he
wasn't really talking to her at all, but it frightened Naia,
and she turned into him, pushing herself even closer to
him so they were lying body to body under the tarp.

'Come on, come on,' he said, as the planes droned on
and away from them. They lay quiet like that for a long
time after the last sound had faded. She clung to him like
a lizard to a rock, knowing this would end, knowing that
he would get up and leave when the time was right, that he
would brush her off him like a piece of lint off his shirt. He
did get up in a bit, saying to her, 'Go back to your room.
I shouldn't have dragged you out . . . I was afraid if they
saw the buildings they would drop their load on us. I will
send men for Yehudi. Don't worry, I will come and see you
in the morning before we leave. Try to get some sleep. Are
you feeling okay?' She nodded miserably at him. 'Didn't
you say I should go with you?'

He was contrite, but not so much that she could make
him change his mind about that. 'I was worried then.
Things don't look too bad, they were just flying overhead.

Probably some old Russian transport planes. Which means they belong to the tribesmen. Opium-runners, probably. I overreacted, all of us did. It will be safer for you here, and you're not entirely better. When you are, we can talk about all this. Now go inside, and stay there.' They were standing at the door of her room, and he opened the door and pushed her in. The moonlight was so bright, she didn't need to light the lamps. She made her way to the cot and got under the covers, shivering from reaction. He waited till she was settled in, and then shut the door behind him as he left. She knew there was a guard outside her door, a wild-looking, fair-haired man with a very old and nasty-looking gun. She was safe, she supposed. In any case, she was so tired that she fell asleep before she had a chance to think about any of what had happened.

Samaad left her room and immediately called a short meeting of his men. Everything had gone well. They had been just plain lucky that the planes had gone over them when not just most, but all of the fires, had been out and all the lamps had been extinguished. Although it was called Samaad's camp, a name that had stuck because that was what it had started out as, it was a large village, after all. There were families, children, life being lived there. He was angry with himself for having reacted the way he did. He was unaccountably, irrationally nervous, and he was making everyone around him skittish as a result. He decided, after talking to Jabra and some of the other men, that they needed to gather some information. They needed to put some ears to the ground in Delhi, find out if there was any talk about them, any stirrings of trouble, any rumours. They needed to reassure themselves that they were still below the radar. He should go to Viren, he thought, and then changed the subject in his thoughts, as though Jabra would read his mind.

Jabra stayed in Samaad's room after the others had left. The brothers drank endless cups of tea and talked about this and that late into the night. Samaad was still awake after his brother left. He would have to change plans. He would have to send Jabra up north for the arms. He had a feeling, an instinct about it. The planes were a wake-up call for him, if not a sign. He needed to go to Paris himself. But he had the feeling that he should not leave the village, the camp—most of all the mines. Jabra agreed with him on this. Samaad sat by the window, staring into the dark, looking for answers in the shadows and light on the mountain outside. As the sun rose, he heard voices. The men had returned from the mines. He heard Leon's voice, his American peppered with local words as he tried to make himself understood to the men. Samaad narrowed his eyes and then smiled in the dark. He called out, 'Yehudi!'

That week for Naia was a blur of dream-filled sleep, small meals, short walks, all punctuated by the pill. She spent some time with Leon, when he could find the time, but there was too much for him to see and do. He followed Samaad everywhere, and when Samaad was not moving, he followed Jabra, who had been gone for a time and had returned. After trying to keep up, she admitted to herself that she was really not entirely well. The altitude did not help much either. She found herself breathless after a few minutes of walking. She gave up and stuck to her own schedule, which was mostly sleep.

Leon came into her room one morning. She knew it wasn't just for a visit as soon as he walked in.

'I'm going to Delhi. It's an errand for Samaad, he can't leave here right now. I will be back in a week, Naayo, it's not that long.'

She was in tears. Leon had never seen her like this. They had been talking since he got back. He had told her that she should stay there until she was fully recovered, until she felt no more need to seek out the drug that had almost got her hooked, but not quite.

'It's too easy to get back into it if you go back to Delhi. You should stay here.'

'But I could go with you and come right back when you do,' she said.

'Look, you know I'm right,' he said.

Samaad had known she would try. 'She will want to go back for it, be prepared to say no,' he had warned.

'If Samaad hadn't told us, we would never have known. You were going to hide it from me, and then it would have been so much harder to get you off it. He has been a real friend, Naayo, you have to understand he didn't have to do this. All he's saying is that you stay until you are really clean. What can you possibly not understand about that? What are you afraid of?'

She didn't know. It was not that she didn't want to stay. She did. She was excited and afraid and felt like she was high, higher than any drug could get her. She was just confused, and still felt the alien-ness of the past few months. Leon was her only link to her life, even to her identity, and she was a little afraid to be there without him.

'Will you go see Viren?'

'If you want me to, but I'd rather not. I'll have to explain to him why you're not with me. What do you want me to say? That you are at the Jihad branch of the Betty Ford centre?'

'Leon, you're full of shit. I'll be fine, I'm just nervous. I don't want to be here without you. Not that you have been around to talk to.'

He shrugged. 'I promised Samaad I would leave you alone until you were clean. However long that took. I trust his judgement about this, and I am going to do what I said I would do. The only reason I came to see you was because I'm leaving, so I wanted to say goodbye, and to ask if you wanted anything. Do you? Gum? Coke? You know . . .'

She started laughing. 'Gum? Coke? You idiot, I don't want anything. No, I take that back. I want socks. Lots of socks. And wet wipes. As many as you can carry. And newspapers. All the newspapers you can find. And a radio. And moisturiser. You know what, if you get nothing else, get moisturiser. I have got to have some. Okay?'

'Okay, Naayo. Yes. I want to ask you something. Will you try to be honest, give me an honest answer?'

She was taken aback by his seriousness, his gravity, as he frowned at her. She nodded, waiting for his question.

'Do you feel like I let you down? That I should have stayed with you in Delhi rather than gone off with Samaad? Because I have to tell you . . .'

'Do you want my answer?' she interrupted him. He nodded.

'Yes, I do. I think you should have stayed with me. I didn't know them, Viren and Saroj. I was lost. Everything was new and strange. And then there were all those reporters and people that I had to deal with. And Saroj, you have no idea. You were the only thing that held me to my life, who reminded me who I was and where I was from. You should have stayed with me.' She was crying, and he was at a loss. He held both her hands in his, but couldn't think what to say.

'It's okay, now, Leon, no need to apologise or wallow in guilt,' she said, wiping her nose and eyes. He was puzzled, and then remembered his own words to her a lifetime ago. They laughed, and the moment, thankfully for him, passed. He took the opportunity and stood up, brushing down his wrinkled but newly-washed pants. All his clothes had taken on the colour of the dust. They were all variations on the grey-brown of the hills that surrounded them. They had been washed in the river running along the camp. Leon had taken Naia's clothes out to the cold bank with his own at men's washing time. He would squat down with the other men there and scrub and rinse and then put the clothes down on the grass with river rocks holding them down in case of winds. He would go back in a couple of hours to bring them back. It was dry and sunny, so the clothes were stiff, but they smelt wonderful, of grass and earth and rain. If they could put that in a detergent, she thought, it wouldn't even have to get clothes clean, it would sell anyway.

'I'm going to have to wash my own clothes,' Naia said to him, and he laughed again.

'Throw away all your panties and bras, I'll bring you new ones,' he said cheerfully. The moment had really passed. They had resolved their issues in minutes, as they always did. She knew she would be fine there with Samaad. She knew what Leon meant when he said he trusted him. It was a feeling of letting go. Of giving yourself up to someone, she thought, of knowing you were in their hands, and wanted to be there no matter what the cost.

'Bye, then, and take care. And I'll be clean as a new whistle when you get back. Leon, wait.' She stopped him suddenly. 'Bring my computer from Tara's apartment. I left it there and haven't even missed it until today. I came into my room and fell asleep last night, but then this morning I wanted so much to write, and I didn't have even a piece of paper.'

'I'm not leaving this instant. But in a few hours, Jabra will drive me down to where the bus comes.'

They hugged each other and he was about to open the door when Samaad knocked and came in.

'You look so—did you go and bathe in the river?' he asked Naia.

Naia laughed. 'No, I wouldn't dare, with all those guys doing their thing there. Leon rigged up a shower for me behind my room. I now have my own restroom.'

Samaad laughed his low rich laugh. 'I'm glad. Maybe he could build me one too.' Then he was serious again. 'Leon will be gone for this whole week. Did you want to go with him?'

She paused for a moment before she answered him. 'No. Well, yes and no. I want to stay with you,' she said, looking into his eyes. 'I want to see the mines. Will you take me?'

Samaad laughed again. He said, 'No, I won't, but if you ask Jabra he will take you. He has a little boy, you might have seen him. You might enjoy meeting him. Did you get those apricots I sent for you?' He opened the door and went out and came back immediately with a basket of tiny, perfect fruit. Naia bit greedily into it and closed her eyes. The nectar spilled out when she cut the skin, the flesh filled her mouth with texture and tartness and sweetness all at once. She opened her eyes to find Samaad laughing at her childish pleasure.

'These are unbelievable,' Leon said. He had eaten three to her one. 'I was in Split,' he said. 'We were tired. Soul-tired, from war, from seeing the pain of children, young men ... there was an old woman in the market, she had a basket. Covered with an old towel. A blue towel. Her face—it was like the oldest face in the world. She had seen everything there is to see. She opened her basket and gave me strawberries. I remember eating them by the fistful, pushing them in my mouth with the leaves and all, squashing them on my face like they were the last thing I would ever get to eat ...' They were quiet listening to him, getting a rare glimpse into his world, seeing through his eyes in words rather than photographs. 'They were so deep—the taste, the colour. They stained my jeans, the juice was all over my clothes. And the next day, when I washed and hung out my clothes on a line, the gypsies stole them. Cigani, cigani, everyone said, when we found the clotheslines empty ... in the middle of a war! The gypsies stole our clothes!' He started laughing, and so did Samaad and Naia. The apricots were all gone when Leon finally left, the basket was full of pits and the room was glowing with the morning sun.

Naia got dressed in a shirt and pants. She put on a huge bulky sweater that Samaad had given her. It was heavy wool in a nondescript biscuit colour that obscured her body and

came down halfway to her knees. She brushed her hair and
tied it back with her one precious covered rubber band that
she put on the knob of her cot every night. She carefully
squeezed out just enough moisturising sunblock for her
face and hands and rubbed it in. She had no mirror, so she
couldn't see her face. If she could she would have seen pale
skin, unhealthy from almost two weeks without much
sunlight, a dark bluish stain under her eyes, cheekbones
more prominent than usual, the gauntness emphasising
her eyes and already large mouth. Her eyes, she would have
noticed, were bright and clean, and that was what had
brought on Samaad's comment on her looking better. She
pulled on socks and shoes, checked that her Oakleys were
perched on her head, pulling them down over her eyes as
she went out of the room into the always blinding sunlight.

Jabra waited at the wheel of the jeep. She had seen him
around the camp, but she hadn't made eye-contact with
anyone, not even him. A boy of about seven sat in his lap.
He turned and got out of the seat as soon as he saw her.
Samaad came over from the group of men he was with and
re-introduced them. It was a little re-birth ceremony. Of
course she knew Jabra, and he knew her. But it was time
for her to start from scratch, as if the past weeks had not
been at all. Samaad was solemn. This was his little brother
Jabra and his son, Munna. Naia looked at Jabra clearly for
the first time. He was even taller than Samaad, who himself
stood at least six feet four. He was muscular where Samaad
was ropy, bulky and slow-moving where his brother was
lean and quick, moving fast but giving the impression of
languor. He had a beard and no moustache, and his hair
was dark, like his eyes. They were not quite his brother's

eyes, Naia thought as she smiled and nodded at him, they didn't have the blue sparks or the velvet depth. She turned her eyes on Samaad surreptitiously through her glasses. She found his eyes on hers again, laughing.

'Enjoy yourselves,' he said. 'Be back before sundown. That means leave an hour before, at least. Jabra, be sure you do. You must not have your lights on while driving. And bring back that bloody old Moin bhai, he's been there for a whole week now, and needs to get some rest. Naia, take care.'

The drive was hard on her back, bumping along in the back seat. Someone had put an old mattress on it, which made it a lot easier than it would have been without. The little boy talked all the way, pointing out birds, flowers, rocks, clouds, giving her fistfuls of walnuts and dried fruits from a bag on his lap. She was having a wonderful time. She had never really been around a child that age other than when she was herself that age. She tried making conversation with Jabra. He was shy, and said little, and his English was odd and broken and he often stopped mid-sentence when he couldn't find or didn't know the word for something. They did talk, though. He explained to her that the brick buildings at the camp were built by the men in the village. She was able to understand that the bricks were made there on site with dirt from the area around the camp, that the roofs were made from material they had brought up there in trucks, from their old village and others in the area, some three years before. She gathered that they had not situated this new village too close to the mines because the mines were much higher in altitude, and would become uninhabitable earlier in the winter when the snow would cover everything and the wind would blow them all away, and also because Samaad did not want the men from the village to be able to get to the mines too easily.

He drove skilfully through the gullies and avoided the large rocks. He steered them over the gravel and kept on going when she was sure there was no way through. She thought they were following a dry riverbed. When she asked, he said no, that there were no dry beds during the late spring, they would all be flowing. This was just a lucky route, and it would soon be time to stop and walk.

'Not long, only thirty minutes' slow walk,' he reassured her. 'It takes me about ten minutes, but you are not well ...' and he stopped, embarrassed for having alluded to her sickness. She smiled and said, 'Thank you, it's okay.'

They parked the jeep as close to a large outcrop as he could get it, and then they took what she had thought was the mattress and opened it out. It was a big tarp the same biscuit colour of her sweater and all the rocks around them. They covered the jeep with it. Munna carried his fruit and nut bag, and Jabra hefted a huge jerrycan of water, and they started on the last bit of their journey.

Naia breathed in, and the air flowed into her lungs like water, it had no taste, no smell. It was perfect air. It was a perfect day. She thought how much her mother and father would have loved it here, how they would love it that she was here. She decided then that she would look at everything as they would have. She would do it for them. She would cherish every perfect blue sky with its streaky cloud lines like the contrails of some giant astral plane. She would sink into every flower in the carpets laid out before her, woven

into intricate fractals of colour and pattern. If only Viren
could see these carpets, she thought. The ones he had,
even the very best, were just a shadow of this, mere human
representations of something much older, much bigger.
These carpets had evolved over the ages, growing, seeding,
multiplying, changing, drinking the water off these powerful
and sacred mountains when they released it each spring,
when they pushed off their blanket of snow. And finally,
she wished Samaad was here beside her, so she could tell
him, thank you for sharing your flowers with me, and your
mountains, and your air. Thank you for bringing me back
from where I was, or at least where I was going. Thank you
for giving me back my life, she thought, I think I would
have lost it. An eagle wheeled over them, screaming into
the valley, a thin long sound that echoed on the rocks.
When someone saves your life, you belong to them, she
thought, I belong to him now.

Naia had been ignoring the chatter between Jabra and
Munna. She had noticed the road getting narrower and
narrower as they went on, and soon they were squeezing
themselves against the wall of the mountain, walking
sideways, with their back against the gravelly rock. A few
steps of this and they came to the end. She found herself
looking over Jabra's massive shoulders into a shallow long
valley. There were men everywhere, crawling all over the
rocks, some with small jackhammers, some with hand-held
tools. She could hear the clink of metal on rock. She could
also see that every man and woman there was wearing the
same sweater that she was, her cherished gift from Samaad.

On one side of the valley ran a small stream. A group of
people that looked to her like women, were at the stream,

working at something there. Jabra began to climb down the
incline towards the cluster of tents that sat directly below
them. Munna and Naia followed. There were goats penned
there too, and children playing. Some women were cooking
on two big fires. They were waving at Jabra and Munna,
shouting their names as they got closer to the camp. It was
barely ten minutes before they were down, and were
surrounded by the children. Munna soon became one of
them and they ran off in a cloud of dust and screams. Jabra
spoke to the women. One of them grabbed the sleeve of
Naia's sweater and pulled her toward the nearest tent. She
went inside. It was bigger and more spacious than it looked
from the outside. Carpets covered the floor. There were
several cushions on the floor too, and the woman motioned
to her to sit. She did, and was surprised at how good it felt
to put her bottom down, to take the weight off her legs.
The woman went out and came in with a cup of the
delicious tea Naia had begun to love, and a plate of some
small square cookies. Naia ate and drank hungrily, and
then stretched out to rest her body for a moment. The roof
of the tent looked like it was made of fuzzy warm light, and
she closed her eyes. When she awoke, she found the
woman still sitting by her, looking at her. She smiled when
Naia looked at her, a sweet young smile and shockingly bad
teeth in her beautiful face. Naia thought she must be no
more than sixteen. Her skin was true apricots and cream,
but it was all cracked and brown at the cheeks from the
winter dryness. The imperfections and her obvious
unawareness of them made her even more beautiful to
Naia.

'*Chalo*,' she said softly, pulling at Naia's sweater.

They got up and went out. Naia was relieved to see that she had not been asleep too long, not even an hour, but she did feel better, the tiredness had mostly left her. Jabra was all the way up the mountainside. He saw her and waved, shouting her name. She started the climb up, excited that she would finally get to see what she had come all that way for—the sapphires.

'Did you have an interesting time?' Samaad asked her as soon as he saw her.

'It was beautiful, really. Thank you so much, Jabra, for taking me . . . and Munna.' She bent down and gave him a hug. He was a lovely little boy, full of talk, bright and edgy as a kite in a stiff wind. Even though Naia hadn't understood most of his language, he gestured and mimed and almost danced to make himself understood, and she thought she understood a lot of what he had been saying. He had been sitting in the seat next to her all the way back, old Moin bhai had been in the front with Jabra. They were engaged in talk, quiet and grave.

'You look very well,' Samaad said to her. 'The sun has done you good. You must be tired. Do you want me to get some hot water put in your shower?'

She was delighted with the idea of a hot shower. The novelty of Leon's shower rig hadn't worn off. A hot shower would really be a luxury. She had got used to her toilet arrangements, but she knew she would never like them. They had dug a hole in the ground and put a slab of stone on either side so she could squat over it. Then she would cover up with fresh dirt from a pail in the corner which she would fill up every day. This whole thing had horrified her when she first realised there was no running water. Leon

went in the woods or on the rocks like everyone else at the
camp, but that had been too nerve-racking for her, squatting
among the rocks, worrying that she would get bitten by
something, or worse, that one of the men from the camp
would stumble upon her. Leon built her bathroom, complete
with a wooden door left over from the camp supplies.

The hot shower was relaxing and refreshing though
short, and she slipped into her nightclothes and brushed
and flossed her teeth. She was running out of floss, she
wished she had told Leon to bring some. She had had
dinner with Samaad and Jabra and Munna and the old
man Moin, in Samaad's room. It was more like a house,
with a separate bedroom, and a gathering room with chairs
and carpets. It was a simple and quiet time. They ate, they
talked, Munna fell asleep on the floor. Samaad explained
everything to her that she had seen. He told her what the
men were doing, how they dug out the sapphire from the
rock face, how they brought it down and washed it in the
stream, how they probed deeper and further in the rock
face to expose the veins of blue that they now knew ran
through the whole area. When the night had grown really
old, he said to her that she must be tired and should go to
sleep. They had all said goodnight then, and she went back
to her room to shower and to bed, the guard outside her
door as always.

The days went by like a primitive dream vacation for
Naia. She woke early each day and brushed her teeth and
carefully arranged herself in bed to be ready for Samaad
when he brought her tea. He always kept the door to the
room ajar when he was in alone with her, but that did
nothing to affect her feeling that they were alone in that

world, the two of them, up in the mountains where no one could reach them. She ignored or put out of focus the fact that there were all kinds of wild warriors all around her, that they were all there for a purpose quite removed from her and her fanciful ideas. She walked in the valleys and sometimes even climbed into the lower skirts of the mountains to look down into distant meadows and fields of wildflowers. She took food with her sometimes and ate and napped among the rocks under the open blue Himalayan sky. She took the notebook he had given her and scribbled in it. She knew all that she wrote was useless to her, it was all full of dreamy romantic thoughts and ideas, flung so far from reality as to be unbelievable, even to her, when she reread it. But she got stronger, she felt no need at all to smoke, felt no drug pulling at her nerves anymore. She got thinner and darker, the mountain rays gave her a high colour and shine that emphasised her best features. Her teeth shone in her smile, and she smiled often. She went back to the mines twice. She loved being with the children, the women were fascinated by her, asking her obviously lewd questions and then laughing amongst themselves, especially the time she had gone with Samaad. She thought of Leon often that week, hoping he was fine and enjoying the luxuries of a city, especially running hot and cold water and a porcelain toilet with a flush tank. He'll be back tomorrow, she realised suddenly that morning, and was happy.

That night, as she put her feet under the soft cotton sheet, she thought again of Samaad, and wished terribly that she could see him, right then and there. She got out of her bed and tiptoed to the door. She pushed the door

open and looked outside. There was no one there. She
went out and quickly closed the door. She hugged the wall
and stayed in the shadows, walking softly all the way to his
room. She met no one on her way there, and she pushed
his door open and slipped in, bolting the door from the
inside. There was no one in the room. She went into the
bedroom. There was no bed there, just a mattress on the
floor. He wasn't there either. She went back to the front
room and unbolted the door. Then she lay down on his
mattress and covered herself with the sheet.

She was fast asleep when he came in and got into his
bed. She felt his surprise, and tried to hold him, but he sat
up and lit the lamp beside his bed. He looked at her for a
long time, and then stood up.

'You do not know the beauty of restraint,' he said, but
she did not know what he meant.

Naia stood before him in her white bra. She came up
almost to his shoulder. She turned up her face at him for
a kiss. He seemed to consider it, but only roughly held her
chin and bruised her mouth with the rough of his thumb,
not looking at her. She took a step closer, leaning into him,
but not touching him. And then he put his hand on the
small of her back, held her hard against him, pulling his
hand up along her back, into her hair, gripping her skull
easily, his hand so wide he could have crushed it. She
wanted to put her arms around him, started to, but he just
pushed her onto the mattress, a hand on her thigh,
holding it down to make way for himself, still holding her
head, and then she could hear the uh-uh of her own
breath, and she thought of the jackhammer tearing into
the mountainside in search of sapphire.

TWENTY-ONE

Leon woke up in a first-class seat twenty-two thousand feet in the air. In spite of the crowds at the airport, there were only two other passengers in the first-class cabin, so he had not only the luxury of his seat, but privacy as well. He remembered feeling apprehension mixed with mounting excitement when he had embarked on this journey. His emotions had settled down somewhat after a few good French meals on the plane, but the fire was still lit. He opened his camera bag and checked again, as he had done several times since leaving the village, that the black pouch was still there. It sat beside an identical pouch full of camera batteries. He slipped his hand inside and felt the pebbles, forty of them. They were large, and he was astounded when Samaad had told him how much they were worth.

The past twenty-four hours had been strange, to say the least. He thought about his meeting with Frank, and Frank's boss. He had had eight hours to kill before he needed to report for his flight, so he had decided, on a whim, to check out Naia's hang-out, the International café. The first person he spoke to, or who spoke to him, was Frank, the German. The guy responsible, in Leon's mind, for Naia's addiction. Leon was amazed that Frank came right up to him and invited him to a cup of coffee. Leon said yes out of curiosity, and then stayed for lunch and several more cups of coffee because he just liked the quiet, self-confessed heroin-addicted German. He said some interesting things about Naia's addiction when Leon broached the subject. Frank had ignored Leon's initial hostility and answered questions calmly, and without any rancour.

'I have been a heroin-user for almost six years,' he said in his quiet German accent further softened by his tone and his gentle demeanour. 'You don't see me dying from overdose or missing any single day of work. Governments like to make big deal about heroin because they want to take attention away from other things—war, alcohol addiction, nicotine addiction, joblessness, failure to stop terrorism . . . it's not so big or so bad. Naia's addiction was what you Americans call "small-time". How long it took to get over? A week? Is nothing.'

He was candid about everything, and casual, unruffled. He reminded Leon of some of the veteran war correspondents he had met in his career. They were not jaded, just worn. They seemed to protect their nerve endings by coating them with acceptance of the human condition, of the things people do to each other. They were all addicted to a drug, he thought, Frank to heroin, the others to war itself, and danger, and being so near death. He didn't make the connection to himself, however.

As they sipped their coffee and exchanged notes about the world, Leon noticed a man come in. He was fifty-ish, very wiry, full of confidence. He stood by the door with a frown on his bearded face and looked around him. He took off his cap and dropped it into the enormous canvas bag hanging across his body, and peered impatiently into the depths of the café. The light was against him, Leon could see him, but the sun in his eyes made it hard for him. The man did not look like he was used to waiting.

'Who is that guy?' Leon asked Frank. Frank turned around to look, and when he saw the man, he stood up hurriedly and said, 'My boss,' and waved him over to their table.

When they were all introduced, Frank excused himself to go to the bathroom. Gabriel Hallam turned to Leon and matter-of-factly asked him, 'You NGO too?' Leon had met many like him. These were tough men, they worked hard for very little personal monetary gain and barely enough funding for their cause, whatever it was. He knew, too, that they had more than one purpose usually, when they were in the difficult zones, as in Bosnia, or Angola, or Thailand. He shook his head and said, 'Photographer'.

This seemed to satisfy Gabriel for a few minutes, he drank his tea and continued to peer inquisitively at Leon.

'What are you photographing here?' he asked finally.

'I'm with a friend in Kashmir, actually,' Leon told him, 'photographing wildflowers'.

'No,' Gabriel said. 'Wildflowers? You taking the piss? You up in the LoC area?'

Leon was taken aback by this line of questioning. He was usually the one with the questions.

'No, we are a bit far away from there.'

'Well, what are you doing down here? You done there?'

'No, I'm going to Paris to meet some people for an assignment. I will be back in the mountains in a week.'

Gabriel drank some more tea. Leon waited, he knew the questions were forming in the man's mind. 'You seen anything fishy?' he finally asked.

'Fishy? What's that? Are you English?' Leon asked him.

'Irish.' He actually snorted. 'Only you Americans would

dare ignore the difference. Fishy meaning, any—uh—unsavoury activity, any extra-legal goings-on, you know what I mean? Any bloody nonsense with the tribals and so on? Are you getting me, old bugger?' Leon felt like he was in some warp. He did understand the gist of Gabriel's questioning if not every word of it, and it unnerved him. He was at a loss for what to say.

'Why do you ask?' he said, to buy some time.

'I always ask, it's my job, you know. There's allus something with those bastards up there, the Pakis, the bloody Indians, the Kashmiris, and when all those are quiet, then the bloody tribesmen get going, don't they?'

Leon started to smile in spite of himself. 'What is your job?' he asked Gabriel.

'Monitoring, lad, monitoring. Keeping an ear to the ground, listening to the rumblings. And, we also distribute medical supplies. Not the emergency stuff. We do more like prosthetics, things like that. Just distribution, mind you. And, lad, I recruit. So I suggest you meet me on your way back from your important meeting in Paris. I may have something for you. Where's that bleeding Kraut now? Him and his fucking vile habit. He's a good lad otherwise, mind you, but I don't think he can ever leave Asia, the dumb fuck.'

He gave Leon his card. It said nothing on it but Gabriel Hallam and a cell phone number.

'Call me,' he said.

Leon smiled as he thought of Gabriel, he had a charming way about him. Leon didn't quite get what he did, or what monitoring was, for that matter, but he had some idea. He knew these NGOs and monitoring agencies, and the line between them was often blurry. He thought of Global Witness and others like them. He remembered reading something about them being the ones to expose the timber trade in Thailand or Cambodia and the diamond trade in Angola. He suddenly felt a flutter in his gut as he made delicate, as yet tenuous connections between himself and the sapphires and UNITA and diamonds and Gabriel Hallam and people like him. He wondered, too, how he had ended up on the side of what he would normally have thought of as the bad guy.

In Paris, thousands of miles from the Himalayan foothills where Naia fought her addiction to heroin and replaced it with an addiction of a different sort, the weather was fine, birds were everywhere, and spring was in full bloom, almost bursting into a warm overblown summer. Leon walked down the road and delighted in the Frenchness of everything and everyone around him. He had eaten an entire baguette for breakfast, and coffee, served to him in a tiny cup. He liked that about the French. The coffee was treated as a prized commodity, not re-filled endlessly like it was dishwater by some relentlessly cheery waitress insistent upon telling him what kind of day he should have. He liked that food was in small servings, but of a quality that sent his taste buds on a journey. After all the Indian spices which, although he enjoyed immensely, had clobbered his senses somewhat, the subtlety of French food appealed to him. He liked that he had to search out the flavours and smells rather than be bombarded by them. The food was expensive, compared to both India and back home, but he didn't mind that.

He walked down the street looking for the address that

had been left for him at his small hotel, scribbled on a piece of hotel stationery. It was one of a row of old stone buildings tucked away on a street with the river on the other side. He was glad he had walked when he saw the line of cars on the kerb as far as he could see both ways. He rang the buzzer and waited, feeling in his bag again for the pouch.

'Mr Leon?' An unaccented male voice came tinnily through the small speaker.

'Yes, I am here to see . . .' The speaker crackled off before he could finish and the iron grille door buzzed open. He went up the stairs and in through a frosted glass door that had the numbers on it in gold, placed vertically on the wood frame.

There was a front office with a marvellous old carved table and chair. They looked like they had been there since Bastille Day. An old rotary-style telephone sat on the otherwise empty desk. The office was entirely without adornment, but none was needed because of the giant wall-sized window with its view of the river. Leon was confused by the lack of personnel, but then noticed the man in the adjoining office through the open door. He had his ear to the phone, he motioned Leon in and gestured that he should sit. He soon said 'Goodbye' and put the receiver down.

'Okay. Show me,' he said, with no preliminary.

He reminded Leon of someone, but it wouldn't coalesce in his mind at that moment. He took out the pouch.

'You are Jean Cahi?' he asked, just wanting to have that verbal confirmation before things went too far.

Jean Cahi nodded yes, leaned under his desk, took out

a velvet tray and emptied the stones into it. Then he
produced a loupe from a pocket on the inside of his jacket.
He turned on the odd-looking desk lamp and began to peer
at the stones. Leon just sat there and watched the top of
his mostly bald head.

He was a large man in a dark suit. Dark, but not quite
black. It fit him perfectly. Unlike the suits on fat people in
California, this one seemed to be made for him. Leon
noticed the blocky ring on his finger, gold, with a yellowish
looking stone that threw out sparks of all colours with every
movement of his hand.

'Yellow diamond. Argyle,' he said, without looking up.
'One of the first from there, you know, a gift.'

Leon had no idea what he was talking about, but let it
pass. He tried to place the accent, but couldn't.

'Hmm . . .' he said, and then looked up at Leon. Leon
got the impression that he was seeing him for the first
time. He seemed to have found a reason to imprint Leon's
face in his memory.

'So. This is what Samaad is up to now.' He went back to
the stones, checking each one, turning them, even smelling
one.

'What about carpets? Does he not do that business any
more? It would be a pity. My best ones are from him.'

Leon was oddly relieved to hear Jean Cahi mention
Samaad before he did. It immediately took away the feeling
of disconnection that he had had since walking into that
office.

'I will send the money to your hotel tonight. Do you
have any preference?'

Leon was confused. 'Will you be keeping the stones?' he

asked. The man started laughing, didn't seem to know how, and soon stopped.

'You can take them, I can have them picked up when I send the money. Or you can leave them here, they will be safer. This is not old stock dug up from some collection? There is more?' he asked very casually, but Leon saw the gleam in the otherwise dead eyes.

'Lots more, but only I have them. They are not on the market, no one else will get them if we can work out a deal.' He was surprised at himself, but the man smiled.

'I will know if someone else gets them, and you will have no deal. These are very fine, very large. It will not be a secret for long. Kashmir Blues cannot be passed off as anything else. Why do you try? People usually try to pass inferior heated gems as Kashmirs. You are doing the opposite. Why is that?'

Leon panicked. 'We need some more time, to consolidate our operation,' he said vaguely.

Samaad had told him that they could not be passed off as anything else, and that was a disadvantage for now. But they would not get the price they needed if they sold to the small-time buyers who bought the stones as packets of blue sapphires without asking or caring where they were from, and sold them as individual stones later. This man knew what he was looking at. He would pay a high price, and Leon knew he wanted to be their exclusive buyer. Leon was not at all sure he was at liberty to give out all the information the man was asking for. 'I will contact you again in a month, I will bring you more. Till then, don't talk about Kashmir, I can give you a discount for your cooperation in this matter.'

Jean Cahi really did laugh this time, and Leon knew who he was reminded of. It was Ariel Sharon, prime minister of Israel. But balder.

'I need no discount. I am paying you too little for this quality stone. You promise me five hundred carats more next month, you have a deal. I will not sell, only make ready the gems. You will see next time you come. I will take you to my—shop. It is outside Paris, in the country. And next time I will take you out to dinner. You should have stayed one more day. We have some good restaurants here.'

He stood up and gave the pouch back to Leon. 'I will meet you again tonight, your hotel. I will come with my son at ten-thirty. Then we will drive you to the airport. We can do our business on the way.'

He shook Leon's hand. Leon felt the dry, soft hand enclose his in a firm, short grip. He smelt the expensive perfume. It was of the quality that didn't decay as the day's bodily secretions broke it down, but rather, became more subtle, more manly. He smelt the cigar smoke on his clothes, and then Jean Cahi put his other hand over their clasped ones, and Leon looked down at the yellow stone on his ring.

'Be careful with those stones,' Cahi said. Then, for the second time in as many days, Leon received a card with nothing on it but a name and number.

Jean Cahi and his son came to his hotel in the morning, as promised. Cahi looked at the pebbles again, took them, gave Leon an alarming amount of money. He began to feel sweaty at the thought of walking through customs with it on him.

'You have to set up an account. We cannot do business this way. I cannot pay cash next time,' Cahi admonished Leon. Leon had dropped any pretence of knowing what he was doing. He was grateful that Cahi was as good as Samaad had said he was, and that he was not interested in stealing the pouch and throwing Leon's lifeless body in the Seine. Cahi's last words alarmed Leon terribly. 'Has Samaad found a source? Is he mining these?' Leon stared at him in stunned confusion. He heard Cahi's laugh one last time before he got out of the beautiful car. 'That fox,' he said, shaking Leon's hand, 'that bloody fox'.

The trip was uneventful for one of such purpose, and he supposed he should be grateful that everything went off smoothly. But on the plane back, Leon admitted to himself that he was disappointed. There was nothing exciting about what he had done. Nothing had happened to him. Nothing had threatened to happen to him. His guts did not turn to vinegar. The high was not from that feeling, it was from having the feeling gone. When you knew you were safe. That something could have happened but hadn't. There was none of that on this assignment. There must be thousands, no, hundreds of thousands of such transactions happening every day in the world. He came from a separate layer of the world from this, with occasional forays into that other layer of danger and conflict. He had always known—in a theoretical way—that everything was connected. Now he was a connection, a thread between the layers, joining them. The thought lessened his disappointment, but gave him little satisfaction. He felt in his jacket pocket for the cards. He knew he would call Gabriel Hallam as soon as he was out of customs at Delhi airport. Samaad wasn't expecting him back for another three days. He could do a lot in that time.

Whatever he had planned to do for those three days dissolved from his mind the moment he got off the plane. A man in a white uniform came up to him and politely confirmed his identity. He told Leon to follow him, and said nothing more. Leon did as instructed, he followed the man's greasy head through the innards of the airport. The fifty thousand euros in his backpack were burning a hole in his back and brain. He frantically went through explanations in his mind that ranged from the absurd—he had picked up the wrong bag from the overhead storage bins, to the absurder—he found the money in the airplane toilet. He attempted to unwish his wish that his trip had been more exciting. He imagined all manner of things that could happen to him, from being held incognito for the next ten years, to being tortured for information he did not have. He tried to reassure himself that this may be a case of mistaken identity, a problem that would be solved in minutes, but the reassurance was instantly replaced by memories of stories of people who had never solved the problem, or at least not until they were beaten beyond recognition and forgotten or given up for dead by family, friends and government. He got angry with Samaad for thinking a white man was less likely to be searched if he walked through the green channel with a smile. They arrived at their destination in five minutes, but thoughts are faster than time, and Leon was numb with apprehension by the time the man knocked on a door and was told by a voice inside to enter. He opened the door and let Leon in, and went back the way he had come.

The room was an innocuous, if seedy, office. Sitting across from a clone of the man who had brought him there, looking relaxed and drinking tea, Karan smiled at Leon. He stood up and said, 'Leon, good to see you. I've been waiting hours for you to show up.'

Leon said nothing. To the man at the desk Karan said, 'Thank you very much for your help, sir, I will tell my father.' The man stood up and shook hands with Karan, and Karan took Leon by the arm and guided him out.

'Do you have any baggage?'

'No.' His backpack was still on his back, he picked up his camera bag.

As soon as they were outside in the sunshine, Leon turned to Karan in bewilderment.

'What the hell are you doing here?'

'Get in the car,' Karan said, not unfriendly, 'I'll explain'.

In the car, Karan waited until he had navigated through the crowds and the dysfunctional traffic before he said anything. Leon sat in the seat next to him and looked out at the chaos that never ceased to amaze him. He saw a brown dog in there in the midst of it all, walking calmly just off the sidewalk, going about his business. He smiled to himself, remembering his panic attack of a few minutes ago, and thought that whatever be Karan's reason for being there, he had got him safely out of the airport with his precious cargo intact. Karan lit the joint he dug out of the ashtray. The car filled with smoke when he exhaled, he cracked open the window so he could see. He sucked on the joint once more and handed it to Leon.

'I went to the International café a couple of days ago,' he said. 'I ran into our friend Frank. He said he had seen you there, he said you spent some time with him and his boss.'

'So?'

'So, I asked if Naia was with you. He told me she was up in the mountains. He said you were going to Paris for a few days. Quite honestly, I don't care what you guys do, you know, I figure you know what you're doing, and so does Naia . . . although with her I have my doubts, considering what she's been up to.'

'And? Why are you here then?' Leon was beginning to get impatient with Karan, but also knew there was no hurrying him. He waited.

'Well, I told Dad. He freaked. Don't know why, really, since he knows nothing of Naia's—you know. I didn't tell him. Honestly, for no better reason than—well, I didn't want to deal with the fallout of him telling my dear mother. I love her, don't get me wrong, but, you know.'

Still, Leon said nothing. 'Anyway, Frank told his boss, Gabe Hallam, you know him?'

'We've met, yes.'

'So he came over and met Dad, and they decided that they should at least ask you if everything was alright. You know, Dad was a little concerned that Naia was up there alone with Samaad. I tried to tell them that you guys had known each other for a long time, that you could look after yourselves, but that didn't go over too well. He made some calls, found out when you were coming back, passenger lists or something, and sent me over to get you. You guys are so much trouble, I just want to go back to London,' he laughed, and Leon had to laugh too.

There was not much laughter after they arrived at the house. Viren and Gabriel Hallam sat at the dining table, deep in conversation that stopped as soon as they walked in.

'Ah . . . Leon. All well with the world of wildflower photography?' Gabriel asked, 'How goes it in Paris?'

'Hello Gabriel, hello Viren,' Leon said, already uncomfortable. He was thankful for the smoke in the car now, it had relaxed him somewhat. Viren stood up and shook his hand. 'Thank you for coming, Leon. I just wanted to see you, ask about Naia, how she is. Maybe we over-react. It's been so many years, you know, we had given up on her, on ever seeing her again, it is a little difficult for me and even harder for Saroj.'

Leon wasn't sure how to react to his thanks. Considering he was not really there by choice.

'You are welcome to stay and rest before you go back. We can just talk and catch up, you can put me at ease about my daughter . . . can't you?'

Leon sighed. He did understand, in some small way. He sat down next to Viren.

'Look, Viren, you may be her father, but she has been my closest friend for a lot of my adult life. Jim and Anne were like my mom and dad. We are family. I wouldn't have left her with Samaad if I had thought she was in any danger.'

Gabriel laughed. 'Ah, Samaad, the greatest carpet dealer in the subcontinent. What else does he deal in, do you know?'

Viren put his hand on Gabriel's arm, saying, quietly, 'I'll handle this.'

'Handle what?' Leon was a little alarmed. They couldn't possibly know what he was doing or why he had gone to Paris. There was no way for them to know. And Karan had said nothing about Naia. He began to wonder if Viren's concern for his daughter was the only reason he had been brought here. Concern for her wellbeing did not explain the presence of Gabriel.

'Handle what, Viren?' he asked again.

'Not handle, I just meant I would talk to you. Gabriel is convinced there is something sinister going on at every street corner,' Viren lowered his voice, Leon could tell it was deliberately soothing and quiet. 'Gabe and I have known each other a long time. Coincidence or not, we've been in six countries together. He's always with his ear to the ground, every tremor of every passing car sounds to him like an impending earthquake. He's tipped me off many times. About nothing.'

Gabriel didn't smile. 'I've been wrong more often than I've been right, it's true. But those times that I've been right, you know and I know, Viren, I have been right big. That's how it goes. Constant suspicion helps. This time, it involves your daughter. Maybe you should be a little suspicious too.'

'Look, you guys,' Leon said, 'there is nothing to be suspicious about. I know the area is inherently dangerous, what with the insurgency and all. We all know that Samaad himself has been involved in skirmishes—but who in that area hasn't? So I do understand your concerns. Our time there has been totally uneventful, to the point of boredom. I shoot wildflowers. Naia takes walks. The area is absolutely stunning. We have our own quarters. Everyone there seems to know and respect Samaad.' He began to feel like he was overdoing it.

'If your concern is about Naia being up there alone, she made that choice herself, she didn't see the point of making a long tortuous bus journey only to go back with me three days later—she also made the choice to go up there with me in the first place, if you remember. That's all I know. I sure would appreciate it if you all now let me go to bed, or go find a hotel room. I'm really tired and jet-lagged and have that long bus journey ahead of me tomorrow or the day after.' He rubbed his face for effect. He felt pretty good, actually, not tired or jet-lagged at all. But he certainly didn't want to spend any more time than he absolutely had, to reassure Viren about Naia. He began to feel a grudging admiration for Gabriel Hallam's instinct though.

'You guys are in what business? Prosthetics, you said? Distribution? And monitoring?' he asked him, and almost immediately regretted that he had shown any interest. This would mean more talk, and less sleep for him.

'Yes, monitoring, we just collect information.'

Karan, bored, stood up. 'I need some food. You hungry, Leon?' Leon said he was.

Karan left the room, rather rapidly. Leon didn't blame him. He didn't see a way out without being rude, or insistent, and that, he thought, might have started something else.

'What is your organisation called?' he asked Gabriel.

'At the moment, "Third Eye", but that will change before you can find it on the Internet. Do you have any more questions?'

Leon said nothing for a moment. 'Wait, Third Eye? Are you shitting me? Is that for real, man?'

Gabriel laughed. 'This one was my idea. I've been in this part of the world for too long, I guess. You know where that comes from? Shiva has a third eye that he opens . . .'

'Yes, I know, which he opens when he gets angry with the mess in the world. And then he burns everything. Can you guys burn anything? I thought you just monitored.'

Gabriel laughed again. But he didn't answer Leon. They all seemed to be dancing in circles around their own personal fires, their orbits touching and sparking, but not overlapping.

'Viren?' Saroj's voice came from the doorway that Karan had just gone into. Viren sighed audibly. Gabriel stood up at once, sending something from his lap clattering to the floor. It bounced on the wood floor and landed by Leon's feet. Leon reached under the table, staying there a moment, to take a breath. He reached for the phone that Gabriel had dropped. It looked like a cell phone, but had a fat antenna, and had a peculiar heft that made Leon take another look. He had never seen a satellite phone before, but he knew that is what it was. He handed it back to Gabriel, who took it and kept standing, looking at Saroj. Leon hardly knew him, but Gabriel's whole attitude seemed odd, he seemed tense, almost quivering.

Saroj came up to the table and stood by Viren.

'Hello, Leon, Mr Hallam,' she said, looking at each of them in turn. 'Can I get you some tea?'

'Well, Karan said he was feeding us . . . some tea would be nice too, if it's no trouble,' Leon told her. Gabriel said nothing, just stood there looking at her.

'Where is Naia?' she asked.

Each of the three men waited for one of the others to answer her. The question hung between them. They all knew the answer had the potential for minor destruction. Leon knew it had to be Viren who would answer her, neither he, nor did he think Gabriel, had any idea what she knew of Naia's whereabouts.

'She's still in the mountains,' Viren said after an uncomfortably long pause. 'Leon had to run an errand, he was nice enough to drop in and let us know that they—she— is fine and that they are having a good time ... anyway, nothing to worry about, she's with Samaad, enjoying the mountain air ... would you like to have some tea? Or lie down?'

Gabriel snapped out of his trance and pulled out a chair for Saroj.

'Thank you, Gabriel,' she said, looking directly into his eyes. Whatever it was that passed between them made Leon feel as if he had stood too close to a lightning strike. He felt the not unpleasant current in his vicinity, a voyeuristic thrill from the overflow of someone else's emotions. He was puzzled. Viren seemed not to have noticed.

Karan walked into the room right then, laden with a huge tray full of plates and bowls, and Leon saw his face cloud as soon as he saw his mother sitting at the table. Leon understood that feeling, it was, in quality if not detail, what he felt when he saw or even thought of his own mother. But he did see Saroj, for the first time, as a woman. And this was, he thought absently, the first time she had not been either upset or hysterical or sedated. He looked again at Gabriel, now quiet and introspective, a completely different man from the sarcastic interrogator of a few minutes before.

Saroj served bowls of tiny black chickpeas sprinkled with finely chopped onions, cilantro, green chillies and lime juice, with a dollop of yogurt on top. A maid brought in cups of hot tea. The tension seemed to dissipate. Karan talked of his trip to Ireland the previous summer, of eating calf liver cooked in whiskey and cream, he went into raptures over colcannon and sharp Irish cheddars. Something reminded him of Frank.

'Where's your sauerkraut Nazi?' he asked Gabriel.

'He had work to do,' Gabriel said, rather tersely. Karan heard the ice in his voice. He didn't pursue it.

Then talk turned to the mountains and wildflowers and, before they were ready for it, the tension slipped like a snake back into the room, reminding all of them of why they were there together in the first place.

'Why are you all so concerned about that area anyway?' Karan, the most artless of them all, or perhaps the one with the least to hide, asked Gabriel. It was his father who answered him.

'Well, if some third party gets too much control in that area, it will undermine both Indian and Pakistani claims. Not to mention China's. It becomes problematic if tribals or Kashmiris get too uppity. I do wish Naia was not up there alone . . . I have heard reports, you know, not just from Gabriel. Samaad himself said to me that . . .' he stopped as if he had said too much. Gabriel looked at him for a moment, and then laughed quietly.

'This guy has played you all,' he said. 'Do you think he would have agreed to take her up there if she had been an American tourist? Viren's daughter! This was a godsend for him. It is like having a low-maintenance hostage who doesn't know she is one—what could be better? Do you all not see it at all?' He looked at Saroj, perhaps wishing he had not spoken. But it was too late. She began to weep silently. Viren got up, went to her and guided her out of the room. Leon just shook his head at Gabriel. He waited till Saroj was out of earshot and said, 'Well done, Gabriel. But do tell me. What are you talking about exactly? What does Samaad need hostages for? What has he to do with Viren other than selling him carpets? Gabriel, I think you are overreacting to all this. Really. I was there, for three whole months, I didn't see anything going on that could possibly be dangerous.'

'Really? And if you did see something would you come running to tell me?'

Leon said nothing. Karan stood up. 'I need a smoke,' he said.

Gabriel stood up too. 'Let's just go outside. I'll tell you some things you don't know. About Viren, Samaad, and carpets. If you are going back up there, you should know what you are going back to.'

He picked up his teacup and they followed him outside.

TWENTY-TWO

Newspapermen and photographers swarmed outside the gates, policemen inside. The gates themselves, once imposing wrought iron extensions to the fortress-like, glass-studded wall around the estate, hung on mangled hinges. They were melted, burned, and beyond repair. Though the press didn't come inside, it was not the gates that kept them out, it was the aggressive police presence. White Ambassadors were parked all along the driveway, each with its driver standing officiously next to it. There were black cat commandos alongside each car indicating that these were not low-level government officials. There were a few olive-green army vehicles as well. The drivers of these stood off to one side, aloof from civilians. Even out of uniform, Indian Army personnel have a military aura about them, a hauteur, a way of carrying themselves, from the freshest jawaan to generals.

Viren's beloved carpet of flowers was destroyed. Shredded plants and clods of earth were all that remained. Viren was ensconced in his study with the army chief of operations and several of his officers, as well as the defence minister himself.

Leon, Gabriel, and Karan sat at the table again. They were all mostly unhurt except for slight powder burns on Gabriel's and Karan's faces. The device had gone off just as they stepped outside. It seemed to have been more of a message than an intent to kill or wound anyone. But the message was a little too strident, it seemed, when the perpetrators had chosen to send it to someone as influential and senior as Viren.

They all thought it was really a stroke of bad luck for the two men that had been killed in the blast, they were in the wrong place at the wrong time. As was everyone who was killed in every way but of natural causes, Leon thought. He had heard the defence minister and Viren dismiss the death of the two men without too much discussion, and was struck by their callousness. Then he corrected himself and put it down to part of the very character he loved and admired in all these people—Viren, Samaad and his men,

Abu and Shankar, the old men he had met at Mushtaq
bhai's—a sort of fatalistic acceptance that everyone would
die, and the ones left alive might as well get over it quickly
when the inevitable happened. He wondered not for the
first time if the conviction that this was not their first or
only life had anything to do with it.

Viren did not want it coming out that Naia was in the
hands of some 'crazed fanatic from Kashmir', so this time
he kept the press out and let them stick to the little they
knew, which was that a grenade had been lobbed into his
garden by unknown parties. The two bodies, or parts of
them, had been removed, the blood had been bleached off
the driveway where the two had been standing, sharing
beedis and gossip in their last moments. The press had
been too late to get any pictures of the gore. He had
warned Saroj in no uncertain terms to keep her mouth
shut about the whereabouts of Naia. She, in any case, was
not up to saying much, she had been shaken by the
incident. She had been sedated heavily and put to bed.
Leon thought, as he listened to Gabriel, that Saroj had
become hysterical and then been sedated and put to bed
now every single time he had met her. It wasn't surprising
this time though—they were all shaken by what had
happened, and she was more fragile than most. He wondered
idly what she was really like, what made her tick. He found
himself more than a little intrigued. She had, he thought,
a hollow, underseasoned quality to her. No amount of top-
salt could redress the inherent lack of it. But there was
something there he wanted to know. And there was
something about the way she and Gabriel looked at each
other that really made him very curious. He had to put the

thought away for later. Gabriel's voice was making it hard for him to think, he was forced to listen. Leon thought he might like to be sedated and put to bed too.

Gabriel had lost his temper with Leon, his accent got so thick that Leon had trouble understanding what he said. He shouted, he banged on the table with his hand and fist to emphasise various points that he wished to drive into Leon's consciousness. Leon saw the men and cars outside leaving one by one. Gabriel spoke in a peculiar language that Leon did not quite understand. He kept asking Leon for any information so that they could 'achieve action' against the 'new targets in an already fragile and very sensitive area'. Leon and Karan listened quietly. Viren came out of his study. None of them, including Viren, standing quietly, teacup in hand, felt much like saying anything.

'You need to think about what you are doing with these people, laddie. I have tried to brief you on what it all means. I hope you have understood enough that you will try to help us. You Americans are new to all this. We have dealt with this all over the world, and in our own country as well. Do you know anything about people like this? You people just fall in love with causes and then end up mucking about in things you know nothing about. You people sent money to the IRA, and to people sending Jews home to Israel from east Europe. I know your kind, you just muck about. You think you are doing something to help a noble cause. Do you know what kind of collateral damage there is? Are you getting all this? Do you have anything to tell me?'

'No, Gabriel, I do not,' Leon said, bone-tired, wishing

someone would rescue him. Again, he had a vision of
sedation and bed, this time involving Gabriel. But Gabriel
stopped his tirade and said no more, perhaps finally
overcome by reaction to the day's events. Everyone was
silent, avoiding eye contact with each other.

'I have some new information,' Viren broke the silence
quietly. 'The men that threw the grenade had nothing to
do with Samaad, Leon. Gabriel, they are a new group,
none that we know, definitely foreign mercenaries, they
have been picked up already and are being held and
questioned. They were on bicycles, so they didn't get far. I
will be kept informed if they learn anything from these
two, but we know for sure they are foreigners.'

'Why don't you just go ahead and say that they are Pakis?
Why do you people persist in calling them foreigners?'
Gabriel said. He spoke softly this time, but still with some
heat.

'Why would someone bomb your house, Viren? What do
you have to do with any of this? Does it have anything to
do with . . . me? Or Samaad? How does anyone find out
anything?' Leon blurted.

Viren looked at him for a few moments from under his
eyebrows that he had scrunched together in concentration
just like Naia did. Leon felt a chill fear on the back of his
neck. He wondered if Gabriel Hallam was right and he was
wrong about Samaad. He wondered if his gut feeling of
friendship and love for Samaad was just misplaced, based
on misunderstanding on his own part, or worse, deliberate
deception on Samaad's. Gabriel Hallam, after all, was an
old hand at this. He did know more about groups with
agendas, not just in Kashmir but all over the world. The

feeling passed with his next breath. He knew, in his gut, and in his heart, that he was not wrong to trust Samaad, with his own life and Naia's. Samaad could be the best friend he had ever had, his protector, the man who gave meaning to his life. Or he could be the one that took that life away. But not like this, not with deceit and lies. He would ask for it, and Leon would give it. He had begun to understand this in his first days in the mountains with Samaad, but the realisation only increased his attraction to Samaad, his desire to be with him, know him better. Moth to flame. It was not something that had coalesced into a single thought, more of a growing light in his mind, illuminating his time with Samaad. Again, he thought, there was nowhere he would rather be. He was impatient, suddenly, to be gone from among these people he was with, this table he was at, this house, this city. He wanted to be in the mountains breathing the clear air, walking with his friend on the flowering earth, drinking flowing snow. He closed his eyes for a moment.

He was brought back to the conversation by Viren's voice, answering his own question, which he had forgotten.

'Information gets out through domestic employees, through gossip, sale and casual exchange of information by people who don't intend, necessarily, to harm me or my family. Quite often they are not even aware that they are giving out any information, they are just talking to people at tea stalls or people delivering the newspaper every morning. It is not hard to gather information in this part of the world. There are people everywhere and it is not considered rude to ask personal questions. There is not the same obsession with privacy, with personal space that you have in your country.' He directed that remark at Leon, who nodded. He knew exactly what Viren meant. 'So, for example, anyone could have found out about Naia and you being here even if it hadn't been all over the press about her. Samaad has been coming to my house for about five years now, he is my best supplier of carpets, he has contacts in the north that not many of the dealers in New Delhi have. To see you together with him, to put two and two together, just luck, I think. But this is not making sense to you, I see. This is just how we think, try to put things together that may have no significance, and a picture emerges. Nothing so far, I have to say. It does not make any sense. This seems like just a truly random act of violence.'

Karan shifted uncomfortably in his seat, and asked if he could leave and go to bed. Gabriel shot him a poisonous look, but said nothing. Karan seemed unable to sit still, fidgeting and itchy. Viren took a look around at everyone, and came to a decision.

'I'm tired too,' he said. 'Let's go to bed now, and we can all talk in the morning. Gabriel, if you need a ride home, my chauffeur will take you.' He stood up, effectively bringing an end to the evening, before Gabriel could disagree. 'Goodnight.' He shook hands with Gabriel and patted Karan and Leon. He left the room, and they both hurried out in his wake.

Leon went to his room and sat down on his bed. He put the camera batteries to charge, that was second nature to him. He turned off his bedside lamp. He was tired, more than he thought possible. He had seen victims of violence before, in larger numbers and worse condition than the two men killed that day. That was not what had made him feel drained the way he did. It was more a feeling of despair and foreboding that all good things were coming to an end. He put his head in his hands and wondered if there was any point in going back, if there was any point in anything. He knew that this was not the kind of feeling that would go away by taking a pill, but he did get the urge for some of Samaad's finest-in-the-world hashish. There was a soft knock at his door, and Karan came in.

'Hey, you awake? Leon?'

Leon snapped the light on. Karan stood blinking just inside the door.

'Dad said I should check on you. And, that I should drive you to wherever you want to go.' He smiled then, and Leon saw the family resemblance again. 'Where do you want to go?' He said it casually, hands in his pockets.

'What do you mean?' Leon asked, cautious, though he knew.

'You want to go back? To Naia? And Samaad? I'll take you, all the way. Dad said I should. You want to go? Now?'

'Yes.'

TWENTY-THREE

Viren sat across from the minister watching the peon serving their tea, using the time to gather his thoughts. The summons had been sent that morning, and the car and driver waited for him and insisted on taking him right then. Viren had had such summons before, he knew it was useless to argue. The man had his orders, and they were to return with Viren or not at all. So he had come, and found the minister literally waiting for him.

As soon as his peon left, he started talking. He was angry.

'Viren. We have been hearing and receiving constant reports from the BSF that there is activity in your areas. I have had no word from you on this for over two months now. Have you had any information, Viren? If you have, we should know.'

Viren sat impassively. The minister waited. Finally, Viren had no choice but to tell him something.

'I have a few sources. I have heard nothing at all about this. What exact area are you hearing about?'

'We are hearing that a lot of money is being spent. A lot of weapons being bought. A lot of ammunition. We suspect it comes from the north, maybe foreign money. I think this may be just a new way of operating, you know, buying entire villages and taking them over, controlling a large population quickly and surely. You know, I sometimes wish we had a religion that directed us to convert at any cost. It works very well for world domination.' He laughed, in a self-deprecating way, but Viren was appalled. He didn't reply, or even smile.

He was a clever man in a basic sort of way. He knew Viren had more information than a normal 'retired' diplomat, he knew Viren had some link to some agency within the government, or foreign service. Viren had seen many ministers come and go during the course of his career, this was the most hands-on man he had seen in that post. He was surprised at this direct an involvement, in so small a matter. He thought there must be something there that he did not know, actually bigger and more important than the man was telling him. He was also quite sure that although the minister was in on some things, this line was coming from somewhere else.

It would be easy for him to find out where. To anyone outside the system, the Indian Foreign Service, and the whole workings of the government looked like a complex bureaucracy, a tangled mess of hierarchies and echelons. Viren's genius lay in his ability to see all this clearly. He knew the road through the whole power structure. He could negotiate his way to that nerve centre and touch it with the exact pressure that would get him the response he wanted. He understood his own role in that system well, what threads led from him and where they went. His career postings had taken that talent into account. He could find, in a relatively short time, the ear that could make the difference between being insider and an outsider. He understood systems that had been built layer upon layer, antiquity visible in their complexity, over centuries of government. The thinnest veneer of Westernisation sometimes sat upon all the tradition, but he understood that it was for show only. He knew how to keep up the pretence and get to the right level without breaking skin. Which is why he had been recruited by RAW early in his career. No one in the foreign service knew this, and very few within RAW itself. It was classified information, of course, and had stayed secret for years. His family did not know it, and this minister certainly did not. So this could be coming from his own agency, but from someone who did not know he was part of it. Or that the minister would come to him for help. India's shadowy secret service agency was easy to understand compared to the rest of the central government. Everyone knew where lines drawn from themselves went. The rest they didn't need to know, didn't want to. It kept things simple. Simplicity made secrecy that much easier.

Viren was retired from the diplomatic corps, but not so long that he couldn't make the calls he needed to get to the bottom of this. All his mates were still in place. Most ambassadors were deliberately kept out of the secret service loop. Some of them because they wanted it that way, and some of them because they were not capable of dealing with the intrigue, dishonesty, even violence it inevitably involved. Viren was not one of these. He had been ambassador to countries where information-gathering was almost more important than diplomacy. The governments in these countries knew perfectly well what was going on, but there were unspoken agreements and underground deals that covered all that. Viren had lost a few operatives over the years, he knew how it worked. The minister did not know. They never did. They would never understand. The diplomatic service had long since resolved that ministers and other elected officials were too temporary to be brought into the inner, real workings of government. RAW did not even bother with them. He had recruited and handled operatives in all these countries, and he had done his job efficiently and with minimum exposure. He had been brought back to New Delhi when things in Kashmir began to fester, officially he had been given an early retirement from the diplomatic service. But his job in the past two years in Delhi had involved operatives in Pakistan and along the northern frontier. Samaad was one of his. He would have to find out, now, whether he was still with them or had gone his own way. He knew the answer, but his thorough nature required him to have intelligence, and then proof, that they could act on. He simply didn't believe that Samaad was on the other side. He made small talk with the minister and slipped away before the man had realised that he had got nothing from Viren. On his way home, he made two calls on his cell phone and set up meetings for the next day. He had started a centrifugal motion that would soon suck him to the centre, where he needed to get.

'Someone is here, there's a car blocking the way, saab,' the driver said to him. Viren got out. It was Gabriel Hallam's Ambassador. Why the man didn't employ a driver was beyond Viren. It wasn't as if he couldn't afford it. He knew the organisation had funds enough to pay for whatever Hallam needed. Viren had sent a lot of information his way through his people and got as much back. Maybe it was time for them to stand face to face, share what they knew.

Viren wasn't looking forward to meeting Gabriel. He was too volatile, too unpredictable. He was going to have to tell him that he had let Leon go, in fact had sent his own son with him. But that was the only sure way he could think of to bring Naia back. He walked up the broad steps and in through the door, noticing the very fine old Sarouk runner warm in the sunlight. He sighed with pleasure. He thought he should re-arrange his carpets so that they would draw his eyes again, surprise him. He had stopped looking at them, he was so used to them in their usual place. Like being married to a beautiful woman, he supposed. One could get used to beauty as easily as ugliness, he thought, and then felt a little guilty. Saroj wasn't ugly, she had just been a shy, awkward, very young girl when they married. No, she wasn't ugly at all, he had just been disappointed when she had raised her pallav off her face and he had seen her after the ceremony. It wasn't the first time he had seen her, but it was the time he understood the finality of that face. He knew she wasn't what he had imagined and dreamed about, was all. He had only to look at his two children, he knew their beauty had not come from him.

Gabriel stood up when he saw Viren. Viren told him right away, and held up his hand to ward off any forthcoming lecture. 'He's gone, he left last night. I don't know why, or how, I have no wish to discuss this any more. Really, Gabriel, I am worried and upset about my daughter.'

To Viren's surprise, Gabriel said nothing about Leon's departure.

'Viren, please sit down. I have some information that may alarm you. And yes, I would like some tea. Please. Thank you.'

Viren rang the bell for tea. He wondered idly where his wife was. He asked the maid that came out to answer the bell.

'She went out, sir, someone came soon after you left, she went out with them. She took the car and the new driver. No, she did not say when she would come back.'

Viren was momentarily puzzled by this. Hallam waited for the maid to leave the room and then came and sat next to Viren on the brocade sofa.

'There's something going on up there, Viren. Right where Samaad is. Right there. They have been buying weapons, an enormous amount of ammunition. Right where Samaad is. I am really sure about the location. Really, really sure.'

Viren sighed. 'Yes, I know. I've just been to see the minister. They have the same information you have. He wanted to know what I knew. To be honest with you—I *will* be honest with you, Gabe—I was embarrassed. I should have been the one giving him information, not the other way round. What am I going to do?'

The maid came in with the tea, and they both waited for her to leave. 'What I don't get is, where the fuck is the money coming from? That's one thing I can't put my finger on. Not a word about that. Not a word.'

'Well, Gabriel, I'm the wrong person to ask,' Viren answered him. 'This once, I had no idea about anything. In fact, I have dispatched my son after my daughter, to the place I now find out is the most dangerous in the country.'

Gabriel stared at him incredulously. 'You did what? You didn't. You sent Karan up there?'

'Yes,' Viren said. I thought he could bring back Naia. He is the only one I can trust. It made sense. It still does. I know Samaad, he won't harm them.'

'Are you all crazy? Or stupid?' Gabriel stood up and began to pace the floor. 'Why would Samaad not harm them? Why would he not? Explain, Viren, please.'

Viren knew he would not convince Gabriel, but he tried anyway. 'I have known him a long time, Gabe. I just know.'

'You just know? What does that mean? Instinct? What? I know what I know too, Viren. There is someone up there doing something big. There is no one else who could be doing this. Use what you know, Viren. We know it has to be Samaad.'

TWENTY-FOUR

Leon had woken Karan when his arm and leg had gone to sleep under the weight of Karan's sleep-heavy frame. Karan was not in the least bit embarrassed when Leon showed him the pool of drool that he had left on his shoulder. They had been confined in the car for so long that they were both beyond politeness. They were both very stoned. There was nothing else to do but smoke, and talk and sleep. Viren had hired the car, a roomy Ambassador with leather seats and air-conditioning. He had insisted on two drivers so they could push on without rest breaks. They stopped at truckers' stops and ate with Sikh truckers that patronised those joints, sitting and eating on charpoys. There were no tables or chairs. Karan chatted easily with them in Punjabi, translating everything for Leon. The food was basic. Thick yellow lentil purees and gigantic rounds of hot flatbread made of millet or corn. They ate hot green chillies and piles of roughly sliced onions that were served at every place, and at every place the truckers complained loudly that the chillies were not hot enough, nor the onions pungent enough. Leon took it to be a mark of manliness, the quantity of high-heat chillies you could consume. At one place the bread arrived with a lump of fresh white butter melting on its hot surface. Leon asked for it everywhere after that. In one small town the truck stop was an actual restaurant, with tables and chairs. There was meat on the menu—ground mutton floating in an evil red oil that Leon ate several plates of, and the truckers smiled at him with respect as he chewed through mounds of chillies, sweating profusely and turning slowly redder with the growing burn of capsaicin. Even the skin on his fingers tingled from repeated dippings in the spicy gravy.

'Make sure you don't touch anything delicate when you take a piss,' Karan said to him grinning evilly, 'It could burn off.'

They arrived at a large village that looked as if it had been built at the top of the mountain and then thrown down the side. It spilt over the slope, grass huts and sheds and low mud boxes with red roofs, each neat in itself but scattered haphazardly with no relation to any other. Cows grazed in the green spaces between the buildings, and there was a sign in English on the road that said 'Highest Mountain Dairy in the world'. They both cracked up and were unable to stop. 'Highest two guys in a weird Indian car in the world,' Leon said, and they fell on each other laughing. The two drivers exchanged looks for the thousandth time. They asked if they could stop for tea. There was a little tea shop there, and to their delight, two European hikers were sharing a huge chillum with locals. Karan and Leon did not correct the assumption that they were hikers too. They did not have enough language in common to make very serious conversation anyway. Karan spoke Spanish, but that didn't go far. The hikers, a Swede and a German, recommended the fresh milk being served. They explained with gestures and all the languages they had in common that the cows ate the ganja that grew wild on the hillside, and that since everything comes out in milk, the milk was highly spiked and would make them extremely high for hours. Karan and Leon had a relapse into hysteria. They laughed and yelled about high cows and high mountain dairies as the locals stood and watched with some amusement and a lot of head-shaking.

These roads, travelled with this new companion, were different. Leon barely noticed the terrain, he never took out his camera, he just talked and listened to this man, so familiar and yet a complete stranger to him. Karan was easy. He had his sister's face. He had lost his rubber band somewhere, and had knotted his long hair at the nape of his neck, making him look like a modern-day Buddha with his now rumpled but elegant once-white cotton shirt hanging out from his linen Armani suit pants. His eyes, though just like Naia's, were longer, shaped like some fantasy fish, the pupils huge and black from the constant high.

'Why did your parents call you Karan?'

'What d'you mean why? It's a common enough name in north India, plus, my mother loves that character in the *Mahabharata*.'

'That's what I mean. Why would anyone love that particular character? I don't mean to be rude, but, he just doesn't come across as a hero, just not someone to be named for, at least.'

'Really? You've read the book? I'm impressed, because I have not only not read it, I never, in my whole life, stopped to think what that Karan might be like. So tell me, I'm too stoned to be offended.' He stretched his legs as much as he could in the cramped back seat that seemed to be shrinking with the miles. 'And while you're doing that, tell me again why we are here?'

Leon laughed. This was a most unexpectedly delightful person, and he wondered fleetingly what Naia would have been like had she grown up as his sister and Viren's daughter. And then he thought of Saroj again.

He said to Karan, 'Here's a deal. I'll tell you about Karan and why we're here, and you tell me about your mother.'

'My mother? What about my mother? I'll tell you what I know about her, which is very little. I didn't really spend much time with her after I was about five or six. Here's something—last night, when I was driving the doctor home, he told me something strange. He said she refused to take her pills. And she wouldn't take a shot either. He said she was very calm, more than he'd ever seen her. So he didn't insist.'

Leon was curious. 'Did he tell Viren?'

'No, I don't think so . . . anyway, he didn't seem worried. He's known her a long time, man, and if he's not taking it too seriously, I wouldn't either. So go on, tell me the story of Karan, then.'

Leon was quiet a few moments, looking out of the window. He saw a brown dog in his peripheral vision. He thought it was déjà vu. Either there were brown dogs running around the length and breadth of this country, or one was following him. They had started approaching the winding mountain roads. They were close now, only a few hours away. He had lost track of time, the motion had become internal. They had both accepted this journey as endless. The mountains were visible in the clear blue distance, and his spirits lifted almost physically. He sat up straighter and began to talk, educating Karan about the great poem of his own culture.

'Karan was born to a young princess, before she was married. She had been granted the power to call on any god to father her child. She called on the sun god, just to try it out, to see if it would work.' Karan nodded, listening

with wide eyes. 'I mean, wouldn't it be an honour to bear
a child of the sun god? An immaculate conception, of a
kind. On the other hand, maybe, just like a normal
woman, she just had this child with some secret lover . . .'
Leon was quite stoned too, so he lost track, and took Karan
with him.

'Was the father the sun god? Or the royal gardener
then?'

'I don't know, Karan. I'm pretty cynical about these
immaculate conceptions, children being breathed into
unresisting virgins by gods. But, what do we know? Maybe
you can enlighten me. You must know some stuff just by
virtue of being Indian, right?'

Karan shook his head. 'I went to boarding schools and
then to England. I don't know shit, man. I just know my
philosophy. Tell you the truth, I may even have avoided all
things Indian. You go on. No, start at the beginning, with
my illegitimate birth.'

'Not yours, Karan's. Don't start taking on this personality.
The story, it's nothing like yours. Okay, so. Karan is born
to this young, unmarried princess. Whoever the father was,
that much is true. Being unmarried, she floats the child off
into the river in a basket with, like, cash and gold. Actually,
in the story, he is born with gold earrings and a coat of
armour, a gift from the sun god.'

Karan laughed. 'What? That's just weird, man. How
could a baby be born with armour? That would hurt.'

'Look, it's mythology. Which means it is either fiction,
or analogy. Which is why I am so confused.'

'The story, Leon,' Karan said.

'The story. A poor low-caste charioteer, himself childless,

finds the baby and brings him up. Karan then spends his life running from that low-caste life, looking for his "true identity" as a man of the warrior class. He finds out eventually who he is, his mother tells him. But by then, it is too late for him to actually be a true warrior, he has not been brought up as one, he is quite without the warrior code. He is eventually killed in a battle where he is on the wrong side, and just not good enough to avert defeat and death at the hands of that greatest of all archers and warriors, his own half-brother, Arjun.'

Karan listened, and then said 'Wow. Tough life.'

'I'm telling you, I don't get why anyone would name their son after this guy. He's really unfortunate. He always encourages his friends to do their worst, he's a good archer but not the best, and when he's not unlucky, he's a liar and a loser.'

Karan looked quite disturbed for a second, and then smiled. 'I'll ask my mother. He sounds tragic to me, and that's just right down her alley. A tragic prince on the wrong side, high-born but lost, brought up by low-caste people from across the water . . . sounds like Naia's life.' And they both started laughing, sharing one more joint, filling the car with smoke. Both drivers hurriedly rolled their windows down, they had got used to it after the first fifty miles.

They were almost at their destination.

TWENTY-FIVE

Naia walked out to the edge of the outcrop and looked down. She was high up the mountainside, and the height scared her, making her tingle. She put her backpack down and laid down her small blanket. She lay down on it and closed her eyes. She would have a small nap before starting back, she thought, she had walked more than normal that morning. She fell asleep listening to the sound of eagles.

She dreamed of lying down beside Samaad, but he had his back to her. She tried to nudge him and turn him toward her, but couldn't. She wanted to see his face, desperately. It became a desire so intense that she woke, and was unnerved when she saw his face right beside hers, looking at her. His eyes were dark. She could see the sky reflected in them.

'This is too far. It's dangerous, you could slip and fall and never be found. What would I tell Yehudi then?'

'Is he all you care about?' she demanded, half laughing.

'No, I care about losing a fine wench like you too, but another can be arranged without much trouble,' he said seriously.

She was startled, more because she had seen humour in him for the first time than because of what he had said. She put her hands on his face and pulled him down for a kiss. He put her hands away and began to sit up.

'Samaad,' she said, 'please don't turn away, or else tell me what's wrong'. He put his hand on her mouth as he had done before. 'Nothing is wrong. Nothing.' And then he looked into her eyes and replaced his hand with his mouth, gently at first, but she was the one that was desperate, and it was as if she had never been kissed until then, this was the only mouth she had ever wanted on hers, and she closed her eyes and lived in that moment.

They made love on the mountain's edge, over and over, till the sky began to darken, and the cold started to get through their heat. He stopped, finally, and wiped his mouth on the back of his sleeve. It was stained with blood, and he was puzzled, looking down at it and then feeling his lips. They were bitten through.

They walked down toward his house. He held her hand for safety, gripping it at the wrist.

'I love you,' she said, and he hushed her. 'You saved my life so now it belongs to you.'

'Naia,' he said quietly, 'you are going back to Delhi, to Los Angeles. We have no use for each other.'

She was quiet. She thought of Raoul. Why was it always about use? Or was it just a way to get rid of her? She wasn't going to let it go this time. She would stay and die if she had to. Then she wondered why her death had come into it.

'Yehudi should be back soon,' he said, bringing her back to reality. She had been uprooted, and now she was adrift on some quiet but swift-flowing current, unable to anchor in harbours she passed. He walked her to her room and saw her inside. He held her a moment before leaving and stroked her head, like a father would a child's. Then he said goodnight politely and left.

She lay down on the bed and stared into the darkness outside. The night was turned blue by moonlight, and she could see the valley fettered by the rising peaks around them, snow on the very tops where there was no summer ever. If she was confused when he had left her room, she wasn't confused when she fell asleep, dreaming of the mountain ledge and him.

She awoke to insistent knocking and rattling on her door. She sat up and yelled, 'What?'

It was Samaad. 'Naia, open the door.'

She went quickly and opened it. He was angry. Frank stood beside him.

'Jabra found him in Srinagar, at the bus station, asking how to find me. So now he's found me. He says he's your friend. Is he?'

She was disoriented, but found herself smiling. 'Yes, Samaad, he is my friend. Frank! Why are you here? Are you looking for me?'

'He's Hallam's kid,' Samaad said roughly, pushing Frank in.

'Who?' Naia moved aside for them to come in. 'What are you talking about? Frank is my friend, I met him in Bombay. At a lumber yard that Leon was photographing. I met him again in Delhi, and he and I became friends.' She sat down on the bed again.

'I'll get some tea, you two can talk and figure out who's who and what's what. And I'll tell you what you don't know. And Frank will tell me what I don't know.' He loped out of the door in a way that made her think of a large cat. They heard the bolt being drawn.

'You okay? Not hurt?' Frank came close to her and peered at her.

She was puzzled by this question. 'No, Frank, not hurt. Why would I be hurt? I'm not smoking anymore either.'

'Cold turkey?'

'No, he gave me some pills. He said they were French.'

'Ah. Suboxone. So. You got any left?'

'Pills?'

'No, hack. You have any?'

She suddenly understood and pulled him down to sit next to her. She put an arm around him, though she knew that wasn't going to help him, but she couldn't help herself. She couldn't imagine what he was going through, but she knew it was going to get worse.

'No, Frank, I don't have any. He took it all away. But I can ask him for some pills for you.'

Frank was rubbing his neck and arms and kept wiping his face. She knew what was coming, and she wanted to cry. She had never thought of Frank as her friend, he was too easygoing for that. But he was her friend, after all, and she cared that he was in pain.

'Who is Halley?' she asked him, hoping he would answer some questions and distract himself.

'Hallam. My boss. He sent me to find out about Samaad. Something going on here he needs to know about. You know about this?'

Naia's throat felt dry. She needed to brush her teeth. She needed to talk with Leon. In that order.

'Frank. Have you eaten? Are you hungry?'

'No. Do you know about anything?' he asked again.

'Yes, I do, but not now, Frank. He'll be back soon. I will tell you when . . . well, not now.'

Frank just sat there, slumped, scratching himself absently. Samaad pushed the door open and came in. The man following him, Naia's bodyguard, was carrying an old metal

tray with food and tea. Another man came in with a
folding table and set it up, and then fetched two chairs.
Samaad motioned them out. He poured three cups of tea
and told them to take some. Frank didn't.

'Drink the tea, Frank, you're going to need it. When did
you have your last fix?'

'Four hours. I have no more. You can help?'

Naia looked at Samaad from under her eyebrows without
turning her head. She didn't want him to know she was
looking at him.

'No, I cannot help you. I can give you a room and a man
at the edge of the village. You can work it off there. Then
we can talk. I think you are not much use to me like this.
Drink the tea.'

Naia saw the set of his jaw. She saw the cold blue sky in
his eyes. She looked away. To her absolute horror, Frank
began to cry.

'No Suboxone? I feel bad . . .' he said between breaths.

'Can't you help him?' Naia said in a harsher tone than
she intended to.

'No, Naia, I cannot. I want to know what he is here for.
To whom he reports and why. I have to know. These
bastards of Hallam's snoop about and carry information to
both sides. They pretend they are here for our good, for
social work. I have dealt with this shit before. You stay out
of it, and do not attempt to intervene on his behalf. He is
that bastard Hallam's boy. You see how he is? That guy has
made sure for I don't know how many years that this boy
stayed hooked. He could have cleaned him up. He didn't.'
He threw a look of contempt at Frank, who was beginning
to contort his muscles to ease the cramping, water running

from his eyes and nose. Samaad's face was dark, lips snarling as he spoke. She thought again of a huge cat hissing before a strike. She got that familiar feeling of falling down, emptying into space, hollowing out into a husk of nothingness. She held on tight to the sight of the mountain outside the window in her peripheral vision as Samaad stood up and called in his men, as they dragged Frank, falling, whimpering, out of the room.

'Naia,' he said when they were gone. 'This is my life, my people's life, he threatens. There is nothing more important than that. I don't expect you to understand.'

'I guess I don't.'

'Well, it does not really matter whether you understand or you don't,' he said, turning to walk out.

'I know, but maybe you could explain anyway? Just to humour me?'

'What is it you need to know?' he said, still reaching for the door.

'How someone like Frank could possibly harm you, your people, your precious mines, or your divine purpose.' She was half frightened herself, unable to stop the words, the poison in her voice. He turned around and leaned against the door and folded his arms across his chest, waiting. She felt an odd menace in his stance, and realised it was more of the cat image which had begun to come up in her head. She didn't think he would do anything to harm her, but neither did she think he would hesitate if he had to. She knew now that she was not enough of a threat to him to bother. She felt like she had just been released from her addiction, opening her eyes after a long underwater swim. She could see clearly and she could breathe.

'What about me? Yehudi?' she said, forcing that hateful name out, asking because he expected her to, not really caring about the answer. She looked him in the face. It was the face she knew again, calm, intelligent, dark-eyed, compelling. With ugliness lurking beneath the ancient beauty of generations, clearly visible if you knew how to look. Like those pictures that you stared at to find a hidden dimension. You stared and stared until you unfocussed, and then, there it was. And once you had seen it, it wasn't hard anymore.

'I told you we were no use to each other, Naia. Yehudi—that is between me and him. You are not part of that.'

'Should I just leave, then?'

And he just considered her for a moment. He made no reply. And turned and left the room. He pulled the door shut and she heard the bolt being slammed into place.

TWENTY-SIX

The camp was full of activity when Karan and Leon were escorted in by the two guards. People were doing the things they did every day, washing clothes, cooking, buying and selling stuff at little 'daily needs' shops, children were being taught their daily lessons. Naia had walked through the two parallel and one cross lane and was on her way back to her room after breakfast when she heard the noise of children running screaming toward Samaad's house. She stepped longer and faster to get there and find out what was up. She began to run when she saw the cloud of dust and children who had surrounded a group of men. She could see Leon's head over everyone else's. She yelled, 'Leon! Leon!' And he turned around. The crowd parted, and she saw Karan there beside him. They were both grinning at her, and stood there watching her as she ran up to them. She ran straight at Leon and hugged him hard. Then she turned to Karan. After a moment's pause she hugged him too, holding him close and smelling an unfamiliar smell of dust and food and hashish. It was a smell she would never forget. She would recall it years from then, and conjure up the image of Leon and her brother, standing there, both tall and bearded, Karan brown and Leon white, the children around them nothing but a blurry background to her eyes, her two most beloved people in the world.

'Hey, hey, are you okay?' Karan spoke into her hair, and then stroked it down so he could breathe. 'What's wrong?'

She didn't know what to say. Everything came to her mind in clear images that shifted and passed before they could be turned into words. They came out as tears instead. They were faster and sharper and hurt less than speaking. She was in a haze of misery, and its sudden onset took her by surprise. Her mother's soft smiling eyes, her father's laugh, Elijah, Raoul, Tara, girlfriends from first grade, Samaad, Frank, all wove in and out in a stream of colour and texture like an old carpet in her new father's house. She had broken under the intense relief of seeing not just Leon, but her brother as well. Karan looked at Leon over her head, still holding her, sobbing into his shirt, a question in his eyes. Leon just shrugged slightly, and shook his head. It had been only a few seconds, and the children still swarmed about them, unaware of the unfolding emotions. Samaad was there suddenly.

'Yehudi!' He was glad to see Leon, he had missed him more than he had thought he would. He had missed his incessant curiosity, his naïve yet incisive questions, his unspoken support, no judgement in his eyes or his heart. He was glad to see his friend back. He had not been sure Leon would return, even with Naia as insurance. Then he saw the pleasure in Leon's face, the smile, he saw Leon take big, sure steps toward him, and then he enclosed him in a tight hug. And he knew it was not Naia who had brought him back.

'I have the money,' Leon whispered in his ear.

'What's the matter with Naia?' Samaad whispered back.

'I guess she's happy to see us?' Leon said, and released Samaad.

'Naia,' Samaad said sharply, and she turned her face to him, but stayed close to Karan's chest.

'What, Samaad?'

'Are you feeling unwell?'

She said nothing, and then sighed, resting her head back on Karan's chest.

'I need to go lie down. Can I have another bed in the house? For Karan? And Leon's sleeping bag is already there, so we'll all be fine.'

Samaad nodded at her and said something to the guards. 'Tell them if you need anything else, they will get it for you. Karan, welcome, I hope you have a good stay. Maybe tomorrow Jabra can take you up to the mines.'

'Cool. Uh . . . what mines?' Karan said, surprising them all. And then Samaad loved his friend a little more, because he knew then that he had told no one, he would tell no one.

'You'll see,' he said mysteriously to Karan.

Karan and Naia followed the guards to their room, leaving Leon with Samaad.

They went to Samaad's house. Leon was thrilled to see a fat blanket-covered velvet couch there, and threw himself on it, groaning with comfort. Samaad smiled. 'Jabra brought that up from my father's old house in Srinagar.' Leon put his feet up on it, stretching out full length.

'Man. You have no idea how long this journey has been,' he said to Samaad, then sat up and reached for his backpack. He took the fat envelope full of money and gave it to Samaad. He fanned the notes, and the five hundred euro notes made a crisp whirr. 'Pretty lucre,' he said smiling, 'paper for stones. How did it go?'

'Good, Jean Cahi is every bit as good as you promised. He is sharp, knew what he was doing, spotted the origin of the stones as soon as he laid eyes on them.'

'What did he say exactly?'

'He said that they were Kashmir Blues, Samaad, my man, there was no denying it. And he was not interested in telling anyone, in fact it makes sense that he wouldn't, he doesn't want us going to anyone else. He also said he was paying us too little for the size and quality.'

Samaad laughed. 'Of course he is paying too little, but that's because we wanted to keep it secret. We have no choice really, we can't afford to have it known.' He began to count the money. 'Why is Karan here?'

'Viren sent him to bring back Naia. He was waiting for me at the airport, they had found out that I was going to Paris on an assignment, they were worried because I had left Naia with you. And then Hallam really got on me that

night. He raved and ranted about you and your type, he
kept saying, and me and my type . . . didn't get why he was
so angry . . . and then the explosions . . . but really, though
Karan was sent to take Naia back, I think he was curious.
I think he was intrigued, and wanted to come see for
himself.'

'I know about the explosions. You were not close by,
were you? You're fine? Do they know who did it?'

'I think they know that it wasn't you.'

'Me? What the hell would I get by throwing grenades
into Viren's house? Are they stupid? I wonder where
Hallam's brain is, sometimes. That stupid motherfucker
had his guy come out asking about me. Jabra caught him
at the Srinagar airport. Dumb fuck.'

Leon stared at Samaad, not getting a word of this.

'Who?'

'Frank. German. He's here. He's a fucking heroin addict
to boot, so he's sweating his drug out at the other end of
the village!'

Leon was clearly amazed. He had never heard Samaad
swearing that much before, and that amazed him too.

'Frank is here? Does Naia know?'

'Yes, and she tried to get me to give him the medication
I gave her, to help him along. For fuck's sake!'

Leon urgently wanted to go and talk to Naia. He said as
much to Samaad.

'Yes, good idea. Go talk to her, find out what's going on
with her. I am glad you're back, my friend, I really am.'

'I'm happy to be back,' Leon said to him. He went out
into the dust to find Naia and Karan.

Karan was standing by the window making a smoke

when Leon went in the room. 'I took some from that chunk Samaad gave you,' he said, grinning. 'Man, it smells good.'

Naia scowled at Leon. 'What did I do?' he said, and she just shook her head and looked away.

'What? What? What?' he said to her.

'Oh, she's teed off because Samaad wasn't nice to Frank,' Karan offered, and she actually snorted.

'You guys don't understand. He wasn't not nice, Karan, he was vicious. Poor, poor Frank, he's—you know, uh . . .'

'A heroin addict?' Leon said.

Her scowl deepened. 'Yes. And all he wants is some stuff, or some medication . . . I know what he's going through, Leon, you don't . . .'

'Guess why you know what he's going through Naia?' Leon cut in loudly. 'If you can't guess, I can tell you. Because Frank shared his stuff with you. You lose all perspective, you have no idea what's going on. Don't forget, before you start telling me what a villain Samaad is, that he got you off the shit. Keep that in your head before you start calling him vicious. And, before you take Frank's side. That's just backwards, Naia.'

Karan stood watching them. He was rubbing the hashish with his thumb into his palm, crumbling the resin and releasing a fresh green smell, enjoying the simple action while absently taking in the animosity building up between his sister and her best friend.

'Leon, you don't understand. You are blind when it comes to him. You didn't see him. And Frank—he was in pain, he was . . .'

Leon held up his palm to ward off her words. 'Naia. I am

not blind. I know what is going on here. I know what Samaad is doing and why. I understand it. I want to be part of it. But never mind that. Why don't you tell me what Frank is doing here. Then we'll talk.'

'He was dragged here by Jabra.'

'Really. And Jabra just decided that Frank would make a good addition to their team? Or is there another explanation?'

Naia was almost gritting her teeth. 'You don't get it Leon, I trusted him. I thought . . . I thought . . .'

She stopped suddenly and began to cry again, in great sobs and heaves. She put her head in her hands and stayed that way for a few seconds. Leon was caught in his anger, unable to make the transition to comfort her, and Karan stood and watched. He finished making his smoke and stuck it in the side of his mouth and started patting himself down for a lighter. Naia took her hands off her face and wiped her tears on her shoulder, streaking her sleeve. She blew her nose on the front of her shirt, exposing her middle for a few seconds.

'You have abs,' Leon blurted, and they all laughed. 'You get them by living here,' she said. Then she took a deep breath, jagged from sobbing. 'I fell in love with Samaad too, Leon,' she said, looking into his eyes. 'I feel how you feel about him, and more. I felt like I would die if he didn't love me back. He didn't. And see, I didn't die. I would have followed him anywhere too, just like you would. But Leon, you didn't see his eyes when he was looking at Frank. He didn't care. He didn't care if Frank lived or died. Or if he was in pain. You didn't see him turn away as if Frank didn't exist.'

Leon said nothing. He produced a lighter from one of the many pockets on his shorts, and took the oversized joint from Karan's mouth. He thought about everything Naia had said, turning it all over in his mind. She fell in love with Samaad? That made him smile. Were they lovers? Probably, and that explained Naia's odd behaviour, her reactions disproportionate to the incident she reported. He smiled some more. He couldn't see Samaad as a lover, let alone Naia's lover. And then he sighed with pleasure at the slowing down of time, the glowing edges of everything, the outer stupor and inner clarity that came from the clean mountain hashish. He wondered how he could begin to make Naia understand Samaad, where he was from, what he was about, and the irrelevance of Frank to all this. He did not dislike Frank, in fact quite the opposite. He didn't wish him ill, but he couldn't, in all honesty, elevate him above Samaad's vision. He handed the joint to Karan, who took it, smiling into his eyes. Leon took it back and held it like he had seen Mushtaq bhai do in Bombay, with all five fingers. Then he cupped his other hand around it. He touched this two-handed fist to his forehead in the manner of Shiva devotees and sucked from a gap between his thumb and forefinger, straight into his lungs.

'Thank you, Samaad,' he said reverently with his out-breath.

The next few days were hard on Naia, exciting for Karan, and heaven for Leon. Naia hardly came out of her room after she had done her hour-long morning ramble. She looked for Frank but did not dare to ask Samaad about him. In fact she hardly spoke to Samaad at all. If Samaad noticed this, he didn't show that he did, preferring to talk

to the two men and Jabra, bantering with the families and
walking around the village ruffling children's hair, sharing
smokes and having small conferences with his militia.
These were now clearly distinguishable from the family
men by their weapons and dusty clothes, but mainly by
their demeanour. They tried, as per Jabra's instructions, to
fade into the walls, mingle with the dust, stay in the
shadows, letting the people live their illusion of normalcy.

Leon had taken out his cameras again, and wandered
about looking through his lens, the digital chirp that
accompanied him everywhere a familiar sound to everyone.
He thought how things had changed from when he had
first walked into that same village months ago. Karan had
not yet decided when he would return with the package he
had been sent to retrieve—his sister. He hadn't even told
her why he had come. He was happy to let a few days flow
by, long and lazy. Naia spent a lot of time with Karan, and
writing her journal. She was civil to Samaad, and she found
that it wasn't hard to avoid being alone with him. He
didn't talk to her unless she did first, but he was never
awkward as she was, he was his usual smooth self, polite,
gentle, and except for one time, soft-spoken. The one time
was when she brought up Frank as they were talking about
going up to the mines.

'When is he going to come out of that room?' she had
asked him directly.

'When he is ready,' he said, and everyone else heard
in the low abrupt answer the warning not to pursue this
topic.

'Can I go see him?' she persisted, and Leon tried to catch
her eye to shut her up. Karan didn't do anything, he

watched the situation going bad with that odd curiosity he
had, an amusement almost, at everything around him,
good or bad.

'You want to see him do what? Vomit on the floor?
Crawl around begging the guards to shoot him? Have
screaming fits about how he is dying and to get him a
doctor? And you won't even understand half of it, unless
you speak German. You want to go?'

'Yes, Samaad, I do. He's my friend, and I want to help
him. So I can go? Will you instruct the guard to let me in?'

Samaad turned on her and raised his voice just enough
to give her a belly clench. 'Yes. Go see him. And tell the
stupid fuck to drink all the water in the can and eat as
much food as he can get down his miserable throat, he will
get over it sooner. I need to ask him questions.'

Naia had turned and left, and then gone to see Frank
the next morning.

He was not bad at all. He was lying on fresh sheets, he
looked as if he had just bathed and changed. 'Hi,' she
smiled at him and settled at the foot of his bed. His
breakfast sat half eaten on a tray on the floor. It was the
same that she had eaten, eggs scrambled with onions and
tomatoes and coriander and green chilies and spices. Samaad
had been sitting across from her so she hadn't eaten as
much as she would have liked, so she picked up the plate
and began to eat from it. Frank looked young and sad, but
definitely better than she had expected from Samaad's
description. He seemed to be over the worst of it, and she
was glad she had come.

'No one hurt you did they?'

'Hurt? No, no. They bathed me, cleaned my vomit, a very

old man gave me massage. He rubbed my legs and arms when I had cramping, and he fed me too. I have not seen him today, I wish to see him, to say thank you. I think I am good, but I must have something. You cannot help me?'

'Frank, there is nothing here. Samaad burned my stuff when he took it, he didn't keep it, so he doesn't have any. I don't know about the pills. You are going to have to get over it cold turkey, there's no other way, I am so sorry, Frank, really.'

He stared at her, panic in his eyes. Then he smiled, only as he could, purposefully banishing the fear from his face and eyes, accepting his situation, even, finally, beginning to enter into the adventure that had been thrust upon him after such a long period of dormancy.

'So,' he said. 'We are in the middle of nowhere, but this is a very important nowhere to a lot of people. I must find out about this place. Also about this village—who owns it, who runs it, and so on. Also, I must get over this sickness soon, or I will be no use to Gabriel, and he will be right.'

'Right?' she said, puzzled and fascinated by the transformation she could see happening before her eyes. What amazed her was that he was effecting the change himself. Like a chameleon which had sat on an unfamiliar surface and had just understood it, and figured out how to rearrange itself to hide on it.

'Gabriel Hallam always said I would not be able to—be well when he really needed something. He said my habit would kill me. I always said I would be good with or without it. It is nothing, only a drug. My body will recover, if my mind wants it to recover. You understand?'

'Yes,' she said, whispering. She couldn't have explained

what he had told her to anyone, but she understood, emotionally. 'I should go, Frank. You need anything you let me know. I will come and see you again later. You look like you need to sleep. A lot. And, I should give you Samaad's message, in case it is important: he said you should drink a lot of water. Okay?'

'Okay. You go. I will be okay in two days. I need to sleep, two more days. Bye, Naia, see you.' He was smiling as she left, more to himself than at her, like he had found something he had misplaced.

TWENTY-SEVEN

Karan and Leon had lost their sense of time. Karan had a walnut walking stick given to him by Jabra, and they both walked everywhere, all the time, tramping up and down the valleys. The paths made by goats grazing the lower hills for hundreds of years were visible now that the snows were completely gone, and they followed these. They explored far afield of the village, sometimes even spending the night in a cave or under an outcrop of rock. They didn't really need any shelter. The nights, though cool, were pleasantly so, and a single blanket was enough cover. Samaad went with them sometimes, and they would lie down under the Himalayan sky, always aglow with a blue light that held back the pitch from the night. He would point out constellations that they knew, the obvious ones like Orion and Taurus, but also stars and planets they didn't. Canis Major, Regulus, Aldebaran. He told them that Betelgeuse, in Orion, was bigger than the orbit of the earth around the sun, was so far away that it might have gone supernova without anyone knowing it. He told them that pelicans die because their eyes take a beating from a lifetime of plunging into the ocean for fish, go blind, and then starve to death. That polar bears have black skin and transparent hair.

'Man, Samaad, I have to ask you a very important question.'

They lay lazing in the pale afternoon sun on blankets on the hillside. Karan was definitely asleep, there was no movement or sound from him other than a steady breathing. Winter wasn't close, but had moved from being last year's memory to being the season impending. The afternoon sun was pleasant now, welcome, where it would have been unbearably hot and bright just two weeks before. Samaad had had his men carry a huge flask of tea and biscuits up to the ledge. Lunch had been particularly good—rotis and kababs made on a recently built open-air tandoor. The hashish, as always, was perfect, it seemed to be made for the kind of weather and camaraderie they were having. Leon wished Naia would get her act together and join them, but she would not forgive Samaad for his treatment of Frank, or what she perceived as his rejection of her, and Samaad did not care one way or another.

'What?' he asked Leon, yawning loudly and long.

Leon had forgotten his question. 'Did I say something?' he asked Samaad, after a while of contemplating Karan's peaceful, slightly fluttering eyelids.

'You said you had to ask me a very important question,' Samaad said.

Leon had begun to yawn now, and his eyes watered from

the enormous expansion of his jaw. He couldn't stop yawning, and finally laid his head down and closed his eyes.

'I'll ask you when I remember,' he said, and was asleep almost before he had finished his sentence.

An hour later Samaad woke them up by calling their names softly as though they were children. The sun had moved while they slept, slanting onto their eyelids, so they were on the verge of waking up anyway. He poured tea for them and then himself, and they slurped the kahwa in companionable stupor for a while.

Samaad got up and peed off the ledge, careful to aim away from them. He came back and sat on his haunches and lit them a pipe.

'I remember what I wanted to ask you,' Leon said suddenly, gulping down the last of his tea and stretching out his cup to Samaad for more. 'I was wondering if it was at all possible that a brown dog has been following me since I landed in this country.'

Karan and Samaad both shook their heads and started laughing, quietly at first, and then, to Leon's irritation, began to whoop and slap their thighs, getting almost hysterical, encouraging each other to keep going when either showed signs of sobering up.

'Would you guys shut up?' Leon said to them. 'I am serious, I have had a brown dog following me. Every time I go somewhere new, I see him in my peripheral vision. It's not funny.'

Samaad held up his palm to Karan, and they both settled down a bit, Karan wiping his eyes. 'Yehudi, do you realize how ubiquitous brown dogs are in India? They carpet the country from end to end, north to south and east to west. They are called pi-dogs. They are mongrels, they are everywhere.' Leon started to interrupt him, but he held up his palm again, and between more laughter, kept talking. 'Most of them even have the same two or three names, if they belong to anyone—Raju, Moti, Tiger, if they have a bit of brindle, and Kalu, if they are dark or black. But mostly they are brown. They are like crows, Yehudi. And you are quite fantastical. How long have you had this amazing notion? That one particular brown dog was following you, I mean?' And he and Karan started to laugh again, and this time Leon joined them.

The hashish reached deep into their minds, connecting them, reawakening old forgotten parts of their memories, visions from other times they had been there.

'I'll tell you what you might see in these mountains,' Samaad said, suddenly serious. 'You might see Shiva. Or his wife, Parvati. Or any of the other gods and goddesses. They walk about in the mountains, and if you are quiet and unassuming and have no expectations, why, then, you might see them.'

Neither Karan nor Leon laughed. If they did not believe him and thought of saying so, they both thought the better of it and stayed quiet, waiting. They knew there was more.

'I was walking through the pass on the Garud hill up there.' He pointed to a peak barely visible through the cloud cover, high up to the east of their hillside. 'It was late winter, everything was snowed in, I had been up here for two months on my own, and was trying out that pass to see if I could get through and down the other side where the old village was, where Jabra was. I came up to a cave. Murky

sounds emerged from the depth of the cave, as though the
air inside were thicker, trying to hold back the terrible
sounds, keep them from me.' He paused and looked up,
remembering.

'When I heard those sounds, Yehudi, a fist closed
around my heart, squeezed, till it felt as though the veins
were closing up, so water flowed from my eyes. I could not
stop it, I could not turn away. And then he came walking
out of the cave, blue as sapphire, tall as the mountain, the
cobras hissing around his body, terrifying me. And then I
knew who I was, what I was meant to be.' He stopped
talking again, and they saw his eyes, glittering in the
indistinct light of the fading sunset, and they both realised
it didn't matter whether it was true or not, what Samaad
had seen. It was what he felt that mattered.

'I saw a man on the lower edge of the pass, he had come
out of the cave on the other side, so it must have been a
sort of tunnel. He was running away, and he fell to the
ground in the snow. He held up his hands to ward off
something. And the great god had his back to me, so I
could not see. But the hair on my entire body stood on
end. A second later, I saw and smelt the fire, the stench of
burning skin and hair, only for a moment, and then the
swift cleansing of the fire's heat took it away, leaving
nothing there where the man had been, leaving it only in
my memory . . . but in my memory forever . . . the smell of
a soul leaving a body.'

'I waited, afraid for my own soul, but unable to move. I
knew he knew I was there, I felt my presence acknowledged
somehow.' Samaad paused, remembering.

'He sang, then, and it was as if he placed the words

gently on the air, to softly float to my ears, so they entered
my mind, reassured my soul ... I did not hear him so
much as feel the song, and I was glad to my quick, and
ready to walk with him to wherever he may lead me. I do
not know, Yehudi, if there is one god or many, if Allah is
this god or another. I know that this being lives in these
mountains and has seen me and shown himself to me. I
know he has given me wealth and power, but for a purpose.
I know that I will follow my heart, and he owns my heart,
he burned his name on it. Allah is in my heart too, and I
feel no conflict. Do you understand?'

He stopped finally, and looked at both of them, not
really expecting an answer, but waiting anyhow.

'Yes, I suppose I do,' Leon said. 'I have no faith at all,
no god nor religion. My parents are Jewish, Yehudi—they
follow that faith. Devoutly. But I cannot say I have ever felt
the presence of the lord. But Samaad, my dear friend, I
have never felt more alive in spirit than I have here with
you.'

Karan nodded in agreement. 'Yes, I know what you
mean. There is something up here, something that draws
you, awakens you. I have felt it too, like a light has been
shone into me.'

They talked about everything, from geology, which was
Samaad's major in college, to philosophy, which was Karan's,
to the species of flowers growing on the hillside they were
on, to the poetry of Yeats. It was an easy, spontaneous
conversation, and no one listening in would have thought
that these three men were from as diverse backgrounds,
cultures, or goals as they were. They were at ease with
themselves and each other, and even Karan, until then the

third party, became, in the course of those days, one of them.

'I can tell you why Yeats appeals to you, Samaad. It's because he is Irish. His land was colonised, occupied, and his words speak directly to your heart, as a Kashmiri in the shadow of other powers.' Samaad was pleased at Karan's assessment, and Leon was lost: he had never read or even heard of Yeats.

'I'll give you a book when we get back to camp,' Samaad told him. 'He is the most . . .'

He was at a loss for words, but closed his eyes and made a gesture implying heart, knocking on his chest with his fist.

'You are the one who should tell him about Karan in the *Mahabharata*. I tried, but maybe I haven't got it. I wasn't able to understand why anyone would name their child after him . . .' Leon said to Samaad.

'Karan is simple, and complex, depending on how you look at him. I suppose I can see what you mean. He is unable to rise above the events of his life. But in India he has always been seen as a hero, a prince who never got his due. He's like a—"the world owes me" sort of guy. I do see what you mean. I never questioned it before. He could have chosen many paths, but he always went where it was easiest, swept by circumstance.' He turned to Karan, smiling, 'I hope you are not like your namesake, my friend.'

'I hope so too. Maybe I can have my name legally changed to—Heathcliff?' Karan said, and they both laughed.

'That's very clever,' Samaad said, visibly impressed, 'You mean Heathcliff from *Wuthering Heights*, right?'

Karan nodded. 'They are the same, aren't they, Karan

and Heathcliff? That really is very clever, Karan,' Samaad
said again. And again, Leon was out of the loop, but
enjoying the conversation anyway. If he had wished Naia
had been there that afternoon, at that moment he was glad
that she wasn't, to bring her petty emotions into the mix,
souring everything. And he was ashamed of his thought
too, because he did love her and wished she could see
Samaad as he did. He wondered if that would please him
though, having to share his friend with her didn't fill him
with delight either. He shrugged and pushed thoughts of
her away. He was where he wanted to be, and with whom
he wanted to be with.

Karan was telling Samaad how that mountainside
reminded him of some part of England called Grasmere,
where he had taken a girl on a weekend. 'I thought I would
impress her, it was Wordsworth's home,' he said laughing.
'I thought I would get some snogging in that weekend. But
it was so glorious, all we did was walk and walk, and then
pass out.' And then he and Samaad started singing, and
Leon listened to their voices, smooth and perfectly blending
together like coffee and cream fading into the big landscape,
a song he had never heard before, but was familiar and
comforting. They were singing not about England, but here
and now, he thought.

And did those feet in ancient time
Walk upon England's mountains green?
And was the holy Lamb of God
On England's pleasant pastures seen?
And did the Countenance Divine
Shine forth upon our clouded hills?
And was Jerusalem builded here

Among these dark Satanic mills?
Bring me my bow of burning gold:
Bring me my arrows of desire:
Bring me my spear: O clouds unfold!
Bring me my chariot of fire.
I will not cease from mental fight,
Nor shall my sword sleep in my hand
Till we have built Jerusalem
In England's green and pleasant land.'

And then they both stopped and laughed.

'That's not Wordsworth, it's William Blake,' Samaad told Karan.

'Really? I didn't think it was a poem, just a song. You live and learn, you die and burn,' he said.

They spoke of landmines—Samaad explained how they were laid. Shakespeare's sonnets—Samaad said Shakespeare knew things about them that even they did not. They remembered women they had known and loved, and of course they talked about sapphires.

If Samaad had planned those days to bond them to one another, he had succeeded beyond his hopes. When they climbed down off the mountain to the village in the late evening light, they were comrades, soulmates, nothing could come between them anymore. Samaad could have asked them to go to war with him, and they would have, without hesitation. Samaad had a different sort of purpose. The other two men had no reason to be there but Samaad. He was the leader, the one who made them feel, whether true or not, that it was the comradeship between men that they fought for in the end. Not sapphires, or a jihad, but friendship, for their brothers-in-arms. And that was what they were now, even though they were not consciously aware of it. He had recruited them to his cause, which was nothing more than justice and safety for the few people who trusted him, by presenting it to them gently and in a way that they could not refuse him. By letting them be free to choose.

TWENTY-EIGHT

Viren looked worriedly at his watch. It had been almost four hours since Saroj had gone out. It was not like her to go off without telling him. He saw that she had taken her cell phone, she was meticulous about having it either with her or on the charger. He tried calling that, but kept getting the syrupy male voice saying she was outside coverage area. After leaving two messages, he stopped calling. He looked for a note in the house, called some of her friends he thought she might be with, and finally gave up and went to his desk to do some writing. She was with the car and driver, if anything dire had happened, he would have heard by now. He had quite lost track of time when the phone rang. The phone at his desk didn't work, so he had to walk over to another in the living room. He had always hated having all the phones in the house start ringing whenever there was a call, it sounded to him like a hysterical crescendo, annoying him no end. He snapped up the receiver and spoke.

'Yes.'

'Gabriel here, Viren, have you heard from your wife in the last couple of hours?'

'No, why?' Alarm rose like bile in his throat, but his voice betrayed none of it.

'I had a call a few minutes ago. Could mean nothing, but thought I should tell you anyway. She was seen at a checkpoint on one of the northbound arteries. She was asleep in the back seat. Are you aware of where she is going?'

'Why would your people even know about my wife?' Viren asked, still calmly.

'Well, we watch all diplomatic plates, and ex-diplomat's cars, but especially yours since the attack on your house. So.'

'Hmm. Well. What do you have for me?'

'Who is the driver? Wasn't your driver one of the blokes that got killed?'

Viren shook his head, his eyebrows knitted together. He should have thought of that himself. Hallam had a network that had begun to impress and frighten Viren a little. Nobody seemed to have any idea about him. The Indian secret service had a very accurate idea of who and how many foreign operatives were in the country at any given time, where they were, what they were doing. Hallam was special. He had made himself useful to every embassy that Viren had ever been at. He had earned trust. But there was no knowing what he told the other side, or sides.

'Hello? Viren?'

Viren came back to the conversation. 'Yes, I was just thinking, I will check on the driver. He was supplied by the usual people. I am sure they vetted him and know who he is. This is all very strange and sudden. I am concerned.'

It was Hallam's turn to be silent. Then he said, 'I will be there in fifteen minutes, Viren.'

'Yes, come, it would help. I don't know what to do or what's going on. Why Saroj? What use is she to anyone?' he said, into the dead phone. Hallam had grunted and hung up.

He put the phone back on its base and called for a cup of tea.

Viren wished Karan were beside him. He wished he had listened to Saroj. He rubbed his hand over his face. He had always been afraid to step out of the safety of institutions. His marriage, the ministry, the embassy when he was out of the country. He knew of the life that existed outside, he even had control over some scrap of it. The men and women he sent out to work for him. The semi-quasi-government types he met at functions, those men in too-well tailored suits, their too-richly dressed wives, he remembered particular faces, shiny with perspiration, pumping his hand, teeth like marble tombstones in their gums, addicts in doorways, whores in Paris better dressed than any diplomat's wife, even the word whore was outside his arena, on the periphery of his life's vision. A shimmer of sleaze slithered alongside his world, companion to everything he was. His life, like the black embassy cars with the diplomatic plates, whispered through everything, touching nothing, picking up nothing. Then, he had been flagged down by his own lost daughter, and here he was, in some back alley of fear and uncertainty, waiting for someone from those streets to show him the way out. He drank his tea, the fine orange pekoe anchoring him in the safe harbour of his own senses, filling him with its mundane, delicate familiarity. His hands stopped shaking finally, and he was almost the self he knew when Hallam was shown in by the watchman.

Viren waited by the phone, as he had been doing on and off for four hours. He could not fathom what could have happened to Saroj, and all his calls to his considerable network of operatives had yielded no result. Not even the new driver had anything suspicious in his records. Hallam had stayed with him that day and night, sleeping in the guest room and answering every phone call. There had been no further news of Saroj. He had left finally, and promised to stay in touch, and call if he heard anything at all. Viren was amazed at himself. He had been a part of the secret service for close to twenty-five years, and had never reacted this way to any incident before, not even to the loss of his baby daughter. He wondered for a second if the argument they had had some days before could have anything to do with her disappearance, but dismissed that as impossible. She would never do anything foolish like run off.

'You let Naia go even when I begged you not to. Now you are going to send my son too?' She had been beside herself, crying, upset, refusing to listen when he had tried to pacify her, to explain to her that it was not in his hands, that Naia had gone because she had wanted to, he didn't have the authority to stop her. Karan was going because Viren had asked him to, to go and bring back his sister, but certainly not against his will, he had been enthusiastic and eager to go with Leon. The explosion had upset Saroj badly, and that was not surprising, it had upset everyone. Perhaps, he thought, that was why she had overreacted to Karan's departure. He was glad that Karan had driven out and brought Dr Joshi. The man had been a fixture in their lives for so very long. Saroj would speak with him at least once a week no matter where in the world they were. He thought she had been calmer after the doctor had left, but he had been too busy getting things back in order to pay too much attention to her. He felt a pang of guilt, but not for long. He was too worried to be guilty.

He had been close to hysteria when he had finally admitted to himself that she had not gone shopping, or to meet a friend. When he knew that something was very wrong, and Gabe Hallam was probably right. Hallam had seen that Viren was taking it badly, and had been as supportive as a relative stranger could be.

Viren wondered how to get in touch with Samaad. He thought about the satellite phone that Hallam had given to Leon the day they had left, maybe that would work. It was becoming the only thing on his mind. Samaad was looking more and more like his last resort, his only option. If he was somehow involved with Saroj's disappearance, or even responsible for it, Viren thought that would finish what little faith he had in his operatives. He had always known that in that region, the agents were temporary at best, highly susceptible to being drafted by the other side. Men joined the jihad to be with their friends or brothers, to be on the right side of their religious beliefs. It had been hard for him to hold on to agents, but losing Samaad would be a huge blow. Besides bringing him a lot of very valuable information, Samaad had insight and an understanding of his land that was rare. Viren had admiration for him, and a liking which had turned into affection over the years he had known Samaad. Plus, and the thought made Viren smile, Samaad had brought him his finest carpets. Viren did not really believe that he would turn to the other side.

If in fact he had ever been on theirs. He was not a man to be on any side but his own. As thoughts chased each other through his tired unresisting mind, a picture began to form. Of Samaad, his sparkling intelligence, his fine understanding of everything, his ability to pick out the best carpets, his sapphire eyes. And then, Viren stood up and reached for the phone.

The room was dramatically lit by slanting evening light coming in from the cracks in the bamboo blinds covering the windows. Twelve chairs surrounded the table, only one was unoccupied. Viren walked around to it. The nine men and two women at the table were all known to him only by sight or reputation, except for one, his immediate boss. They were all looking at him expectantly. They were all, he knew, thinking that this had better be good, there had better be a good reason to have called this lot of people together in one room. He thought there was. The attack on his home was a good starting point, they had all heard about that. It was probably why they had agreed. Not one of them was surprised by it, and neither was he. It had to happen sooner or later, and he had escaped for longer than most of his colleagues. Rogue agents, sale of information about senior officers in the service, revenge . . . many had lost lives, family members, staff, property. He had been fortunate that he had been mostly in Delhi, living in his own home. Those living in troubled areas were most vulnerable. Kashmir, Pakistan, Sri Lanka, Nepal. There were kidnappings, disappearances, bombings, shootings.

'My wife has been kidnapped . . .' Viren began, and then, suddenly tired, he sat down heavily in the chair. He drank the entire glass of water in front of him, wiped his face with his large white handkerchief, and then, having collected his panic and put it away, he started talking.

'Gabriel Hallam came in today with information that she—my wife—had been spotted being driven north. But that is not the most important information he had. He tells me that there is something going on in one particular area that is close to the border ... that someone there is, and has been acquiring, a small arsenal, and a small militia.'

His superior started to talk, but Viren held up his hand.

'My daughter is there too, in this particular village, and her friend, both American citizens. Now my wife has disappeared. Look. I know that we need to secure that area. A hostage situation is good reason for us to send in a small force. If they respond with arms, we can keep backup ready.' He put his hand down and looked at his boss. He was shaking his head.

'You are really amazing to me, Viren. Are you saying your daughter is with these people?'

'Yes. She went as a tourist, she did not know what she was getting into. Maybe she does not know she is a hostage. You know, sometimes these people will keep them as their guests ...'

'And all you can think of is strategy? That's what has kept you where you are.'

The man was smiling, and so were all the others around the table.

'Old habits,' Viren said, smiling tiredly too. 'Very old habits ... putting my family last ...'

The man patted his arm. 'Well then, let's get on with it. We have the opportunity, we have the right reasons. We get to secure that area before our friends from the north even know what is going on. What I would like to know is, how is it that it went on for so long and you had no idea, Viren?'

Viren had been afraid of that very question, and these men were too astute to not ask it.

'The man running the operation is one of mine,' he said gloomily. 'One of my best. For almost several years. If he is in fact the one responsible, the leader, and I think he might be, then it stands to reason that I did not receive intelligence. He deliberately kept me in the dark. But then there is Hallam ... it seems hard to hide anything from him for very long.'

There was silence at the table. Viren was far too senior and far too well respected for anyone to say anything more. His pain and embarrassment were palpable.

He came home to find Hallam pacing outside his front door.

'Well?' he said aggressively to Viren before he was out of his car. 'Any news?'

'We are going to investigate the matter,' Viren said to him.

'Investigate the matter? Aren't you concerned about Sara—uh—your wife?'

'Saroj. Her name is Saroj. Yes, Hallam, I am concerned. But when there is nothing more I can do, when I have done what I can, all I can do is ... do you want to come in and have a cup of tea?'

Hallam stared at him incredulously for a moment, and then said, 'Yeah, alright. Tea.'

Inside, Viren excused himself. 'I need to make a few calls, and I really need to freshen up. I'll just be twenty

minutes. Is that okay? I'll order some tea, you go ahead.
Thirty minutes at most, I promise. And I'll tell you
everything I know.'

Gabriel Hallam sat on the couch and looked out of the
window. He had been sitting there only a few minutes, but
his thoughts were swift, and confused, spanning decades
and continents but chasing just one person. He remembered
the first time he had seen Saroj, he remembered that
clearly. But he had never reconciled that meeting, that
person, the time they had spent together, the mornings in
his bed, the afternoons walking the streets of Madrid, with
the person she had become today. She had been the most
painfully shy woman he had ever known, but she also had
an innate curiosity about the limits of her senses. She
enjoyed the painful or unpleasant as much as the pleasure.
She understood instinctively that what was painful to her,
such as putting caracol—the disgusting snails that everyone
ate with obvious relish—into her mouth, had a small chance
of turning into pleasure. She took risks for that small
chance. And he found himself laughing at her, but also
found himself more and more willing to go where he
himself had never been. She had been a delight in his
male-dominated world. The only women he interacted with
were those he paid to give him information, or to sleep
with him. He smiled when he thought of the day trips they
had taken together from Madrid. Segovia and Avila,
aqueducts and iglesias, little towns where they had done
nothing but sample cheese and watch people, Toledo,
where she had turned to him and said, 'No more ancient
monuments Gabe, let's buy a bottle of wine and get a
room.' That was the first time she had tried something she

had never tried before, and he had never asked her to. 'It can't be any different than the snails,' she had said, 'and those were disgusting and delicious.' He had laughed so much they almost had to abort the whole effort. But it was the sweetest memory he had. Of anyone. And then in later years, though they had lived in the same countries, they both understood that their time was over, that they had different roads to travel. And he had met her once, in London, with Viren, and a baby boy of about three. She looked happy, filled out, and a grown-up version of that girl he had known and loved. She had been an unexpected gift in his intentionally solitary life. He had enjoyed her, he was glad they had what they had. He hoped he had given her a memory worth going back to, as she had him. But he had not wanted anything more, with her or any other woman before or since.

And then he thought about how he had been excited when he had heard that Saroj and Viren were back in New Delhi. He was curious to see her again, to see what and who she was after almost three decades. He had seen and even had dealings with Viren in the interim. He knew what had happened with their second child. He had heard that Saroj had not taken it well, and that she had never recovered from it. But he was unprepared for what he saw. She was nothing like the woman he had known. It was as if that woman had left, and taken with her not only the spirit and sweetness, but the physical beauty as well. Saroj was a small dry sparrow, brown and almost ugly in the sorrow that had consumed her life. He had been shocked, but also ashamed of his own reaction, his recoil from her. He had looked at himself in the mirror that day and seen, for the first time, how much he himself had changed, aged. He supposed that the man she had loved had left him too, taking the colour of his hair and the shine of his eyes with him. They met a few times after that, but never spoke much beyond polite social noises.

He heard Viren closing a door somewhere and began to pour a cup of tea from the pot the maid had brought in at some point. He had been lost in thought.

'Well, what I can tell you Gabe, is that we are doing the most we can. I am so afraid you may have been right about my friend Samaad. This time I wish you were not . . . but I have no option other than to act on the assumption that you are.'

Gabe glanced out of the windows. The garden was pretty enough, but the spectacular carpet was gone. It would take time and effort before it could be replaced, regrown. Maybe Viren wouldn't even try to restore it. Maybe he would be content to remember it as it had been.

Gabriel Hallam listened to Viren, but only one thought filled his mind. He hoped that Saroj would walk in the doors of her home unharmed.

TWENTY-NINE

The flowers on the hillside were the prettiest blue she had ever seen. She had never actually seen that blue before. The climb was hard on her legs, and the loose legs of her salwar made it harder because they kept getting caught in the rocks and pebbles. She had tried folding them up, but they wouldn't stay up. Her sandals, though they were causing her shoe bites and blisters, she had to keep on, because she had to have something. She wished she had been more sensible about her shoes, but she hadn't had comfort on her mind when she had left. She had tied her dupatta over her head to give her a little protection from the sun, but she was overheated and panting in spite of the cool air. She had been climbing a moderate grade for two hours, and knew that she had another two to go. She knew she was not lost, because there were stacks of flat river rock like sentinels along the way, all she had to do was follow them. She knew too, that there was one group fifteen minutes ahead of her, and she knew there must be people behind her. Most of the people on that trail were on their way to a large Shiva shrine that was as old as the mountains it nestled in. She was looking for a different deity. She was looking for Green Tara, goddess of wisdom. She didn't want any more advice or good fortune bestowed upon her by the opposite sex, even if he was a god. Even if he was Shiva.

She took small frequent sips from her canteen. She wondered if Viren had missed her or even realised she wasn't in her bedroom. Drugged, as usual. One day the pain would recede from her head as it did when she took those wonderful pills. It would recede, and never come back. She would be free from it. She wouldn't care anymore whether her baby was alive in some tiled room in the red-light district on Faulkland Road. She had been driven through once, when some stupid pompous American senator had wanted to see it. She saw those young girls, or maybe they really were boys as their driver had informed them, all

made up with some awful chalky pink powder, bloody
mouths leering, paan-stained teeth, eyes as old as sin,
gesturing, beckoning with theatrically sexual movements
that would have been funny if they had not been so
pathetic, so small, so minutely ugly in such a big world.
One of them could have been her Menaka, she had
thought, and then had begun to weep, screaming at the
guest what a fat slob he was, pervert, white, fat, slob, sick.
She remembered nothing after that, and there were no
further incidents of that sort, Viren made sure of it. The
psychiatrists, the medication, the help she got made sure
she never embarrassed him again.

Until Naia came. His daughter. He forgot everything
then, when she came. He forgot all his pain, that he
claimed he had felt, that he hid so well she didn't believe
he had it. But he didn't have the imagination that she had.
He didn't see their baby raped by some street psychopath
at the age of three, four, five. He didn't see her dead in
every heap of garbage. He didn't see her alive everyday
either, as she did, cradled in her arms, smelling of talcum
powder and baby oil, her skin impossibly smooth, so she
had to keep touching her, stroking her cheeks, her hair. He
was silent, pain-free. Talking helped her. It removed her
from the pain, as though while she was talking, reality was
held away, as if it was just talk. And so she talked about it
to everyone. She talked out her soul. But it didn't go away,
the pain. There were short periods when she forgot. She
would be talking to someone—the gardener, the maid—and
suddenly it would come back, and she would realise it had
not been with her a few minutes. And she would feel relief
because she realised it could be gone. And then guilt, for

having forgotten. She had hoped for years that time would heal, the pain would fall away, but it always came back. The healing was not clean, it didn't just leave a scar. The wound went so deep that the scar tissue obscured the person she had been, could have been.

'Imagination,' she thought, 'that was the thing that took away my breath. I would rather see a body, know what happened to her than imagine it every hour, every day. There is nothing I have not imagined. Sometimes I thought, the truth cannot be as bad as what I have imagined, and I was right. But I have lived through all that as though it were true, each horror I imagined was true for me. I must wipe it all away, nobody will repay me for all the anguish I have lived, I must find myself and live, I must find myself. Always there is a higher power we can go to. Always. Someone up there. Father. Husband. Doctor. God. Not this time, this time I will be the higher power in my own life. I am Saroj, and this has been my life. My past made me what I am, I have been loved, wanted, beautiful once, and I will learn to love myself again.'

She had been walking steadily, thinking, talking aloud sometimes, sipping her water, wiping only the sweat that dripped in her eyes, but not the rest, it cooled her. She had to sit down, she had to take a rest. The man at the bottom of the hill had instructed the three parties starting out that they should rest ten minutes for every hour of walking. She had walked more than that. She found a smooth rock and sat on it. The relief was intense. Her legs shook, her back went limp. She let herself down full length so she was lying with her back curved against the stone, looking up at the sapphire sky. She took deep breaths of the empty air. She fell asleep. When she opened her eyes, all she saw was blue. She lay there for a while, staring up, examining herself internally as she did so. She ran a mental check within herself, feet, calves, knees. A little face appeared over hers, blocking the sky. She didn't move, still lying in the awkward-looking but very comfortable position, head back so the blood flowed and throbbed in her eyes, a pleasant massaging sensation. The child looked into her eyes with her own slanted almond ones. They were green like the hills around her, quiet, yet dancing, smiling.

'You are not sleeping,' the child voice said, but Saroj didn't see her lips move.

'No. I am awake. You have beautiful eyes, child,' she said, without moving her lips.

'That I do. They are grass eyes, today. I can have sky eyes, or water eyes, or fire eyes too. But today was a grass day. For you. I could have mud eyes, but those are hard to see through. The worms and pebbles get in the way.'

'My little girl had mud eyes,' Saroj said, and wished she could sit up and talk to the child face to face.

'Let me help you,' the child said, 'sit up, and we can talk face to face'.

Saroj felt herself sitting up, but couldn't remember having moved.

The child was a cloud of grass, not dressed at all, a naked cloud of green. 'Where is your mud-eye girl?' her voice sounded green to Saroj. She began to feel confused, and then decided to think about it later, and was not confused any more.

'I lost her, she went away. I looked for her everywhere, but she was gone.'

'Everywhere?'

'No, no one can look everywhere. But I looked in all the wrong places. And I was glad she was not in those places. I looked as far as I could look. But I did not find her.'

'You didn't look where you could find her?'

Saroj began to be annoyed by the voice now. 'I didn't know where she was,' she said, a little stiffly.

'Where did you first get her?'

'Get her? I gave birth to her!' she said, angry now, but trying not to be that way with a child.

'She was within you?'

'Yes.'

'Did you look for her within you, then?'

Saroj didn't say anything. She thought of her pregnancy. The gurgling, the kicks, the hiccupping movements of the child in her. The birth, so full of pain, yet so perfect, the only pain that she knew would end in something good. The milk coming down filling her up, the child sucking on her breast, kneading her breast with two little fists . . . 'She is not within me now,' she said to the green child, louder than she meant to. She seemed unable to recover the polite tone she had always had.

'She is, she is. Did you not find her just now? When you felt her move, come out of you, suck your milk?'

Saroj said nothing.

'Was she hurt, dead? Like you had thought?'

'No, she came back. I lost the baby, but she came back.' She began to cry, but did not feel tears, or her face move, but she was crying.

'Menaka lives in you. If you refuse her, she will die, be forgotten. You can let her live, let her go into the world,

let her find her way. And then you could hold her hand,
go with her, find your way too.'

'Yes,' Saroj said.

'I too must go now. Goodbye,' the green child said, and
touched Saroj's face with the side of her own. It was as if
she had been brushed with a cat's tail, a puff of steam.

Saroj felt her arm being shaken. She woke up with a
start, and found three men from the party in front of her
standing over her worriedly.

'Are you okay, madam? Some water?'

She sat up hurriedly, adjusting her dupatta, rubbing at
her eyes. 'I am fine,' she said, 'I just fell asleep, I was tired,
and very hot.' She gratefully took her canteen from the
man and gulped water, letting it flow out of her mouth
onto her neck and chest, wetting her shirt.

She looked around her. She was leaning against a wall
green with a light layer of moss. She was confused now, she
didn't remember seeing any structure when she had fallen
asleep. There was an intricately carved door standing open,
but only small enough for a child to go in, or an adult
kneeling. They all crawled through the door. It was like
crawling into a cave. They crawled downward on a gentle
slope, and then it leveled out. The shrine was a large space,
but with a low ceiling. It had been dug out below grade. It
was cool and dark inside. A lucid green light, like sunlight
filtered through deep jungle foliage, filled the space. At the
end of the room was a seated statue of the goddess. It was
wood, with deep, articulate carving that must have taken
time and devotion. And, Saroj thought, someone who had
seen the goddess herself. The gold-painted ornaments and
the emeralds in her ears and around her throat were the

only things not covered by the light moss that made the figure a living green. Her eyes seemed to be looking at all of them. They were grass eyes, sky eyes, water eyes, mud eyes.

As they all walked out of the shrine, one of the men said to her, 'I am happy we came to look for you. We found the shrine of the Green Goddess. You know, not everyone who looks for her finds her. Only those who she wants to find her, will. So thanks to you, we got Devi's blessings.'

Saroj smiled at all three of them. 'Blessings,' she said. 'And, I think I found a new life.'

They started the long trail down the mountain, and not one of them was tired or hot any more.

THIRTY

Samaad, against vociferous but reasoned objections from Jabra, decided that Leon and Karan would go with him to the weapons bazaar that would be open that week on the border. Jabra ranted on about the safety of the two men, that they would compromise the safety of the others, that there wasn't enough space, until he realised that there was no changing his big brother's mind. Once he was resigned to their tagging along, he became as friendly and helpful as if it had been his own idea from the start. Karan loved that about him, that he was simple and quite incapable of carrying the unnecessary baggage of grudges and suchlike.

Karan almost declined the offer to go, but Leon's excitement was catching. He was apprehensive at the

beginning of the drive, and afraid for the rest of it, but said
nothing, and watched everything. He and Leon rode with
Samaad in the Jonga. Two old US Army trucks that had
arrived the night before their departure followed them.
The convoy made its way north and east through small,
and, Karan was sure, unmapped mountain roads. They
squeezed through claustrophobia-inducing passes. The Jonga
went through easily, but the trucks slowed down to inch-an-
hour speed to make it through, sometimes scraping their
sides on the rock walls that reluctantly let them pass. That
explained the gouges on the metal bodies. Karan and Leon
had joked that someone had keyed them while they had
been parked at the Himalaya Walmart.

Hours passed, they went from waking to sleep so many
times that they lost track. The terrain took on a wild
severity that made them inexplicably melancholy. It was a
land abandoned by all but those who wished to hide from
the world. The colours had leeched away into the snow,
leaving only white and ashen mountain faces and dark
slopes of rock. The sapphire sky above them was the only
colour, and it, too, was darkening. The drivers took four-
hour shifts, and there were two to each vehicle. They slept
in the back of the trucks. Leon and Karan did too, at night,
rolling against each other with every turn, their bodies
loose and rattled into relaxation and deep dreamless quiet
sleep. There was no goal left, no purpose but the one right
before them. To be where they were.

In the early morning of the third straight day of driving
with only bladder or bowel relief breaks, they awoke because
they were no longer moving. Leon opened his eyes and
thought he was still asleep and in some black and white

dream. And then, as he lay there in the back of the truck, everything slowly began to take on gentle colour as the sun rose and illuminated the stark and lonely place they were in. Leon climbed out of the truck and looked about him. As far as he could see, there were tents, trucks, vehicles of all sizes, he even thought he could see tanks in the misty distance. He could see the movement of people who were beginning to wake, like himself. There was smoke in the air, from burned-down fires that must have been lit in the night. There were still stars in the sky. He squinted to catch the last of their fading light, fast being outshone by the rising sun. He could see that they were parked at a vantage point above a long valley. They must have been the last to arrive, there were no vehicles behind or above them.

'Well, what do you think?'

Samaad was standing beside him with two cups of tea. Leon gratefully took one and had a long pull from it before replying. The tea was, as always, delicious. It was quite different from the aromatic kahwa they had every morning. This was milky and not as sweet, and Leon wondered aloud where he had got it.

'There's a guy that comes to all these bazaars and sets up a tea shop. He has quite a bit of food too, and charges the earth for it. I suppose people who are here to buy Saqr missiles and RPGs aren't going to worry about the price of tea.'

Leon looked at him carefully. There was a tightness in his voice that he had not heard before. 'We have had our morning tea together forever, haven't we?' he asked Samaad.

'Yes, and I hope we continue to do so forever,' Samaad said, also sensing some unspoken anxiety in his friend. 'Come on, let's go see what we can get.'

They strolled down the hill together, Samaad in his
flowing tunic and pants, Leon in jeans and a hooded
Lakers fleece jacket. They got barely concealed stares from
men lounging against cars and trucks, smoking, talking in
low voices, secretively. Turbaned and bearded, most of
them, just as Leon had expected. They walked past the
parked vehicles down into the valley where the weapons
were. What Leon had thought were huge boulders turned
out on arrival to be five massive tents. There were armed
guards at the entrance of each, but other than staring at
the two of them, no one attempted to stop or search them.
They walked into the first tent and Leon was unable to
hold back his gasp.

There were heaps of guns, rifles, missiles. Ammunition
was piled on top of wooden crates indicating what was
inside them. The crates had Soviet, Chinese, American,
Indian markings on them. This was an international bazaar,
Leon thought. Samaad walked up to one of the heaps of
what looked like rifles. He began to talk to the man
squatting disinterestedly by them. After a few minutes, they
walked on. Samaad picked up a gun from the heap.

'AK47,' he said to Leon. 'This is the most popular and
easily available weapon in these parts.'

'I saw a lot of them in Yugoslavia too, or is it just similar
to something used there?'

'Of course you saw it. Kalashnikov. I don't know how
many have been manufactured, and how often it's been
modified by how many countries. They make some of this
lot out in a village south of Peshawar, from leftovers and
bits and pieces. They are very good.'

'How many are we getting?' Leon said, half serious, still

not completely comprehending that they were there for that very purpose—to buy weapons.

'Oh, I have a couple of hundred. Jabra knows the exact number, and he also knows where each one is. The hard part is the ammo. We have to load up on ammo for everything we have. It's not so hard to get the weapons. I can have those delivered in a pinch, for a small extra fee. But the ammo is heavy, and, it gets used up. In drills, practice, you know. And we need it. It will get used up, obviously, if it comes to that. So we come up whenever there is a bazaar of this sort, just to stock up on ammunition.'

Leon stared around him.

'How much do you need? How do you know how much you need? How much do you have already?'

Samaad laughed and put his arm around Leon's shoulders. 'I have enough. I will have enough so that if we are attacked, we will be able to hold out long enough for Jabra to get non-fighting people out. I will have to do something to protect the mines. I have to think of some way. Cut a deal with the other side, maybe.'

'What? Why would you do that? Which other side?' Leon asked, louder than he intended, and the guard outside the tent pushed the flap of the entrance open and looked in. Samaad waved at him and said something to reassure him.

'Yehudi, do you think these stones are for anyone else to have? They are for me and my people. They have been given to me for a purpose. I will not let anyone else get to those mines. They will control the very land that I want them to leave alone, they will turn it into a factory for their own profit, they will contract it out to the highest bidder from Europe or America . . . what then will be the point of having found those stones at all?'

'How did you find them?' Leon asked him.

'Shiva gave them to me,' Samaad said, smiling.

Now he could hear the constant sound of scattered gunfire, weapons being tested, reverberating and bouncing off the mountain walls that surrounded them. It was unnerving to Leon. He thought about being hit by a stray bullet, but that only added to the sensation of fear and apprehension that he so enjoyed.

They had strolled to the end of the tent, and finding a way out on that side, walked out and found themselves on the opposite end of the valley from their trucks. There was a small tent there, and Samaad explained that this one was where they sold non-working guns.

'Why would anyone want non-working guns? To repair and use?'

Samaad laughed. 'No, they buy these scrap weapons by the kilo, and take them in when militias are being disarmed. So they can collect money from the government for disarming, and keep their own weapons. The junk weapons get destroyed by public burning in the name of decommissioning. Ingenious and tragic. But, that's how it goes.'

Leon never ceased to be amazed by the education he received from Samaad.

'We should be getting back to Jabra and Karan, Yehudi, I should not have left him alone for so long. It has been an hour since we left. Hopefully they aren't still sleeping. I know Jabra will be counting boxes by now, but the drivers were dog-tired from the drive.' He started walking briskly

along the edge of the valley back to where they had parked.
Leon had taken out a small tourist camera and was taking
pictures when Samaad turned and looked back.

'What the hell are you doing?' he whispered urgently.

'What? I shouldn't shoot?'

'Shoot all you want, just get behind that rock where no
one will see you. They will shoot you if you are seen, and
it won't be with a silly camera. What is that thing? It
doesn't look very professional to me . . .'

Leon positioned himself so that to anyone looking it
would look like they were standing and talking. 'It's an old
Olympus XA camera. Film. It came out in the Eighties, and
I have had it since. Takes some pretty good pictures too.
Cute little bugger yeah?' he said, imitating Samaad's accent.
Samaad laughed and posed for Leon. It was a great shot,
Leon knew as soon as he took it. Samaad had looked into
the tiny lens, his face open, a smile crinkling his eyes, his
hair feathered in the mild late morning breeze, the valley
below and behind him full of trucks and tents and weapons
of war.

The way back was somehow shorter than the way there.
Karan said as much to Leon as they lay on crates in the
back of one of the trucks, looking out at the second truck
following too close behind them. He had been fascinated
by the experience. He had followed Jabra everywhere like a
silent shadow. He had seen Jabra expertly go through boxes
of material that he himself, other than recognising as
weapons and ammunition, didn't know anything about.
He saw Jabra negotiate, bully, argue, back down. He sat
quietly through it all, till the final handshake and exchange
of money for goods. Then men would come to their trucks

with wooden crates and load them up. This went on the whole day until late evening, when their trucks were completely filled up. Then everything was over, and bonfires were lit. Men circulated around, sharing and selling opium and hashish. Samaad bought what looked to Leon like a few kilos of hashish all neatly wrapped in goat skin. They sampled before he bought any, and it was all good. Samaad and Karan discussed the quality in excruciating detail, being quite stoned. Some was mellow and fresh and gave them a fine clear high, sparkling like champagne on a cool summer evening. Some was dark and musty, drawing them into its sultry depth, like a lover's sulk. The stuff they finally bought was what Samaad called an honest resin, straight and true, with a good body and taste, no frills, no pretence, just plain simple hashish that took them up and brought them down as smoothly as a jumbo jet in fine weather. It was predictable, and that was what Samaad said he looked for when he bought a large amount. Leon laughed at all this talk. 'It's not wine, you guys,' he said, laughing, 'or marriage. It's just hashish to me. High's a high.' And that had started a whole new conversation about wine, highs, relationships, jazz, and religion that, along with the joints that Karan rolled so expertly, helped the miles rattle by that much faster.

They got back to camp early in the evening, approaching from the north, slowly making their way down the final bit of road to the valley that lay below them. Leon realised he loved that sight. The glow of oil and kerosene lamps lighting the windows, the slow flicker of outdoor fires scattered almost artistically, hinting at the activity below. They were in the Jonga, the three of them, on that last part of the journey. He made Samaad stop for him to take pictures. The trucks went on ahead. Dinners were being cooked. The air coming up to them was smoky with the smell of charred meat and rotis. Back at camp, something had changed. Men were waiting for Samaad, and Leon noticed a new obsequious attitude in the militiamen that he had not seen even earlier that day. Jabra came out of Samaad's house as they approached it, and there was a terrible, visible tension in him. He was quivering, holding back his bunched muscles. He said something to Samaad that Leon didn't understand, but Karan's sharp intake of breath told him something was up. The men crowded outside Samaad's house as he went in. 'Come,' Samaad said to Leon and Karan when they hesitated outside. 'We all need to talk.'

THIRTY-ONE

'They are coming,' Karan said to Leon.

'Who? Who are coming?'

'I don't know who, but that's what Jabra said to Samaad. I don't know who, but I think we need to think about leaving here, Leon, it doesn't sound good.'

They sat by the door waiting for Samaad to finish his conversation with his men, and though Karan could understand some of it if they spoke very slowly, this was beyond him.

'We are not going anywhere, Karan. At least I am not.'

Karan stared at him in some amazement. 'Leon. There

may be armies coming in here. They could be ours, in which case we may survive, or they may be from the other side, in which case I don't think we have a chance. Why on earth would you want to hang about? Do you want to get killed?'

Leon thought about this for a few moments. 'I don't know, Karan, but I am not leaving Samaad here by himself. I have to stay with him.'

Karan took a deep breath. 'Are you stoned, man? Do you really want to die? I don't want anything to happen to him either, but look, I am not ready to die for him.'

'No? Are you sure?'

'Yes, I am sure. And what about Naia? Where the hell is she? I haven't seen her in hours. We need to get our shit together Leon, and we must get out of here.' There was a gathering panic in his voice, an urgency, and yet Leon could see that he was trying to keep it down, stay calm. His eyes were wide, pupils dilated with excitement. Leon wondered whether he had stopped to think about what he was saying, whether he even knew what he wanted.

'Yehudi!' Samaad called from the inner room as the men filed out, too silently, Leon thought. He pulled Karan to his feet and they went in. Samaad was sitting on his khaat. He patted it for Leon to sit beside him. Jabra got up to leave, making space for Karan. He bent down and Samaad stroked his head and kissed him. Leon had never seen the gesture before, but he knew it meant something. Jabra nodded at them and left the room, closing the door behind him.

'This has been a special time for me, meeting you, Yehudi. You too, Karan, I think we may have become friends, in another time and place, perhaps.' He paused and looked down, and Leon caught a glint in his eyes that he had never seen before. He said nothing, because he did not want to interrupt what was obviously hard for his friend to say.

'You must leave, Yehudi, and you too Karan. And take Naia with you. And Frank must leave too with you. You must leave immediately.' Leon started to interrupt him, then, but Samaad reached out and put his hand on his mouth as he had done before, up in the mountains, when Leon had first realised that Samaad could be the best friend he had ever had, the protector of his life. Or the one that took it away.

'I know what you are going to say, Yehudi, that you would not miss this for anything. But you cannot stay now. They are coming. I do not know which side it is. I can guess. But it will not be easy, and not many will be alive at the end. So you have to leave. I do not want you to be hurt, and I do not want to be worried about you. You will be a burden for me and my men. So it is time we have to say goodbye. You have to go now.' He looked up at Leon finally. There were tears in his eyes. He was afraid. The realisation made Leon shiver. Karan sat without saying a word, just looking at Samaad, thinking his thoughts as always, letting circumstance have its way with him. 'At least I don't do the worst thing I could do, like that other Karan,' he thought.

'I am not missing this for anything, Samaad,' Leon said, his voice a whisper, unwilling to leave his throat for fear of being heard. 'I'm not leaving,' he said, firmer this time, defiant.

Samaad laughed. 'Do you know what is going on here?' he asked, softly, but there was anger in his voice.

'I do,' Leon answered him.

'No, you don't. You don't know that I have been an informer to Viren for almost five years now. You don't know that he has been protecting me without knowing what I have been up to. You don't know what the sapphires are really worth. You don't know if someone has found out, informed Viren, or someone from the agency, and now they are coming down on us with all they have. Don't you see? They will kill us all to get to the mines, if they know. They have to, if they want to own them. And they have to own them. It is worth too much.'

Leon and Karan stared at him. 'My dad's informant? What does he need information for? He is a retired diplomat,' Karan said, but the doubt was in his face. 'Tell me,' he said, knowing, admitting that he knew nothing.

'I don't have time for this Karan,' Samaad said, 'but I'll tell you. Your dad is too clever to be retired. I met him when I sold him a spectacular carpet some years ago. He asked me if I would tell him things. Keep an eye. On the region, like, because he knew I travelled for my work, because I knew people and they trusted me. He knew that I wanted both countries to leave my land alone ... he knew I wasn't on the other side even if I wasn't on his. So I brought him news along with carpets. Information. Weapons bazaars, large population movements, plans that floated about in the communities, whispers of plans for attacks. I was valuable to him. I know I was. But then I was given a chance to do more, and I took it. And I had to keep that secret from him. Because he is not on the other side, but he is not on my side either. And now maybe they all know, and they will not let us be. Even if they don't know about the mines, and this is unlikely, they won't let this go, once they know about it. Maybe it was all the weapons we have been buying. But I think it has to be the mines.'

He put his head in his hands for a moment, tired. But only a moment, and then he was straight and tall again, eyes alight, lips set hard.

'But what does my father do?' Karan asked him again.

'He is in the secret service. He runs agents, about a hundred of us, I think, some just simple informants, some that have been embedded across the border. In Pakistan, in Afghanistan, even Russia. All related to Kashmir, though, that's his domain. And I know that he loses them occasionally, more and more these days, as they fall into the jihadi cells. They are not cells any more, you see, it is the way of life. I can't blame them, when you live amongst people, you lose touch with what you left behind. Anyway, Karan, you will see him soon enough, and then you can ask him yourself. But you must leave now. Jabra will take you down to the road, and then you're on your own.'

He stood up. So did Karan. Leon just sat there. It was as if he had not heard any of what had happened.

'Come, my friend, let's go get Naia and Frank, and then you can all get going. Yehudi! To your feet, sir.' He pulled at Leon's shirt. Leon didn't move. So he turned to Karan and said, 'You go get Naia, I will be out with him in ten minutes.' Karan nodded and left.

Samaad sat back down next to Leon. 'You must go,' he said again, softly, and there was no command in his tone at all.

'No, Samaad. I cannot go. This is what I am here for. For the good time, and it has been very good, and now for the bad. I will not go. You can drop me off at the end of the road. I will walk back. So you might as well just let me be, man. I will not go.''You are sure of this? There will be no one to take you out once the fighting has begun.'

'I am sure Samaad, I have never been so sure in my life. I know what it means. I will stay. So please just let me stay. Please let me just be with you. Through whatever happens. I have to see this through. I have to. Samaad? Okay?'

'Yes,' Samaad said.

Naia folded the pink shawl into a small square package and held it up to Samaad.

It had been an hour since Leon had come into her room without knocking, and had announced to her that she was leaving and he was not. She stood in the middle of the room that had been her home for a time. She looked out at the mountains through the small window. The size of that window had been of no importance. The view outside was so enormous and sweeping that a tiny pinhole would have been enough to look out of. She said nothing to Leon. In the time they had come to India, he had grown slowly into someone who took no orders from her. Or even suggestions. She traced it back directly to the day he had first laid eyes on Samaad. That man had taken Leon's hand and led him into something she did not share. She knew too that she had not wanted to share it. What little she had got from Samaad was enough for her. She had felt that severe attraction too, but she had never had the death wish that Leon carried with him. She thought he had left that part of him behind, but it had caught up with him again.

Because here he was, rooted to a spot that was about to blow up. She was filled with sadness and dread that she would never see him again, that she would be so utterly alone in the world. She wanted to drag him away from there, from those dark mountains, the fierce awesome beauty of Samaad's home, the magnetic passion in Samaad's eyes that had brought them both to this place, this place geographically and in time, at a crossroads where she had no choice but to turn away from her best friend and only family in the world. She knew she should have said something to Leon, but she didn't. She knew they would be only words, falling into the chasm between them, lost, meaningless, misunderstood. And they were too precious to her to waste, throw away. So she said nothing when he told her he was going to stay there with his beloved Samaad, to die if it came to that. He didn't actually say that. They promised to meet later, in Delhi, or in Los Angeles—'back home' he had said, but, she thought, this is his home, this is where his heart is. With Samaad and his sapphire eyes. And she hugged him for as long as she could, and she let him go.

Samaad came in then, and they were suddenly alone there in that space, with that window and that view the backdrop to what must surely be their final meeting, so fitting it could have been a movie. She held out the shawl to him, and he took it. He shook it so the folds fell away, and he wrapped it around her shoulders. She remembered and felt as she had when he was that close to her, but he had converted that intimate gesture into an impersonal one, as he had done to everything between them. As if he were merely a mirror for her feelings, with none of his own.

'I gave it to you, Naia, you keep it. May it keep you warm whenever you are cold.'

'Thank you Samaad, I will keep it always,' she said seriously. And then they both looked at each other and started laughing.

'Oh, life is so strange,' she said between fading giggles. 'Could you just have loved me, and then we could have had a normal life, marriage, with a house in Malibu canyon and children that I drove to school and soccer?'

He didn't say anything at all, and she thought that her words had fallen into that chasm, wasted.

'Yes, I suppose it could happen,' he said then, 'but not this time, Naia, not this time. I have another purpose this time. Be happy, Naia, I will think of you.'

'No, you won't,' she said. 'You never did, and you never will. But that's all right, Samaad. Could I ask you a favour before I go?'

'You can ask, I'll see what I can do.'

She considered him. She was going to have to waste these words, she thought. Just in case.

'Would you please send Leon back when you are finished with him? I really love him, and need him. For my life.' She was crying then, her body and soul had found out what only her mind had known till then. She was leaving Leon behind. She would probably never see him again. She turned away from Samaad and ran out of the room to Leon, where he stood by the Jonga with Karan and Jabra.

'Leon, Leon, please come back with us, please, don't stay here, please?' And she saw his eyes, the regret, the apology, and she knew she had wasted those words too. She hugged him again, and then got into the jeep. Karan hugged Leon too. They thumped each other on the back as men do. And Karan shook Samaad's hand and got in the front with Jabra. Frank walked out to the jeep and put a small bag carefully on the back seat. He shook Leon's hand, and then Samaad's, and to everyone's amazement, put his arms around Samaad.

'Ich danke Ihnen für mein Leben,' he said. Samaad only smiled. Frank got in the back seat, and Samaad signalled Jabra to leave. Leon turned away at once and went inside. It was Samaad who stood and watched the Jonga till he could see it no more.

THIRTY-TWO

There are no probables and improbables in fiction or in life, Leon thought. Anything can happen, and anything will happen. There is nothing holding back fate, or destiny, if there are such things, nothing to stop events from unfolding as they will. He lay on his bed listening to one of Samaad's jazz tapes. He hadn't seen cassette tapes in years, but he had got used to the old player and its scratchy and somehow authentic sound. He was delighted with all the music Samaad had. He wished he had known earlier. Samaad had a great depth of knowledge about classic jazz too, and was quite happy to share his views with Leon. They sat one night, listening to some combo playing jazz standards. Samaad had taped them as they played in a club in London. Leon fantasised that they were in the club, the sound of people talking on the tape made it easy.

'See, they have your attention now. The thing with it is that every solo must hold that attention. The trombone here will lose it for a moment, but be patient. He will draw you back in gently, and hold you quietly. You will fall into his velvet tones, you will wish it never ends . . .' He was right. Leon listened, entranced by the music. He was not surprised, but made a mental note that a Kashmiri in the Himalayas was teaching him to appreciate jazz. Samaad was concentrating hard on a file full of papers he had open on his lap, squinting slightly in the amber light of the old hurricane lamp between them. Leon opened his eyes when the joint he was holding out did not leave his hand for a whole minute. Samaad shook his head no when Leon offered it again, and Leon was curious. 'What is that you're reading?'

'Stuff, as you Americans say,' Samaad said.

'But what? What makes you say no to the world's finest hashish?'

'I'm going to get through this tonight, and I want to be able to remember it all tomorrow morning. Blasting and detonation. I want to get it right. I can trigger explosions remotely. By radio, I think. I don't know how it works, but I want to do it right so that it will work. So I am going over it once. That way, when we are working on it, I won't be seeing the terminology and parts for the first time. Saves time. We're going to have some help, but I still like to know what's going on.'

'Help? Who from?'

'From whom.'

'From whom, Samaad?'

'A guy I met a long time ago in Paris. I was out there

with some kilims, and I made this guy a really good deal. He said I should call him if I ever needed to blow up anything, so I did.'

'You have strange friends, Samaad,' Leon said, smiling.

Samaad just looked at him, and they both started laughing.

'Do you really think Indian forces are going to attack us?' Leon asked Samaad. The words left his mouth before he could stop them, and he regretted them, because the music became tinny, the mood fell away, reality opened the door and a cold wind brushed away the perfumed air that had held him in its gentleness.

'Yes, Yehudi, they are. I hope you believe me, because if your wish is to live through this, you will have to wish very hard. I will do my best to make your wish come true, but I may get busy with other things, and for that you will have to forgive me.'

He said all this smiling, and the heaviness in Leon's heart somehow vanished. He got his old feeling back. He remembered his reason for having stayed with Samaad, and he began to look forward to what was coming, better or worse. Impending danger always brought him to life, his senses awoke, he felt every nerve and muscle being, doing their job, living. Although his bowels rebelled and made him so very uncomfortable, he lived for this feeling. He lapped up every particle of life because the uncertainty of it loomed right there in front of his face. He sighed with pleasure and sucked on the roach held delicately between his fingers. Samaad shook his head and went back to his reading. Morning was not too far off, and he did want some sleep.

The Spaniard was due in the morning. He was to take a

flight to Srinagar where Jabra would meet him and drive
him up. Samaad wondered if he should ask Leon to go, just
in case. In case Jabra was already a target. He was sure Leon
was a target. Viren would have given them his description.
They would want him out of there for his own safety, but
that was probably secondary to the main reason—Leon had
more information than anyone else they could easily acquire
before operations commenced. He weighed the options.
Perhaps they didn't need any more information. In that
case Jabra was more valuable to them than Leon. He could
imagine the headlines—'Right-hand man and brother of
notorious and dreaded terrorist Samaad captured by RAW
agents in Srinagar'. He smiled to himself. The agency
wouldn't, of course, ever let it be known that Samaad
himself was an informer to a RAW agent. That would be
too complicated for the public to sort out, and would taint
the direct glory of his capture. He smiled some more.

'What?' Leon asked him.

'Nothing, really. I was thinking about how all this would
end.'

'I'm glad it made you smile, then,' Leon said, and closed
his eyes and went back to the music.

He slept well that night, Samaad sitting in the room
awake made him feel secure, like a child asleep in its
parents' bed, he supposed. He thought of his own mother
and shuddered. He could never dream of sleeping in her
room, with its smell of lavender, or was it lilac, he never
could tell the difference. When he awoke early the next
morning, he found himself covered with a soft old sheet
and a wool blanket, and he was so warm he didn't want to
lose the feeling that he was in a safe cocoon, so he closed

his eyes and held on to it a little longer. He fell asleep, and awoke an hour later to find Samaad by his side again, with tea for them both.

'Hmm. Good morning to you, Yehudi, you seem to have had a good sleep?'

'I have. The best. I have never slept so well in my life as I have in this room, Samaad, and I think it's because of you.'

'Me? It's not me, it's the mountain air. And the food. And the fact that you walk about so much that you are tired and ready to rest when you do. But, if you think it's me that makes you sleep well, then that's fine too.'

He sipped his tea and watched Leon rouse himself and arrange his blanket so that he had all of himself covered except for the hand that held the tea.

'What time do you wake up? Or don't you sleep at all?' he asked Samaad.

'Of course I sleep. I just wake up early. I have to bathe before I say my morning prayers. I say them before sunrise. So I am always awake before you, who says no prayers. Am I right?'

'Absolutely. I say no prayers. But I might begin to pray to you. You must be a God, to wake up, bathe, and talk to Allah all before the sun rises. Actually, you must be insane.'

Samaad laughed. 'I have a favour to ask you. You can refuse if you like.'

'For the man who brings me tea every morning, I refuse nothing. What is it?'

'I want you to go down to pick up the man who is coming to help us with the explosives. He is a Spaniard, and it will not look suspicious if two white men travel together. In case they are watching us. You go with Jabra, and be aware, they might be on the lookout for him. Will you go?'

Leon sat up. 'Now?'

'Not immediately, but very soon. You'll go?'

'Of course! Do I drive?'

'You decide. You'll have a nice drive there and back.'

'The Jonga?'

'Yes. The trucks are taking all the women and children and families back to the old villages, where they lived before I brought them here.' His face crumpled for a moment when he said that, and Leon, for the first time since he had met Samaad, saw defeat in his eyes. It moved him almost to tears, and some other, as yet unrecognised, feeling unsettled his breathing and made his eyes burn. He said nothing to his friend, though, and waited for him to continue speaking. But Samaad was silent, his head bent down, his eyes in shadow.

'Samaad, how are they all going to manage?'

'They have sapphires. Enough to see them through a few generations, if they are wise about it. And the men in the mines are still working the veins, very hard. They will get out as much as they can before . . .' he stopped there, and Leon did not ask him to complete the sentence. He knew Samaad could not. They would have to wait, both of them, and time would complete it for them.

The Spaniard was the only foreigner at the airport, other than Leon. He waved and smiled at him and Jabra when he saw the card with his name on it. He was younger than Leon had expected, and blonder and whiter too. He was from the north, Leon realised, and so not the dark-haired

Mediterranean type that he had expected to see. The security man was going through Machuca's bags, meticulously, removing every article and examining it carefully. They had driven through four checkpoints to get to the airport, and had been frisked twice before they had got to the passenger-receiving area. He was treated a little gentler than was Jabra, who was taken away at once for a body search. He said it was okay, when he came out smiling as usual, to Leon's immense relief. He had insisted on being the one to get Machuca, and would not listen to Samaad about sending someone else. The barbed wire around the airport buildings made it look like a war zone, both soldiers and policemen patrolling the walls, visible on the tops of buildings, armed with those same AK47-type weapons. Leon looked out of the windows as they waited. The sun was up, and everything outside was clear, the visibility high, every last tree stood out against the spotless blue, late-summer sky. So much beauty, Leon thought, was incongruous with the oppressive atmosphere in the airport. There was a man in black pants and a white shirt leaning against a wall and staring into space. His hair was a shiny black, the glint on it had drawn Leon's eyes in the first place. He was smoking. He seemed distracted and tired. Leon observed him for a moment. He supposed the man was waiting for someone to arrive. He had that air of endless waiting, of having sunk into his unchanging situation. Leon began to imagine who the man might be waiting for, when his own waiting came to an end.

Ion Machuca finally walked out with his bags, smiling ruefully, striding with the confidence of someone who has seen all this so often that he took it for granted. Leon had wondered aloud to Samaad if his being from the north of Spain meant that he was involved in ETA.

'Yes, of course, Yehudi,' Samaad had explained patiently, 'except that Machuca is not directly involved in anything. He gives practical support to them, specifically explosives. Remote detonation is his thing. That's what he's here for.'

They shook hands and walked out, Jabra carrying the bags and walking a little ahead of them, as if he were their driver, and they were tourists. They smiled a lot at each other and all the soldiers and police they passed. None of them smiled back, they just nodded grimly and waved them out. Once in the car, they had to stop and be searched twice on the way out of the airport, and Machuca had assured Leon that there was nothing on him to find. 'Samaad will provide all materials, I only show how,' he said.

They began the long drive back. It was really a camp, Leon thought, now that all the kids who ran around in the alleys between the houses had gone away, the women no longer hung around the stream gossiping and doing laundry. The little tent village at the mine was empty of families too, only a skeleton crew of men worked the mine, gathering up what they could of the precious blue. Jabra chatted a little in his sketchy English, but stopped when he got no more response than grunts from Leon. Machuca had tilted his head back and fallen into a deep sleep as soon as they got out of the city and onto the open road. Leon was tired too, nodding off but struggling to stay awake. They passed a small village that reminded him of how the camp used to look. They turned a steep corner, and he turned his head to take a better look at a brown dog running away among

the trees. There was a truck some distance behind them, a
common enough sight on those roads. On the straight after
the turn, a car swung out from behind the truck, and Leon,
still craning to find the dog, caught a glimpse of the driver.
It was the waiting man from the airport. He was sure of it.
He didn't say anything to the others, though it did occur
to him that it may be more than coincidence. There was
only one road going north, there were other trucks and
cars on the road, and on second thought, he was not
absolutely sure it was the same man. So he kept quiet, Jabra
drove on, Machuca slept on, and he kept turning and
trying to confirm that he had made a mistake, that no one
was following them. He was glad that Jabra was there. And
he began to nod off eventually.

Jabra suddenly pulled off the road onto a dirt track,
swerving hard, throwing them against the side of the Jonga.
The door handle dug hard into Leon's side, taking his
breath away. Machuca was awake, looking around him with
bright eyes, curious but unperturbed. Jabra manoeuvred
the car into a small gully behind a mound of rocks, and
stopped. He didn't turn off the engine, and said nothing.
They just sat there for a few minutes, waiting.

'Did you lose him?' Machuca asked him.

'Hmm, I think, yes,' Jabra said, looking in the direction
they had come from.

Leon said nothing. He just sat there holding his side,
trying to bring his breathing under control.

Machuca lit a cigarette from his pack of Gitanes. He
pulled the smoke in long and hard, and Leon saw a tremor
in his hand as he lowered it from his mouth. It was the
only sign of nerves that he had seen in the man, and Leon

didn't think he was aware of it. It seemed more physical
rather than from his state of mind. Leon longed for one of
the cigarettes. He had smoked them in Europe, filterless
and utterly satisfying. Even the way they sat between the
fingers, fat and yellow, was somehow reassuring. Machuca
must have felt his need, because he passed the one in his
hand to Leon for a drag, and Leon took it gratefully. He
coughed from the bottom of his lungs. It wasn't as gentle
as Karan's joints were. But it felt good.

'What now?' he asked.

'We wait for him to come here behind us, and he is
alone, so okay,' Machuca said, and then to Jabra, 'Okay?'

'Okay, we take him,' Jabra said, reaching under his seat.
He took out Samaad's handgun and put it under his kurta,
on his lap. Leon began to feel alarm at these developments.
He was beginning to lose control of the situation. Or, in
truth, he thought, he had never been in control.

'What can I do?' he asked, and his voice had become, to
himself, uncertain, reminding him of his miserable teenage
years. They both turned on him in unison, two guys who
had never met before this day. They spoke different words
with different accents, but they said the same thing. That
he should sit tight and do nothing. Let them handle it.

The car, a small Japanese or Korean one, came quite fast
around the small bend and into the gully. They saw him
before he saw them, and when he did, he braked and
stopped. He swung out of the car along with the opening
door, and the speed and fluidity of his movement terrified
Leon. Machuca pushed Leon down so he was crouching in
the space between the front and rear seats. Then he
opened the door on the passenger side and, crouching, half
stepped, and mostly fell out of the vehicle.

'You stay there,' he whispered loudly to Leon. The engine was still running. They wouldn't hear the man's approach, but neither would he hear them. Leon suddenly realised that Jabra was not in the vehicle. He was confused, he didn't remember seeing him leave. And then, if things had not been going fast enough, they speeded up even more. The man's face appeared right above Leon's, disappeared, and was replaced by a gun pointing at him. Then that disappeared and Machuca's face appeared instead. Then Jabra opened the door from the driver's side, and slid through and around the car. Leon could now see him standing tall with his back to the car, his shirt billowing slightly, pointing his gun at the ground, where presumably Machuca had pinned the man.

Leon got up and got on the seat. He opened the door on the opposite side and got out. He walked slowly around to the men. Jabra had not moved. Machuca had the man's gun. The man just lay there doing nothing, saying nothing. There was a smear of blood on his forehead, his eye was beginning to swell and look purple, like a smashed aubergine.

'Get string,' Jabra said to Leon, without looking at him.

'String?' Leon was unable to think straight.

'Rope!' Machuca said.

Leon got the neon green nylon rope that he had shared the back seat with. Jabra had bought it on the way in. He had said it was a clothesline. Lucky they had needed a clothesline, Leon thought.

He helped tie the man and sit him up in the back. Leon didn't like the idea of having him beside him all the way back. Machuca then went to the man's car and drove it further down the gully, so it would be harder to find.

Then they all got back into the Jonga and Jabra drove them on. Machuca was in the back seat with their captive. He promptly fell asleep.

None of them spoke to the man, and he didn't speak to them. Leon was unbearably curious, but something stopped him from asking any questions. Machuca and Jabra seemed to know the man, or at least knew what he was there for. He would wait till they got back to camp. Samaad would answer whatever questions he had, he was sure of it. He turned and looked at the man in the back seat. He was asleep too, moaning occasionally. He looked contorted and uncomfortable with his hands and feet tied up in the insistently green rope. Leon turned back and there was a green afterimage of the rope pattern on his retina. He glanced at Jabra. There was no expression on his usually cheerful face. He just stared ahead to where the sky met the road. Leon had a thought that the man they had captured was in trouble. Then he dismissed the thought as irrational and spoke to Jabra. His own voice startled him again.

'How long? To camp?'

'Four-and-a-half, five hours. You take rest,' Jabra said.

Leon folded his Lakers sweatshirt into a pillow, held it against the side of the car and rested his head on it. He closed his eyes and was asleep before he had completed his thought, of how he couldn't possibly sleep in those circumstances. He had used up all his reserve, and his body snatched the opportunity to build it back up.

THIRTY-THREE

The summer sun rose urgently and began to beat heat down on the city. Sweat-basted, people roasted in the glare, forgetting the cold days of winter when they had actually longed for heat. A collective lethargy lay like a weight holding everyone down. The power had gone off in most areas, gone off or had been turned off by the power company to save electricity. Load-shedding. There was no relief from the oppressive humidity then, no air conditioning, not even fans. Everyone drank very hot tea, strangely satisfying perhaps because the weather, in comparison, seemed illusively cooler.

Karan sat in his chair fanning himself with a copy of *India Today*, making the new American President's serious, intelligent face flap back and forth. He stared at his mother as she listened to his father lecturing her about her irresponsible actions. He was in a stupor from the heat and confusion of his parents' role reversal. He glanced at Naia laying on the tiles of the floor between two rugs, trying not to move except when she had sucked the coolness out of the spot she lay on, and she had to slide to the next one.

He looked again at his mother. She reminded him of someone, he thought. He gave up trying to figure it out and had another sip of his tea, slurping off the surface to avoid scalding his tongue.

'Can't we have kahwa?' he asked, wishing for the Kashmiri tea that Jabra would send over to him many times each day. He had loved, and then grown accustomed to, its fragrance. It went very well with the joints.

His mother stopped listening to his father and turned to him. 'I don't remember how to make it,' she said, 'but I am sure someone in the staff can find out. I'll get you some.'

The interruption seemed to have ended Viren's tirade. He said to Karan, 'I haven't said this to you, but I am very relieved that you are back. I am glad Samaad did not hold you hostage there.'

Naia sat up. 'Hostage? Why would he do that? He insisted that we leave. He said something was up, and he didn't want us to be in any danger.'

Viren looked puzzled for a moment. 'Really? He asked you to leave? Good, good. Did he say anything else to you two? Did he seem . . . upset?'

'Dad, he didn't send any message for you. He is ready to die for what he wants and what he believes in. And I am aware of what you do and your connection with him. It's time you told us all that.'

Saroj looked around at all of them. 'What does it matter?' she said softly. 'He has to do what he does. That has been his job all his life.'

Viren looked at her speechless, as if he was seeing his wife for the first time. And it came to Karan whom she reminded him of. It was herself, but many years before, miseries ago. She seemed to have shed years and lines and had no tightness around her mouth as she spoke. She was serene, a person who had accepted life. Sad, but serene.

'What about Leon? Why did he not return with you?' Viren asked.

Karan was getting very drowsy, and the conversation was branching away from him and he could not stay with it. He yawned and stood up. 'I am going to take a nap,' he announced. 'I have had no sleep for a while, and I cannot tell one person from another. Will you wake me in a couple of hours?' he asked his mother.

'I will,' Viren said, 'I have to go meet someone at lunch, I will wake you then. This is all getting very tense, Karan. I will tell you news of your friends when I return.'

'What do you mean? What's going on? I thought they were being attacked from the north, by the Pakistani secret service. That's what he led me to believe. Is that not true?'

'No, Karan, it's not true. He is on our side of the LoC, this does not concern them. It is our men who are going to try and secure the area.'

Karan wasn't sleepy any more. 'What do you mean secure the area? It is secure. It is just a village, Dad, with families living there. Little kids, families. That's all.'

Naia stared at him, surprised by this response.

'What about the guns?' his father asked him quietly.

Karan sighed, and was quiet a moment. Then he spoke again, louder this time. 'The guns? It's a dangerous area, Dad, people keep coming down from the north and threatening these guys. They have to have guns to protect themselves. The Indian army sure wasn't there to do that, at least when I was there.'

'They don't need that many weapons. Not the amount they have been amassing. And where is the money coming from, son? To buy all this stuff? Did you see anything? That would explain it? Were there people from the north there at all? Did Samaad go out to meet anyone?'

Karan said nothing, just shook his head.

Viren said gently. 'Don't worry, everything will be over in a week, we will secure the area, and we will have Samaad in custody. No one is going to be hurt unless they resist.'

'Resist? Of course he will resist—why would he not resist?'

'Because he values his life, and the life of his people?'
Viren regretted his tone, but couldn't take it back. His
children had had strange times while they had been gone,
and he should be gentle with them. He knew Samaad. He
cared about him, wanted nothing bad to happen to him.
He supposed Naia and Karan felt the same way. He
wondered how Naia was really taking all this. He glanced
at her, sitting on the floor with her arms wrapped around
her knees, almost foetal. She was looking back at him, and
there was an aloof curiosity, he thought, in her eyes, but
nothing that alarmed him about her state of mind. Then
he looked at his son, and found him looking back too.
Karan's face was more intense, lines of strain and tiredness
only deepened his beauty, gave it a lean edge that Viren
had never seen. He had little twitches around the mouth
that he seemed unaware of.

'I am going to lie down for a while, wake me if I fall
asleep,' Karan said again, and walked out of the room,
patting Naia's head as he passed her. He hoped she would
say nothing to their father about sapphires, about mines. It
didn't matter anymore anyway. It was all over, finished.

He went to his room and dropped like a full sack onto
his bed. The heavy damask bed cover felt hot and suffocating
even through his shirt. He pushed and pulled and got it off
the bed from under him without getting up. It fell softly,
heavily off the bed and lay in a heap on the floor. He
watched it lying there, the soft purple folds piled up like a
creature asleep. The heat was palpable. He began to feel
sticky from the sweat. He thought about Jabra, his round,
cheerful face smiling and waving at them as he drove away

from them. He thought about the time they had been at
the weapons bazaar up north. Samaad and Leon were
scouting together and he hadn't really wanted to hang
around with them, with their coded conversations and
obvious feelings for each other. There was no place for a
third person in that space. They seemed to feed off each
other. They had developed a language between them that
was sometimes difficult for him to understand. He had
enjoyed the days with the two of them, but had tired of it,
had preferred to stay away. He had also been physically very
tired, and laziness had made him stay with the trucks
rather than walk around the camp looking at ammunition.
He was glad he had stayed with Jabra. They had talked, in
two languages, which they balanced out between them into
very good communication. Karan had found that Jabra was
not the loutish oafish personality he seemed to project
around his sharper, more angular, more educated, more
refined, more obviously beautiful brother. Jabra had the
same quick mind, but he was just more self-effacing,
diffident. And he did trust Samaad implicitly with their
lives. He was colourful, had had experiences that Karan
dug out of him like gemstones from bedrock to start with,
but when he got him going, he was unstoppable. He was
also very funny. Karan found himself laughing out loud at
Jabra's way of looking at things, his quirky opinions, his
remarks about passers-by that came thick and fast when he
realised he had a one-man fan club. He thought of them
laughing between the crates of ammunition that were
being loaded onto their truck that day. He thought of Jabra
as a man who laughed a lot, ate a lot, and said his prayers
five times each day. And who made good tea.

'Good luck, Karan bhai,' he had said before leaving, and had given Karan a hug that had surprised him and brought unexpected tears to his eyes.

Karan was almost asleep in the heat haze when the fan started to spin. He sighed with the relief of having the heat swept away from the room. The hum of the air conditioner sent him into a deep sleep.

He dreamt he was Karan on the battlefield at Kurukshetra struggling to free his chariot wheel from the mud and slush and the blood and bones of dead warriors that held it fast, Arjun bearing down, taking aim with his magnificent bow, no mercy, no quarter in his eyes. Karan's life flashed before his own eyes, as it must before it is gone forever. Jabra, Samaad, Leon, little children, brown dogs, mountains, sapphires, all came and went, and there was a story there, and there was an ending, but he did not know it yet, and he had to find out what it was. He had to make choices, not go where he was sent, not follow where he was led. Arjun's arrow came flying towards him, he saw Samaad, Arjun's charioteer, with his hot blue eyes. That arrow would surely find its mark in his heart. He never knew nor ever would know who he was, or why he was. And he left Karan to his inevitable life and death. That was not his life or death, he did not have to be there. He was not that Karan.

THIRTY-FOUR

'Sir. You have to stay here with the truck. We cannot leave a guard for you, but you cannot come any further.' The young jawan gave him the radio and began to explain to him how to use it. It was simple enough, and he said again and again that Karan should drive away if they told him to.

'I will, don't worry,' Karan lied again, as he had been doing to everyone since this whole thing began, starting with his father.

'Karan. This is a covert operation. You have to promise to stay where the command tells you, and with whom they tell you. If you promise me that, this can go further.'

'I promise,' Karan had replied to his father. 'What time do I have to be there?'

'The first trucks are leaving now, you take a flight to a small airfield close to your camp, I do not know where, they won't tell me. The only reason they are taking you is because I made some calls and some calls were made to them. They are not happy about this, so you had better toe their line. Are you rethinking this?'

'No, Dad, I am not. I should not have left them in the first place.'

Viren had put his arm around his son's shoulders and pulled him close. 'I am glad you did, this way you will be safe. They won't let you go back to the camp. You will be close but away from any actual action. I feel better about it.'

'Is Mom okay?'

Viren had smiled. 'She is fine. I mean she is really fine. I mean she is more fine than I am. She said I should let you go if that was what you really wanted. I don't know what devi she has been possessed by, but it is miraculous.'

It was pretty amazing, at least, if not miraculous, the transformation in his mother. His father said she had been on a long trek to a temple of a certain goddess in the mountains. She had left soon after Karan had, and had been gone for days. This goddess, apparently, was reputed for her ability to cure insanity. People did this sort of pilgrimage all the time, to the many temples in the northern ranges. But still, Karan found it strange, and too simplistic, if not fantastical an explanation, not only that his mother had done such a thing, but also that she was suddenly 'cured'. And his father's relief when his mother walked in a few minutes after they did, was peculiar, to say the least. He did not say much, but took her into their bedroom at once. When they came back out, she was as calm as she had been going in, and his father was quiet, but seemed puzzled. He kept glancing at his wife.

His mother was almost as she used to be when he was a little boy, before Naia was born, before she was lost. He remembered her then—not confident or emancipated, but happy. Shy, yes, but not nervous, not the neurotic mess of a woman that he had known for most of his life. Almost as she used to be, he thought. Because she was different, she was strong now, she was bright-eyed. She seemed to have somehow found her feet. He was happy for her. He hoped it was not some temporary cure that would be gone with the next episode. He didn't think it was, judging from her reaction to his departure. She didn't seem driven anymore by the loss of that child a million years ago. She was unhappy that he was going back to those dreaded mountains, she asked him not to go. But she didn't become hysterical. She didn't go off the deep end and lose all perspective. She talked, she listened, she accepted his decision, she hugged him goodbye, she told him to be careful and come back safe. Not like someone who was afraid for herself, for her own feelings, but for him, for his safety. Like a mother. All mothers.

It was Naia who tried to tell him not to go back. He didn't really understand her. She seemed to love Leon, she seemed to care. But she also seemed able to disconnect from it all, to withdraw into herself, to live normally without tears, without the outpouring of emotion that his mother was prone to. He couldn't tell whether she even felt anything after the emotion of the moment. In that they were different, his mother and his sister. One felt deeply and forever. The other, he thought, perhaps uncharitably, felt it on the surface and then it slid off her like a shawl when the day grew warm. He had hugged her goodbye and whispered in her ear, 'Don't tell anyone anything more than they already know, Naia. Don't give them the blues.' He hoped she had understood, and if she had, that she would do as he asked.

The twenty or so jawans jumped out of the back of the truck, one by one, like wind-up toys. They filed off behind their leader down the hill, never looking back at Karan, alone there by the truck. The sound of their boots fading and the light of day disappearing with the sunset made him feel like he was losing his senses. He had a plan, and that exhilarated him. It was a new and wonderful feeling, to have a plan. He laughed at himself and his own childishness, but he was unable to shake off the delight that filled him to brimming over. He was alone, he had a truck, he had a plan. He got back in the truck and lay on the front seat, thinking he would at least rest, if not sleep.

Leon followed Machuca and Samaad and six of the biggest men from the camp around and around the hillside.

He watched as they dug deep holes, put in explosives and some kind of remote device in each hole. He had watched Machuca all that day gaze at the mines, make notes in a large red book that was being carried for him, along with his water, by one of the older boys who had stayed behind. Machuca took measurements, consulted with Samaad, walked around tirelessly.

'Why are you doing this?' Leon asked Samaad, when he realised that Machuca was not going to ask. It was not so much a question as a whine. He knew it as soon as the words left his mouth. Samaad just smiled and patted him on the back. As you would a moron child, Leon thought, and he felt he deserved it. The mines would have to be blown up if they lost control of them. There was no other choice for Samaad. He could not let them fall into the hands of either government. Samaad had explained this to him, but the truth had not sunk in as it did now—actually being there, seeing the mines again. He shot a few pictures. Machuca shot him a warning look, and Leon nodded at him. He had kept to his word that Machuca would not be in any of them, or if he was, he would not be recognisable. He wondered why Machuca believed him. It had occurred to him that Machuca did not expect him to live through what was coming, but he dismissed that thought before it came up too far in his consciousness.

'He will find me and kill me later,' he told Samaad, thinking of Machuca's speed and strength. He had tackled the man from the airport easily, effortlessly, even though he was twice Machuca's weight and much taller, even though he was very fast and obviously well trained. And what frightened Leon about Machuca was his apparent lack

of reaction, of nerves. All he did at the end of that episode
was to fall asleep. And again, when they had come back to
the village. And Samaad and Leon had watched as the man
had tried to disarm Jabra. He had been brought into one
of the houses, empty now that everyone was gone. Jabra
stood at the door, gun in hand, and Machuca stood
smoking inside, next to a guard. The man, his hands and
feet untied, suddenly jumped Jabra, and actually had the
gun in his hand when Machuca, in moves that Leon could
not reconstruct in his head after the incident, dropped his
cigarette, snatched the Kalashnikov from the guard, shot
the man once in the leg, sending him screaming to the
ground, and then, minutes after the situation was settled,
was asleep on the nearest khaat, everyone still milling about
him. No, Leon thought, he would not break his word to
Ion Machuca. He was not afraid of him, he just admired
him. No, he thought, changing his mind, he was afraid of
him. He was glad he was on their side. Or at least was
being paid by their side.

That night, as they sat in the tent in the valley below the
mines, Machuca explained the layout of the explosives to
Samaad. He assured him that it was as Samaad wanted.

'There will be nothing left to mine if you chose to
detonate the devices. There will be nothing and nobody
left alive in a kilometre radius, Nada.' He was smiling.
Leon watched as Samaad shook his hand and gave him a
familiar black pouch. Machuca shook some of the stones
out of the bag onto his palm. Leon saw his eyes light up.
The stones threw little blue sparks on his face as he
brought his hand closer to look at them.

'I am helping you to finish off this?' he said to Samaad,

and Leon thought he looked sad. But then he smiled, and
then put them away. 'They will be worth more if I wait a
couple of years, no?' he said, and Leon knew he was wrong.
Machuca was not the type to look sad. Or feel sad. Or
anything else. When Leon awoke the next morning to the
smell of kahwa, Ion Machuca was gone, and Leon knew he
would never see him again.

Leon crouched in the corner of the room, his camera
bag in front of him, like a dam between him and the world.
The man from the airport sat on one end of a khaat on the
opposite side of the room. Leon shot off a few frames of
him. The man stared directly into the lens, directly into
Leon's eye. His straight black hair fell across one eye, a
swatch of heavy silk. The eye that looked at Leon was pale,
almost colourless, like rainwater in a ditch, framed by dark
smudgy lashes. There was an arrogance in his face that
reminded Leon of Samaad. He put the camera down when
Samaad walked in. Jabra, sitting on the other end of the
khaat from the man, leaning against the wall half asleep,
sat up straighter. Leon did not see anything pass between
the brothers, no signal, no word spoken. But Jabra stood
up, went up to the man, and hit him full in the face with
his open hand. The man's head snapped back, and a whuff
of breath left him. And nothing else. Leon, who had not
taken his eyes off him, saw nothing change in the face. A
welt began to rise on his left side. He didn't say a word.
Neither did anyone else. The sound of the slap hung in the
air, and Samaad let it. He seemed to know what he was
doing. He had that look on him. Leon had seen it before.
There was concentration, but no discernable emotion.
Unless determination was an emotion. Leon picked up his
camera again, a reflex action.

'Who? Who am I dealing with?' Samaad said, after a full five minutes.

The man just shook his head, no. Leon saw him brace, shrink back almost imperceptibly, his lens framing everything else out.

Jabra's hand whipped into the frame and out, the man's hair moved, revealing his other eye, jammed shut, and then came down heavily again, like a crow's wing. Leon was fascinated by the hair. He focused on it and became centred on it, seeing and hearing everything outside his frame only physically. His kept shooting, he wanted neither to engage in the moment, nor lose it forever.

'I can't tell you that. If you want to talk, I can make you a deal.'

Leon was confused. He heard Samaad's distinct English accent, but not Samaad's voice. It was the man speaking.

'I am Waseem,' he said. 'You want to talk?'

Leon kept the camera up to his face, and, in extreme close-up, watched the skin puff and turn purple around the already bruised eye. Jabra had added to his own handiwork, or Ion Machuca's. The pinks and blues ran together around the cheek and jaw of the man's face. Leon had narrowed his vision and focus on the man's face. He could not, did not want to, see Samaad's face, or Jabra's. He wondered fleetingly why Samaad let him stay in the room, why he let him continue taking pictures of what was going on. He didn't dwell on it. He was too busy recording the moment.

Samaad sat down next to Waseem now, they began to talk as if nothing had happened between them, as if they had just been introduced. They both had the calm, quiet speech of men in a gentlemen's club.

Leon was fascinated.

'You will have to tell me whom you are representing.'

'No. I cannot tell you that. But if you listen to what I have to say without that bloody ox hitting me, you may not need to know whom I speak for.'

Samaad considered him. He made a sign to Jabra to move back. He looked at Leon and shook his head, telling him not to shoot any more.

'Alright, I will listen to you.'

Waseem smiled. It obviously hurt him to do so—the smile became a wince before he even completed it.

'Can I have a fag, please?' He said to Samaad. Samaad nodded at Jabra.

Jabra left the room to find some cigarettes.

'You know, I knew he would bring me to you. That's why I followed him. We didn't know any other way to get to you Samaad bhai.'

'How did you know they would be at the airport?'

Waseem smiled again, broadly this time, but again, this time too, the smile was short-lived.

'Gabriel Hallam. He is the only one who has enough money to spread his people everywhere. They don't depend on khabris. They have enough resources to employ and train their own people. Once we got in touch with him, it was no trouble tracking everyone and everything ... You holding his German lad?'

Samaad said nothing. He just looked at Waseem, waiting.

'We want to offer you a deal. A simple deal. You keep everything you have here, you stay, you run your mines. All we want is assurance that you will sell only to us.'

Leon looked at Samaad. He was filled with hope by this

offer. It seemed to him to be perfect, everything that Samaad wanted really. A measure of relief began to form around his edginess. He became aware of how nervous he had been as the nervousness began to dissipate. His belly was still clenched, still hurt, but he had removed it from his immediate consciousness.

'What do you think I am doing here?' Samaad asked Waseem, quietly, almost whispering.

'I don't know, I don't care. We don't care. Samaad bhai, I need to do this quickly, I need to contact my people and tell them if you agree to this. I need to go soon, the sooner the better.'

'Yes, I know, I know we are short on time. I know that the BSF has already come up to the southern pass.'

Waseem held up his hands, still bound by the green rope that Machuca and Jabra had tied on him. Samaad reached under his kurta and brought out a small knife. He cut the ropes. They fell on the packed earth floor. Waseem rubbed his wrists. Leon noticed his hands, long fingers, smooth oval milky fingernails.

'So. What is it to be. You need to move on this, Samaad bhai, you have very little time.' There was a high note of urgency in his voice.

'What do I get?' Samaad said.

'Protection. The freedom to do what you please. No one will come around here, we are willing to guarantee that. We won't even bargain about the price. All you have to do is give me your word that you will not sell to anyone else. Just your word. That is all I need from you right now.'

'I need to know who you are,' Samaad said.

'No, I cannot tell you that. You will eventually know

with whom you are dealing. But not now, I cannot tell you that now.'

'Then we cannot have a deal,' Samaad said. And stood up.

Waseem stared at him, taken aback by this answer. He seemed shaken for the first time since Leon had seen him at the airport.

'Samaad bhai, you are in a bad position right now. You have maybe two days. The Indian army is snapping at your heels. You have no choice but to deal with me.'

The little relief that Leon had felt began to fade as rapidly as it had come.

'Why won't you take his offer, Samaad?' he blurted before he could stop himself.

Samaad turned only slightly toward him.

'You, Yehudi, have understood nothing.' He walked to the small barred window and looked out of it at the mountains. 'I cannot deal with them. I do not know who they are.'

He turned to look at Waseem.

'If you are from the north, I will be selling you my soul. If you are from the south, I will only be postponing what is going to happen now. If you are a private party, you need to tell me, I will deal with you.'

'I cannot tell you, Samaad bhai. You will have to take my word that we will protect you from all sides. It will be in our interest to do so.'

Samaad shook his head. There was a silence. Waseem stood up and walked over to Samaad, facing him and looking directly into his eyes.

'If I tell you who we are, how will that help you? What

do you want after all? To be left alone? To live here, mine the sapphire, sell it, buy arms, have enough money to last you forever? Travel as you please? You will be the warlord, chieftain, of this place, you will have the power to do whatever you please.'

Waseem paused dramatically, theatrically, but it was a necessary pause, nicely done, and gave Samaad time to formulate an answer. The camera moved now to Samaad's face, watching him, waiting for his thought processes to end, for the words to come out. Leon recognised that he was beginning to lose touch with reality, he was beginning to leave the situation he was in, the huge joint he had smoked was causing him to hallucinate. He was beginning to disconnect from the immediate and therefore, if that was possible, see more clearly.

He saw Waseem and Samaad standing close to each other, almost touching. He saw Samaad hold up his palm and close his eyes, telling Waseem to wait while he completed his thought. He heard the door open and turned his head away from the two men to see Jabra enter the room. He saw the expression on Jabra's face change rapidly, something about the narrowing of the eyes began to make sense to Leon, he foresaw what would happen next even as it unfolded. Jabra reached under his shirt, and then fired a single shot at Waseem. Waseem looked directly at Leon, confused, and Leon saw the ditchwater eyes turn muddy as he crumpled to the dirt floor.

Karan jerked awake almost exactly an hour after he had closed his eyes, surprised at himself for having fallen so completely asleep. He uncovered the truck that the jawans had camouflaged so carefully that it was invisible unless you

were up against it. Then he took a look around and made
sure as best he could that they were not close, and started
it up. He hoped that he would find his way back. He had
a good idea where he was. He also hoped that when he got
there, they would recognise him before they shot him.

He steered the truck carefully around the base of the
mountain. The spurs were getting closer together, and the
road was nothing but a series of hairpin bends. It was
getting to be less road and more dirt track. He began to
think that he was lost. Either that, or driving on this road
was so much harder than being a passenger, that it was
making everything seem unfamiliar. Or it could be the time
of day that was making it look different. The sun had set,
and it was getting very dark, he had to go so slow that he
was making hardly any progress. At one point he stopped
the truck and turned the headlamps off. An eerie blue light
caught the edges of the mountains. They glowed. He felt as
if he was underwater. Or inside a sapphire, he thought
fancifully, and then laughed aloud, startling himself. It
should be two hours to the camp, he had already been
driving for about ninety minutes. On the other hand,
going was slow, so it could be longer. He began to feel
tired, and wondered if there was any water or food in the
back. He thought of Jabra and decided he would drive a
little longer.

'I am coming, Jabs, hang on,' he said aloud, and it felt
so good that he said it again, louder, and again, yelling as
loud as he could, driving away his fear and anxiety by the
sheer volume of his voice in his head.

'Jabra, I am coming!'

And then, when he was quiet, the tendril of thought
came back. Did Jabra even want him to come?

'He must, he must,' Karan said, talking to himself again, reassuring himself that his feelings were not his alone, that Jabra would be happy to see him again. And so would Leon, and perhaps even Samaad. He strained to see the road and drove on between the rocks and into the gloom.

He sang to himself to make the miles go by faster. He had never been so alone before. He felt like the whole world was empty but for him and his truck rattling along from nowhere to nowhere. He saw a shadowy movement on the edge of the mountain and squeezed his eyes to make it out better. It seemed to be an animal, large, just standing there, its head turned to the sky. It could have been a goat or a wolf, he couldn't tell. But he didn't feel so lonely anymore, and he drove more easily after that.

An hour later, he was close to the village. He could feel it, he knew for sure now that he was not lost. He knew those familiar outcrops of rock, he could even see a distant amber glow of lamplight when he turned down his headlamps. He would have to be careful from then on, Samaad might have snipers in the rocks, and they might not wait to see who it was. Plus, he was in an army truck. They had no reason to hold their fire. He wondered what to do. Finally, as he approached the last bottleneck in the mountains that would open into Samaad's valley. He turned the light on in the cab so his face would be visible, and drove very slowly into the narrow opening. He was sweating and shaking, but he was afraid to stop. He heard nothing but the sound of his engine and the wind going through the front windows and out the back of the truck. He slowed even more, and then more, so he was almost at walking pace. Still there was no sound of gunshots or voices. He couldn't quite believe he was in, parking at the point where the truck couldn't go any further. He was about to get out when four men with their weapons pointing at him came silently out of the shadows.

'Karan bhai?' one of them said, amazed.

'Yes, it's me. Can you tell Jabra I am here?'

The man signalled the others to put away their weapons. There was a sound from the truck then, crackling and a man's voice, 'Karan sir, come in sir.' The weapons came back up in a flash and the men ran swiftly to the truck and began to search it. One of them stayed with Karan, gun on him again. 'It's the radio,' he said, but they didn't pay any attention.

Finally satisfied that there was no one there, they pushed him roughly toward Samaad's house.

'What the hell are you doing back here?' Leon and Samaad were there, eating their dinner, staring at him like he was a ghost.

The men still stood at the door, waiting for instructions from Samaad. The radio crackled up again, 'Karan sir, come in.'

'What is that? Who is it?' Samaad said.

'I came in with the army. They told me to stay put. I ran off with their truck.' Karan said, and began to laugh, Samaad, Leon, and the four men looking at him in consternation. They joined him when he wouldn't stop. Finally, Samaad got up and came to him. He drew him down to sit and poured him some tea from the flask by his side.

'Here, drink this. Have you been driving long?'

Karan drank. 'Very long. Hours. I thought I was lost,' he said, and then put his head in his hands.

Samaad asked the men to leave, and to send word for
Jabra to come.

'Where is he?' Karan asked.

'On the north side, patrolling that pass. He will be here
in five minutes.'

The radio began to pop again, and Samaad reached for
it. Karan got to it first.

'I had better answer that.'

And then they both looked at each other and smiled.

'Karan here, come in,' he said into the radio. The smile
on his face was wicked.

'We're going to be in touch with one of the units, we'll
know exactly where they are and what they are up to. They
won't be here for ages, because I drove, and it took me four
hours—they will take twice as long on foot, right?'

'Wrong,' Samaad said. 'They will come straight up the
pass, they don't have to hairpin around the mountains.
That's why they left the truck where they did. And there is
a shorter way even by road, but they don't know it, we did
that when we moved here. You took the long way, my
friend, but they won't.'

'Karan here, come in,' he said again, waiting for an
answer.

'Sir. We are near the village awaiting word from the
other units. There is no word so far. We will wait it out
until morning. If there is no word we will wait until sunset
of tomorrow. You will have to stay with the vehicle, sir. Do
you read me?'

'I read you,' Karan said, 'go on'.

'We will not attack until dark sir. We have orders to wait
four days until all units are in place. There is food and

water in the vehicle, you will have enough. Is there any question, sir?'

'No questions, captain, I will be fine. Thank you for your help. Tell me if your situation changes. Bye.'

'Yes, sir. Over and out.'

Jabra had come in and was listening incredulously to this whole exchange. When it was over, he hooted and rushed in and gave Karan a bear hug.

'Jackpot, man,' he said, clearly excited.

'It's nice to see you too, Jabra,' Karan said, smiling, but meaning it more than the big man realised.

Leon, who had watched all this quietly, suddenly stood up and went to the corner of the room where his bags were. He opened his large camera bag. He then held up a cell phone, looking directly at Samaad.

'What is it?' Samaad said.

'Satellite phone. It's from Gabe Hallam, I had forgotten about it till now. Can we use it?' He was clearly excited.

'We probably can,' Samaad said, taking it from him, 'but I'm not sure how or for what'. He turned it over in his hands. Then he laughed. 'They tracked Osama by his phone and nearly got him, remember?' Everyone was quiet, waiting, unsure how to react.

'I wish they had,' he said, laughing some more. 'They might have left us alone then.' He looked at his friends and brother, who were unusually silent.

'What is it, you guys? You think I'm Osama bin Laden? Lighten up!'

They all laughed, a little nervously, except for Leon. He didn't even smile.

'You shouldn't even turn the phone on, Samaad,' he said

seriously. 'It isn't Indian army issue. This is given by Gabriel Hallam, and it could be nothing more than a device to pinpoint your location. I'm glad you brought up Osama, I could've got us all killed.'

He snatched the phone from Samaad and threw it on the floor and stared at it as if it were a poisonous spider.

'Yehudi, calm down. We aren't that easy to pinpoint, signals don't carry as well in the Himalayas, even satellite signals.' He put his arm around Leon's shoulders and sat him down next to Karan.

'You guys shouldn't even be here, but it looks like you are not leaving. So we need to have a council of war now, and figure out, seriously, what we do next. I know you think I have it all worked out, my men certainly do, but the fact is I don't. And the fact is that they are going to get in here sooner or later and take over those mines. So the question is: what do we do?'

Every face in the room was turned to him. They were all, to a man, surprised at least. There was no verbal response from any of them. They waited for him to continue. He looked around the group. Yehudi, sitting with his hands on his knees, serious as always. Karan, with his slanting brown eyes, so like his sister, and yet nothing like her, full of confusion, nuances, always torn between one thing and another. Coming back was probably the only firm decision he had made in his life, and it may turn out to be the one that cost him his life. And then Samaad saw Karan's eyes flicker toward Jabra. And he understood why Karan was back here in the mountains, risking his life. He was here for his brother. And if Jabra was Karan's brother, then Karan was his own brother too. He looked at the faces turned to him and realised that he could trust every one of them with his life. And that they all trusted each other with theirs. And he realised that he could not throw these lives away.

'I will surrender,' he said.

There was a collective intake of breath from the three men in the room, and then, after a moment's silence, all three of them began to talk at once. Samaad let them talk themselves out, answering none of their questions, saying nothing more until the men were silent again, their arguments and questions done, waiting again for him, their leader, their captain, to speak. It frightened him, it strengthened the feeling that he was doing the right thing, going in the right direction. He was not, after all, the leader of a terrorist organisation. All he had ever wanted was peace. And so he had to draw back from the escalation, he had to draw back from any action that might lead to violence, death, loss of any lives, especially these three lives, that had somehow become, surreptitiously, so precious to him.

He held up his hand, palm forward. Leon looked at his dark eyes and thought of a stone Buddha. Samaad was still, his normally sparkling eyes dark, like black water, nothing visible on the surface, full of thoughts and creatures, so full that they seemed empty.

'There was to be a place, a valley of freedom, of strength,' he said, and his voice, like his eyes, was so full that it came out flat, cold, silent. 'Where we could be what we wanted to be. Where there would be no one telling us how to be, or who our gods were to be. The sapphires were given to me to make this happen. I tried to keep them secret. I tried to cover my tracks. But Kashmir sapphires are too big, too precious to keep hidden. Someone heard, someone told, before you know it, it's all over. As I knew it would be. I prepared for the end, I was ready for it, I thought. But I am not. I do not want any of my people to die. Not even those that came into this knowing they might. And certainly not you, my friends, my brothers. It lasted two years, my village. But now it's over, and we must give it up.'

He stood up and reached for Karan's radio. 'Call them, Karan, and tell him I want to talk. Tell them to come into the village and that we will be unarmed and waiting.' He turned to Jabra. 'Call the men outside, gather them all here, and tell them I will come out and talk to them.' Jabra nodded and left.

Karan got the captain on the radio.

'Karan sir, where are you sir?' was the man's alarmed question when he realised what was going on. Karan explained.

'I will have to co-ordinate with the other two units, sir, I will radio you again in fifteen minutes.' He sounded excited. Karan thought this must have been his first possible combat situation, and he must be relieved that it had ended before it had begun. They took the radio and went outside to listen to Samaad address his militia.

A bloated yellow moon poised close to the horizon, a ball thrown up to the sky in that moment right before gravity pulls it to earth. Impermanence. Forward movement. Even if things got worse, it was still forward movement in time. Leon thought he was like that moon, that ball, life itself was that moment. Thrown up, soon to fall. Life was as long as that moment of neitherness between up and down.

He got behind Samaad and stood on a rock so he could get shots of the whole scene. In the gloom, the men's eyes caught the light from the lamps making them glow, making Leon think of a huge pack of hyenas. That was an unfair comparison, he thought. These men were nothing like hyenas. Wolves, maybe, brave and dark and certainly as hairy as wolves, waiting for their alpha to show them the way. They were all ready for war, to defend their home to the death. They didn't know that the leader was going to disband the pack, sell them to the zoo. Leon was suddenly full of dread. He wondered if the men would now turn on Samaad. He shrugged. He would wait and see now, what happened next. That was what he had come here for, what he had stayed on for.

It seemed that it was all over before it had begun. He had been ready for whatever was going to happen. His erratic body tics spoke of suppressed fears that hadn't surfaced into his conscious mind. His stomach like a fist clenching and unclenching in anticipation of a fight, giving him diarrhoea and cramps that he ignored. His continuous need for small sips of water to ease the parchment dryness in his mouth and throat. His sweat glands working overtime, letting off a stink of fear, a sourness on his breath that disgusted him and made him brush his teeth many times a day. He knew everyone else had noticed over the past few weeks, but no one commented on them except Samaad himself, who gave him herb teas, strange soaps, advice, and of course hashish to ease him. Everything helped, nothing helped. This feeling of anticipation was what he lived for. So he put up with the ugly messages his body sent him because the pleasure or pain that his mind got from all this was more than worth it. And now it was all over. He felt that familiar twist in his bowels, but he ignored it. He didn't want to be squatting in the scrub when Samaad told his men that it was all over. This, anticlimactic as it was, was the climax to all that had happened since the day Samaad had walked into Tara's house to sell her a carpet. So he would stand there behind him, and even though he knew he would not understand the words that Samaad spoke, he would feel the mood of the men gathered there. He wouldn't miss this for the pleasure of emptying his bowels.

Samaad began to speak. Without the words, it was, for Leon, like watching a silent movie. He shut off the sound and watched. There was a silence in the valley that unnerved him. The men seemed to be holding their breath. They shifted softly in their spots. Some of them put their guns down as the minutes passed. They seemed to sag collectively as Samaad's voice fell on them like a soft warm rain, a blanket over their war spirit. Then he paused. He had them in his hand, like a politician. Like a jazz musician playing a solo to an entranced crowd. He had paused, Leon thought, to give weight to his punch line. They all waited, and then Samaad spoke again. So softly that the men moved forward, leaning as one great creature toward their leader. And when he was done, they released their breath. And sound came back for Leon. They all began to murmur and whisper among themselves. And then Jabra stepped forward. He spoke very loudly, like a commander. The men responded instantly by becoming quiet. Then Jabra said a few lines and stopped. They held their guns over their heads and chanted as one voice. It filled the valley around them, vibrating the rocks and ground, echoing and bouncing off the buildings. Jabra joined them. Samaad just waited. Then the men moved forward toward Samaad and Jabra.

Leon's stomach lurched again. He took an involuntary step back. He kept his eyes on Samaad. He saw Karan move toward Jabra, and stand right behind him. He realised that Karan must have understood most of what Samaad had said to his men. The men in the front row moved forward. The closest one put his gun down by Jabra's feet. Then he hugged Jabra. Jabra put his hand inside a bag that was slung across his body that Leon had not noticed till then. He took out something and put it in the man's hand and then embraced him. The man moved on to Samaad and embraced him too. The next man came forward and did the same. And on and on until there were piles of weapons by Jabra's feet. When they were done, the men dissipated into the shadows of the mountains like smoke, leaving nothing but the guns. As if they had never been.

Samaad turned to Leon.

'Well, Yehudi, it's all over now. They are gone.'

'You just let them go? Where will they go?'

'Wherever they want, wherever they came from. Some of them will go over the border, some of them will just go back to their families, to the lower valleys where they came from.'

Leon ignored the tears in his friend's eyes.

'What did Jabra give them?'

Samaad turned to look at Jabra and Karan. They were carrying the piles of guns to the army truck that Karan had driven up. They were talking softly to each other.

'He gave them two sapphires each. It's not much, but it will see them through the winter, until they find work.'

Leon nodded. He didn't know what he could say.

Samaad called out to Jabra and Karan.

'I have to go, Jabra. You know what I have to do now.'

Jabra said nothing. He turned and almost savagely enclosed his big brother in a hug, holding him until Samaad pushed him away gently.

'Khuda hafiz, Jabra.'

'Khuda hafiz, bhaijaan,' Jabra said, turning away briskly, wiping his eyes.

'What do you mean?' Leon asked.

'Yehudi. It is time for you to go now with Karan and Jabra. They will drive the truck down. They will surrender the weapons to the army. You will go with them. There is nothing more for you here now.'

This time Leon heard the command in Samaad's voice.

'Where are you going, Samaad?'

'I can't take you with me Yehudi, I can't.'

'But where are you going, can't you tell me where you're going?'

Samaad turned away and started walking toward the Jonga. Jabra and Karan got busy with the guns.

Leon stood for a moment and then ran to Samaad.

'I am going with you Samaad, wherever it is you are going. Do not stop me now. I have come too far in this to not know the end of this thing.'

Samaad got into the Jonga.

'Well, get in then Yehudi, we have to go now,' he said.

They made good time. Samaad had the headlamps turned off, and they growled through the dark, hoping that no one would see or hear them. He would turn them on every so often when he wasn't sure of the road. They parked on the ridge as always and got out. The valley below them was crawling with men, the lights dancing fireflies from their vantage point on the mountainside.

'What are they doing?' Leon asked Samaad.

Samaad put his hand on Leon's mouth. 'Softly, speak very softly. They will have snipers positioned everywhere. They'll hear us.'

Leon nodded, silent.

They started down the hillside, scrambling quietly. They needed to get across the valley and up the other side. Samaad whispered to Leon that they would go halfway down and then work their way around the rim, that way they had a better chance of avoiding detection. The rocks felt jagged, the gravel made them lose their footing again and again, sending them several uncontrolled feet downward each time. They were down sooner than they expected because of it, though, and were crawling toward their destination rapidly. Leon had a sense of not being there. He looked up at the stars above them, and saw the Milky Way washing a swath of light like a carpet to the other side of the valley. He heard wolves speaking to each other in the far distance. He saw the men Samaad had let go running wild in the peaks, sapphires instead of eyes, free at last, from the guns and dreams that had held them for two long years. He smiled to himself in the velvet dark. And then, he lost his footing again, and began to slide down. This time he was unable to stop, the lights at the bottom of the valley coming closer and closer to him very fast, he could even hear the voices of the men holding the lamps.

And then they heard or saw him, or both, and began to point and shout into the darkness that had held him safe, their lamps swinging toward him, throwing shadows and streaks of light across his eyes, blinding him, his eyes unable to adjust to the bright-dark confusion that was getting louder with every passing second. Then he heard a sound that he never quite understood, that he had heard before and was intimately familiar with, but yet could not identify, like a voice that you couldn't put a face or name to, a song that wouldn't come up from memory to sound. And he heard the sound of his friend's breath like a moan leaving his body for the last time.

'Samaad, Samaad are you okay?'

'Yes, I've been shot somewhere . . . it hurts.'

They lay quietly while the lights and sounds of the men came closer. And then, a dark shape ran past them into the crowd of lights, barking.

They heard the men shouting and eventually laughing, and then turning away and leaving, walking slowly away from them. They seemed relaxed and casual, all the urgency and confusion over.

Leon heard a sound from Samaad. He thought he knew what it was.

'Are you laughing, Samaad?'

'Yes, Yehudi. But not too easily, because it hurts. They went away because a dog ran out from here toward them. Your brown dog. They thought he was what had made all that noise. Your dog. You know,' and he stopped and took a shaky ugly breath that went into his lungs reluctantly, 'I think you did have a brown dog following you. Like an afreen, an angel . . .' and he coughed and took a rest. The men in the valley had gone away to the tents, their lights faded into the canvas fabric. Their voices no longer reached Leon.

'We must go on, Yehudi, help me up.'

Leon stood up carefully and helped Samaad to his feet. They had very little ground to cover. They walked, Samaad leaning on Leon's shoulder, his shirt wet with a darkness and an iron smell that Leon recognised but didn't talk about. He gave his friend sips of water that hurt him to drink. They came to the rock that Ion Machuca had placed there as a marker, and Leon was glad that he had. They would never have found the spot in that darkness otherwise.

'Do you know what to do?' Samaad asked him quietly.

'Yes, I think so.' Leon sat Samaad down carefully and lifted the rock off the hole. He found the device and held it out to Samaad, who shook his head and told him what to do.

'Is it done?' Samaad said ten minutes later, and the pain vibrated in his voice.

'Yes,' Leon answered him. 'We have to go now, and try and get as far away as we can.'

'I can't go any further. Yehudi, you go. I will stay here.'

'And die? Samaad? I can help you. We have to go. Jabra and Karan will wait for us. Samaad, I won't leave you here. I won't.'

Samaad seemed to have no air left, and no blood. He got up with Leon's help, but began to slide down to the ground, unable to hold himself up. Leon looked in Samaad's bag. He took the length of rope he found in it and tied their hands together, like handcuffs.

'The sky is getting light. We must do it soon, Yehudi. You go on, my friend, I cannot come.'

'No. Samaad, no. You have to come.'

Samaad tried again to get up, and Leon dragged him up

by the rope. They began to make progress, Leon almost carrying his friend forward, pulling him away and upward where he knew they might be safe.

'The stars are going out, Yehudi, look. One by one they are going out.' Leon thought Samaad was losing consciousness, and then he realised he was really talking about the sky, the stars disappearing as it got brighter.

They were almost to the top of the ridge, the tents that once belonged to the mine workers and their families laid out below them, the familiar and beloved ring of stone, battlements circling the valley below glowing in the distant breath of morning sun.

'We are far enough, do it now,' Samaad said.

'Yes, Samaad, I was just looking at your beautiful valley, your mountains, your sapphire sky. I love it all, and I thank you for letting me be a part of it all, Samaad.' Leon held Samaad close to him. He could see his eyes now, still sapphires, but with the milky inclusions of life loss, blood loss, straining to see the Himalayan sky that was his home.

Leon pushed down hard on the black square that protruded from the device Machuca had given him.

The sky lit up a bright orange that momentarily blinded them both. He saw Samaad's face, burning with the glow. And then the hillside collapsed and slid silently down upon the tents below, turning them dark and silent. The explosions came like a chain of flowers blooming one by one along the hillside toward them, a hundred feet below. A garden planted by Machuca, Leon thought. Again and again, the fierce heat lit up the sky, shouting at the rocks and valleys and stars, coming closer and closer. And then the ground below them shook, and slipped gently away.

Leon dug his feet hard into the rock. It slipped away, and then there was nothing below his feet. He tugged on the rope, and felt the weight of his friend. And then the world exploded around him, and he was blind and deaf and numb. He came into a dark consciousness of pain and thirst, his mouth felt black and dry. He could see only sky and a morning star, bright and spiky. He could feel his arm, it was being pulled off his body slowly, a distant rapidly approaching red flower of pain blooming in his brain. He began to scream as the pain came on him, and the sound of it violated his every nerve. Samaad was at the end of his arm, dangling over the ledge that he was anchored to. He passed out again, unable to tear himself away from the soft comfort of the blackness that beckoned to him. A field of red flowers woke him again, and the pain was not so intense anymore, his arm was growing numb.

'Just hold on a little longer my friend, a little longer.'

Leon was looking upward toward the mountain, but he couldn't see anyone coming. He had no strength left to shout anymore, his voice was a hoarse shadow. The sun was taking its time coming up. And then he realised it was not morning, it was late evening. He had been unconscious for hours. He felt his head instinctively with his free hand. There was a huge lump there that hurt obscenely. He left it alone.

'Samaad?' he said, suddenly feeling alone, wanting to hear his friend's voice to comfort him. It was getting dark and the temperature was falling. He could feel his sweat begin to chill. Like condensation on a glass of ice water, it clung to him. He was sure that Samaad was secure on his arm. Now if his arm didn't rip off, they would last another few hours. He could hear gun shots in the distance, but the time between them was longer. His arm began to throb again. He realised that Samaad had not answered him. He had no idea when he had last spoken to his friend.

'Samaad. Talk to me,' he said. There was no answer at all. So he turned his head carefully and slowly without shifting his body weight to look at his friend. Samaad's face was turned up to him. His eyes were open, glittering in the darkening gloom. They looked like holes with the sky showing through them, sapphire blue Himalayan sky. He had been dead for a while, Leon did not know how long. He unwound the rope tying them together. As the blood began to return to his arm, with each un-turn, his arm throbbed harder and hurt more and more till he was screaming with the pain, only he had no voice left to scream with. Samaad was finally free, and he was free too. Samaad dropped away quietly into the chasm. There was no sound at all ending the fall, just deepening, tightening silence that grew like a sound filling his mind. Leon turned back to the mountainside and there he was, tall as the mountain itself, blue as the sapphire sky, cobras hissing around his body. And he smiled at Leon and said, 'It was not to be. This time.'

EPILOGUE

Leon slammed the Balinese door knocker hard, smiling at the moon face smiling at him. Anne had had an aversion to electronic singing doorbells, he remembered.

'If there is no power, how will I know someone's at the door?'

'Annie, my love, your door is never locked, they will turn the door knob and walk in,' Jim had said, laughing.

Leon knocked again, thinking still of those hot summer afternoons that cooled into evenings and nights full of talk and food and wine and, in spite of Anne's objections, potent hydroponically grown California spliffs.

The door opened suddenly, and Dog flew out at him, drooling and peeing and unable to contain himself, still a puppy after all his years. And Naia just stood in the doorway, laughing.

'Stop, you slimy cur, get off me. Watch the arm. Naia, call him off, please?'

She did. And then she came out and hugged him too, and they stood that way for minutes, just happy to actually touch after almost three months, confirming each other's physical presence.

'Come on in, I'm sorry I didn't come to the airport to get you.'

'It would have made no sense. I didn't know my arrival time or anything, it's just as well you didn't. Plus, the 405 was truly a nightmare, I had forgotten how bad. I can drive, but the arm gets tired.'

It was bandaged, the fingers showing at the top.

'I'll get you a drink, then let's just sit so I can look at your face.'

She got him a glass of wine and a bowl of tortilla chips. He recognised Jim's bowl, the signature blue swirl that had dominated his work in the Seventies and made him famous.

She was about to sit down beside him when the phone rang. She went to get it. He watched her walk barefoot on the wood floor. She looked fuller than when he had last seen her. The flowery pink cotton slip she wore was Anne's, he remembered her in it. He watched her talking on the phone, silhouetted against the Pacific glare coming in through the picture windows, smiling, excited, absently rubbing her tummy. Something about her was different. He wasn't paying attention to her words, Dog was nudging his hand to stroke his head, and then suddenly it clicked. She put the phone down and walked over to him, slightly flat-footed.

'That was Adam. He wants us to go over there, there's stuff there for both of us. I had given his address for our mail to be forwarded to, remember? I keep forgetting to change it back. Actually, it's a good excuse to go see him every few days. Come on, he wants to see you too.'

Leon picked up the wine and chips. 'You drive, I'll just eat and drink.' He watched her movements as she reached across the counter for the car keys, confirming his suspicion.

In the car, they were quiet, both remembering the last

time they had driven together on that stretch of PCH toward Adam's house. Dog panted rhythmically on the back seat, stopping at precise intervals to slop up his lengthening drool. They both laughed out loud when he had done it for the fifth time, like an engine, in perfect beat. He looked offended and howled.

It was midmorning. Adam was waiting at the door. Naia got out and hugged him. 'You look beautiful,' he said, pushing her away to look. Leon saw that he knew. He hugged Leon too, carefully gentle with his arm. He examined him like a parent would. He seemed satisfied that Leon was mostly alright.

'Come on, I have a giant surprise for you both.' He walked into the house and they followed him.

Frank stood in the middle of the room. Naia screamed and ran up to him and hugged him, both of them squealing like children. Dog was beside himself, barking and pouncing, catching the mood as dogs do. Leon and Adam just stood and watched, smiling.

They all sat down eventually, and Dog settled down to pant and drool on the cool marble floor.

They talked and talked, and Adam listened. He had met Naia several times after she came back, so he had heard her stories, but now he got a more complete picture, and they compared notes, talked about people and places that began to take better shape—Jabra, who had disappeared into the mountains, only Karan, who was back in London, knew where, Viren, and Saroj, who had promised to visit them. Gabriel Hallam, still in that part of the world somewhere, he would send for Frank soon enough. And Samaad. They didn't talk about him so much as just mention his name, there was no story to be told without him.

Leon watched Naia's face, her gestures. Finally, when there was a lull in the conversation, he blurted, 'Naia, are you having a baby?'

She turned to him, grinning happily. 'Yes. I was going to tell you. Does it show that much?'

Frank and Leon both laughed. 'Yes, it does. And your face looks all shiny.'

'It's called glowing, Leon. Say it: "You're glowing".'

'You're glowing,' Leon said, imitating her, and then was serious. 'Is it his?' he asked softly.

Naia looked confused. 'His?' And then understanding came into her eyes, and she looked so sad that Leon felt his eyes get wet. And she said, 'He really got to you, didn't he?'

'Yes,' he said, taking a deep calming breath to stop the dam from breaking.

'No, Leon, it's not Samaad's baby I'm having. It's mine. I'm sorry. And the father—it's Raoul.'

Leon was confused now.

'Raoul? Raoul? Where is he?'

'He went to Havana. To play a concert for his grandfather's hundredth birthday. And to meet his family. And I don't think he's coming back.'

Leon didn't really know what to say. He wiped his eyes and put away his pain for another time.

Frank spoke into the silence of the room. He was solemn. 'I have something—many things—of yours,' he said to Leon. Naia thought he looked very fit, and very young, his hair looked cleaner than they had ever seen it, his eyes were bright with a joy of life which had been deep inside before.

'He came to my room that night . . .' he kept his face to

the ground, remembering, and they could not see his feelings, only hear them. Leon found himself holding his breath. 'He gave me the pills, a full course. He didn't ask me any questions, but I talked to him anyway. I told him all about Hallam, about what we did. I told him everything I knew. But he knew it all before, before I told him. He just let me talk, it was my need to talk. And then he did not come back for many days, I could not count how many. But I was given food, tea, a lot of tea. And an old man came one time a day to massage me and wash me. And then, that day before we had to leave, he came again. And he asked me to take this.' He touched the worn old leather satchel that sat on the floor beside him, and then stroked it as he continued to speak, as if it were a dear pet. 'He asked me if I would do him a favour.' He turned his face up at them, and they all saw the surprise on it, as if Samaad had just spoken to him.

'He could have made me do anything, in return for those pills. Before he gave them to me. But he waited till I was well, when he knew I would not refuse him, and then he said I could refuse if I wished.' He kept trying to convey what he had felt, why he was so amazed by it. Leon understood, but said nothing, let him talk on, as Samaad must have done that first night. He glanced at Naia from under his eyebrows, surreptitiously. She was listening to Frank intently, arms wrapped around her knees, mouth slightly open.

'He asked if I would deliver this bag to you, Yehudi.' Leon felt his eyes burn when he heard that name. He was tempted to let go, to allow himself the relief of tears.

Frank smiled as they all watched him. He took out a

brown paper bag from the satchel. He just reached over and handed it to Naia. She took it and looked inside. And then her eyebrows came together and she handed it to Leon. 'This is yours, Leon.'

He took out the big black suede pouch from within. His hands were shaking, and he couldn't see clearly through his wet eyes. He pulled open the drawstrings on the pouch. He took a sharp gasping breath and stared for long seconds. He gently put his hand in the bag, grasped a fistful and drew it out. And then opened his fist to show them all.

A cluster of velvet blue stones lay on his white palm. Pieces of Himalayan sky. Love and life and tears and death, locked into pebbles.

6456 /WEST
26/6/10